The
DHOW HOUSE

The
DHOW
HOUSE

JEAN
McNEIL

For Bb, rafiki yangu ele na ishi karibu na bahari

CONTENTS

Prologue 1

PROLOGUE

We are on the dhow. The teak groans with each wave. The lateen sail is taut with wind. He is at the rudder, underneath the slatted wood canopy which throws a weave of dark and light on his face. At our feet is a basket full of shaking bream.

A flare of sun over a blood ocean. The sun rises like a proximate planet, a burning ceramic moon. We have been at sea for so long, traversing the Indian Ocean and its jade archipelagos: Vamizi, Mafia, Zanzibar, Pemba. On nameless islands we maroon ourselves, cook cockles and prawns. Whale sharks bask in our wake. It is the Matalai, the period of repose between the winter and summer monsoons.

He stands to adjust the sail. One foot on the gunwale, one balanced on the tiller. I push him off as easy as I would throw the stone-shaped seed of a mango overboard.

I tell Lucy about the dream. I don't know why. But she is a confiding person by nature — this is probably why she has been so successful in her work.

"You're afraid of yourself. Of what you might do. What you've done." Lucy's voice is toneless, professional. She is used to talking to people about their dreams, to excavating them for meaning. Lucy is right. I am always taken aback when people much younger than me see things so much more clearly than I do. What is the point of experience?

Lucy is a black-and-white photocopy of her brother. She is dark-haired in a country where white women are blond as a matter of principle. She is dark-eyed, too, quick and alert. She stands out here among the local whites and expats, almost without exception beautiful women in linen shirts and skinny jeans. Her haircut is gamine; her limbs have the curious pallor of white people who have lived their lives in the tropics and hide from the sun. Storm is also slender, but he has a solidity his sister lacks. They both emit a force field: the power of the protected.

Lucy now lives in a sandstone-coloured apartment in a gated community five kilometres from her parents' house in Hatton. She has returned to this country from London, against all advice, against history. She would be better off living in South Africa, where her father's money buys her the right to work, or to England, with her British passport. But something has pulled her back. "I'm a white African," she says. "I make sense only here."

We meet in the café in the Usimama complex near the university, a rare democratic space in this city. I see professors — immediately identifiable because here they still carry leather satchels — young executives who work in the satellite TV studios across the street and people from the nearby American embassy, although these days they detach their ID badge before entering public places. The city is under constant threat of attack.

Outside the sun burns through the flame trees with their blossoms of acid orange. In the suburbs are lawns of electric green tended by gardeners and sprinklers, thick with bulbuls and cuckoos; at night we hear the whoop of hyena from the Lubaga National Park which borders the hills. Elephant, giraffe and wild dog are incarcerated there, too, only seven kilometres from the red leather chair where the president of the republic sits. On a clear day he can hear the lions roar. From the café we can see the *milima ya nyuma ya tembo*, the Hills of the Elephant's Back. Two hills curve high over the city's western horizon. The wooded forest that drapes them is stocked with turacos and whydahs and is hacked at steadily by nearby slum-dwellers. The hills are darkening with the late equatorial afternoon. Lucy and I have taken to drinking in this café. We start with a beer and graduate to cocktails. Our meeting again — just being together — seems to require us to drink. By our second cocktail we have become expansive and nearly trusting of each other.

"I've thought of you so often," I say. This is true. Not a day has passed in the last two and a half years when I have not woken up with their faces suspended in my mind. It is not Storm's but Julia's face, an altered twin of my mother's, I see most often.

"Did you?" Lucy says. She sounds unconvinced.

"I felt so . . ." I stall. I can't think of any adjective that would not be repulsive to her.

"Most of us have no idea what our limits are," Lucy says. "Very few people are ever taken to the boundaries of themselves by their experience. They don't know if they are good people, or bad people."

"Do you know?"

"Probably not," she says, after a while. "Or not yet." I think she is telling the truth. Lucy's instinct is for honesty. She was always an intimate person, so much more than the rest of her family. She is the kind of person who sheds light on your flaws and shortcomings. Lucy has standards. The rest of her family knew this and made her pay, I suspect.

"How is — your mother?"

"She's fine. She's living in South Africa. So many of us end up there. It feels familiar, although of course it's a foreign country. She's met someone. It took a while, but she's happy now."

"Did she leave because of the violence?"

"No, that calmed down only two weeks after you left." Lucy shook a cocktail straw into her passionfruit juice, animating its cloudy contents. "In any case, Julia can cope with danger."

I register that Lucy calls her mother by her first name, now. In the Dhow House Lucy had always been a dutiful daughter. She looked more like her father than her mother, but she and Julia are cut from the same cloth all the same.

4

I don't ask about Storm. She does not offer any information, either. Because of this wordless agreement we can see each other, pretend we are still family.

We sit in silence for a minute, as if we are only having a friendly conversation, two cousins catching up. Tomorrow I return to the coast, and in a week's time she flies to Johannesburg to do her post-graduate course in forensic psychology. We could easily have missed each other.

This is last time I see Lucy, probably the last time I will see her in this life. I watch her as she walks to her black Pajero in the car park. She steps lightly on the perimeter of the shadows of potted trees planted to provide shade against the sun. She is as slim as ever. She walks as though the ground is air. When she reaches the car she hesitates. A twin version of her appears — Lucy's reflection in the car's window, which is tinted against the sun. I wait in the edge of shade thrown by a palm tree, I think she will turn at the last moment and wave, but she opens the door and gets in the car.

Tomorrow I will return to the coast, where the mosque swallows arrow through the evening sky. It is the Kaskazi monsoon, summer on the coast, which I've never experienced. I came to this country for the first time in the winter monsoon, the Kusi, when seaweed tars the alabaster sands of Moholo beach and squally days bring cool rain. I have always liked off-seasons, their neglect and melancholy. The monsoon is both season and climate on the coast: it brings summer and winter, tourists to fleece, times of plenty, times of want. On the coast the wind is everything; time itself swings on its hinge.

I

AMANI
SUNBIRD

They lived at Kilindoni. There were more dramatic stretches of coast in the country where Bill's father could have built the house, with ivory dunes, beach bars, ancient houses glowing the colour of phosphorous in the sun. There were more beautiful places, from Moholo in the north to Lindi in the south, all along the coast — *pwani* — that stretches for six hundred kilometres in a shallow arc along the Indian Ocean.

Her first view of it was from the plane, which had flown from the capital and took its approach to the runway along the wave-raked coast. She saw its sweep of beaches protected by a garrison of coral reefs, the jade inlets and tangled mangrove bays. She saw the two giant rivers emptying themselves into the sea, the Mithi in the north and the Sarara farther south. She saw the thin forms of dhows out at sea; from the air they looked like narrow insects with their noses to the wind. All along the coast fishermen still make Homeric journeys, travelling from Moholo to the famed spice islands — Zanzibar, Pemba — in search of the fish they call *filusi*.

The house was the first to be built on that stretch of the coast. Her uncle's father built it thirty years before the first hotel, Fitzgerald's, installed itself on a curving faction of the beach poised between two coral islets. The beach in front of the house was not the most pristine and sandy but Bill's father chose it for its commanding position above the shore, from where it looked out to a black coral headland called Lion's Rock. At one time there had been short-haired lions on the coast who had adapted to the heat, but by the time of the settlers they were long gone.

Between the house and the coastal highway were fields of pine-apple plantations and in a nest of hydroponic greenhouses a Greek-descended agriculturalist named Achilles grew chives for export to France. The white canopies of the greenhouses glinted in the sun, stretched between the coral road that skirted the edge of the land and the access roads of the plantation. In between the spikes of pineapples were fields of a pulsating, almost plastic green where Holstein grazed. The fields were traversed by white-tailed mongoose and hedgehogs, and green mambas whose venom could kill a herd of elephant stone dead in a single bite.

Coconut palms leaned, thin as heiresses, into the sky. Beyond the trees the ocean hissed. White houses lined its shore. In these houses, housekeepers and gardeners wearing green uniforms kept floors of cool cement polished and the branches lopped off trees so that monkeys could not climb inside bedrooms.

It was a place for people whose families had been in the country for generations. Foreign tourists shied away from Kilindoni because the beaches were difficult to find, quarantined by tides; in some places the beach gave way to a network of shallow, smooth cenotes of coral. On either side of Kilindoni the ocean was garlanded with sharp reefs. So it became the preserve of locals, people from the highlands who left the cool upcountry nights and rainy winters to play on the coast.

One night Storm would tell her how forty or fifty years before — for him an epoch away, but for her a graspable previous age — the ranchers and big game hunters of the north would converge on Kilindoni at Easter, at Christmas and New Year, and celebrate the fruit of their destruction by hooking marlin and sailfish off its fertile coasts. Then, the Indian Ocean had been thick with whales — sei, killer, pilot, sperm, humpback — and an abundant marine life had fed on sea grass, including finfish and five species of marine turtle. Its brackish mangroves were studded with Goliath and purple

9

herons, which stepped like dignitaries through mud, feeding on prawns and the mud crabs sold as delicacies in tourist restaurants. The Amani sunbird, the eastern nicator, Fischer's turaco and the green barbet were plentiful, then; they threaded through lianas and sedges in the hot coastal forest where it was thirty degrees by eight o'clock in the morning.

She knew little of this before she arrived. She had only a few hours in the capital, sitting in a corner in Anthony's office, underneath the severed head of a buffalo killed by the embassy's previous owner, and which no one had managed to remove.

But she'd looked up Kilindoni on Google Earth. And so she knew that the plantation extended inland, its rolling hills of pineapple and cultivated sisal feeding on the moisture of the ocean. A parcel of it hugged the coast, and it was here she would find their house. Across a shallow inlet, five kilometres away, was the village of Kilindoni. There, mosques and Christian churches sat side by side, their *mabati* roofs shimmering the heat. From the banks of the creek dhows slid out of the harbour at dawn and pied kingfishers dove into the sea.

"Would you like me to stop so I can throw that away?"

Chocolate veined down her hands and pooled on her wrists. "It melts quickly, doesn't it?" She tried to stem the flow with her tongue.

The night before, in her hotel in Bahari ya Manda, her first night on the coast, the heat had kept her awake, along with the drill-buzz of the fan and the mosquitoes who had staked out her bed before she had dropped the net. But also, she was charged with a sense of anticipation so fierce her heart pounded, an alloy of dread and excitement she had felt only once or twice in her life.

Then night capsized to a tropics dawn. Birds whose calls she could not recognize sang with languid conviction. On the other side of the curtain the sun was already white-hot, at seven in the morning.

The heat was a hot stone slab. In Gariseb the nights were cool. In July and August — the equatorial winter — it went down to ten degrees at night. She would wake in her tent with her breath suspended in the air and scramble for a fleece.

The drive would take an hour, Vincent told her. She had to close her eyes at times, when the juggernaut long-distance buses bore down on them from the opposite direction, their bulk straying into their lane and forcing Vincent to hug the rim of the road. They drove with the windows open and she heard the birds whose calls she had been learning on her computer for some months now. Some were familiar to her: the dark-capped bulbul and the common bulbul, locally abundant birds with melodious, sweet calls. They sounded as if they were arguing — a long-married couple who could finish the other's sentences: *I just said, I just meant, no you didn't . . .*

She felt her body begin to succumb to a kind of melting. The heat alone seemed to want to convince her of this. *Everything will be easier now. You will see.*

The coastal highway shone like a black snake in the heat. They passed ragged towns of evangelical churches and motorcycle taxis, slim women barefoot, skirts made of a bright material, printed patterns of pineapples or suns and moons wrapped tight around their legs.

Black Africa — this was what Mike the army major had called it. The term struck her. "What do you mean 'black'? Is there a White Africa?" she'd asked him. "Sure," he'd said. Mike had been her boss and she was young then, twenty-seven, twenty-eight, and so did not dispute his casting of the continent in chess-piece colours. Before she came to work in Gariseb she'd not thought much about Africa at all, she realized now. She'd taken it to be a continent-country, undifferentiated, like Antarctica or Australia.

"Why are they all dead?" She turned to face Vincent, who drove with stern concentration.

"What?"

"Those trees. Do they always look like that?"

The fat grey leafless forms had begun to appear north of the village of Larona, like bloated skeletons. Their girths were big enough to house a small bar. They looked less like trees than spirits.

Vincent's head gives the slightest of shakes. She saw words moving on his lips before they were discarded into a hesitant smile. He might have learned that to dispute what white people said brought only trouble.

"They're alive," he said, finally.

"It's so hot," she said.

"This is the time we call winter," Vincent said. "In summer it is five degrees hotter. This is, how do you call it . . . the down season?"

"The off-season."

The spiky plantations receded, taking many of the bloated trees with them. Now lush trees with thin cascading leaves draped themselves close to the road. Through them she could see the gnarled knots of mangroves.

"We are getting closer now."

Vincent turned the wheel and a dust lane swallowed them. She still held her chocolate ice cream, now melted to brown sludge. It was her first ice cream in months, bought at the Manda Bay shopping mall café. In the same café, a low-lit, wood-hued place filled with white faces, she'd bought bread, a couple of good French loaves. She couldn't think what else to bring to Julia, for the family. They might have everything.

Now they were driving under dark-leaved drooping trees. She knew the house overlooked the ocean; she could smell salt and kelp. A feeling seized her then, an odd belated sense of remorse. She could tell Vincent to turn around right now. He would do her bidding, just as he had for hundreds of erratic tourists, people from distant, wealthy countries who could not make up their minds and who were never happy.

The first thing she saw of the house was a white wall, perhaps seven feet high. Above its ramparts were the dark heads of palms. As they approached, the white of the wall seemed to gleam brighter, as if lit from inside by some kind of fluorescence. In the centre of the wall was a dark-wooded gate with grilles of inset ironwork, so glossy and black it looked as if it were made of wet ink. Bougainvillea draped over the walls in pink cascades. On the ground their smashed and wilted petals pooled.

She cast a look at Vincent. His mouth was working silently again, practising and discarding words. She'd been about to say — what? — some obscure apology for the opulence they were about to enter. *This is not me. I am not one of these people.*

Then they were through the wall's aperture and the ironwork portal was on either side and they were gliding along a long dark driveway, pursued by a dog. She locked eyes with the dog, which loped soundlessly beside them. He was brown-black, a thick bullish Doberman. She was glad they were in the car. The dog's eyes were seeds.

The back door of the house was slightly ajar. In it stood a woman dressed in a purple sheath of semi-transparent material. This was an aged version of the woman she'd seen in a very few photographs, with her sand-blond hair and trim body.

She got out of the car. She had every intention of walking up to her aunt and putting her arms around her but at the last moment she saw that this was not what her aunt expected. She held herself very upright and thrust her hand out in front of her.

"How fantastic you've come," her aunt said, taking her hand. Her grip was firm. She did not try to embrace her.

A stab in her stomach. It was raw and unexpected. She put her hand to her abdomen.

"Come inside."

She followed the purple of her aunt's dress into the house only to stop in the middle of a very large, high-ceilinged room. Something was missing. Then she understood: the house had no wall. The living room dissolved into a garden; there, palm trees shaded a lawn. Beyond it was a square of tourmaline water, and beyond the pool was the ocean. Along its shore was a fringe of grey ridged rock. She went forward, drawn by the sight of the waves breaking. She found herself standing in front of a swimming pool whose edge dispersed into the horizon.

"What's that?"

Her aunt looked out to sea. "What do you mean?"

"That grey rock."

"Coral."

"Is it dead?"

"No, it's alive. It's low tide now. At low tide the coral is exposed."

The sky was covered in a thin greasy layer of cloud. The ocean stared back at her.

"Nice view, isn't it? We never tire of it." Her aunt's heels — she hadn't noticed she was wearing shoes; somehow shoes seemed useless in this open cathedral — slapped against her feet. Her aunt was wearing those shoes with no back; what were they called? She had forgotten her entire shoe vocabulary. She had worn one pair of trainers and one pair of flip-flops for the last four months.

Through her aunt's purple kaftan she could see her swimsuit, a bikini balanced on coat hanger hips and aquiline thighs. Julia might be fifty-five, even sixty. There was not an ounce of fat or wrinkle. Looking at her aunt ignited an unfamiliar trill inside her, a tinny vibration.

"Are you alone here?"

Her question sounded wrong, but it was too late to recall it.

"Bill is in town, on business. The boys are out fishing. Or sailing. You'll meet them all tonight."

"The boys?" She was sure Julia had a son and a daughter.

"Storm and his friend."

"Oh," she said. "Thank you so much for having me."

The look that passed across her aunt's face then, and which was almost instantly banished, was one of annoyance. It was replaced by a bright smile. "Nonsense. You're family."

For the last few days she had been trying to remember Julia. In the end she failed to conjure up a single image. Her mother's sister had come to England every two years, "to shop," her mother had said, with a brittle laugh. She must have been twelve, thirteen, and this fragment had lodged itself in her mind, even then. *Distant relatives*, she remembered her mother saying, the hurt sing-song in her voice, *we were never a close family*. These phrases — *distant relatives, close family* — had rung in her mind for weeks afterward. She did not know enough about family to ask her mother how a sister could ever be a distant relative, no matter how far away she lived.

A thin woman wearing a flowered dress and a pale scarf around her head appeared and she was shown to a room upstairs. Everything in the house was the colour of sand, or variations on it: ivory walls, a bleached white mosquito net, skirting boards painted the palest of peach. She saw wooden sculptures, gnarled pieces of driftwood tucked in cool corners. On the walls hung baleful African masks. Some sort of lantern made from Bombay Sapphire gin bottles were placed at intervals around the house where they threw a swimming pool light.

When the woman — she hadn't caught her name, but she was almost certainly Julia's housekeeper — left, she sat on the bed. The river of thought flowed again, as if it had never been dammed.

Why had she thrown herself on these people's hospitality? She'd seen the bar as her aunt led her out onto the house's stage in front of the ocean. Three types of whisky, four brands of gin. Gariseb was dry. She had gone four months without even a beer. The night before in Bahari ya Manda she'd been too tired to down the Duma beer the barman gave her, inexplicably, as a gift. She drank three mouthfuls and went to bed, even though sleep eluded her.

Kitten heels. Yes that's what they were. She'd never liked them; they were dainty and threatening at once. Only a certain kind of woman would wear such shoes, a woman under the impression that she would not have to run for her life, that she would not have to walk home for twenty miles along the side of the highway after her car had been commandeered by rebels.

The sea roared. It was closer now. She'd imagined the Indian Ocean would be calm, a minor ocean, pacified by warmth. But sharks patrolled the waters here — bull sharks, blacktip reef sharks, even great whites had been known to stray north from their usual feeding grounds in the cool Mozambique channel. This was another thing she learned from Google, in Anthony's office, after she received Julia's invitation.

She went to the window. The tide had come in, fast. The breakers had disappeared and the sea undulated now, its surface unbroken by coral. Waves pounded the low cliff on which the house was perched.

She sat on the bed. On the desk by the window were two photos. They sat in frames made out of dark wood. Their original colour was faded by the sun.

She picked one up. A boy stared at the camera as if it were an adversary, his face static, a fish dangling from a hook in his hand. Behind him was a beach. Hair spiralled from underneath a baseball cap. A girl's photo showed her seated at a long table of other young people against a stone wall — a castle or stately home. England, for certain. She knew Julia's daughter had studied there so this must be Lucy. With her dark hair and dark eyes, Lucy looked like a different species from the boy in the other photo, who must be her brother, Storm. She studied their features and could find little, apart from Julia's patrician nose, in common. Lucy would be coming home soon, Julia had said in her email, in the middle of August. They would meet each other then.

The middle of August. What would she do in this house for a week, let alone two months? She would have to make an excuse to leave early. She would find some way of staying in the capital until she returned to Gariseb. By then enough time would have passed.

She sat back on the bed. Her duffel bag stared at her. It contained two pairs of shorts, three shirts and one dress. In the bottom of the bag, underneath these meagre possessions, was the object Anthony had procured a permit for with only a day's notice. If you were important enough, and paid enough money, you could do that.

She lay her hands on its outline, swaddled in a red and purple checked blanket. They had waved her through at the airport with Anthony's underling as her escort. She had placed the bag in the scanner and seen its outline on the screen, halfway between a triton shell and an impala horn, those trophies tourists were always trying to smuggle out of the country.

She shoved the bag underneath the bed and lay down. The bed's crisp ironed sheets were turned down at the corners, as in a hotel. The mosquito net gripped its perimeter. Mosquito nets always made her think of wedding dresses, of bridal chambers; they reminded her she wasn't married, and within that thought was the possibility, stretching into the future, that she might never be married. That there were women who men had always wanted, would always want, and this was established while they were still girls, or even earlier, when they were still mere amoebas in the womb. Her aunt was one of these women, she knew it immediately with her bleached blond streaks in her hair, her rigid stomach, the khaki eyeliner she wore to complement her taupe lion's eyes.

She did not remember falling asleep. The sound of the waves drew her away from herself, lured her into another realm.

She and Ali are reading *Macbeth*, his copy, half-destroyed, a gift from the British Consulate in Gao when he had been a teacher, is in her hand. Beside them a hurricane lamp hisses. He is gaunt, more so than in life. She wants to ask him why he has lost weight, what has happened to him, when a pistol is pressed against her temple.

She gasped, tugged awake by a sound, a slim bell ringing in the distance.

"Rebecca." Her aunt's voice reached her over the sound of the waves, how much later she didn't know, waking her from the hasty dream. "Come and have a drink."

E ven before she walked down the stairs she knew the house had changed. She paused at the top step where she would be unobserved. Here she could see the sweep of sofas below, their crisp eggshell embroidery ranged around the ocean view. She'd slept later than she thought; two of the Bombay Sapphire lamps were lit. Dusk lapped at the edges of the light.

She heard voices — urgent, loud, male voices. Her aunt's flute-like voice. A drawer or door being opened, the scrape of a knife. A figure crossed the living room. The figure was tall and wore blue shorts. She heard the slap of bare feet walking quickly across tiles.

She meant to put her foot on the top step of the staircase but a reticence held her back.

Slap, slap, the feet came back. She glimpsed them, although not the body they were attached to. They left glistening narrow footprints on the floor.

The pool gurgled into silence as the pump was turned off for the day. Then a crash of laughter. The sound rushed toward her. Some note in it frightened her.

"There you are," Julia called from the kitchen. "Come and say hello."

Two shirtless torsos, backs to her, stood on the other side of the breakfast island. Their faces swivelled around, then lunged toward her and shook her hand. One was the boy from the photograph — a man now — who looked like her aunt, so much so that he might be a copy. He was six foot one or two, long-limbed; there were parts of him yet to be soldered together. He had light brown hair with a metallic glint, a vein of colour like brushed chrome. His eyes were the depth-less blue of swimming pools. He had a strong face, not a young man's face. There was an Easter Island stasis about it, as if he had spent his formative years looking out to sea.

As she took her cousin's hand, she felt briefly unsteady. The sea roared so suddenly she started. She heard water birds screech. Then a strange, dead moment of silence.

"When did you get here?" he asked.

"Today. Well, not long ago. I fell asleep."

"Awesome," said the other, immediately friendly, face. "Great to meet you."

How old would they be? Her mother had never spoken about Julia's children. Julia called them boys only as a term of affection. She used her medical student yardstick. Her cousin was not quite as old as a newly qualified doctor straight out of med school, who was twenty-five or six, an engaging age. They were intelligent, chatty, charming. They still had the newly minted quality of the young.

She heard herself say, "It's great to be here. It's so much hotter than up north."

She had not worn shorts or bared her arms at night for four months now, and for a very long time in England, either. She felt almost giddy. She could not convince her body to forget the notion that she would not need a pullover or jacket soon. She was used to that moment in Gariseb when the sun was deflected by the horizon, followed by an automatic cooling, as if the day had been a charade.

The young men reassumed the rhythm she'd interrupted. She continued her conversation with her aunt, but her eyes tracked their movements behind her aunt's shoulder.

Her cousin moved in a series of explosions. He opened the fridge door, took something out — she missed what it was — plunked it on the counter, went toward the pool, grabbed his phone off the table. His friend — he'd said his name but she had instantly forgotten it

— stood stock-still and kept her under a steady gaze that was a combination of warmth and wariness. He looked younger than her cousin. He was an *ephebe* — a word she had learned in her classics elective in her first year of medical school, and which she had instantly loved. Only his face, held tense and self-protective with a certain masculine pride, gave away his age.

"Bill will be home in an hour," Julia said. "Do you want a drink?"

"What have you got?"

Her aunt shrugged. "Everything."

She perched herself on a stool as her cousin and his friend flitted away. She looked around to find them gone. "Where did they go?"

"Who knows?" her aunt shrugged. "They come and go like the wind."

A flare of noise tore the sky open. She sprang off her stool and ducked her head.

When the noise had swallowed itself she emerged from her crouch to find Julia peering at her. "They fly low on the way back. I'm sorry, I should have warned you."

"Who was it?"

"Army, returning from over the border. They go and come back every day. In England it would be illegal to fly that low, but here the army do what they like." Julia paused. "I thought you'd be used to this kind of thing."

"I am. I was. I haven't been around fighter jets in a while."

Julia's slim silver mobile phone emitted a discreet chime. She took it and walked into the living room, toward the garden. Julia returned, the phone clutched by her thigh. "Bill's stuck in town on business. We can all have our own suppers."

"I really don't feel like eating. I think I'll just go to bed."

She retreated to her room. There, she sat on the edge of her bed, her head heavy from the afternoon, from encounters with strangers who were so familiar, and yet so removed.

Julia had certainly met her. Her mother had shown her a photo of her three year-old self, snug in Julia's lap, taken on one of her aunt's trips to England, lemon sunshine behind them, which had struggled through the bay window of their north-facing flat in the spring. In the photograph, Julia had worn a beaded necklace and a white shirt open to display a shield-like breastbone. She would have been in Africa for no more than five years at that point and already looked like a different species.

She had certainly never met Storm. But he seemed so familiar. As she'd taken his hand she'd felt an odd buzzing in the pit of her stomach.

From down the hall came the same explosive laughter she'd heard in the kitchen. The sea had receded. She could hear its distant rasp, and within it, an echo of the jet that had exploded into the house at dusk. She had caught a shadow of the plane in the corner of her eye as it tore through the sky. Julia was right, it had flown much lower than would be allowed in Europe, as low as in the theatre of war. They must have been taking the scenic route home, getting a thrill from strafing the waves.

The plane would have taken ten minutes to fly from the border 130 kilometres away. She had never been there, but she knew the terrain from satellite images, how the coastal road wound north from Moholo, dipping inland at two wide river deltas spanned by concrete bridges. North of the Mithi River the landscape changes abruptly, becoming dry and treeless before reverting to the mangrove-choked lagoons of the coast. The road arrives at the town of Puku, a tourist gem of whitewashed mansions, their cool courtyards arranged around tinkling fountains and lined with captive Fischer's lovebirds huddling in cages.

North of Puku the road continues, but no one maintains it. Only one kilometre outside of town potholes begin to appear. Soon after the road becomes impassable to anything but a four-wheel drive or a tank.

Puku itself is a place of women — the men are at war. Women wear *buibuis*, their faces visible behind a delicate grille. The men who have stayed are either too young or too old, men with slim faces, their almond eyes supported by two strict sails of cheekbones. These men wear full-length *kanzus* and move like cats — spring and recoil, spring and recoil. Some have cicatrized faces, swirling patterns carved into their cheeks.

The border is thirty kilometres beyond Puku. In those thirty kilometres stand five army roadblocks. You begin to see herds of camels grazing on the dunes, Ali had said, plucking what little they can from the saltbush, the spiky sea grass. The sea comes in blue shards, fronted by foaming yellow dunes. Women's dress changes there, becomes more raucous, they wear *abayas* of fuchsia and orange. The faces of the women harden with their eyes ringed in thick kohl, their parched lips.

Yes, she can feel its presence, the border, even in Kilindoni, and the country that lies beyond it, like a black sword poised above their heads. This is the country that serves up the thin men she operates on, far away in the Sahel, near another section of desert border. This is the country that has wiped itself off the face of the earth, a process of erasure that began not in a war or an invasion but an implosion. She has never been there but imagines it sometimes, its gutted stadia and decapitated minarets. But these are not her own images, somehow. They are being projected to her from elsewhere, so that she may filter and broadcast them to her own mind.

She can see him, the generator of her false memories, walking toward her that day in Gariseb when she is surrounded by three of her colleagues who try to protect her. He strides with that matchstick gait the fighters she treated there have. She is beginning to sweat and has lost control of her bladder and a warm stream of pee runs down her leg. *No*, he says — she understands the word, *la*, but it is elongated, strung out in Ali's mouth, *laaaaaaaa*, then many words of haste and reprobation and the grip is loosened slightly, her hands unbound, her colleagues restrained behind a chaotic cordon of men, the buzz of a pickup waiting nearby. Ali's words ringing like dark bells in the air. *No*.

Julia stirred a pitcher of passionfruit juice. Morning sun formed a halo on the patio floor. She sat on a kitchen stool. She saw her aunt studying her. The discerning note in her eye had been replaced by something a shade warmer.

"I was just thinking," Julia said, not meeting her eye, "about your reaction yesterday." She paused. "To the jets."

"I'm sorry. I'm a bit nervous these days. I've had a tough four months."

"But you aren't near any fighting in — in the north. Where was it you said you are working again?"

"Gariseb. Near the border."

"I thought all the western donor agencies had pulled out of there after the attacks on aid workers last year."

"They did, but two medical corps stayed."

Julia seemed to be considering something — whether to believe her, perhaps, even though everything she said was perfectly true. Julia might know that in the company of someone else — a colleague, or someone better informed — she would not have resorted to such pat explanations. The truth was that all the international NGOs who had worked in the area for twenty years — Oxfam, Save the Children, even the UN — had decreed the area unsafe for their personnel, even though it was now a demilitarized zone.

"It must take guts to be somewhere everyone else has left."

"Only certain people can do it," she agreed. "But when you've had as much experience in conflict zones as I have, it's almost a relief to be on your own. And there's no jets there," she said, trying a rueful smile.

The careful note had returned to Julia's gaze. Her aunt was wearing another beach dress, this one the sand colour of her eyes. Her feet were bare. She wore no jewellery apart from a pair of glistening earrings she assumed were diamond. Julia's pageboy haircut made her face look delicate and strong at once. Her body appeared hard, planar, but also somehow yielding, as if it had retained its memory of fleshier incarnations. Something of her mother's cast — a very minor echo — the slope of her aunt's cheekbones, perhaps, pressed upon her memory.

"How did you come to Africa?" she asked.

"Work, initially."

"Weren't you a model?"

"Did your mother tell you that?"

The sharp tone made her back away. "I don't know where I heard it."

"I was a photographer."

Julia told her the story in a slightly famished monologue, as if she had been rehearsing it, as if she'd had no one to tell her story to in years.

She started with her parents — Rebecca's grandparents, who she remembered not very well, they had both died when she was twelve — how they were inattentive bohemians, useless at university applications, no money. About her confusion about what to do after university, a sudden passion for photography, a chance decision to try to find a destiny, a flight to a city she had never heard of before, then called Lourenço Marques.

"I thought it sounded like the name of a dictator, and it was, in a way." Julia's chime-like laugh hung in the morning breeze. Julia told her how she had cut her teeth in Madagascar — a long-forgotten failed revolution — then on floods in Mozambique and finally in Zaire, photographing child soldiers. It was this last assignment that had finished her off, as she put it. "The look in their eyes," Julia said. "I've only seen eyes like that on snakes."

She watched her aunt absorb the memory of what she had seen. It temporarily weighted her, and for a second Julia became a different person — a version of the woman she might have been, perhaps, if she had stuck with her job. Julia with a blue UN flak jacket. Julia wearing a necklace of cameras and binoculars.

"Why did you stop?"

"Digital came in and I couldn't keep up. I couldn't adapt. Everything was so *fast*. I used to have to persuade businessmen to take my photographs back to New York or London with them. I'd put the rolls of film in an envelope and write 'useless if delayed.' Everyone did that then, all the AP and Reuters people, until they got satellite. I bought a digital camera in London but I never liked the process. It was too easy. I think the magic was destroyed, for me." Julia was silent then, heavy with something unexpressed. "It got too real. I saw people killed."

Julia's lovely, unlined mouth tensed. "I decided I wasn't built for it," she went on. "I couldn't get what I'd seen out of my mind. Other people I worked with could. Mind you they drank more than I did. On one of my last assignments — it was in Brazzaville — I met Bill."

"How did you meet?"

"Around the pool at a hotel."

That moment when Julia and William encountered each other appeared to her fully realized, as if she had lived it herself. The green glasses containing weak gin tonics, the scruffy palms on the street outside, the unhealthy algal glow of the pool, and a man, Bill's blue eyes shrouded in sunglasses, looking so much like the son he would eventually bear with the stranger in a blue-and-white striped bikini sitting two tables away.

The light had thickened. It fell into the kitchen in a yolky wedge. "Rebecca?"

Her name, in Julia's mouth, sounded old, settled. As if it belonged to another person.

"Yes?"

"You're tense. You know, you're as stiff as a board. Any little noise makes you jump. We're worried about you. Maybe it's right that you've come here. You need to relax."

Julia's face flared. "You look like you're going somewhere."

She turned around to see Storm walk across the living room wearing a black T-shirt and a pair of shorts. He moved with purpose, a rangy, long-legged stride.

"You look a bit groomed." Julia all but winked at her. "For Storm that means he runs a hand through his hair."

"I thought I'd make an effort for your party."

"Didn't I tell you?" Julia swivelled toward her. "We're having a small cocktail party. Only thirty people or so. I'd like you and Storm to circulate. Bill can't be here, so we're going to fly the flag."

"Isn't he coming home today?"

"Unfortunately, no." Julia cast a glance in Storm's direction. "He's still away on business."

"I'm happy to help," she said. "What should I wear?"

Julia shook her head. "Wrong person to ask." She pointed to herself. "Old person."

Storm had not greeted her or even acknowledged her presence. He seemed magnetically attached to his mother. He gave his mother a smile, then. His face was exploded by it, dislodged from its stasis and thrown into another dimension. "You're not old," he said.

She spent the afternoon reading. She had bought a novel in the capital, a famous book she knew about but had never gotten around to reading, the story of a Frenchwoman who had come to the country to work with a wildlife conservation organization. She had raised several leopards from cubs. Everyone had thought her mad, they had expected her leopards to kill her. Leopard were the most wild of cats, was the accepted wisdom, she read. They could not be tamed. The woman had been killed by her assistant, a local man. Her story had recently been made into a film.

She looked outside the window to where a coconut palm leaned over the ledge of the land. The light was foil-like yet liquid, a green-gold colour she had not seen anywhere else.

At six o'clock she descended the stairs to the living room to find twenty people assembled. She had time to observe them before she was seen. The older people among them were not tanned and had a strange pallor. Blue patches mottled their brows, the edges of their faces. On closer inspection she saw these patches were milky freckles; some sort of reversed melanistic adjustment to a lifetime in the tropical sun, perhaps. The edges of their faces — their hairline, the perimeter of skin around their lips — were lightly crisped, like crème caramel.

The teak dining table was laden with food. Sweating hunks of cheese squatted on plates. Strawberries sat defeated in bowls on a bed of ice, their pores hairy and dilated.

The housekeeper, whose name she had learned was Grace, approached her with a glass of champagne. Grace held it like a chalice, cupping the bottom of the glass in her palm.

Julia's voice rang out. "Rebecca, would you mind taking that chair upstairs? It's getting in the way down here. I'd ask Storm, but I don't know where he is." Julia pointed to a large rattan armchair. People were still arriving and her aunt shuttled back and forth to the door. She went to the chair — she had supposed she might be called upon to perform such tasks in the house. She would be with them for two months, she had to pay her way somehow.

She put the chair at the end of the corridor, in a large alcove. On the way back, she saw Storm's door was open. Without thinking, she walked in. She went to the dartboard on which he'd pinned photographs; more, in frames, were arranged on the table underneath.

There were many photographs of Lucy — or rather Lucy and Storm's friend who she had met the day before, Evan; she had heard

Julia say his name, or at least it looked like him — in the light of a full moon on a beach, a party by the smudged look on their faces. Another showed Lucy in London, she supposed, swaddled in a thick knitted scarf, drinking a coffee at an outdoor café.

On the edge of her perception she saw the light move. The torso of her cousin solidified out of the darkness.

"What are you doing here?"

"I thought you were downstairs. Your mum asked me to move a chair. I saw the light was on."

This was a weak explanation, more a list of unrelated facts. She saw his face decide something. Whether it was to believe her or distrust her, she could not say.

She cast her head in the direction of the photograph of Lucy and Evan. "I didn't know they were a couple."

"Since last Christmas. I think they'll last." He said this with a defensive finality, as if she'd suggested they wouldn't.

She gestured toward the chair, uselessly. "Well, that's done. Let's go downstairs."

They rejoined the group. Several men were having an energetic discussion. She hung on its fringes. The men were all of Julia's age, she guessed, their thick wrists gripped by metal watches. They were discussing a development close to Bahari ya Manda, on the last remaining strip of beach unoccupied by a hotel. It would be secluded, they avowed, looking out as it did onto a headland. From there you could see the curve of the coast, the limitless glass-blue of the Indian Ocean. They would call it Paradise.

"Do you know what it means?"

She had inserted her comment awkwardly, in a bid to enter the conversation. Julia gave her a blank look. "Of course, Rebecca. It means a perfect place. Perfection."

"It's a Persian word for walled garden."

"How do you know that?" Storm was beside her. She hadn't heard him arrive.

"I learned it in *Paradise Lost*. I studied it in school."

"Is that a book?"

She returned his stare. "Yes."

The conversation moved on, to mangrove draining, environmental impact studies, contractors. Storm continued to stare at her from across the table, a flat, unreadable stare that could have been anger. He might have felt shown up by their exchange, she thought. Perhaps he didn't care about books.

Night congealed. It came in stages here, she had observed. Beginning at five o'clock when the shadows thrown by the five coconut palms at the edge of the garden lengthened. The sun sank on the side of the house that faced inland, into a stand of gauzy casuarinas. The sea held the light longer than the land. By seven it was completely dark. In England now, there would be sunlight until nine o'clock. For the first time in months home tugged at her. She missed summer evenings when you needed sunglasses at eight o'clock in the evening.

Julia had lit lanterns and the gin bottle lamps. The house looked most-compelling at dawn and dusk. It preferred in-between times, but it needed night. When dark triumphed she could almost hear the house breathe a sigh of relief.

Her phone blinked. Four forty a.m. The time when the body's circadian clock is at its lowest ebb. The time when people died in their sleep.

She remembered where she was. The tide sounded as if it were at the steps of the house, as if it might crash into the living room. The wind pounded the louvered windows. She got up to look outside. In the trees beyond her window she saw the huddled forms of sleeping monkeys sheltering against the wind.

She could remember the remnant of a dream. In it, Storm was staring at her, much as he had done the previous evening, but she could remember nothing more about it.

She was still awake an hour and a half later when a greasy dawn soaked the sky. She went to her window and saw lunkheaded clouds moving fast across the sea. The ocean was a cold jade. Geckos slalomed headfirst down the walls, freezing mid-crawl when they sensed her gaze on them. They were mucous-hued, two black beads for eyes. She inspected the rust on the mesh protecting her from the fan's blades, the paint drooping in buttery flakes from the ceiling.

Her eye was drawn back to the horizon. Wherever she went in the house her eye searched for the ocean, as if she were afraid it would disappear.

The sun had risen and the sky was carved in strata: a layer of lime near the water, then rose, then tangerine. Over the horizon was the wedge of the Arabian peninsula and its desert cities: Dubai, Sana'a, Jeddah — those names like sheer curtains trailing across a floor. The ocean was peppered with islands — Pemba, Zanzibar — which, much farther away, splintered into archipelagos: the Comoros, Seychelles, the Maldives.

She heard the familiar grind of a helicopter. A blue and silver bubble appeared out of the sky from inland. She watched it chop through the rough wind parallel to the beach. She jumped up from the bed, her heart thudding. But there were no children to immunize against measles, no pulmonary edemas to drain.

She felt a burning take hold of her. This is the only way she could describe it — a light but insistent immolation that started on the epidermis and then moved to her core, where it boiled.

She was in the living room, suddenly, almost running down the spiral staircase, then into the garden, still expecting to encounter a door or lock somewhere. The house's security was its tall wall, the razored glass that studded it, the *askari* keeping watch at night, the alarm tripwire around the perimeter of the plot of land, and finally — and most effectively — Charlie the guard dog. Luckily for her, Charlie was kept in check by the night watchman. Still she heard his stiff barks as she crossed the garden.

She walked the length of the beach in the opal morning light. Its sands were littered with pearl-like flower petals. She picked one up. It had an oblong chamber made of gristle the colour of milk.

She returned to the house. Sounds were coming from the kitchen. There was something about their urgency that didn't sound like Julia, who moved quietly, almost regally.

Suddenly a man was walking toward her and she only had time for an emergency impression to form — but he's not so much older! — before she found herself shaking her uncle's hand. His grip had a vigour she recognized from the military men she had treated. Bruise-coloured veins snarled his forearms. He had a flared jaw like the bottom of glass soda bottles, and Storm's severe blue eyes.

"I'm sorry I couldn't be here to welcome you."

"That's fine. I was welcomed." She smiled.

"We'll take you sailing this weekend, how about that?"

"That would be wonderful."

"You must have seen some terrible things up north. We're all very proud of what you're doing up there."

No one ever said such a thing to her, except perhaps at diplomatic receptions.

"Thank you," she said. They smiled at each other.

He was older than Julia, *much older,* she can remember her mother saying, her eyebrows raised, voice arched. Even then, at twelve or thirteen years old, she might have understood this was a comment about money. Her mother must have told her that Bill had been a farmer, but not of a common cow and goats variety, rather an owner and director of a vast plantation. Then, after he sold his farm to the government, a property developer, then a financier — that was the word her mother had used and her twelve-year-old self had hoarded it away. It sounded debonair, French, as if raising money might be a sublime event.

"We're so glad to meet you," her uncle said, "after all these years."

She found she did not know what to say.

"So how have you been keeping yourself busy?" her uncle asked.

"I've had time to read for the first time in years. In the mornings I've gone running. It's a pleasure to be able to put one foot in front of the other again."

"You can't do that in the north? Are there mines?"

"No, the mines are over the border. But there are bandits. Lions. Stray RPG fire from over the border. Plus I'd probably be kidnapped and held to ransom."

Her uncle's gaze stayed on her. He might have been expecting her to laugh, to say it was all a joke.

"Hey, Dad. When did you get home?" A sleepy voice, the yawn still in it, reached them from the stairs.

Storm walked toward them. Again she had the impression he only had eyes for his father. Sleep clung to him. His eyes were huge and glistening. He looked very young, like a child.

"I was just telling Rebecca we'll take her sailing."

Storm drifted to the refrigerator. On the way he stopped to give his father a kiss on the cheek. She had to look away. How long had it been since she had seen a young man kiss his father? In England, never. The young injured men she treated at Gariseb would cover their eyes with their hands when they spoke of their fathers, who had stayed at home to tend their goats or who had been killed in rebel assaults. Tears would emerge from between their fingers.

"How did your meetings go, Dad?"

"Fine, but I had to drive all night to get home."

"You should have waited, or flown."

Her uncle's smile was quick and rueful. "This is what happens at a certain age, Rebecca; your children start nannying you. You don't have any children, do you?" The expression in her uncle's face was mild, but some note in his voice made her heart beat faster.

"No."

"Well, there's still time." He turned to Storm. "What are you up to today?"

"I don't know," Storm yawned. "There's a party Evan and I want to go to."

"Why don't you take Rebecca with you?" Her uncle turned to her. "Would you like to go?"

She saw Storm's body reach the pool and falter, almost imperceptibly. Then he kept walking.

"Ah, he didn't hear you."

"That's fine."

"No," her uncle gave her another kindly, open, yet somehow manufactured smile, "I'll tell you what — we'll go sailing, if not this weekend then the next. As a family."

The sands of the beach were warm, even though a layer of high translucent cloud hid the sun. *You have to keep an eye out. Don't go too far from the house. The tide comes in quickly. When it comes in there is no beach. You don't want to be swimming home. The undertow will take you down.* Julia's many warnings — about the tide, the motorcycle taxis, the mini-buses squashing twenty-five people in a space designed for twelve — rang in her mind.

She set out walking to the headland, perhaps a kilometre away. Beyond it was a cove she'd seen from the terrace of the house. The cliffs she passed were of a fine-grained peach sand, pockmarked with pied kingfisher nests. The birds appeared in the entrance of their holes, shook their heads at her, then crept back into their tunnels.

Houses lined the low cliff above in two or three-acre intervals. Each of these was connected to their parcel of beach by a stone staircase. The stone was weathered and pitted almost to pumice. She had read that these staircases were once a supply route; dhows would sidle up to the cliffs and deliver goods to the house and to the villages beyond. There were few roads in those days. Life was conducted by sea.

She saw a figure in the distance, someone sitting alone, hunched over on the sand.

As she approached, the figure did not lift his head. Nothing in Storm's posture or demeanour suggested invitation. She stopped several metres away from him.

He stood with a jolt. On the sand where his legs had been was an oval. In the distance it had looked to her like a rock, a piece of driftwood. It was shiny, olive-coloured. Its edges were neatly scalloped.

She leaned toward it and the oval-shaped object moved.

"They retract their head and legs when they're threatened." He leant down to pick it up.

He turned the oval. She peered down a dark funnel. She saw a glint. Two small eyes stared out at her from the darkness.

"There you are," she said.

He raised his eyes toward her and gave her a shocking smile. "The tide's coming in," he said. "There you go. Take it easy."

The turtle crawled toward the tideline. At the lip of the ocean it hesitated. The turtle was washed by a single wave; it floated, buffeted by sea. Then, with a jolt it began paddling. They watched as it melted into the waves.

They walked back to the house. He told her about the turtles that nested along the coast, how the females lumbered up the beach under the cover of darkness to lay their eggs, how he had helped countless hatchlings run the gauntlet of gulls on their arduous journey to the edge of the ocean. The sun came out. Under its glare the sea turned a hot garnet.

When they arrived back at the house Julia was getting out of her car, a dull silver Land Cruiser. Julia wore a white semi-transparent shirt, a green and turquoise bikini beneath it. A slim silver bangle rested on her upper arm.

Julia's eye flickered over them. "Where have you two been?"

"I went for a walk on the beach and bumped into Storm." Her explanation was completely true, but Julia's eye shuttled back and forth between them.

"Can I help with the shopping?" she offered.

"No, the staff will bring it in." Julia pressed the horn twice. Grace and Michael, the gardener, appeared. Julia turned to her. "I thought we could do one of our little walks."

She had begun to help Julia on her patrols of the house to dust and rearrange its many objects. They both seemed to delight in this. The orphan part of her enjoyed following her aunt around the house; she was an audience, but perhaps this is what children are, she thought: audience and adoring companion.

Julia looked so much like her mother from behind, her trim legs, which emerged from hips perched high in a slightly swayed back. But when Julia turned around the illusion was shattered. Her hair had been expensively coloured in striations of dark honey, platinum, even a faint note of pink. Her mother's hair had been naturally golden in the sun, and her nails had always been unvarnished, bitten at the rims, unlike Julia's perfectly manicured hands.

They walked from one end of the five-acre parcel of land to the other, where seedlings grew in the herb garden encased in mesh to protect it from the monkeys. Plated lizards scattered at their approach; she saw only the chevron of their tails and their stout babies' legs thrashing away through the undergrowth.

Julia recited the names of the trees and flowers that flourished in the perimeter and gardens of the house. There were neem, mbambakofi and Indian almond trees, as well as the fern-like casuarinas, which grew well in sandy soil. The coral creeper, its warm pastel pink flowers, climbed high into the upper branches of the neem. Three types of palm grew on their land, the golden, lala and coconut palms. Two small baobabs grew on the terraces down to the ocean. "It will only take a thousand years for them to mature," Julia said.

She marched behind her aunt, the gold axe of the sun cleaving her head in two. "Hibiscus," Julia said, pointing to a crimson flower, so bright it almost throbbed. "Allamanda — that's the flower that grows through the louvers in the downstairs bathroom." They stopped by the cerise desert rose and thin urns containing a narrow-growing plant called mother-in-law's tongue.

The showpiece of the house were the clouds of bougainvillea that fell over its white coral walls. It grew in three colours — fuchsia, a deep, rich red and a delicate white. It was these leaves that blew down the nighttime corridors of the house to be captured by Grace and her broom in the mornings.

"It's so fertile here."

"You can grow anything, but the monkeys will eat it. They trashed the hibiscus last year. Bill had to shoot them away from the golden palm fruit with his air rifle."

"Really?"

"They look tame, but don't be fooled. They're vicious."

She had seen them in the trees a couple of times already, looking at her with their amber eyes. She didn't understand how monkeys could be vicious — mischievous, yes. But then she imagined Julia had fought and lost many wars with them, losing papayas left to ripen on the kitchen counter or cooling cakes uncovered within the grasp of the louver windows.

"Lucy never took an interest in the garden, and my friends live in the city." Julia gave her no sense of how these two statements were related or what had provoked them. "They come down twice a year, at Christmas and August." Julia looked away, toward the sea. "It's too exotic for some of them. They can't handle the fact that a plated lizard darts out from underneath the freezer. And lately of course they're afraid for other reasons. They don't want to risk running road blocks."

Julia stopped and squinted unhappily at a fern-like plant in a pot whose tips had turned a grainy white. "Look, the *dudus* are after my bonsai golden palm."

She thought of the threads of spider webs that parted against her skin as she walked through the house. Spiders wove webs everywhere overnight — on the stairs, in the corners of her room. Morning exposed the overnight missions of ants, who had found mysterious lucre hidden under Julia's prized goat hair carpet.

They came upon a cone-shaped anthill of dust. This was the efflux of the white ants that were eating their way through the house, and which were also in the process of shattering Julia's prized mangrove sculptures and the timber beams, as well as pulverizing the thick-spined leather volumes on the bookshelf by the *baraza*. Thin rivers of ants poured into the house from the garden, everywhere.

"I've never seen so many insects in my life."

"I rub the walls with cloves, that's the only thing to do, it goes back to the first Arabs who came here," Julia said. "Ants hate the smell. Still, I wonder if one day I'll be walking through the living room and I'll just hear a giant whoosh!" Julia threw up her hands in the air, startling her. "And the house will collapse around me like a piece of scenery."

It rained that afternoon. A hush came over the garden. Even the constant sigh of the sea was muted. To quell her restlessness she helped Grace sweep the patio and pull up the weeds that pushed their way through the thinnest of fissures in the tiles. Through all of this Grace looked at her with an absent wonder, as if a giraffe had suddenly appeared and started sweeping the floor.

On one of these cleaning missions she dusted the bookshelf. She ran her eyes along the books, their titles in faded gold emboss: *The Conquest of Lake Victoria*; *An Encyclopedia of Seashells*; *Vanishing Africa*.

She pulled out an imposing book titled *Dhows*. On the flyleaf she saw Bill's name and then, *with love from Julia, in memory of Dar to Zanzibar by dhow*.

The introduction told her that the boats were first sailed by the Sumerians and the Phoenicians; it was thought that Noah's Ark had been a dhow. The names of their designs sounded like diseases or incantations: *Sambuk* and *Baggala* were large, cargo-carrying dhows that looked like Elizabethan galleons; the *ngalawa* were an outrigger canoe-type fishing boat favoured by fishermen all along the Indian

Ocean coast; the *jahazi* was a small fishing dhow and was the version favoured locally. The dhow's sails looked triangular but were actually quadrilateral. They were made from a cotton called *madrouf*, the book told her. The mainsail was called a *lateen*.

She heard the castanet trill of the yellow-rumped tinkerbird. Then the nasal slew of the trumpeter hornbills as they swayed back and forth in the thinnest top branches of the casuarinas, hooting as if on a funfair ride. She found a pair of binoculars on the baraza just in time to spot an Amani sunbird, a small woodland sunbird with a bottle-green head, white breast with a flash of scarlet near its wing. In Gariseb her observations of birds were confined to the hours just before dawn or at dusk. In between rounds, operations, medical team and logistics meetings, lunch breaks and tea breaks consumed her time. The fact that her days were now free to observe animals and birds elicited a furtive guilt.

Where was Julia? It was five o'clock. The refrigerator's hum filled the empty house. Julia usually left a note on the table. There was never any salutation, no *Dear Rebecca*, only instructions: *There's dal in the fridge. There's fresh lemonade. Help yourself.*

She went into the kitchen. Storm was leaning on the counter.

"Where's Julia — where's your mother?"

"She told me to take you fishing."

"She did?"

"Yes. The day after tomorrow. The tides are right. We need to get up at four thirty."

"Oh." She looked around the house, as if someone might appear to help explain this puzzling turn of events. "Fine then," she said. Then, "I'd like that."

She turned and realized as she did she didn't know where she was going. She walked across the living room with the unmistakable sensation of being watched. His eyes were on her back; their impress was light, questioning. She stopped to look at five small

discs of wood mounted on the wall of the house. She had seen them
before, but in the way of the house, so full of driftwood sculptures,
lanterns and fabrics, she had tuned them out. Two showed a cres-
cent moon and a star. Three seemed to have a miniature ship in
their middle.

"They're the eyes."

She nearly jumped. She hadn't heard him follow her.

"Eyes?"

"Of the dhow. All dhows have them. This one," he pointed to the
star and moon combination, "is on one side of the bow, the eye is on
the other. The moon and the stars symbolize navigation; the eye is to
ward off the evil eye."

"What's that?"

"You really haven't heard of the evil eye?"

"I'm a doctor. A rationalist," she added, for good measure.

"Bad spirits."

"Oh, a superstition."

"No, more real than that." He turned back to the eyes. "I got them
for Mum in Puku. They're from two dhows that were scuttled. They
were about to throw them away. They've been at sea for hundreds of
years, some of them. When they take apart a dhow it's almost as if
they're dismembering a person."

She was transfixed by the look of sorrow on his face, then, by the
way it had cast steel shadows along his brow, his mouth.

Outside, mosque swallows cut through the air. He stared into the
sky, following the birds. "They're heading home for the night. They
nest in the minarets."

"What other birds are around now?"

"Trumpeter hornbills because the neem is in flower," he said.
"There's an osprey that fishes right in front of the house. And a
Wahlberg's eagle or two down the beach."

"I love their colour. Like salted toffee."

"You know them?"

"A little."

"Why are you so interested in birds?" he asked.

"There are so many of them, and they're all different. It seems a miracle of evolution that in one place you have a starling with a scarlet breast, and in another place it's golden. They're not really part of our lives. They don't belong to our dimension."

She waited to see what he would make of this, watching his face for clues. "I like them too," he said.

He walked back into the house. She watched him go. He never said hello or goodbye, he never excused himself in any way. Perhaps this was the reason for the strange abandonment she felt whenever he left the room.

A brochure lay on the dining room table. A note was scrawled on a Post-it: *Thought you might be interested. Jx*

She told Grace she was going into town. Before she even reached the road a motorcycle taxi sidled up to her; its driver had spotted her walking down the lane. She could not walk anywhere on the main road by herself without twenty motorcycle taxi drivers stopping next to her within minutes. *Want a ride? Want a ride?* When she said she did not they were affronted. She relented eventually and hopped on, riding pillion behind a thin young man.

He left her at the entrance fifteen minutes later. She braved an onslaught of young men selling coconuts at the gate. She looked into one man's eyes, which were rimmed with red. He lopped off the top of a coconut to reveal a reservoir of water. She was not thirsty but she bought one anyway. As soon as she had, the others pressed around her. She handed them coins, which they took in the pale centres of their palms and stared at as if she'd just handed them an insect.

She walked down a lane shaded by tobacco-hued sycamore fig trees. The ruined city came upon her slowly; a square arch eaten alive by the root of one of the fig trees, a low maze of chocolate stones, ankle height, the foundations of what would once have been a street. After the steel heat of the town, the ruins were cool and quiet. From its margins she heard the clicks of monkeys. She became aware of lithe forms winding themselves around branches.

"Cool day, isn't it?"

The voice came from behind her. She turned around to see a woman dressed in black sitting on the perimeter fence of the ruins, surrounded by a group of grey and russet monkeys.

"It's pretty hot."

"I meant cool as in nice."

"You're American."

"Sort of. You look new," the woman said.

"I am."

The woman made no move to descend from the fence. Four monkeys flanked her on either side. The woman exchanged a knowing look with the monkeys, who cast their faces downward and looked uncertainly at their palms.

"Don't come any closer for the moment."

"Why not?"

"The monkeys don't know you."

"Will they attack me?"

"No, but they might run away."

"Do you work here?"

"I do. I'm an archaeologist." The woman was slight, with dark brown hair just visible under her hat. Her eyes were large and glossy. She looked like a fawn. She might be very young, or her own age. She had nothing to do with her mental picture of an archaeologist — hard, sunburnt women dressed in khakis. "How about you?"

"I'm a doctor."

"Oh, cool. Do you work here?"

"No, in the highlands. I've been there for four months. I'm down on the coast visiting family." She had been practising this litany for just such an occasion. It rolled off her tongue convincingly smoothly.

The woman remained sitting on the stone wall. The sun drilled into her. She moved into the shade.

"Aren't you prevented from being here? All the embassy staff have been forbidden to travel to the coast. Didn't your organization put out some kind of directive?"

She found it difficult to read the woman's tone — inviting yet wary, seemingly casual but with a sharp note buried within. "They did, but I got special dispensation," she added, "because my family lives here."

"You look a little young to be a doctor."

She laughed. "Everyone says that."

She was close enough now to see the monkeys' faces, how their expressions differed. One had a sage look. Another's forehead was knit together, as if with worry. Its face was narrow, fringed by orange bristles, like an eighteenth century gentlemen's sideburns. Its fur was blue-grey, luminous.

"So are you here from the States?"

"Well, yes and no. I did my doctorate on these ruins. I'm Margaux, by the way." She slid from the fence. This caused apprehension in the monkeys, who darted glances from the woman to her. "I'll give you my number. We can go out for a drink. It's not so easy to hang out on your own as a lone woman in this town."

She absorbed that Margaux's invitation came wrapped in self-interest. But she could not help feeling grateful; she might need a friend, someone outside the house.

Margaux said she would take her on a tour of the ruins. They walked under the tall figs, their trunks gleaming in the afternoon light. Black-breasted starlings and green barbets perched in the trees' plate-shaped leaves.

45

"Watch your step," Margaux cautioned. "There are stones every-where." Most of the city was rubble now, apart from two crumbling archways, once the entrances to the sultan's palace, Margaux said.

"Who lived here?"

Margaux stopped at the threshold to a structure, no more than her height. They stood in the shell of what once might have been a doorway. "That's the mystery. No one is quite sure. It was a kind of secret city. No one knew about it, apart from the residents. The Portuguese built Moholo and Kilindoni and had their main fort only ten kilometres way, but they had no idea it existed."

She tried to take the measure of the city. The ruins were around two kilometres inland, she guessed — close enough that the ocean appeared as a blue slice in the distance. She had been to the ruined cities of the Maya and Aztec in Mexico and Guatemala. The air of imperial grandeur, and behind it, of cruelty, was absent here, with its quiet, draping lianas and wide, shaded avenues. Even the monkeys seemed to revere the place. They were less antic than at the Dhow House.

"So it wasn't a trading post?"

"It was, but the sea was probably farther away then, up to ten kilo-metres even, so they would have unloaded the boats and walked every-thing through the forest. *Siri* — its name means secret," Margaux said. "It was abandoned around 1650. Nobody knows why."

"Is that what you are trying to find out?"

"In part. Archaeologists are not mystery solvers, although you'd be excused from thinking that depending on how many Discovery Channel documentaries you've watched."

"The ruins are not as ghostly as they are in Mexico."

"Well they didn't practise wholesale human sacrifice here. So that helps keep the ghost count down. As ruins go, they're pretty friendly. Although now and then when I'm here in the early morning or at sundown I get a sense I'm being watched."

"By who?"

Margaux shrugged. "Like I said, it's a feeling. It's not real."

It was five o'clock. The light had thickened. She felt the tug of evening. A breeze appeared from nowhere — certainly not from the direction of the ocean. They drew to a halt underneath a tree and looked out to sea, just visible beyond the palm trees that fringed the ruins. The cloud had cleared, revealing a horizon broken by breakers folding over a distant reef.

"Here's my card," Margaux presented her with a damp rectangle. "Give me a call anytime. We can hang out."

"I will," she said. "I'm afraid I don't have a card but I'll text you."

"Great," Margaux said, although there was no particular energy in her voice. Rather she sounded languid, almost sleepy. "We'll have a blast."

By the time she returned the electricity was off, casting the house in solemn twilight.

Julia greeted her at the door. "We've run out of diesel for the generator. We'll have to do with candles."

Julia looked exhausted. Bahari ya Manda was only an hour away, but the road was bad, and traffic could clog the city so much so that travellers regularly missed their flights from the airport even if they left three hours early. This was one of the nuggets of information she'd gleaned from her conversation that afternoon with Margaux. "The roadblocks have made it worse," Margaux had said, her face sheathed in a pool of shade thrown by her wide-brimmed hat. "A trip to the supermarket is a four-hour affair now."

Julia made them each a gin and tonic. From the patio grounds came the intermittent screech of a bush baby. "Well, cheers." Julia lifted her glass. "I always need a drink after the supermarket trip."

"Where is Bill?"

"He's away on business." Julia's eyes had turned olive in the evening. She fixed her with a frank look. "He's having to spend a lot of time in the city because of the banks."

"Which banks?"

"His bank, Pan-African. Well, his money is mostly offshore — this is the local bank; it's been seized by the government."

"I haven't heard anything in the news."

Julia laughed. "Oh, you wouldn't. It's not like in England — a free press, journalistic standards. They've got that very much under control here. It's being kept quiet."

"What's the issue?"

"Fraud. Insider dealing, supposedly, but that's a set-up. The Central Bank has their eye on the money so they've concocted the story. They've frozen the assets of a million citizens."

"Can that really be true?"

Julia's head rotated stiffly. "You don't believe me?"

"No, it's just in England there'd be a riot, or a national outcry at least."

"But this is not England. Do you think there's a financial services authority to guarantee your deposit? Do you know that so-called politicians have nearly bankrupted the national airline to line their own pockets?"

"No," she said. "Is there a substantial amount of money at stake?"

"Not in pounds sterling. But here, yes, a small fortune."

"I'm so sorry."

Julia shrugged. "Fortunately our necks aren't on the line. We'll have to raid the Guernsey account for a while, that's all."

"That's not so bad then," she said.

Julia gave her a look she could only describe as suspicious. "This country is becoming ungovernable."

She thought of the slim folder Anthony had pressed into her

hand. It had contained printouts of bank account statements and tax declarations, proof of non-domicile status. There was nothing irregular, he'd said. But she could remember seeing nothing about Pan-African bank. She did remember the file informed her that twenty years before, Bill had set up one of the country's low-cost airlines. What was it called? Zoom, Zip, something like that. She'd had only ten minutes to scan the contents. She was not allowed to take a copy.

The fridge stuttered on. The electricity was back. She and Julia floated around the living room, snuffing out the candles, which gave small exhausted hisses as they were extinguished.

Julia's phone rang. She walked into the living room. She spoke for only a few seconds, then returned. "You'll excuse me, won't you, Rebecca? Bill rang, he needs me to go up to Moholo. I've made a prawn curry for you and left it in the fridge."

"Thank you, you didn't have to."

"It's the least I can do. You'll have to hold the fort tonight. You don't mind, do you?"

"Not at all. I need some time on my own, in fact."

"I know you do. I can imagine you're not used to this —" Julia swept her hand around the empty dining room "milling about."

Alone in the house that night she heard many sounds normally masked by the presence of people; the mechanical chirr of the slender-tailed nightjar, the low scoping cry of an owl, half-strangled sounds of alarm she could not identify.

She awoke — how much later she could not say — and sat up with a jolt to a crisp gunshot sound. She listened intently for a few minutes before she was sure it was only a shutter snapping against its frame, somewhere down the long corridor of the house's second storey. The house swallowed the wind and funnelled it to the back. The house was an amphitheatre, every sound magnified by its wall-less mouth, open to the sea.

She stood. She didn't know where she was going; she didn't care. She had no talent for ambivalence, for inhabiting this in-between place. She had spent all her life on the edge of accomplishment, of finality. She had no talent any more for process.

She started walking down the long passageway, lined by louvered windows on one side and nut-brown wood on the other. It led to the master bedroom where her uncle and aunt slept. They must have come home at some point before the midnight curfew. At its turn, on an L-shaped bend, was Storm's room. In the strip of light visible under the door shadows flitted back and forth.

She returned to her room quickly and had nearly closed the door behind her when another opened with a crack. She leant back into the shadows.

Two bodies emerged. Through the crack in her door she saw them in the dim corridor as they serpentined down the spiral staircase. When their outlines had disappeared down the stairs she went to stand at the top step.

She could see only a rectangular piece of the living room. In view was the top of Storm's head. Evan — she knew it was him from his voice — had walked away. She heard the fridge open and shut. Storm sat on the white sofa, his back toward the stairs. A hand appeared and worked its way through Storm's hair. It lingered on the crown of his head. Storm's paler hand clasped it, arrested its progress.

She stumbled backwards, hitting her heel on the wrought iron balustrade. She had to breathe in sharply to avoid crying out.

"What was that?"

"I don't know."

"I heard something."

Then the padding of feet, coming to the stairs, mounting them — feet that were used to owning the house and the night.

She flung herself into bed. She darted out her hand and drew the mosquito net closed. A crack of light appeared in the door. Then the door shut.

"It's nothing," she heard Storm say to Evan outside her door, the only sound now the lean palm trees battering their heads against the house. "They're all asleep."

II

BLACK-
BELLIED
BUSTARD

A tall ginger-haired man was coming toward her, striding fast. "You alright?"

She shook her head.

"It's forty-four degrees in the shade. It gets to you here." He put a hand on her elbow. "You look like you're about to swoon."

"Swoon." Silver stars sparked and died in her eyes. "I haven't heard that word in a hundred years."

"Well, you look old, but not that old. What are you doing out here anyway?"

She had walked to the edge of the compound to escape camp, its disinfectant smell, the tinny radio that sang with local pop songs, always, from the nursing station, the scabbed knees of the patients, the issues of the *Economist* and *Prospect* on her desk and which she had read so many times their edges had curled.

"Here," the man held out a bottle of Gatorade.

"Where did this come from?"

"Alabama, probably, courtesy of the UN." The man's face carved itself into a dismissive grimace. "You got to hand it to the UN; it sure knows how to cart bottled drinks around the globe. I wonder what the carbon footprint of this one is."

His words didn't quite cohere in her mind. She drank it in one go, its sickly lime slipping down her throat. "I'm out of practice," she said. "The heat," she added, for measure.

"I heard you were in Helmand. Weren't you in Iraq, too?"

"News travels fast." *Andy*, that was his name. It came to her. They had been introduced briefly that morning. "How did you know?"

"Don't worry about it; it's probably hotter here."

"I've been in England too long."

"I know, I try to spend six months in the place, max. Long enough to file a tax return, short enough not to be corrupted by money and house prices."

She had to smile. There were always characters like this, everywhere she worked — thin, ironic men who survived on a diet of sardonic quips and servitude.

The field hospitals were always the same, too, remote colonies, advance parties sent to the moon. A generator, a water filtration unit, a backup generator. Transparent plastic boxes full of documents stacked high and forming a maze in the logistics tent like an art installation in the turbine hall of the Tate Modern. These were full of procurement orders, Hilux truck manuals, health and safety procedures.

Andy disappeared. The sun was levering toward the earth, just beyond the accommodation tents. She took an inventory of this new home. All present and correct: generator, back-up generator; refrigerated portakabin where freezers for the blood and plasma stock were kept; a much smaller rectangle where the food freezers hummed. The triage tent, ICU, recovery bay, processing tent, staff compound. It was a functional version of the travelling circuses that used to cluster in the summer near their house just off Clapham Common. Here, the circus animals were Giacometti copies of their tiger and elephant cousins: scrawny goats that tottered around the tents and the donkeys and the camels, floating regally on the outskirts of camp like a bored imperial guard.

She had arrived at Gariseb in early February, just after the hottest time of year had passed. With summer — December and January — came the *Jilal*, the season of no rain. The heat became more intense with each day until it could not be withstood. She shied away from the sun, fleeing to the scrawny shade offered by the three haggard acacias. The spindled trees, the dull ochre hills and their copper ridges cooked in convection waves. She hadn't thought such heat possible, apart from furnaces, or the epicentre of a solar flare.

The high plain on which Gariseb sat was surrounded by green knuckle-shaped mountains and stately equatorial skies. The camp straddled a border in the desert, a straight line as arbitrary as any drawn by an imperium. Across these invisible boundaries, famished people materialized daily. They appeared first as dark question marks flanked by goats and pitted camels, or alone, burdened only by the hump of what they could carry on their backs.

The wounded were transmitted to the hospital in pick ups. The camp had a trio of dingy tents, shaky prefab lozenges that housed the camp office, the satellite phone, the one and only computer. There was no mobile signal, not even a local radio station. No news reached them or would, she knew, other than the BBC World Service, which they could listen to on the satellite internet connection, and occasional telephone calls to the capital city. Emails came once a day in a consolidated block via satellite phone.

For the first two weeks at Gariseb she dreamt of helicopters; the angry angel of the American Black Hawks or the ashen UN beasts of burden, plucking out the souls who made the mistake of staying too late. She couldn't bear to fly in helicopters. It was the way they came down. She'd seen it, more than once. They dropped from the sky like stones.

The battlefield was different here. It was mobile, a fluid stain in the empty quadrant of the south of the country. Her previous postings had been farther from the fighting, and an army, British or American, had been either on-site or nearby. In Gariseb they had no backup; the British army base was three hundred miles away. The violence from which the casualties were envoys could easily reach out and engulf them. Even as they ate their lunch of goat or camel in lime and chili she would keep an eye on the door of the mess tent, expecting the snouts of AKs to appear at any moment. At night she slept fully clothed, a full army-issue Osprey water bottle beside her bed in case she had to flee into the desert.

It was two months before she acclimatized. In the afternoons, when the heat was at its peak, she would stand in the spiky shadow thrown by an *acacia mellifera*, the sweet-thorn tree. The ground was pitted with tracks — the tiny Vs of dik-diks, the unmistakeable tire tread of a puff adder, hopefully now far away. The fissure valleys that surrounded camp had been cut by rivers, long dried up. She imagined lions lurking behind the ridge, watching her.

"Don't even try to understand this situation," Andy told her on one of those nights when they both stood outside, waiting for the cool of evening to offer respite. "You'll get nowhere."

She understood well enough. She had the advantage of a specialist weekend seminar, held in a village whose name she was sworn not to repeat, located in one of the flat minor shires northwest of London. There she had sat in a Chequers-like mansion surrounded by people like her, plucked ripe on the professional tree, who two weeks later would pitch up in Manila or Lahore or Erbil, all of them looking wistfully out the window, already nostalgic for the moral certainties, forty kinds of yogurt and imported Sauvignon blanc of home.

There, experts informed her that Gariseb was located in a blasted vector of semi-arid scrubland, seasonally desertified, between four countries. To the north was a stable country of water and vine-choked terrazas. To the northwest, a newly formed nation that had split from its larger cousin and was busy prospecting for oil. To the east was a country that had imploded, ungovernable, a "failed state," a "haven for international terrorism" in US State Department–speak.

In the failed state/haven, aid workers were taken as spies and informants and were at risk of being shot on sight. To the west, in the newly formed country, aid was still vital to the project of nation-building, and welcome. But there, in the last two months, old rivalries between the major ethnic groups of the country, the Bora and the Nisa, had erupted. Pockets of random, non-state violence — a cattle raid here, a shoot-up about profits made from a palm-wine shebeen there — had left hundreds of young men dead.

The conflict seemed to have taken its cue from the landscape. It was gaunt, half-hearted. The real war was in Gikayo, a hundred kilometres away, and in the coastal city of Gao, which looked out into the Arabian Sea.

In Gariseb the days started at six a.m. The sun appeared without warning, a clouded disk that had been hovering in the sky all night. But within a minute it charged, heraldic, into the equatorial sky. She took three bucket showers a day. The dust clumped in her nostrils; if she blew them in the arid air the tissue came away black.

At night the shadows were stone. She stood on the perimeter of the light thrown by the generator's striplights. Sometimes she thought she saw shapes, bundle-sized, moving from thorn tree to rock; child goat-herders on the outskirts of their employers' land, straggling behind their quick-trotting charges.

The land was heartless. Or rather, it could have little use for them, for anyone. This indifference was so absolute it was almost cleansing. The brassy ridges of the hills broadcast a curious pulsing intent, like a heartbeat. The hills knew they didn't belong there; they had never seen their kind before, these medical colonists with their moon tents and solar powered walk-in refrigerator and strong boxes and provisions flown in twice a month. The long resinous grass that came and died the one week they had rain wagged its head in disapproval in the rare wind. *I know you*, it seemed to say to her, with its bare hills that leaned so readily into the night. *I know what you are doing here.*

"Okay, I think we're almost there. You can finish up?" A question curled in Rafael's voice, but he did not stay to hear it answered. He was already behind her, shucking off his gloves.

In the two months she had worked alongside Rafael, she had managed to glean that he was a Madrileño. He certainly looked the part: thin, edgy, a smoker. There was a bit of the dandy to him, if only because his goatee beard was always perfectly trimmed. Harsh glasses concealed fine caramel eyes. In the evenings he set himself personal building projects, working with the mechanics in the shed, fiddling with drills and old light bulbs. He produced light fixtures he referred to as "sculptures."

Rafael had been an anarchist in university; he was arrested and held for five months after a student protest, he'd told her. She wasn't sure if that experience explained the narrow, hard streak within him. As a surgeon he was fussy, exacting. She had the sense that he might have perceived she was the better seamstress, where arterial surgery was concerned, and resented her for it.

That day's casualty came late, at four o'clock. Rafael unwound shrouds of gauze, sticky with flesh, to reveal a sabre wound to the tibia. It was deep — this is what distinguished it from a normal knife wound. Sabres were invented for a reason; they could slice cleanly through sinew and tendon and bone.

They set to work. It proved a surprisingly easy job. She sutured under Rafael's exacting eye. They were done within an hour.

She pulled aside the curtain and threw her gloves into the hospital waste bin. Out of the corner of her eye she saw a sack — rags, perhaps — on one of the few rusted trolleys. It was parked beside the tent, against the billowing walls. As she approached, the bundle twitched.

She put her hand out and touched it. The bundle turned over and revealed a dark face. Dull eyes stared at her.

She asked her name. The dull eyes followed her lips. She pointed to her ear. The woman shook her head. Two claw-like hands emerged from the bundle and went to her ears, then quickly apart. *Boom*, she mouthed in a soundless oval.

"I will find you a bed," she mouthed. She lay her head sideways on her folded hands.

The woman closed her eyes. The expression on her face was indeterminate. It ought to have been relief, but it looked like sorrow.

The following day she went to check on the woman.

"I can hear now," the woman said. Her voice was deep and strong.

"Temporary deafness — a bomb."

"Yes, yes." Then a stream of words in a dialect she couldn't understand. She called for Lenjoh, the interpreter.

The woman, Aisha, told her story. She had walked from her home, crossing grassy mountains inhabited by sociable baboons, cutting thin valleys with her miniature camel train, walking for ten days without food and only a little water. She'd slept only two or three hours a night. Her animals began to suffer: first from sleep deprivation, then hunger, then thirst. But Aisha had kept going. She'd brought three camels and five cows, her only remaining animals. She'd heard there was a food station on the other side of the border.

By night she hid her animals in the bush and slept inside a thorny acacia. Twice men with guns walked past her, looking for her. They'd seen her tracks but she'd been careful to erase the last several hundred metres with a makeshift broom of thorns.

By day she walked through the bush. She'd seen people — black stick figures, she'd said — coming toward her and panicked. But they turned out to be apparitions.

Three of her sons were dead, killed fighting Al-Nur. They had been coerced into uniform by the state. "They were herders," she said, through Lenjoh. "Men of peace." By the time she had made it to camp, only one camel was alive. She had seen this camel tethered to a tree just outside camp, heard him lowing painfully day and night.

"Please take care of him," the woman begged her. "I cannot feed him."

For the next ten days she took her staff ration of UHT milk and fed it to the camel via a makeshift funnel given to her by a sweet Irishman on the mechanics team. She gathered leaves from the few acacias in flower, swaddling her hands in thick gloves to avoid the thorns. She plucked sparse grass, as Aisha had instructed her to do.

At first the camel swivelled its backside at her, and she feared it would kick. But after he'd taken the first draught of milk he let her approach. When he saw her he made a deep rumbling noise that could have been pleasure or pain. At night she fed him water.

She was forty-seven, Aisha told her. She looked seventy. When Aisha was strong enough she was given a small tent from their store of fifty or so. These were lime green Vango tents from the UK. Aisha had stared at it as if she'd just been given a four-bedroomed house.

The camel stayed attached to a nearby stunted whistling thorn, which it quickly stripped of its leaves. In her breaks she led the camel out to pasture as far beyond the camp as she dared and stayed there while it fed, leading it back to Aisha's tent at night. During one of those breaks she watched a rainbow form, far away. A sudden wind swept dust in a spiral, erasing its beams in an orange haze. In the distance was the scrawny valley where it was rumoured lions lived.

The sun set as it always did, hurling itself over the horizon. It was dark within ten minutes. The moon rose and the corrugated landscape bathed in silver strips. She stared into its gleam, thinking how the detail of her life was so unanticipated — she had worked in barren, blasted places before, of course, but they were almost always military hospitals, run by rote and fear. She never spent her off-hours tending to a lone camel as if she'd been appointed its guardian angel, trying to read the expression in its indifferent eyes. It pleased her to be so disrupted from her sense of herself.

"How is the camel doing?" Rafael appeared next to her. She was startled. In three months he had never sought out her company, other than to discuss the surgical rota for the day, the new nurse arriving from London, or logistics.

"He's getting stronger."

Together they watched the camel orbit the acacia. He didn't seem to mind the hobbles, stepping around them delicately, padding back and forth with his cushioned, dinner plate–sized feet.

"I wonder if the lions would go for him," he said.

"I know. I'm thinking I should put him in my tent, and I'll sleep outside."

Rafael gave her a quick sideways glance.

"It's a joke." Although, as she said it, she wondered. The Bedouin's camels slept with them. She quite liked the idea of settling down on a rug beside him.

"Ah," Rafael nodded. "I don't think the logistics people would permit it, actually."

She watched Rafael walk away to his makeshift workshop where he struggled with his sculptures.

The moon had risen. It hovered in the east, low-slung, peering at her with its censor eye.

Yes, Gariseb had been this, so far, strange dislocation. It was not merely a more remote version of other field hospitals she had worked in. In Gariseb she treated Christians and Muslims side by side, and in the recovery tents or the canteen a détente ruled: there were no skirmishes, not even arguments. It seemed the wounded found common ground. In any case she was uninterested in religion or ideology. She normally traversed far more intimate terrain — the flooded blood vessels, the exploded retinas, the tributaries and marshlands of flesh.

She ought to have felt harassed, or at least discontented by the camp, its isolation, her straitened circumstances, her sudden demotion to camel herder. But she was glad to be back in the field. If she had stayed in her job at St. Thomas', she'd never have understood any of this — but what? She still could not identify it exactly, this suddenly pressing truth. It was like a dark, sleek animal, glimpsed only before it disappeared around the corner.

S he had been there for nearly four months when he appeared. She was working fifteen-hour shifts. Sleep had become a dreamless refuge.

She emerged from one of these nightly comas into an orange morning. The camp was quiet at six a.m. There were no twelve-year-olds who would soon be footless, no pickup trucks of bleeding villagers. These began to arrive after seven a.m., the casualties of dawn assaults.

She ate her customary breakfast quickly — coffee and a small bowl of porridge. The diet had become oppressive. Every day lunch was the same: sorghum flatbreads and goat stew. The organization made a gesture to western cuisine in the form of chicken legs, flown in on the UN plane every month and pushed to the bottom of the vault-like meat freezer. She had eaten no fish. She found that a dull desire, not as sharp as a craving, had taken hold of her bones. There was an oily base to the hunger.

She walked to the triage tent. Out of the corner of her eye she caught sight of a man leaning against the wall. She couldn't remember seeing him before, couldn't remember pulling him out of the flatbed of a pickup truck.

He approached her. He was like a greyhound, quick, aquiline. There was a flash in his eye, a firmness to the slant of his mouth. His age was hard to judge, but then it was, generally, here. The twenty-eight-year-old doctors and logistics managers who worked with her looked twelve. The thirty-two-year-old Bora and Nisa she soldered back together looked sixty-three.

He reached her. "I would like to show you something."

His English hit her like a blow. She had yet to meet an insurgent who would admit to having learned a word of the infidel's language, although many did speak it more than adequately, a result of their training in Yemen. Anthony had shown her surveillance drone photographs of a neat foldaway camp in the mountains two hundred kilometres from Sana'a, in a hill fort that had been the British cavalry headquarters at the turn of the century.

He took out a notebook. It had black covers and ruled pages and was bound by a black elastic. Bound tight to the notebook was a pen. "I will have to translate." He leafed through it. He gave her a hesitant look.

She studied him. His lean frame suggested he was a Bora, although he was not particularly tall. He was most likely from the coastal city of Gao. Most of the men who evaded their questions were from there. She had never been to the city but she had read books and seen photo essays on the once grand resort city. The photographs she had seen were from the 1930s and showed wide, tiled avenues fringed by thin palms. It looked like Rio de Janeiro. There was even an art-deco cinema in town, sandwiched between two Italian restaurants; the names were visible in the bleached black-and-white images: the *Terraza Roma*, the *Toscana*.

The city was between the desert and the same ocean she would come to know in the Dhow House. But the city had lost any sense of its original geography. Entire blocks had vanished in the civil war. Gutted hotels surveyed the Indian Ocean like open-mouthed old men. Former foreign consulates stood roofless to the scald of sun. Gao's salmon-coloured buildings had once been garlanded with second-storey balconies fringed by filigreed stonework. Its mosques had been as white as those she would later see in Kilindoni, their minarets traced in green trim. The beachfront had the same ivory sands, shallow warm waters patrolled by blacktip reef sharks, the desert rose growing on its edge.

The man proceeded to read from his notebook. It was a story he had written, he informed her. The story was about a man who died from shark bite — one of the many sharks that scissored the cold waters off the coast of Gao — only to be reincarnated as a pair of spectacles. Everyone put him on their faces, the man told her, and their sight was instantly corrected. Widows saw the reasons for their husbands' deaths and thanked God for having given them the opportunity to die as martyrs. Children saw their true vocation as soldiers of God. They stopped longing for the streets of the old capital with its bars and Italian magazines, its DVD stalls and mandolin players.

"And the sharks?" She asked.

"The sharks are too big to wear the spectacles, so they go on killing senselessly."

She listened in his voice for any note of irony. Finally she said, "So it's a parable. You are the man who becomes a pair of glasses."

He gave her a solemn, nearly nostalgic look. He was not strident. He didn't seem to have the self-destructive stubbornness others of his kind displayed. His manner was mild but watchful.

The sun's tangerine flare caught his face and turned his skin to bronze. He pointed toward the dressing swaddling his left abdomen. He must have been operated on two or three days before.

"How long will I take to heal?"

"I'll do an examination tomorrow and tell you then."

"I must go home. My father is waiting for me." He named a village not far from Gao. His face lightened at the sound of its name, but his eyes remained two pieces of coal. "You won't tell them?"

"Tell who?"

"Who you speak to, over there," he flung his right hand north, an errant compass.

"We are doctors."

She saw his eyes search her face and fail to find what they were looking for.

He gave his name as Ali. She struggled to picture his body on the operating table. She must have operated on five different men the morning Ali arrived. With his clipped, martinet stride she would recognize his walk in a crowd of similar thin, impala-haunched men. His skin was darker than most, he was not particularly tall or commanding, but he had a commanding quality. He was very thin, a result of his wounds, lack of food, years of loping through the desert and the natural physique of his tribe, the Bora. "We are all like camels," he said. "We need no food, only a little water to keep us going."

There was no appeal or gratitude in Ali's eyes, but no disgust either. He was not like the others she had treated, who looked at her — a woman — with a confused wash of fear and distaste. They squirmed, sometimes, told the interpreter they wanted a man. "There is no man. She treats you, you live. Or you can refuse and die."

Ali's wounds had not been so severe, she recalled. Bone was incredibly strong. If a high-velocity bullet entered a body and hit a bone, it could be deflected, even if the bone itself were shattered. Then the bullet went on a zany trajectory, sometimes travelling up people's forearm, through their shoulder, and out the other end, leaving its trail. If it failed to hit the soft tissue of a vital organ, the casualty might be saved.

There were other wounds, invisible, that only a surgeon would see. The kidney smashed into overripe watermelon, so that the flesh became almost granulated, slipped through her fingers with its ooze of juice and blood. When they hit organs, bullets pulped them. Then there were the bullets that kept on going through the body, having encountered no real resistance, shattering out the other side of a shoulder or an arm, taking with it a triangle of flesh, then carrying on into the body of the person behind them, passing through a shoulder or a neck again, penetrating the skin of a third. These bullets kept going for an average of 2.2 kilometres — another statistic her dry Major boss had taught her, nearly ten years ago now, in Kandahar.

In Ali's case there was a neat exit wound from an AK round which had skirted his abdomen and exited his back, tearing his lateral muscle but missing his spine. She had traced the bullet's cavity, sewed the exit hole, and thought, that's another one ticked off.

The following day she stopped by the recovery tent. Ali sat on the bed. She examined him and pronounced that he would be well enough to leave in two days' time.

"Thank you," he said, in his precise English. In one eye was an inquisitive, even kindly, expression. The other eye's direction was random and interrogating. This astigmatism unnerved her. When she spoke to him sometimes she would focus on the left eye, sometimes the right. It was as if her mind refused to take him all in at once.

That afternoon she was stirring masala into a cup of tea when Andy called to her, telling her she had a visitor.

Ali hovered on the threshold of her office.

"Would you like some tea?" She said, in her best Arabic.

"Thank you," he returned, in English.

"Please, sit down." She offered him an orange plastic chair, regulation issue, coated in dust, like everything else.

He levered himself slowly onto the chair without wincing, but his pain was evident in the twitch of his deltoid.

"You are not quite healed." She knew he was planning to leave the following day. They could do nothing to stop their patients dispatching a goat herder as a runner to the nearest village with a message to send a truck. In the old days they'd had to return people across the border or into frontlines beyond the field hospitals, a dangerous task.

"I am well, thank you."

"I am glad to hear that. *Allahu Akbar.*"

He frowned. "Are you a Muslim?"

"No, but I thank Allah for his grace."

"I wanted to ask you if I could listen to the BBC. It is where I learned my English, from the World Service. It would give me great pleasure to hear it again."

"I'm not sure I can do that."

Ali lowered his cup and fixed her with a grave, certain look. "I only want to listen to the English."

"I believe you. But I don't know if my director will."

Ali put down his cup on the ground. "I thought you were in charge here."

"No, I'm only a doctor."

They looked at each other. The formality of their conversation, the upright, manufactured tone of his supposed radio-learned English, the gravity of Ali's eyes, were for a moment so overwhelming that it threatened to tip over into the absurd. She had to fight against an impulse to laugh. She might be a bit hysterical, with the heat, the hours, the pressure. She hadn't laughed in a month.

"You need to get your bandage changed. Go see Alan in the nurses' tent. Announce yourself first. He is not expecting you."

Ali smiled. "We are none of us expecting anything here."

She watched him cross the courtyard. When he was out of sight she took out the notebook she carried in a money belt–type pouch next to her body and wrote: *Ali. Nom de guerre. Speaks English. One for AC?*

Among the ten days he was in camp were days she would later forget. Or rather it was not that she forgot — each day was subtly different in the dilemmas it presented: a case of anemia, two children with rickets, an elderly man in the grip of malaria — but days when violence did not tear the fabric of their lives somehow failed to cohere in her mind.

"You need to get into the habit of keeping a diary," Anthony had told her soon after their first meeting in London. "Make it a medical diary, but write anything that comes up in code. Decide on one — medicines, procedures, parts of human anatomy. I leave it up to you."

She had enjoyed this part of her task. She decided on arteries for news she heard, anecdotally from her patients or in her eavesdropping missions around camp — *Carotid artery presents oxygenated blood flow. Platelets advancing to hippocampus* translated as: news heard that Al-Nur is advancing from the interior to the coastal capital, Port Al-Saidi. She came up with an emergency code consisting entirely of anti-malarials: chloroquine, atovaquone, proguanil hydrochloride, doxycycline.

It must have been later that week when she finished a repair job, not particularly challenging. Femoral artery of the left leg, frayed but not severed by metal shards from an exploded RPG. Shrapnel came in several disguises, but the blackened residue at the edges of ragged epidermis betrayed the culprit.

She peeled off her gloves and went to stand at the door of the tent. The sun fell on the perimeter of the tented verandah. She wanted to smoke, to drink, to stand on her head. But the nearest cigarette was 270 kilometres away, and she didn't smoke anyway. She tried to remember if a swash remained in the bottle of the contraband vodka she and her colleagues kept stashed under her bed, away from the breathalyzer eyes of the Christian logistics organization. She might have downed it the week before in a similar frenzy of remorse, she couldn't remember.

A bustard — black bellied, she guessed, from the dark shadow on its underside — winged across the sky like a scar.

She went to visit Aisha. She had been living in the Vango tent for two weeks. She refused to speak to men, Andy had told her.

They sat cross-legged on the ground in the meagre shade thrown by a whistling thorn. The camel sat next to them, its long legs folded primly under its body.

"Do you know about the *Wir?*"

La, she said. *No.*

"You people call it luck," Aisha said.

"What is it, then?"

Aisha thought for a moment. "Justice."

She knew the word in Arabic — *eadala*. She knew that people who lived ruined lives clung to justice over luck. She could hardly blame them for being unconvinced that ordinary humans were responsible for their suffering.

Two months before she had left England, an expert from the School of Oriental and African Studies had come to speak to them, a strikingly handsome professor with dark malachite eyes. For the Bora and the Nisa alike, he'd told them, spirit possession meant being in the grip of an external force much more powerful than yourself. Attempts to tame or understand it were futile. For them, these forces represented not ecstasy, nor exorcism, nor possession, only a geometry of the soul and a restitution of order.

She'd worked in places in the grip of similar beliefs: spirit-dogs that stalked the living, harbouring souls of the dead; vultures that were actually someone or other's great-grandfather given wings. Dark fortune lapped effortlessly at the edges of villages razed by rebel forces or visited by famine. She was chastened by the relentlessness of this moral system and she was too tired, these days, to challenge another culture's shamanism. So she did not tell Aisha what she herself believed: that nothing else existed other than human order and morality, human cruelty and human chaos.

She lacked the Arabic to say all this, besides, she no longer had to be right, she no longer wanted to change things. She felt muted, she had felt this way for some time. She seemed to be entering a new phase of life. She was getting used to existence, finally. She felt the pleasant authority of maturity settle within her, but also, connected to it, something dulled, like old silver.

She excused herself and rose. Aisha smiled and thanked her for

71

her visit. She had filled out, somewhat. Her vital signs and iron count had improved.

She walked toward her office. The wind picked up, ruffling the valence of the giant tent. She ought to do paperwork. She didn't know why she was standing, looking out again into a land that gave nothing back, save for the edge of a burning column of setting sun.

Aisha's camel levered himself to his feet at the same moment she had risen. He floated toward her. For him the sight of her had become the equivalent of passing a Sainsbury's on a wet night. He plodded in her direction.

"Aren't you afraid of him?" Andy had materialized beside her. "Camels are vicious buggers."

"Not this one." She waited until the camel filled their vision with his worn doormat nose and chocolate eyes. "I've named him Montague."

Andy nodded. "He looks like a Montague."

"Stay still or he'll know you're afraid," she instructed. The camel's long neck extended in Andy's direction. Andy shrank back. She put a hand on the camel's nose. Immediately his neck drooped. He uttered a low rumble.

"You've gone right native," Andy said.

Andy left and Montague wandered back to the umbrella thorn he had been stripping of its leaves. Her eye caught a smudge in the sand near the operating theatre tent. Its glossy hue meant oil, diesel or blood. Possibly all three. The heat was thinning. In the sky was a watermelon sunset.

"I'm sorry to disturb you."

He stood in his white shirt and torn black trousers. His beard was immaculately trimmed and a pencil was shoved behind his ear. He looked like a village schoolmaster.

"My people are coming to get me."

"You are not yet healed."

"This camp is not well defended."

She stiffened. "Is that a warning?"

"They might think that you will not give me up. I can't communicate with them to tell them otherwise. I need a radio."

"I can't."

"Are you a Shakespearean?" he asked.

"Not particularly. Why?"

"I have a quotation that might interest you. Something I learned on the radio."

A voice called her name with the sharp urgency of something gone wrong. She bolted. After two strides she turned back to Ali, but he had melted away behind her. She never discovered which play he was so eager to recite.

III

RED-
CHESTED
CUCKOO

"I planned the dinner party long before you came," Julia said. "Before we even knew you were coming."

She nodded. "I hope it's not inconvenient."

"Of course not." Her aunt gestured to the fridge. "You're just going to have to fit in. Would you mind taking the prawns from the freezer?"

She rummaged in the depths of the freezer, groping past tuna steaks, Italian ice cream and a frosted bottle of Jägermeister.

Julia sounded annoyed. She felt trapped. What could she do? She called Margaux that afternoon, but she was away in Bahari ya Manda, renewing her visa.

She stood, awkward and exposed, in the living room as the guests arrived. There were two couples, neighbours who lived in Oleander House and Zanj Mansion up the road. Then Evan's family arrived. Although she couldn't be sure if the man was Evan's father or his uncle. No one introduced themselves. They seemed to expect that she should know who they were. After an hour of conversation she could still not fit faces to roles. She drank four glasses of wine in quick succession. She had an impression that she'd always been there, around Julia's dinner table, but for some reason the hundreds of dinners she had eaten had been erased from her memory.

Julia gave her a place across from Storm at the table. The table was lit with hurricane lamps. Julia had placed the lamps inside sprays of bougainvillea. The light was filtered through the delicate cerise flowers, casting them all in its glow.

At one point she turned to Julia, intending to offer some automatic pleasantry about the food, and ran into Storm's gaze.

"Why did you become a doctor?" His question was thrown across the table like a challenge.

"Because I want to help people."

"And do you?"

"I hope so."

She did not know if anyone had overheard them. In the corner of her eye she saw Julia flash them a steady, practiced look. She turned to talk to Evan's uncle — at last she had determined this was what he was. He had been a road engineer, he had told her, but was retired now. "I keep my hand in by building swimming pools. In fact I built this one —" He gestured to the black rectangle of water, just beyond the perimeter of light. "It beats camping out for months in Sierra Leone with only warm Coke to drink."

She flicked her eyes in Storm's direction. He was laughing, open-mouthed, at something Evan had said.

"These young people," the man said. "They're all so competitive now. It was never like that, for me. We didn't have much to compete over — no GoPros, no Canon Mark 6s, or whatever the model is now. I have to buy them all for my son, just so he can keep his mates' respect. That's what he tells me anyway. In my day we were lucky if we had a car. In fact I had to ask to borrow my father's, and he charged me for petrol."

The hurricane lamps fizzed with random flares of paraffin, *mafuta ya taa*. Julia had taught her the Swahili term, along with *mshumaa* — candle. She loved the swish of the words, how they sounded reluctant to let go of themselves.

As they spoke she tried to catch Storm's eye. She didn't know how to read his tone, she realized. In fact she had no idea what he was thinking. All the clues she had learned to decipher and which had worked so well in her favour — the angle of a glance, the set of a mouth, a drift in the eye, a restless right hand — failed her with him. With another corner of her mind she registered Storm's astonishing

77

effect in the dark light of the dinner table. He was at that fleeting point in life where beauty had the immovable density of fact, like wars or diseases.

The beauty she encountered in this country was not of any stripe she had met before. In part it was the sun, she supposed, the climate and the outdoor life they made possible. In England these people would look quite ordinary, but here they had taken on the sheen of demigods. She had never trusted beauty; beautiful people's faces were sculpted by other people's gaze, by the certainty that they will be looked at, and so they never fully belonged to themselves.

The guests went home at eleven. She woke hours later to a thud somewhere within the house. It was difficult to tell where the sound, dull and insistent, emanated from. She padded down the stairs.

A figure gleamed in the twilight. It stood next to the pool. In its hand was a rope. Storm turned at the sound of her step. Beyond him, over the lip of the low cliff, dawn was soaking the horizon with opalescent light. His body was dense with shadow. He held up the rope, which spasmed and twitched three-quarters of the way down its body.

She took a step back just as he turned and walked out to the edge of the patio, beyond the infinity pool. She watched his shoulder blade tense. He drew his arm back and released it — a taut, powerful throw. The snake went flying over the cliff.

He did not turn back toward her, but walked out into the garden.

She stayed at the bottom of the stairs, a shock reverberating through her. He did not want her in the house, in the family; he did not want her anywhere.

She returned to her room. She thought of what she had witnessed the night before from the top of the stairs. Did he know she had seen them? Was that the reason for his hostility? But what had she seen, exactly? Young men could have tactile friendships — she knew this from the field, from the army — and be intimate with each other in a way that women seldom were. She could not say what Evan's hands on her cousin's head had been about. Only that the gesture she had witnessed carried a charge. Their nakedness, too, had seemed a deliberate provocation — but to whom? To each other? To Julia, or even her?

What spooked her most was the lack of recognition in Storm's eyes when they looked at each other. At times he looked at her as if he really never had seen her before. With this was an absence fellow-feeling so profound it pitched her into a pit of loneliness.

Perhaps she would take his cue and leave. She fell asleep again that night rehearsing explanations: called back to work, called back to England. She would never have the conversations she craved with Julia, which might illuminate her origins, and more. She would never really know Lucy or Storm. Family would remain for her a distant country she had once visited, before a nameless insurrection forced her to flee.

Four thirty a.m. It was the day he had promised to take her fishing. She opened one eye and levered herself out of bed. Downstairs, Storm was waiting.

They left the house in silence. At the boatyard, Storm did not speak but gestured to what he wanted her to do. They worked quickly, their headlamps illuminating the ropes, the rudder of the outboard motor, the luminous white of sails in the half-dawn.

The sea was almost silent. The boat slid through the water. There was no wind. Beyond the breakers the hurricane lamps of the fishing dhows glowed.

They sailed out of the mouth of the inlet. "We have to run through the reef," he said. "The tide is a bit lower than I'd like. That's why I'm not speaking. I have to concentrate." He sounded almost contrite.

Breakers on the reef formed a silver ribbon. He steered the boat straight into them. For a minute the boat was buffeted. It rose and fell sharply; the hull landing with a dull smack on the water. By the time they passed beyond the reef, a pale lustre stalked the horizon. In twenty minutes' time this would become the sun.

He released the throttle. He lunged forward and untied the sail, then hoisted it. Wind caught the mainsail. It billowed with a sound like gas blooming from a stove. He put out the longline; it unfurled from a spool attached to the gunwale.

"I'm going to take down the sail. We'll use the motor. Fishing from sailboats is never easy and the wind's going to pick up. You take the tiller. If I tell you, pull the engine cord. It's going to be a bit unstable for a minute."

He pulled down the sail. She watched his manoeuvres with attention, as if she might be called upon to perform them, unaided, at any moment.

He sat down across from her. "I'll take the tiller; you watch for fish."

"How long do we have to stay out here?"

"Until we get a fish. We have to wait for the tide before running in again anyway."

"Did Julia — did your mother tell you that you had to spend time with me?"

"No."

"What about your father?"

"They thought you'd like to see how we live, what we like to do. So here we are. It's nice in the morning."

"I'm sorry. I'm not very good at all this."

"At what?"

"Keeping still. Waiting."

He turned his face away. She could see the thin muscles of his cheek flexing.

When he turned back toward her, darkness had settled in one side of his face.

"We didn't know you existed. She told Lucy and me by Skype, before you came. Lucy lives in England, although you probably know that. She just said, your cousin is coming to stay, and we were both like, who? I don't think we even realized that Mum had a sister. Or we knew, but we'd forgotten."

The effort of exiting these words seemed to cause him great pain. They both stared at the horizon in silence. There, two early morning kayakers were hardening into silhouettes.

Storm is my cousin. The phrase installed itself in her head, in a different voice. *He is my family.* Until that moment her inner voice had always been her own. She was careful not to reply to the voice directly, to ask, *who are you?* This would confirm that another self inhabited her, an interloper she might not know.

The hollows in his cheeks had deepened. She thought again how the filament of a body's energy, the totality of it, could coalesce in a face. It was uncommon for this to happen. Perhaps it was this intensity, rather than beauty strictly speaking, that made it so difficult not to look at him. His face seemed to be channelling his spirit's intention to live; and not only his, but hers, or anyone's.

The fishing line zinged taut. They both looked at it as if they had forgotten it was there. A silver body sliced through the ocean toward them. Its body tore open the surface in a neat white scar. Suddenly it was in the boat. She saw a steel, panicked eye.

It bounced on the deck, hurtling from freeboard to seat to floor. She stood on the plastic bench ranged around the stern of the boat to escape its thrash. The fish was the yellow of marigolds as it came out of the water. In front of her eyes the yellow turned blue. Its colour faltered and its body shivered. The blue became unstable. Green dots began to thicken on its skin. The fish kept its eye on her, inside it a glossy hope. But the sharp gaze of it was clouding.

Storm turned his body toward her, one hand still on the steering wheel.

"Just whack it. Otherwise it suffers."

"I can't."

"Come on, you're a doctor. Here," he reached with his spare hand and passed her a long wooden club. "Or it will take a long time to die."

"I can't."

He took the club from her hands. She darted her eyes away. She heard a dull thud as he pounded the head of the fish. When she looked back she saw the fish's body was changing again. Its skin shivered, the blue turning to copper. Light rippled along its body, pinks, purples, the speckled brown of trout. Then a cold blue, like the storm skies of the Kusi monsoon, as it died.

They arrived back to an empty house. Storm left the fish in the sink for Grace to prepare, then went upstairs to sleep. The early morning start, the heat and the exposure of the trip had exhausted them both.

That afternoon she had arranged to meet Margaux at the ruins. They took a motorcycle taxi to a shady café with a view over the ocean.

"Don't you find it hot, all that black?"

"It's my favourite colour; I'm hardly going to stop wearing it just because it's a little warm."

"Margaux, it's thirty degrees."

"Could be five degrees hotter. You should come in December."

The day was still and the café terrace was empty apart from a trim tanned man reading the *Guardian Weekly*. Something about him attracted her attention. He wore the usual coastal uniform for men: a T-shirt, surfer shorts and flip-flops, but there was something odd about his square-shaped head and a face that seemed to want spectacles perched upon it.

"The local spook," Margaux said, keeping her voice low.

"British or American?"

"US Naval Intelligence. They're up and down the coast, looking for Radical Islam. His name is Bob and he's a sport fisherman, but he never goes fishing. Maybe the State Department is going through an austerity period and can't advance him the eight hundred dollars a day he'd need to maintain his cover."

She laughed. It was refreshing to talk to someone so cynical, after the hushed, almost clerical endeavour of Gariseb and the devotion to wealth and ease that seemed to reign over the Dhow House.

Margaux winked just as the man turned another page of his news-paper. She saw him take advantage of the moment to inspect them.

"He should try to look a bit more dissolute. He looks like he's just stepped off an aircraft carrier."

"He probably has. Before him was Keith, and before him Gary." Margaux raised her eyebrows as she recited their names, to signal their falsity. "All from Quantico." Margaux shook her head. "Everyone in town knows who they are. Even the waiters, the imports and now you." She gave a satisfied smile. "The chances of an Al-Nur insurgent falling across their path are practically zero."

"Imports?"

"That's what locals call people from the UK, the US. White people from other countries."

"Do imports come here on holiday or come to live?"

"They come to stay. But they'll always be called imports. You don't like the term much."

She shook her head. "It smacks of eugenics experiments. Imported bloodstock. But I can see the logic of it. I've never felt more foreign. In the house they don't know what to do with me. They can't talk business with me; they can't talk about safari trips, lodges in Zambia, horseback riding in Botswana; they can't talk about dinner parties they host in the capital or golf or property developments." She sighed. "I think I bore them."

"I'm not sure I should say this, but I think most people find your aunt and uncle hard to talk to."

"Why?"

"Maybe you don't realize just how successful they've been. Everything they have ever done has turned to gold, from your aunt's interior design business to your uncle's investments. Everyone knows this and is in awe of their good . . . fortune." Margaux said, her hesitation lingering between them. "That's my anthropological assessment of the situation, for what it's worth."

"They see it as good fortune and not good judgment?"

"Judgment doesn't apply in Africa." Margaux's heavy-lidded face drew itself into a sly smile. "In any case, it's all about to be derailed."

"By what?"

"The roadblocks, embassy no-travel directives, the spooks. By Al-Nur, if they get half a chance. So far they haven't been very together. I think they're waging some factional war within. But it's just a matter of time."

She allowed her eyes to drift back to the spook. He was still there, nursing a coffee that had long gone cold.

"So what are you going to do when your two months here are up?"

"I'll go back to Gariseb. I've got another six months. My contract is for a year."

"Then what?"

"I might do emergency medicine in London again. That keeps you sharp. Sharper than a war zone."

"Why's that?"

"More variety of cases, more diagnostic possibilities."

A contemplative look settled on Margaux's face. "I don't think I'd be able to take it. It's too harrowing."

A moment fell between them. She decided she should return Margaux's inquiries about her profession.

"What are you finding in your excavations?"

"Clues to the social structure of the original civilization. Iconography, pottery, that sort of thing. There's evidence people traded widely in the city, but no one can explain how Venetian glass got here. Especially because it carbon-dates to before the arrival of the Portuguese. I suppose ultimately we're looking for why the inhabitants abandoned it. Was it an Arab raiding party on their way to found Bahari ya Manda? Was it local warfare? Nomadic clans from the desert muscling in?"

"When did that happen?"

"In the late eleventh century, then they came back in the thirteenth century, then again after the arrival of the Portuguese. That's when the city became unviable for the last time."

The monkeys surrounded them. She hadn't heard them coming but suddenly they thumped and rustled as they flung themselves from tree to tree, causing showers of leaves and seeds to coat their table.

"They're here, too, even by the ocean."

"They're everywhere there's food to eat," Margaux said. "They were here long before we arrived, and they'll be here long after."

By the time they parted, the spook had left, gathering up his paper and shielding his eyes with mirrored sunglasses. Margaux touched her fingers to the brim of her sunhat in a strangely military gesture. "See you," she called.

She walked the sandy access road to the tarmac. On either side were small patches of cultivated maize, which she'd heard Julia call *shambas*. Sunflowers poked their heads above the maize. She walked through a cage of shadows thrown by thin towering coconut palms. She felt the pull of the house for the first time, heard its message, the magnetic frequency on which it broadcast. Its siren call sounded not unlike the *Asr*, the afternoon prayer that drifted above Kilindoni from the muezzin's towers. *Come back, Rebecca, please.*

They drove the coastal highway, which followed the edge of the land, hugging mangrove-gnarled inlets, salt flats and pockets of dense forest. Villages clung to the perimeter of the road, their houses made of ochre mud held upright by a cage of wattle. They passed men pulling two-wheeled ox carts with unidentifiable heaps in their wagons covered in jute. Shaded groves of young casuarinas shivered in the breeze.

Moholo was the real resort on this stretch of the ocean, she had gathered. Kilindoni had only two hotels used by package tours from the UK, Italy and Germany. In Moholo there were more than a dozen.

As they approached the town a flurry of billboards appeared at the roadside — Five Islands Hotel, Fitzgerald's, Marlin Bay Ocean Resort, the Sahara restaurant and bar. They were sun-bleached and tattered, with the exception of Fitzgerald's, which had its own helicopter pad, someone — it must have been Julia or Margaux — had told her. It was the choice hotel of millionaires, with the best sport fishing north of Durban, and only three hours from Johannesburg by Lear Jet. One South African industrialist flew up in his private plane every week, Margaux had told her, just to hook marlin and billfish off the reefs of the warm ocean.

Storm's face was a study in concentration as he drove. He negotiated the obstacle course the road generated, the motorbike taxis that appeared from side roads and lanes and whose drivers careened onto the road without looking, the tuk-tuks chugging at twenty kilometres an hour, the wobbling cyclists and gloomy cows on rope leashes tended by children carrying sticks.

"You never answered my question."

She darted him a look. "What question?"

"Why you wanted to be a doctor."

"I told you, I want to be useful."

"To whom?"

"To society. To life." She laughed. "There aren't many things you can do in this world that directly contribute to life and not death."

"What do you mean?"

"I mean there is no neutrality in our existence. You can always trace a line from your actions and consequences and know whether those consequences are good or bad."

She turned back to watch the life of the road. She didn't know why she was telling him this. Conversations with him appeared from nowhere and quickly went astray. It made her nervous, how quickly he tempted her into such moral equivalences. She didn't like the sound of her hazy assertions or her sacrificial offerings of vulnerability. In any case, with Storm they failed to provoke intimacy, or even understanding. She had never encountered this before — her well-practiced admissions widened the gulf between them.

"What about the army. Isn't that about death?"

"No. It's about limiting damage, death included."

"So it wasn't actually about being a doctor?" he said.

"No, I love medicine. You can't make it through medical school without having an affinity for it."

This wasn't entirely true — she'd known people at medical school who could just as easily have been stockbrokers, lawyers, army majors. They'd chosen medicine for its social influence and then had to deal with their recoil when they understood just how much information they had to acquire, how much responsibility travelled with it.

"What do you think I should do with my life?"

She looked out the window, considering her answer. Stray piebald goats stared back with their yellow eyes.

"I think you should just follow your instincts."

He shot her a questioning look. Normally she would have been grateful for any sign of ambivalence from him. But now that it came to her she rebuffed it and looked out the window instead, seeing the firefly *makaa* braziers in the forest, the thin boys cycling, tottering on the edge of the asphalt, daring the bus drivers not to kill them.

Ragged memories settled in her like a flock of crows. Gower Street in the rain; cramming on defibrillation from textbooks on the upper deck of the bus; late for class; running computer models until two in the morning, astonished to see the early May dawn; the planet titling on its axis while she tried to control the formulae governing the epidemiology of infectious tropical diseases, how they etched themselves into her mind like hieroglyphs in her dreams.

"I don't know what I want to do," he said. "This country — I can't see where I fit in here but I don't want to leave."

"From what I can see your father owns this country, or some of it." She was startled by the instant anger in her voice.

"You don't know anything about this place."

"Maybe not. But I've stitched back together hundreds of people who are from this country and their blood is on my hands." She held them out in front of her body, for his inspection. "You'll never see it, but it's there."

She turned away. She no longer cared who Storm was, what he thought. She had regained herself. She felt momentarily free.

"I don't know what to say to you." He shot her another sideways look. "That's why I don't talk more. You're older. You're educated."

They turned onto a smaller road. Soon their headlights swept across a sign made of a solid slab of concrete; *Reef Encounters* was written in flowing blue letters that mimicked waves. They passed through the gate. A bass thump greeted them. In a small clearing to the back of the hotel a black helicopter squatted.

The party was on the hotel's front deck but spilled onto the beach.

People stood in strips of magenta, pink, purple; a light deck was turned on the sand. The sea was invisible, lying somewhere beyond the illuminated struts of young people.

Storm lunged ahead into the crowd without a word. She followed him as if blind, one arm reaching for the small of his back. Storm's elbow was snagged by a thin tanned girl, wearing a bikini under a transparent vest.

She loitered for a while on the outskirts of their conversation. The girl swivelled toward her. She had a child's nose and dark eyes rimmed in eyeliner. "What do you do?"

Storm spoke before she could answer. "Rebecca's a doctor. She was in the army." There was an impersonal, tribal edge in his voice, family pride perhaps. She'd never had such a sentiment mobilized on her behalf, not even from her mother.

The crowd was thickening. The young men were tanned, with mops of unruly salt-stiffened hair. There was a uniformity to their faces, which were tanned, light-eyed, with the same static, rigid note she saw in Storm's. The young women looked identical, sisters or cousins in an extended, prosperous family. They were all blond and their hair, while seemingly casual, flowing long and free, was on inspection surgically cut. They were beautiful in a lissome, easily ruined way, adorned with feather earrings and silver bangles they wore above their elbow, in imitation of the austere tribes people of the far north who guarded cattle wearing blood-coloured robes.

There were few black faces in the crowd, apart from the barmen, the busboys and security staff. The DJ was playing trance. Boys pointed kaleidoscopic light lasers into the trees, illuminating the red eyes of frightened bush babies.

She continued through the crowd, her eye on Storm's back.

"Would you like a drink?" She turned to find Evan beside her. "I'll get you a beer; stay here. It's mayhem at the bar."

A surge of people nudged her from behind. She inserted herself into Evan's wake. As she followed him she was struck by a jolt of déjà vu. Each detail of the scene — Storm's swathe through the crowd, Evan's broad and muscular back, the pounding trance anthem on the sound system, the thin boy from London on the turntables, the tubes of plastic-covered fairy lights that entwined the anorexic figures of palm trees — she had lived before, so vividly she could have drawn it.

Evan had reached the bar. Behind him she was shoved, hard, in the ribs by a knot of teenagers. She was unnerved, her heart raced. How could she get out of here? She could get a motorcycle taxi back to Kilindoni, even though that would take an hour, and riding pillion on the highway when the overnight juggernauts of buses were passing was a known way to die.

The sea of young bodies parted. She felt a finger, or a hand, on her elbow. She turned to find Storm beside her.

A press, three people thick, blocked her way to the bar. The crowd behind them intensified. Storm's thigh pressed against her hip and something — his hand? — rested on the small of her back. They were thudded from behind by bodies.

His hand had fallen somewhere near hers. Without any awareness of what she was about to do, she reached for it. She took two of his fingers and encased them in hers.

Her heart constricted. She turned her head to catch his eye, but he was staring ahead. She had made a mistake. If she released his fingers now she could claim she had been seized by anxiety, that she hadn't thought about what she was doing.

But an instant before she did this, he encircled her hand in his and held it. More bodies piled on them from behind. Pinioned in her position behind him, she could not see his face. His hand gripped hers until he had to reach for their drinks, and at last he released her.

She left them and went to the wooden railing that overlooked the beach. She needed to gather herself. Her heart was still pounding.

The tide was in; waves patrolled the concrete edge of the deck.

Julia had told her that Bill's father had built Reef Encounters in the 1950s, when the only tourists on this stretch of coast arrived with camping equipment. She tried to imagine it then, a strip of thick riparian forest, the shallow scoop of the bay speckled with local boats, no flat-bottomed snorkelling boats shuttling back and forth, no whitewashed houses perched like giant egrets on the shallow rise above the ocean.

Near the position she had taken up, three men stood in a row with beers in their hands, looking out to sea.

She tried to look studied and serene, as if she had come only to stare at the ocean. One of the men-boys of the trio peeled himself away and approached her.

"Enjoying the view?"

"It's one of the most impressive I've ever seen."

"It is." He nodded outward, as if saluting the sea. "Here from England?"

"Yes, for a couple of months."

"That's quite a while."

She struggled to make out the detail of his face in the darkening light. He was dark-haired with a receding hairline, a little stouter than the other men at the party, perhaps older, too. On the deck tables small electric candles began to appear.

"I'm Rebecca."

"Tom."

Storm appeared, just as suddenly as he had vanished. He nodded at Tom. "This is my cousin, Rebecca."

"We've just met," Tom said.

"Great." Storm departed. As he left, he cast her an uncertain glance. Tom must have caught it, because he raised his eyebrows to her.

"So what do you think of the party?"

"I think everyone knows each other except me."

"Yes." He gave her a rueful look. "That's a pretty good description of things."

"I'm not great at parties in any case," she said. "I'm always asking people to repeat themselves. As soon as I arrive I start wondering how I'm going to get home. I suppose that means I'm old."

"Not old, just wise." Tom smiled. "I'm staying in Kilindoni. My folks' house is there. I can drive you."

"No, really. I wouldn't want to take you away from the party."

"I'm not up for staying much longer, either. My dad's not well. I said I'd be home by midnight."

On the way out they stopped at the table where Evan and Storm sat. She had to fight her way through bodies to reach them. "Tom is going to give me a lift home," she said.

For a moment Storm looked confused. Then he looked at Tom. "Thanks, man." He put his hand on her forearm, angling her back toward Tom, as if handing her over. She surprised herself by wrenching her arm away from Storm's touch. She saw Tom observe this, as well.

They walked to his car together; the sounds of the party drowned by distance, by the curled roar of the waves.

"It's good of you to drop me."

"Oh, don't mention it. I was glad to get out. They're always the same, these parties — same people, same conversations. Everyone knows that but there's a ritualistic aspect to them that's oddly comforting. I think that's why everyone goes."

"Have you known Storm for long?" she asked.

"I'm a few years older than he is, so we've never been close. Plus I've spent a lot of time abroad."

"What do you do?"

"I sail other people's boats. I have my own, but I need to upgrade if I'm going to win any races, so in the meantime I skipper boats belonging to people with more money. A *lot* more money." He smiled in her direction, but his eyes did not seek out her face. "What do you do?"

"I'm a doctor."

He whistled. "I didn't expect that. No wonder Storm doesn't know how to talk to you."

"Why do you say that?"

"I could be wrong but I spend a lot of time in confined environments. Boats are good for getting to know people you know you won't like, much too quickly. They accelerate everything."

Tom's speech pleased her. She felt relieved to merely hear such words: *ritualistic, confined environments, accelerate.* She felt as if she'd spent the last two weeks speaking a foreign language and had only now met someone who shared her mother tongue.

"I don't know how to talk to Storm, either," she said. "I don't know how to talk to any of these people."

Tom's eyes were dark grey, she saw, open yet resigned to something she would not be able to identify.

"This country is a bit like an island. You have to come from here to understand it. If you move here, no matter how many years you live here, I'm not sure you can get inside."

"Imports," she said. "A friend of mine used that term. It sounds like a word for breeding stock."

Tom laughed, but there was an uncomfortable slant in his voice. "It is, I suppose. Otherwise it becomes incestuous."

"How did these people make so much money?"

"Oh, that happened long ago. Land, mostly. Farming. Most of the people there tonight are their grandchildren. Some of their families are in finance, or own safari companies. That's probably the last cash cow left in this place, for a white person at least." A doubtful look flashed across his face. "Don't get me wrong. There are some fascinating people in this country. I'm grateful for the upbringing I had here. My grandfather was the undersecretary for the PM, before

93

independence. I have values. I'm not sure I'd be so certain of what I believed if I'd grown up in England."

"You'd have different values," she said.

"Maybe. It's difficult here because no one with a white face will ever be in political power, ever again. It's impossible to even get a job. So you have to be a self-starter; you have to make your own way. The president has decided he wants to make life difficult for the whites. He sees us as parasites." He laughed. "But everyone knows the parasites are elsewhere."

Parasites — a word she knew from Gariseb. It had suctioned itself to her, once.

"People here seem so much more . . ." she searched for the word, "vital. So much more themselves than in England."

"That's because of what I've just mentioned. But also they don't need to conform here. The social pressures are not entirely absent, but completely different."

She considered all this, lost in thought for a moment. "You speak very well," she said.

"Ah, thanks." He flashed her a smile. "But that's just my expensive education talking."

They slid through the gate of the house. She was grateful — for the ride, for his conversation, for any exchange that was not the painful, stop-start trade of misunderstandings she had with Storm.

She flicked open the car door. "Thanks for the ride."

"Don't mention it. Here," Tom fished in his pocket and pulled out a damp card, "this is my number. I'm not around for much longer, but give me a call if you find yourself at a loose end."

She lingered on the step until Tom's headlights were extinguished by night, Tom's phrase echoing in her mind. *If you find yourself at a loose end.*

She turned to enter the house. The smell of frangipani was overpowering. The trees grew thick around the house with their dark, rubbery leaves. The grass rustled nearby and a hedgehog snuffled into view.

Julia's voice floated toward her from somewhere far inside the house. "Storm, is that you?"

"No, Julia," she called back. "It's only me."

The tide was out, exposing the reef. The ocean was striped with floating vats of seaweed. Between these were laid strips of light turquoise — sandbars. There, lionfish and blue-spotted rays darted in coral hollows.

At Reef Encounters, four Muslim women occupied the ocean-front deck, sheathed in buibuis, sipping tea on a table littered with sunglasses and mobile phones.

Margaux was late. Margaux was, she was beginning to realize, habitually late. Or perhaps no one took appointments seriously on the coast.

Margaux sat down without apology. She wore her usual costume of a black bush hat, a black shirt, its top panel lacy and semi-transparent, and black trousers that stopped just below her knee. The Muslim women eyed them curiously from their table.

"How's it going up at the big house?" Margaux asked.

"It's quiet. But then I suppose I wanted quiet."

They ordered gin and tonics. Normally she never drank in the day, but in her two weeks on the coast, alcohol had already become a habit. She couldn't believe she had made it through four months in Gariseb without a drink, apart from her contraband vodka.

"This has to be a first. We're the only white people here." Behind her sunglasses, Margaux's eyes must have been roaming over the deck.

"Is it that unusual?"

"Reef Encounters is the colonial hangout, par excellence. I take a kind of masochistic pleasure in coming here and watching them."

"What do you see?"

"Stateless ex-colonials. There's no other community like them anywhere, except maybe South Africa. I had plenty of time to observe them, growing up."

"You grew up here? You didn't tell me that."

"Well, it's not straightforward. I left when I was twelve. My parents were missionaries, upcountry. The local whites always snubbed us. You were one of them or you weren't; you went to the country club, you went to their dinner parties and their retirement galas and weddings on the beach, or you didn't. There was no racial solidarity. It was all about class. Which wasn't surprising, given they were mostly Brits."

"So it's the British you disapprove of?"

"They're hardly British anymore. Their ancestors used this country as their personal playground and they haven't developed much beyond that," Margaux's mouth folded lean and tight over the word. "I mean, there's an election coming up, thousands of people may be killed, Al-Nur is killing a hundred people a month in terrorist attacks, and these guys —" Margaux gestured to the twirling trapezoids of parachute material and guy wires in the sky above the beach — "they're *kitesurfing*."

"What would you have them do, join the army? They wouldn't be allowed. They have the wrong colour skin."

"But doesn't it strike you as dangerous? This is the leakiest border between terrorists and the western world, and there's a whole generation who've decided to hunker down in their mansions."

"They're innocents."

"There is no such thing as innocence here."

"So they're implicated, then?"

"No, not at all. Not implicated, but not unaware, either. These people are very smart. You don't survive here for a hundred years unless you're very shrewd. It's not so much innocence as carelessness. Or thoughtlessness. Believe me, they know what is happening." Margaux sucked on her gin and tonic. "What amazes me is that they stay. They've stayed through an independence movement, a hostile immigration bureaucracy, restrictions on foreign exchange, election violence. And now terrorism, the real showstopper." She looked out to sea, her expression unreadable behind the sunglasses. "But with the exchange rate, if they went back to England, they'd hardly be able to buy a house in the home counties."

"I don't think they see that as an option anyway. Even if their ancestors were English, they're African now. That's how they see it."

She was surprised at the vehemence in her voice. Only a few weeks before, she'd held the same opinion as Margaux. She'd thought, *what are you all doing here, still?*

"That's right, to an extent," Margaux said. "But really it's because they won't consent to be ordinary, to live ordinary lives. That's what England means to them, a life like any other. They're used to being the heroes of their own story, just because they are whites in a black country."

The same thought had occurred to her, but she hadn't been able to articulate it as crisply as Margaux could.

"Why does everyone stop talking when I mention my uncle's name?"

"Do they?"

"Just now, the manager here, he asked where I was staying. When I told him his manner toward me changed. He became more formal, somehow."

"There are so many rumours around this place," Margaux said. "Everyone says something different."

Over the last few days she had found herself poring over her uncle's behaviour. He had not failed to be kind, solicitous, even chivalrous. When he looked at her there was real curiosity in his gaze. But also, she had to admit, suspicion, a thin icicle buried deep inside his being. In moments when he was unaware of being observed — getting out of his Land Cruiser, walking across the terrace facing the cliff, wielding gin and tonics before dinner — she saw in him a dark vitality, a speculative threat.

"Look, I don't know you well," Margaux said, "but how close are you to your family?"

"Julia is my aunt, my mother was her sister. But they were never close. I only met Julia once that I remember."

"Your mother *was* her sister?"

"She's dead."

"Oh, how did she die?" The usual strain of pity was absent from Margaux's voice. Instead she heard the slightly clinical note she associated with people who were used to being surrounded by death — people of her tribe: doctors, nurses, soldiers.

"A car accident."

"Did she die here?"

"No, in England. My aunt came here and married, and much later I came to the border to work; that's the only connection."

"But she didn't marry just anybody. She married into one of the longest-established white families here."

"I didn't know that. I don't know much about Africa, as it turns out."

"Well, this particular version of Africa."

"I know this sounds naïve, but I don't understand how people make so much money here. Most people on the continent are so desperately poor."

She couldn't see Margaux's eyes, but she sensed a shift in her expression. "That *is* a naïve comment, for someone in your position." Margaux's mouth twitched. It was as though she was considering, then discarding, words. "I mean, you're a doctor. A worldly person."

"It's not that I haven't read the *Economist*, but I've never lived here," she said.

"There are fortunes to be made off poor people," Margaux said. "And there are no rules here. Money makes the rules."

This was likely true, and one of the sources of her discomfort. She rifled through the facts in her mind, ordering them into cause and effect, as she had been taught to do: There was a possible insurrection developing, extremist attacks had taken place in the cities and towns of the coast. Foreigners were targeted, as much as locals. Elections were to take place in six weeks. The last time the country had an election, over two hundred people had been killed in violence that the news termed 'tribal' but was actually political. Yet in Julia's house these topics never rose to the surface of dinner party conversation.

The truth was she didn't know what this place was really about. She would never fit into this enclave of white wealth. She passed through her days here giddy like a child, drunk on the novelty of her ignorance.

"Tell me," Margaux said, "is that his real name, your cousin? *Storm?*"

"His first name is Aidan. But he's been called Storm since he was a baby."

"Well, I can hardly talk about heavy names. My mother named me after Margaux Hemingway. She thought she was pretty. And she was. But it's quite a burden to carry around, a name from a family that has either shot, drunk or drugged itself to death."

"I love his books," she said. "They're brutal, but they have such clarity."

"Everyone says that about brutality — that it's clear. As if it were transparent, like gel handwash — you need its astringency to keep the bacteria away. I think brutality is just brutal."

She felt a draining away inside her. She didn't really know Margaux, and wasn't sure if she liked her even, but she needed a guide, a chaperone, in this country. Normally she had the clarity, the natural skepticism, to perform this duty for herself. But the beauty of this place had disarmed her.

They watched dhows bucking over through the *mlango*, the door

— this was what everyone called the break in the reef. The sun disappeared around the headland. A column of cloud was advancing from the southeast. The doum, date and lala palms that guarded the coast seemed to anticipate the arrival of lashing winds, and shrank back.

After sundown they parted. Margaux was heading to the backpacker bar she frequented on Frangipani Road. "You should come sometime," Margaux said. "They cultivate lovage and make nettle tea. It's a blast."

She flagged down a *matatu* on Kilindoni main road outside the service station. *Never take them,* Julia had warned her. *They're driven by lunatics. They pack twenty people in.* She had begun to defy her aunt's warnings deliberately. The local whites treated any European or North American who came to live on the coast for any amount of time like children. The locals needed to peddle their knowledge of savagery and danger, she decided; it made them feel powerful, she supposed. Having eschewed the false safeties of Europe, the country's whites had become resentful and suspicious of anyone who benefited from them.

She buzzed for the night guard to open the gate of the house. He appeared, a stark face beneath a Muslim prayer cap. It was six o'clock and he had been kneeling on a thin prayer mat on the side of the driveway with his shoulders flung east, toward Mecca. She kept her distance. She did not want him to smell the alcohol on her breath.

A car materialized behind her. She turned around and saw Storm at the wheel. She waited for him at the entrance of the house, but when he got out of the car he was on his mobile. He did not look at her until he had finished his conversation — he never seemed to say goodbye; he just hung up.

She opened the back door.

"Three road blocks on the way up."

"Army?"

"Militia."

"What did they want?"

"What do you think?"

"I don't know." She was becoming impatient. "It's your country."

Voices came from the open terrace. Fragments of words she could not quite catch flew toward her.

As soon as they were through the door, her uncle's eye snagged on her. "Rebecca, come and meet our guests." The word, *guests*, in her uncle's mouth had a different sound. It sounded sacred, somehow.

"Rebecca, please have a drink. Grace!" Her uncle shouted. They might have been drinking for some time.

"This is Eugene," her uncle declared. She looked into a broad face. A man with a polo shirt stretched over a stomach so large it looked like he might give birth.

"Where's Storm?" Bill asked.

She turned around. "I don't know. He was just here."

Her gaze was pulled beyond the open living room, east to the ocean and the moon lifting above the horizon. The cool light coloured the water pewter, a sunken, absorbed hue, united with the sky in an ancient wedding. That was it, she thought — this ocean looked old. It was settled, knowledgeable.

"*Rebecca . . .*"

She turned. Eugene was beaming at her. She saw him gathering his powers, like a singer taking in a lungful of breath.

"How long have you been in our great country?"

"Nearly six months." She named her position, the name of the organization she worked for in the north. In Eugene's face a rearrangement took place.

"I see," Eugene said. "You are aiding the insurgency from the north."

"Humanitarian medical aid is non-partisan. We treat combatants and soldiers both," she said, using the terminology of the conflict.

"This family continues to surprise me," Eugene shook his head.

"All this talent. Why have we never met you or heard of you before? Julia?" Eugene had regained his beam and now directed it at her aunt. "Where have you been hiding this child?"

"She's older than she looks," her aunt said, then smiled, to show she meant no harm.

She felt all the guests turn and regard her; the living room of the house was a stage and she a lead actress who had forgotten her line. Because she was in the spotlight she could not see the audience, only darkness.

What would this audience see? After having met her once they are confused as to her exact height, the colour of her hair. She gives an indistinct impression. But they remember her eyes, which are dark grey, the luminous graphite of paint on expensive cars or crushed pencil lead. They notice she has fierce eyes but an approachable, capable manner, and wonder about this contradiction. They imagine she is easy — to manipulate, to convince. Some susceptibility, some minor flux within her sternness of mind, affords them this delusion. They are not entirely wrong.

They are surprised to find that such a small woman willingly hunkers down in the trench that separates life and death. They are intimidated by her integrity, her ambition. She is a serious person, having gone to the most serious of English universities as a hardship scholarship student; she learned there that life was similarly serious and lightweights didn't count. She learned the ways of the wealthy, and their ruthlessness, specifically that there was a ripe clarity to be found in the pure exercise of the power of knowledge. She discovered she found this quality — of heartlessness, which she associated with clarity — attractive in other people. Ruthlessness and bad faith: she judged these qualities worse than cruelty — venal and subhuman, frightening, but sexually beguiling.

The power stuttered; behind her the guests sighed as one. Another coastal power cut. On days with heavy rain the power cut out almost immediately, extinguishing the floodlights that illuminated the terrace. The house had a generator, a small one capable of running the fridges and the lights, but Julia switched it on only if the power had been out for an hour or more; diesel was becoming scarce.

Swahili lanterns, lit by Grace at six thirty each evening, were placed in the grass around the pool. The darkness made the boom of the sea louder.

Storm appeared in the living room dressed in jeans and a white shirt. There was a necklace of leather and a piece of bone around his neck. All the young men, black and white, wore jewellery, she'd noticed: a beaded bracelet, an assortment of copper around it, sometimes a piece of leather or thin fabric tied to the wrist. These amulets jangled each time they moved.

"Rebecca loves birds," Julia informed Eugene.

"Really? Tell me something about birds I don't know."

"To do that I'd have to know what you already know."

"Assume I know nothing."

She realized then what the quality in Eugene's face was, and which that had caught her attention — a veiled, watchful note she was familiar with, from the faces of Anthony, Stuart, the men she knew in her other, secret life.

"The first bird you hear in the morning is the common bulbul," she said. "Then the red-capped robin-chat, which are parasitized by the red-chested cuckoo, which lays its eggs in their nests and the robin-chats find themselves rearing a monster chick. Sometimes this chick kills the legitimate chick, but the red-capped robin-chat keeps feeding it nonetheless."

Eugene shrugged. "The robin is not so intelligent then."

"The red-chested cuckoo has a beautiful call. It's the bird that says, *It will rain, it will rain.*"

"Yes, yes," Eugene said. "We have it in our garden in the capital."

Her aunt rose and went to stand at the long teak dinner table. She called Grace, who appeared carrying a bowl of rocket, shaved parmesan and figs. The table smelled of the citronella candles her aunt set out to deter mosquitoes.

Her uncle and Eugene were now deep in conversation. "The Vilanculos development — I saw that on the VP's agenda."

"Good," Eugene nodded vigorously. "We need to get that off the ground. They're insisting on an environmental audit. UNESCO. The mangrove, Mac." *Mac* was her uncle's nickname here, she'd understood.

"Well," her uncle shrugged.

"I know, I know. It's taken care of."

They were beckoned to sit at the table. "You sit next to your cousin," Julia commanded her son.

Through the meal she felt the pressure of Storm's gaze. She chose her moment when her aunt and uncle and Eugene were deep in conversation about the harbour development up the coast and launched her eyes in his direction, half expecting to be wrong, to find that he was in fact staring at a gecko on the wall over her shoulder, or out into space.

"I'm going to England."

She gathered herself. "When?"

"In September. Before the elections. It's not safe here."

"Is that what Julia wants you to do?"

"I don't like England, but that's where the opportunities are."

"What don't you like about it?"

"Too much indoor life — it's all about making money."

She said nothing. He had a point.

"I'll teach you to surf if you want."

She shook her head. "I couldn't even stand up on the board."

"Yes, you can. Tomorrow." There was a determined note in his gaze.

The patter of rain began outside. With the electricity out, the moon was bright enough that she could see the steel seam of the oncoming clouds as they met the horizon out to sea. The rain began to drum on the satellite dish. It sounded like a steel drum in a Caribbean band. She heard the uncertain chatter of monkeys. In the trees beyond the house she could see their forms, huddled in the forks of branches.

The detail of his face pressed into her. It was stern, as if a larger force were being held in check. His bones were so close to the surface they looked like they might break the skin. But the weary loveliness of his eyes moved her; how he used them like a wall, casting her steel-hard glances. It was a face that knew it was being watched.

The sound of the monkeys came louder. They heard a bush baby screech.

He turned it upon her now, the face that made her vital organs slide sideways in the cage of her body. His eyes had cooled to jade. He said, "They don't like the rain."

Three dhows sleek out of the inlet at the same moment she leaves the house at five thirty a.m., heading into silver breakers and a parchment sky. Dawn comes reluctantly at first, then catches fire. At five fifty the muezzin begins to sing from the small green mosque across the inlet.

She is running through a substance denser than time and space. In her mouth the warm iron taste of need. Already she carries him with her everywhere she goes.

She is back at the house before seven. "Rebecca," her aunt's voice, thin but insistent, calls her from somewhere in the house — beyond the outskirts of her thoughts, its distant, distracted note so like her mother's voice. Perhaps it was her mother after all, calling her from outer space.

She stood at the bottom of the stairs, a black velvet dress dripping from her shoulders, eyelashes stiff with mascara. She had glimpsed her undressing for the bath. It was like spying on a minor movie star with an unidentified addiction: razor clam ribs, spine like a row of slim stones. Her legs were very mysterious. They were flour white, covered with nicks and the smoky smudges of bruises.

She had been left alone at night for weeks now, since she'd turned twelve. She was a reliable child. It didn't occur to her to drink the bleach in the kitchen cupboard or set fire to the house.

She made fish fingers, watched television, did homework and searched her mother's pockets and purse for evidence of where she'd gone. She found bus tickets, a Tube pass, chewing gum, lipstick, loose change. She could have asked the question, but it would be like asking a wild animal where they went at night to find, kill and devour small creatures.

Her mother always came home alone. "I'm going to bed," she said, from behind her nighttime mask. It was seven in the morning. "Your porridge is on the stove."

Her mother was willowy, saved from being thin by her modest curves around her waist and breasts. Her blond hair darkened with the winter. She never came to parents' meetings at school or to the school play or concert band performances. She never took her to Crystal Palace or the zoo or the Science Museum and they never went on holidays. She worked long hours at famous magazines alongside other women whose perfume was worn so liberally her mother returned home with a confused tang wafting from her.

She went to school, she came back. The sky was the colour of mud. Her mother drank a bottle of wine every day. Even so she was not quite drunk. She was not quite *a* drunk.

There were no photographs of family on the walls, and when the phone rang it was about a delivery or a wrong number. *You must have the wrong number*. She learned to say this phrase convincingly by the time she was five years old. When school let out and other children went to grandparents' homes or to a beach in Spain she remained in London, climbing through ghostly playgrounds, orbiting parks where she would look longingly at dogs her mother told her they could not afford.

Don't you have any friends? her mother said.

I don't want friends.

Friends are the only thing in this world that will save you. Without friends you will never get ahead, no matter how well educated you are.

She lay on her bed later, turning over her mother's parable. Her mother never gave her advice or proffered truths. She spoke in a series of warnings. She would have to get a job because she had no friends; she had no family, so she needed friends. Would a job protect her from having friends, or would it be a way to acquire them?

Her mother had always been there, yet she was poised for the moment when she would leave. In her room she hoarded thirty pounds, plasters, a container of water she kept forgetting to refill and which gathered dust on its meniscus (a word she had learned in science class and instantly loved), a telephone calling card, her birth certificate and a stuffed donkey who would accompany her when the day came and she was forced to set out on the road to — where? — because her mother had not come home that morning, her mother had gone to a tent in Devon to learn the spiritual ways of the Sioux Indians, her mother had made an unwise choice among the reedy men lined up on pub barstools that night, her mother had gone to a Buddhist retreat in Snowdonia, her mother had been knocked down by a bus.

Children always knew if their parents were on their side, she came to understand. They could be wayward and bizarre parents, but still you knew if you were safe or not. That even very young children could tell a reliable from an unreliable parent was down to survival instinct, she supposed.

The year she turned twelve she became fascinated by ghosts. She was anticipating something. Death seemed very near to her. She was convinced she could die quite soon. Her childhood was one of serial obsessions — horses, nuclear war, Arabia, feral children, poker — which came and went with the seasons. She knew these were not common obsessions for a twelve-year-old, and she kept them to herself, as much as is possible for the truly obsessed. Life was a forest of secrets, she was beginning to realize, a densely woven wood to which there were no maps. In her mother's life there was always a whiff of impropriety, a doubt about her integrity. She lived as if in a cloud.

She was nineteen the year of the accident. She remembers waiting — waiting for her mother to come home, waiting for normal life to resume, for the blare of uncertainty that had suddenly filled her lungs to disperse. Neither of them had mobile phones. Hardly anyone did — tradesmen, celebrities, yes. It was a different world then, a world of waiting.

The sound of the café where she went to calm her nerves grew to a roar in her ears. It was a Portuguese café; there were many in their area. She waited and studied the moon crater patterns on the burnt sugar surface of the yellow pastry she bought but would never eat.

It was evening when the police rang. She remembers trying to get hold of Julia — an international telephone call to what must have been Bill's office. She can't remember who she spoke to, only that the woman, a secretary perhaps, had said, *She's computing in the hoarse trils. Pardon?* She'd said, over and over. *It's her niece, her sister has died, you must tell her. I can't, I can't,* the woman said in the truncated, tripping accent, her voice fading on the line. *The hearse trils!*

Julia was competing in horse, or hearse, or hoarse, trials in the country club in Hatton. She has been there now, seen its immaculate polo field, the grass kept clipped by a resident herd of Thomson's gazelles, set in the shadow of the dormant volcano. That was where Julia was on the day her mother's broken body was vaporized in a crematorium in Streatham. Julia, soaring over fences, through artificial ditches, the *thump thump* of her horse's hooves, the equatorial sun a knife through her head, hair shimmering from underneath her black riding helmet. At the crematorium they were ushered to the small chapel: Rebecca and three of her mother's colleagues from the magazine were the only mourners. One of the pallbearers, if that's what they were, saw her stricken face and gave her a friendly wink. *Sometimes we get none at all, love.*

Six months after the funeral she was in a lecture theatre, organic chemistry organograms on the PowerPoint screen, a thin professor pointing at them with a red laser.

At university she lived among cadavers of small animals and full-sized human beings, skinless anatomy models, drawings and graphs of the interiors of bodies, and found this was the territory she had hoped to discover when the surface had been peeled away. Life was an elaborate stage set. If you pulled aside the curtain or unplugged the light the inner truth would stand exposed, sudden and vital, a creature that was no more than an amalgam of flesh and ghost. When she became a doctor she would move, all-powerful, the healer, stalking this corridor of chance that separated the living from the dead.

"**D**on't look down. Look at the sky; get a fix on the horizon."

To the south, black clouds were amassing. The sea was choppy but warm. Clumps of seaweed, coconut husks and swollen protea-like flowers floated in water the colour of gooseberries. On the sandbar, matted shoals of small fish swirled.

She managed to get her feet onto the board, but her knees locked when she tried to straighten them.

In the water Storm's hands were the pale lime of fever trees. Their reflections coalesced and fractured on the surface of the water. She was becoming thin and brown.

She looked down into his frown. He stood in chest-deep water, spotting her, hands outstretched.

"Just stand up."

"I can't."

"Yes, you can. Just go out there, paddle. Sit down if you don't want to stand. Come on."

"I haven't been doing this since I was three, like you have."

"Concentrate. I'll swim out with you." He let go of her and powered through the water.

She followed him out beyond the breakers. He raised his head.

"Okay," he said. "Go."

She stood. For the first few seconds, she thought she would fall. Then from somewhere inside her body she found her balance. It moved through her, a gold current. The wave shoved her forward with surprising force.

She looked out to sea. A shape cohered. She hadn't seen it from the water.

"What's that?"

"What?" Storm squinted.

"It looks like a ship."

"Oh, that. Something's wrong with it. Lost an engine. It needs to be towed back to Gao."

"It's from Gao? What's it doing here?"

"There's a lot of shipping between Gao and Bahari ya Manda."

"Even with the war?"

He shrugged.

She turned back to stare at the ship. It was still against the horizon. A freighter, from its bulbous bow, low-slung waist, anchored in deep water.

"How long has it been there?"

"About a week. Nobody knows for sure. They've taken to calling it the ghost ship. At night people come ashore. They've got a speedboat."

"Why do they come ashore?"

"To get supplies. What's the matter?"

"Nothing," she said.

"Let's go in. We'd better get home."

She remained standing all the way to the shore. He swam beside the board. When they reached shallow water she crouched down and slid off; she misjudged her trajectory and splashed into him.

"Sorry," she breathed. She felt light-headed from the heat of the day and from spending so much time in the water. "I'm not used to the ocean."

"Come on, let's go. We've got just enough time to get home before the tide comes in."

She watched him wade through the shallows toward the beach. *He is just an ordinary kid.* The voice again, the one that had first spoken to her only a few days ago. It sounded uncannily like Julia's, or her mother's, even. *He doesn't want to conquer the world. He just wants to live in the country where he was born. But he's not wanted here.*

She was beginning to understand the nature of his dilemma, of all the whites who came from here. She hadn't taken it seriously, until now. She silently addressed his pale, gleaming back. *So what do you want?*

He might have perceived her thoughts. He made to turn around. She darted her eyes away, looking down along the beach, where slim pale people in bikinis and *kikhois* were ambling on the shoreline.

"Come on, Rebecca," Storm said. She heard it for the first time, the snare in his voice. "It's time to go home."

She walked out of the sea and onto the beach behind him.

When they arrived back at the house, Julia was not there. Storm went outside to speak to the gardener. She stuck her head in the fridge on her way to her room. Three flavours of yogurt were lined up on its shelves: passionfruit, vanilla, strawberry. In Gariseb she had dreamed of yogurt, any kind.

She sat in her room, spooning her way through a vanilla yogurt. This would be her dinner. It didn't matter; the heat took away her appetite.

A gust of loneliness passed through her. She could have sought out Storm's company, she supposed, but she was wary of overstaying her welcome. They had spent the entire afternoon together after all.

There could be no purpose to her staying for the two months. She'd have to call Anthony and tell him it was time for her to go back to Gariseb, or home. Wherever that might be. Her flat in Vauxhall with its tangle of high-rise luxury flats-in-progress and Victorian railway arches, perhaps. It appeared in her memory as an abstract space. She tried to imagine herself moving around it, from her open-plan kitchen with its white Magnet cupboards to the living room, its flatscreen television, the plant-less cherry wood plain of her floor. She could never keep houseplants; her work took her away for too long.

Should she tell Anthony about the ship? It could hardly be a secret. If she told him, he might suggest she stay. But she didn't want to be here at all. This was the fact she had been hiding from herself, these past three weeks. She would rather have had a summer in London, of debriefs, psychiatrists, of shuttlings between her flat and Anthony's office only a kilometre away until they would let her go, at first gently, then, when they had no further use for her, they would stop answering her coded texts.

The past three weeks had been unlike any other weeks of her life. She had lived them in slow motion, so that it might as well have been three months, or years. Something had changed within her, shifting her away from her usual balance, the assembly point inside her around which all energies rotated. She didn't know what it was. Only that it had been a kind of previous self, the Rebecca who, on her return trip to the embassy in the capital, where she had expected to be for only two days before returning to London, sat at a computer, Anthony looming over her shoulder, all but dictating her email to Julia, tentatively entitled, *hello*. Who dictated an explanation of why she had not been in touch before, her early granting of leave, her intention, always, to have looked them up. *I don't need to stay for long.* But she did, as it turned out. Two weeks became two months. *I can stay at a hotel for a while*, she'd written, *if that's too long.*

Julia had responded warmly — with more warmth on email than she showed in person, curiously. *We have a big house, you're welcome to stay as long as you like. We are down at the coast for the winter.* Anthony had been pleased. And she found she was pleased, too, for unanticipated reasons: she was relieved to have somewhere to recuperate, to finally have a chance to meet her mother's sister properly. In those days in the capital, for the first time in a very long time, she felt optimistic. Anthony must have seen this and wondered about this woman who was neither old nor young, who was able to rescue herself from one disaster and walk so sanguinely into another.

As she read Julia's email in Anthony's office she formed a vision: she saw herself taken into the bosom of the family, invited to dinners, barbecues and parties; she saw herself not having to make decisions or choices about who she would be with and what she would do. All this had happened. It was not as if she had been excluded. She did not expect to be known or understood, or even accepted. Possibly she had hoped to be tolerated, and that some in the family might display some curiosity about her. As for Anthony, he would get what he wanted, but she did not see this as a betrayal — not exactly. She was owed something. By him, by the universe, possibly, after what had happened.

But the family was not yet complete. She heard the name more and more now that her arrival was imminent. Lucy was five years older than Storm; she was a woman — might she provide some companionship? Her name rang through the house now in Julia's insistent chime. *Lucy.*

Lucy arrived in a blaze of bougainvillea. The rains made the garden glisten in green and gold. The palms leapt toward the sky, and flowers exploded along the low coral wall that separated the house from the garden.

The purr of her uncle's Land Cruiser subsided. She heard a crunch in the driveway, doors opening and shutting, then the drum roll of a wheeled suitcase.

"Rebecca —" Julia's voice rang through the house, that strident tone she used when welcoming guests. "She's here."

The live version of her cousin was identical to the photographic one. Lucy was small and dark-haired. She looked like Bill; she could see nothing of Julia's blondness, her elastic heiress quality. Lucy had something of Storm's severe cast of eyes and mouth, but her eyes were of a much darker blue, so deep they looked black. A pair of skinny jeans clung to a wiry body, a purple shirt billowed over a wasp-ish waist. Lucy's feet were tiny, almost child size. She wore green nail polish on her toes, but her fingers were bare. Lucy was twenty-eight, is that what Julia had said? The sprite girl who stood in front of her could pass for eighteen.

Lucy put down her bags and surveyed the house. "It looks good, Mum." Lucy turned and smiled in her direction. "I'm so glad you're here." She said this with warmth.

She took her cousin's hand. "Me too."

Julia drifted through the kitchen. She was already changed by the arrival of her daughter, like a garden suddenly surged into season.

Storm came down the stairs. He embraced his sister. She was enfolded, her face pressed into his chest.

She felt like an intruder. She would go for a walk on the beach. She had enough time, according to the tide tables.

She headed down the garden stairs. She stayed there; her eyes focused on the top branches of the mbambakofi tree, where she heard the trill of sunbirds.

He was beside her before she heard him.

"Where's Lucy?" she asked.

"She's gone to bed. She didn't sleep at all on the plane. She always watches films, one after the other. Where are you going?"

"For a walk on the beach. To give you some space."

He gave her an unusually tolerant look. He reached out and snagged her elbow very gently. "Listen. Scarlet-chested."

"I can't see them."

"I can tell by the call."

The sunbirds kept up their rapid lilt. They threaded in and out of the tree. From time to time she caught iridescent flashes within the cobalt weave of shadows. They looked like Victorian Christmas baubles, blue-brown glazed glass, then the slash of scarlet next to viridian, then dark amethyst.

"Do you want to come for a drive?"

"Now? Where?"

"I have to go up to Moholo to do some banking and pick up a few things. I thought — since you wanted to get out of the house." He gave her a defiant look, as if willing her to refuse.

"Fine," she said. She didn't know if she wanted to go with him or not. She felt her will evaporate once more, in his company, as if she'd never had a will at all.

The heat cut through them as they got in the car. He revved the engine and they skidded backwards.

They drove north under a tiger sky; streaks of red-brown stretched from the sky to the sea. "Sandstorms," Storm said. "Heading down the coast."

"Where is the sand from?"

"North, the desert. It's not far."

"I know," she said. "I feel it. It's like it's pulling me toward it."

"We used to go on holiday to Gao when I was a kid. Dad had business there. He owned a hotel, the Costa. Everyone stayed there, before the war. Now it's just a ruin. I liked Gao. Everything was pristine, undisturbed. People were pure Arabs. It was like stepping back in time."

Storm spoke in a series of fragments, always. He didn't like to tell stories, she had noticed. It was as if he had lived a history-less life. So when he offered a nugget of past it was as if he were entrusting a treasure to her.

She closed her eyes. His profile carved itself on the inner shade of her eyelids.

"What are you thinking?"

She opened her eyes. "About Gao. How now its name sends shivers down everyone's spine. Didn't you feel afraid there?"

"It wasn't like that then. It was a city of camels and *qat* and dates and Italian newspapers. A real Arab culture. The men sat out in the streets at night drinking tea. The women were allowed to come and go unchaperoned then. There's nowhere like it anymore."

"No," she said as they flashed past women wearing *khangas* and carrying yellow water containers on their heads, past shambas and their floppy maize. Horned cows grazed in the gullies on the side of the highway. "That's long gone."

"You don't like us."

She darted him a look. She was so shocked by this statement she couldn't think what to say. "It's not about liking."

"You're bored here."

"Not bored. Restless. I'm used to . . ." She shook her head.

"To what?"

"I don't know even where to start."

"Tell me about a typical day, when you're at work."

"Alright. I wake at five thirty. The earlier I get up the better the internet is; we have one satellite connection for a staff of twenty. I look at my email, read the charts of the patients on my rounds, try to get information on the conditions and diagnoses I'm not certain about or familiar with." She drew in a breath. "The first thing I do is see who died in the night. Or if someone's amputation has suppurated, if there has been any sepsis. The patients who are critical are kept in a separate tent, and I start there. We get incoming casualties, mortar fire, border skirmishes. Usually this happens after seven in the morning. By then there has been enough light for an hour for either side to start killing people."

She glanced at him to see if he was still listening. He stared straight ahead, his gaze intent on the road.

She had left out certain details — bile, pus, sodden bandages left in the corner and that somehow retained the shape of the limbs they had been attached to, how they lolled like sinister dolls, their appendages at impossible angles. Women who refused to be cut out of their chadors or burkas, girls whose headscarves were wound around their necks like a constrictor. She catalogued the abrasions on their vaginas, the bruises turned black under bloodflow loss, how labia would sometimes twitch to life in the throes of rigor mortis.

"You stopped."

"I know."

"What are you thinking?"

"I'm thinking that — to me, everything I've just been talking about is my life, and all this —" she cast her arm out the window as they passed by the heliotropic signs for hotels, sun, sea, sun, sea "is just . . . I don't know what it is."

"It's a resort. People come here to have fun. Don't you ever relax?"

You became a doctor so you could avoid the reality of life, not to confront it. Alexander the pilot had said this, how many years ago now? The statement had marked the moment he had stopped admiring her, or, more importantly, stopped believing in her.

"Maybe I don't. I can't take much leisure. I need to be put to use. What is the point of good times if you only ever have this, if there's no struggle and sacrifice to set the good times against?"

His lips were pursed. It might never have occurred to him that there was any quarrel with the life he led, that any other life was possible.

"I like having you here."

She was so surprised she laughed out loud.

His look was one of affront. "Why are you laughing?"

"Because I thought you were going to say the opposite."

"No, I really do."

"You've got a strange way of showing it."

He glanced out the window. "It's almost as if you were necessary."

At this she felt — elated. Then instantly burdened.

They had slowed, then stopped, to let a herd of handsome cattle cross the road. In the rearview mirror she watched as a truck approached. Surely it would slow down now. No, *now*.

She had time to glance at Storm, to see his alarm.

Then her own voice, strangled, screeched, then tires on asphalt.

The world receded, as if raked on a giant tide, and darkness soaked her mind.

Lucky, so lucky.

The words swam toward her. She saw a metal trolley. She was in a supermarket. They had gone shopping; how could she have forgotten?

Then she remembered and in the same moment was on her feet. A dark-skinned man in a thin white coat stood beside her.

"You are very lucky. You must lie down again. I am amazed you can even stand." A gentle hand pushed her down. An emphatic, elderly voice. Indian accent. All the doctors on the coast were Indians, she had heard.

"Where am I?"

"Bahari ya Manda. At the clinic," the voice said.

"What happened?"

"You had an accident but you are fine. Both of you."

She remembered she was not alone.

"Where is Storm?" A dull thud in her chest — her heart, staggering. A pain in her left leg, a throb in a cheekbone. They had been wearing seatbelts. She remembered the thrust from behind, her head pushed back with the force.

She saw a window and another hospital bed. He lay there, perfect, as if he was just taking a nap. The rest of the image emerged. She remembered the truck filling the mirror.

"Give me your stethoscope." She tried to pry it out of the man's hands. When he resisted she said, "I'm a doctor." She got down from her bed and moved toward Storm.

"There was a bomb in town this afternoon."

"A what?"

"That is why there are no other doctors," the man said. "A bomb at the bank. Ten people dead, forty injured."

The information slid over her brain.

She looked at Storm, prostrate on the bed beside her. His hair looked unusually dark and matted with sweat. Other than that, he seemed unscathed.

Suddenly he sat up. Then immediately slumped forward. "Dad —"

"You're fine." She took his face in her hands and before she had

time to think, pressed her lips to his. A slight response, a muted electricity, pulsed into her. She let go.

"He is your brother, yes?"

"Yes, he is my brother."

The doctor might think, this is what you do when you realize your
brother is still alive — you kiss him.

"How can we get home?"

"You can call your family," he said. "Use my phone."

"Where are our phones?"

"I don't know. Some people came to the car." Their phones had
been stolen, even while they sat in shock, slumped at the steering
wheel.

"Where is the car?"

"By the side of the road where you had the accident. I would get
an ambulance to take you home, but with the bomb I am on standby."

The muezzin's call to prayer filled the air. She saw a window with
a crack in it. On the opposite side of the street, used bicycles lined up
in three rows. A white structure with lantern-shaped windows, green-
and-yellow stained glass. An unceasing buzz of tuk-tuk taxis with
plates on their fronts announcing their names: *Ptolemy, Julius.* On
their backsides was another plate with their slogan of choice. *You'll
never walk alone.* A man walked down the street carrying a box of
avocados. He passed another man selling bags of rice from a stall
made of planks balanced on old gas canisters. On the corner was a
pile of old televisions and the sad clump of a mule, his hair pitted
and blackened.

All this pressed on her.

Bill sent a driver to fetch them. He was waiting for them at the
house. She would never forget the look on his face when he saw his
son. He gave her a single searching glance before panic flooded his
eyes as Storm emerged from the car.

"You're alive," Bill addressed her.

"We're a bit bruised, that's all. We need to rest." She heard an unfamiliar conciliatory tone in Storm's voice. "Where's Lucy?" he asked.

"She's at Tasha's," Julia said. "We called her but she didn't pick up."

"Like I said, we're fine."

"It could easily have been otherwise." The tone in Bill's voice held them. She saw Storm's neck stiffen. Her uncle's face had collapsed into a dark mask. "But thank God you're okay." A viscous energy seemed to radiate from her uncle. Bill was standing; Julia sat on the baraza. She found it odd Julia did not get to her feet and embrace her son. Julia looked outwardly composed, but on closer inspection something was slumped inside her.

"Don't worry, really," she heard Storm say. "We'll be down for dinner." She felt Storm's hand on her elbow. "Let's go upstairs. We'll take the back steps."

"What's happening? What's wrong?"

He would not meet her eye. "They're discussing something important."

"I can see that. About our accident? The car?"

"I don't know. I don't think so."

There was a narrow white staircase at the back of the house. It was for the house's staff and also served as a makeshift fire exit. Her aunt had shown it to her once; it led to a passageway at the back of Storm's room. They walked along the passageway of the second floor, skirting the edge as if it were the sea cliff. They could hear his father's voice emanating from downstairs. She could not make out what he was saying. At the door to his room, Storm steered her inside. He closed the door behind them.

"I'll show you some photos." His voice harboured a new, calming note.

They sat on his bed. It was low, inches from the ground, and faced the window. Through it doum palms rustled in the breeze.

He spread his laptop across his knees. A series of images unfolded: a door handle, round, wrought iron, against a darkened door, slats in the shape of stars and diamonds carved through the wood; a rope slung across the prow of a faded dhow, the teak once painted purple, now faded to the colour of rose wine; an Arab lamp, tall and slim, like the one next to his bed.

"Did you take these?"

"At Bahari ya Manda, a year ago. Close to where we were today, the clinic, in the old Arab quarter."

She stared at the images. The day appeared to her as pieces of a vexing puzzle.

Lucy's arrival, the sunbirds, their departure, the clinic, Bill's mood, and now sitting next to each other on his bed, looking at photographs. She wondered if he remembered her kiss. She didn't know why she had decided to do it. If he asked her why, she would be unable to say.

She forced her attention back to the images. "You have an eye for detail. You seem to be drawn toward Arab culture."

"I am," he said. "I like it visually, the patterns and the filigrees, the kanzus and the buibuis. I like how people hide themselves. It seems restrained and elegant. Even the language is like that. You speak Arabic, don't you?"

"Not that well, but enough."

He nodded. "Mum sometimes says I would have been an Arab in another life. A dhow captain, maybe."

Her leg pressed against his. She did not try to move it away, although this would have been the correct thing to do. Her body hummed with an unfamiliar current, calm and excited at once. Perhaps this was what it felt like to be part of a family.

From downstairs came a sudden scrape of chairs.

"I think they're going out," he said. Then, sure enough, they heard the start of a car's motor, a rev, the crunch of gravel underneath wheels.

She pulled her leg away and felt a tear within her, as if she were leaving her own flesh behind. She stood. "Are they angry at us for having an accident?"

He shook his head. "It's better you don't know."

"Why?"

"You're going to have to trust me, at some point."

"I do trust you," she said.

"It's something to do with getting their money out of the country. Before that becomes impossible."

"Why do they want to do that?"

"They don't trust the banks here anymore. They're worried about the elections, about what will happen on the coast if the Islamic movement gains ground here."

"But they won't leave?"

He looked troubled. "I used to think they'd only leave the country at gunpoint. That's happened before, but not here. Not to people like them."

"What do you mean, people like them?"

He gave her a strange, mistrustful look. He closed his laptop. It was her cue to leave.

She went to her room and lay down. The events of the day troubled her. She had been cast out of her own existence. This was what accidents, injury, trauma did to people, she knew; it dislocated them from a continuous narrative, like a bridge that has been washed away or a plane that suddenly loses altitude and plummets through the sky. She was still falling.

Alone in her room she heard a distant door shut, then open. The house's sounds were as familiar to her now as if it were her own.

Later — she would never be sure how much time had passed — she jolted awake, her eyes peering into the darkness. She had been woken by the muezzin's bellow from the Kilindoni mosque, the midnight-to-sunrise prayer was early. The clock said three fifty a.m.

The mosque turned up the volume. She put her hands over her ears and lay wide-eyed in the dark. She had once liked the sound of the pre-dawn *Adhan*, had found it comforting, even. Now it sparked alarm. After an hour she lost patience. She got up and went downstairs.

Halfway down she heard a sound she could not immediately place — half rasp, half hiss. Her mind was ready to continue but her body stopped dead.

She saw a movement more as a suggestion than a form. Something was coiled around the lamp next to Julia's pristine white sofa. Slowly, her breath held in her lungs, she backed up the stairs.

At the top step, she turned and looked behind her. What she would have done if the ribbon had followed her up the steps, she didn't know.

She found herself walking down the corridor. She pushed open the door to Storm's room. He lay sprawled on the bed, his arms thrown out on either side of him.

"Storm."

He shifted but did not wake. She put her hand on his shoulder and shook it. A single eye opened.

"There's a snake in the living room. I think it might be a green mamba." She added, uselessly, "I don't know what to do."

He was on his feet in a single movement that was so swift and compact she jumped back. He went to his closet and emerged carrying a spear-like instrument with two oval shapes on the end of it.

"I'll handle it. I've done it before. Just stay at the top of the stairs until I tell you to come down."

"Shouldn't we wake Julia and Bill?"

"They're out. They've stayed at friends. The curfew."

Only then did she notice he was naked. He seemed to notice his nakedness in the same moment because he leaned the tongs against his wardrobe and leapt into a pair of shorts.

She followed him down the corridor. From behind he looked like one of the illegal fishermen she saw on the road and beach during her runs, with their trident spurs for spearing octopus and lobster.

She waited at the top of the stairs until she could not see him anymore. "Is it there?" she hissed.

"You don't need to whisper. Snakes are deaf."

"But is it there?"

She moved two steps down. His back gleamed in the moonlight. He held the spear with the tongs out in front of him; she could make out the body of the snake swaying back and forth, its head clamped in the body of the instrument. He held the captured snake out in front of him, then walked beyond the house and disappeared around the corner.

When he returned the tongs were empty.

"What did you do with it?"

"I let it go. It's not a good idea to kill a snake."

"Why?"

"I was taught that if you kill a snake needlessly then all snakes will know, and they'll make you pay. You're much more likely to be killed by one then. It's a kind of curse."

"Who taught you that?"

"Dad. But everyone here knows that. This is a wild country."

Afterwards they found they could not sleep. They sat on the sofa, posted at either end, legs tucked underneath them. The lamp that the snake had wrapped itself around was at her elbow.

"I was going to come and sit right here."

"Why were you up, anyway?"

"Bad dream."

"What about?"

"About making mistakes. I'm operating and it goes wrong. I puncture an artery by mistake, and blood spurts onto my face. I'm operating and I can't find my instruments. The nurse is wearing a balaclava and holds a gun to my head."

She looked at him, half expecting to see his usual stony middle-distance stare.

He was regarding her watchfully. There might even have been a grain of fear in his gaze, as if he weren't sure what she would do next.

"You seem like you've always known the right thing to do," he said.

"I'm trained not to have doubts."

They both looked out beyond the house, to where the sea was pouring into the world. The lip of the sky was lit with amber.

"Today will be cloudy," he said.

"How do you know?"

"There are patterns in the Kusi. If you can see the sunrise then the day turns cloudy."

"What is the Kaskazi like?"

"It's so much calmer. The mornings are overcast but at noon the wind chases the cloud away. The afternoons are windy and hot."

He described the high cloud of the summer monsoon, an alto-stratus of a light grey pearl, he said. The Kaskazi brought still conditions at sea because the wind came from the north and the currents from the south. This created an opposing force, calming the waves. She tried to imagine days without the cathedral clouds of the Kusi, the olive light they gathered at sunrise and sunset.

He told her about the heat at Christmastime, when even in the depths of night the temperature never dropped below twenty-five degrees, about the ghost crabs that invaded the house, tap-dancing sideways across the cool cement of the living room floor. The mornings were cloudy, but by noon the wind blew the clouds away. The ocean was warm and free of the seaweed that latticed it in the Kusi. Then, everyone sat out late at night under the watchful eye of Orion and the Pleiades, which careened high in the sky.

As he spoke, she felt a rendering inside her. An entity was

separating from its creator, like a space capsule departing from the mother ship. The same sensation had come to her in the car, before their accident. From the passenger seat, she was listening to him speak when she felt a peeling off, a release. One part of her held a sensible conversation, heard him use pleasingly precise terms like *altostratus*. The other part was stunned into a sullen fear she had never felt before. Fear of what? She tried to catch it, put a name to it, but it slipped from her hands. She knew a fissure had been carved through her, a deep cut only he might be able to cure. But he did not seem the curing kind.

"Let's go back to bed."

She let him walk past her, brushing her arm as he did, and absorbed the familiar bolt of electricity strung between them as taut as any power wire. She followed him up the staircase, past her own door, down the hallway toward her aunt and uncle's unoccupied room, past the louvered windows with the shutters drawn against the night wind. She walked for what felt like hours, her life falling away behind her. Her heart pounded even while tiredness lapped at the edges of her body, spreading a paralysis within her. He passed through the door to his room, which yielded to his touch, floating open. She pulled the door shut behind them.

She will have to forget what happens next, before remembering it.

She will not remember how she got from the door to the bed. She will not remember whether he said anything, if he told her to leave, but she will remember the look on his face as he turned to find her in the room with him, that it was not gratification or acceptance, but a look of reckoning. Of manoeuvre, even.

She will remember that her mouth was suctioning his. There was no transition, no moment before this happened. It suddenly *was*. She struggled to grasp the present tense. There was no more present, only an amalgam of past, present, future. In this nameless dimension — more than in his flesh — she lost herself.

She will remember that she has never kissed anyone like this before. It is like starting life again, in reverse, going from old to new. Her mouth no longer has anything to do with breathing or hunger.

They were still sore from the accident, she will remember — both bruised where the seatbelt had pulled taut against them. She might even have cracked a rib, because when his ribcage pressed on hers she cried out.

She will remember digging her fingers in his scalp. She will remember wanting to devour him, everything that made him. She will remember thinking, and yet it being not her thought but an old code that emerged from a deep vault inside her: *I want to be with you.* But she was with him. Where was this yearning for what she had underneath her hands coming from? It frightened her to need so desperately what she already possessed.

Thought deserted her. She descended into a black vacuum. The tension on his face was not like any other expression she had seen — not desire but a kind of hate, a stunned ferocity. They kept their eyes open and on each other every minute. She could not remember being so afraid.

She will remember biting his shoulder hard enough to leave a tooth-shaped brown bruise that he would cover in the following days, when he was careful to wear a T-shirt in the house. She will remember he held her down, he blocked her breathing for a minute, his hand pressed on her windpipe and she began to rasp. Only then did he let go.

She will remember that for the first time since she had come to the coast she could not hear the roar of the sea. Another sound took its place inside her ears, her mind, in the echoing chambers of the damp cathedral of her heart.

A violent rearrangement took place inside her, as if her organs were being shuffled. Kidney replaced heart, heart replaced brain. She wondered if the taste of blue metal in her mouth was blood. She liked his smell. It was familiar to her. They were kin, she could smell it on his skin. He was cool, tasteless. He had fine downy hairs in the hollow of his lower back.

Later they lay under the mosquito net. She tried to trace the outline of the muscle that ran from his shoulder blade down to his buttocks, but he reached out and arrested her finger's slide, capturing her hand with his hand bent behind his back.

She turned her face toward the window and tried to think of oleander, of jasmine, of a sea the colour of green oranges. Everything she has done in her life until now has been so wrong, to a point where her error might tip over an invisible meridian and become truth, and allowed in the world. Or perhaps she has always been a producer of inevitable mistakes, the errors that had to happen so that other things could happen.

Outside, the coastal bush that surrounded the house was dark, thick with negative spaces. At some point he turned out the light, which lay inside a latticed Swahili lantern. Julia had these stationed all around the house. They were a millennia-old design from Yemen, Julia had told her, they came from ancient dhows, where they were used to guide stray navigators in the hours of darkness.

IV

AMUR
FALCON

"That's quite the book."

The man is middle-aged, as are many of the men who come to Moholo in the high season. He is pale and square with bandy legs. It is eleven in the morning; a beer sweats in a glass in front of him. He sits at the same table at Reef Encounters where Bob, or Gary or Keith, the spook who approached Margaux and I, habitually sat, leafing through his newspaper. Margaux is here, too, in spirit, with her broad-rimmed hat and her ankles decorated with henna tattoos, her feet swollen in the heat, grasped by a pair of flip-flops.

"*Birds of Africa*," he reads the title, just visible under my arm. "Keen birdwatcher, are you?"

"I'm studying for an exam. It's for nature guides who want to specialize in birds."

"Are you a guide then?"

"No, I'm a doctor. I'm just doing it out of interest."

"A doctor." His face is suddenly solemn. "You must be good at exams."

"I suppose I am."

I turn my gaze out to sea, to signal that I want to be alone with my thoughts. I take the book out and lay it face up on the table. On the cover are a pair of d'Arnaud's barbets and the names of the three encyclopedic Englishmen who have compiled the book.

"What is it about birds, other than there's so many of them?"

He's not the first person to ask me this question. "They live by their own rules. They're mysterious."

"How so?"

"They appear in the morning and the evening, usually. During the day they disappear. No one sees them, no one knows where they are. It's as if they pass into a different dimension."

He frowns. I sound unhinged, perhaps: disappearances, other dimensions. As if to prove me wrong an African fish eagle launches itself from the neem tree on the far side of the deck, even though it is nearly midday. It sails out over the waves in its Trappist robes, the white hood of its neck sharp against the brown of its wings.

I leaf through the book to find my weak points — thrushes, larks, warblers. I've never been quick to identify the small songbirds. Bird guides usually begin with the sea birds, then move on to the water birds, then the raptors. I don't know how this order has been arrived at, but there seems to be a consensus. The raptors are hard to identify in the field, in part because there are so many of them: vultures, the Secretary bird, the eagles, hawk-eagles, harrier-hawks, snake-eagles, the goshawks and the kestrels, the falcons and the buzzards, hobbies and marsh-harriers.

The lives of raptors are epic and violent. Like the migration of the Amur falcon, a small red-footed falcon with a barred breast. It breeds in Siberia and northern China but flies all the way to southern Africa in its migration. In India, its stopping-over grounds, it is trapped for cheap food.

Aisha took me to an acacia tree once. She had as good a bush eye as any field guide. "Look," she'd pointed into the dark interior branches of the tree. "It was driven there by an eagle."

I saw a dishevelled ball, like a plastic bag that had been snagged on a branch and ripped by the wind. It was the body of a shikra, a small sparrowhawk. "The eagle put it there," Aisha said. The shikra had been trying to escape a tawny eagle, most likely, flying fast, and became entangled with the mistletoe that grew as a creeper up the acacia, then impaled itself on thorns. The tawny eagle is a handsome bird to look at with its yellow cere, its butterscotch feathers.

Its Latin name is *Aquila rapax* meaning "rapacious eagle." It is an opportunist, unafraid of attacking eagles larger than itself. It will go for smaller birds carrying food and harass them until they drop their prize.

"Well, see you around. Have a good holiday. Good luck with the birds." The friendly man has finished his beer. He rises and for a moment I wonder if he is a replacement for Bob. The coast still needs its spies.

"You know . . ." I look up to see the man has paused. He turns back to me. He's now wearing round hippie sunglasses with purple lenses. He looks like a jovial John Lennon. "I've heard bird watching is for perfectionists and high achievers. People who like to get things right and tick boxes. But I'm sure not everyone is like that."

"I'm sure," I say.

He melts into the dark interior, passing under the startled eye of the stuffed marlin.

I move like a fugitive. I find myself scoping rooms, using my peripheral vision, sunglasses on, my hat obscuring my face. I never thought I would come back. I was afraid to.

I am most afraid of meeting Julia. I can imagine the scene: us meeting in the narrow aisles of the local supermarket with its dusty rice-starch smell, seeing her walking toward me in those delicate silver sandals she always wore to go shopping. I am afraid of going to the house, of not going to the house. Afraid of feeling as if time had passed, of feeling as if time hadn't passed at all.

The coast does not feel like somewhere I stayed for two months. It has the density of home. I don't belong here, I would never belong here because I'm not a deep-sea fisherman, I don't run a franchise of whisky bars in sub-Saharan Africa, I didn't found a hot air balloon safari company or run the national division of Mitsubishi trucks.

Crucially, I was not born here. No amount of years racked up here will compensate.

And yet I look back and know that I loved the hours I spent here, trapped in the sordid eloquence of an obsession. I never expected that would happen to me.

Today the sky is a clear Kaskazi sky. The weather is just as Storm said it would be — hot, dry, bringing a stable, unhurried wind. Kitesurfers rip through the waves just beyond the reef. I miss the Kusi monsoon. Then, the sky is a person — you can talk to it with its flexing moods and rains so sudden they feel like a visitation.

I pay and go for a walk on the beach. At the bar the waiters are cleaning jars for the candle lanterns with window cleaner. *Asante sana, tutaonana badaaye.* They thank me, say we will see each other soon. It's good to hear the swish of the language again, to walk under crimson bougainvillea and the arbours of neem and moringa trees draped over the hot sand. Out to sea, just beyond the reef, the isosceles triangle of the jahazi sail leans in to the horizon. Yes, I am back in the land of the *Zanj*, an Arabic word, meaning black, the word the Arabic traders used for the coast as well as for its inhabitants.

Tomorrow morning Daniel and I will walk in the forest. He is the best bird guide on the coast, possibly in the entire country, or so says a website full of testimonies from other students who have studied under him. I have met him before. Storm introduced us one day, when we stopped at the forest reserve where he works. We were driving to Moholo for a party. Suddenly he stopped the car and pulled up on a non-descript stretch of road.

"What is it?"

Storm reached for the binoculars he kept underneath the driver's seat. "A Böhm's spinetail." He pointed to a jet-shaped bird, like a large swift, fluting through the sky above electricity wires.

"It looks like a bat."

"It does — they have an uncertain flight. They're hard to see. We're lucky."

We drove on for a few kilometres, then stopped at the forest station and talked to Daniel, who accepted our offer of a basket of mangoes with a smile. "It's amazing how happy a basket of mangoes can make people," Storm said.

He seemed alive that day. Animated from within.

I have arranged to meet Daniel at the Miombo supermarket at one p.m. I have an hour to kill so I walk. In town, tuk-tuk drivers huddle outside the village supermarket, waiting for fares. The supermarket is cavernous, its shelves filled with boxes of matches, bottles of bleach and bags of low-grade pasta imported from Italy, and little else. The tourists have come back. Italian girls totter down the street in platform sandals, squeezed into beach dresses, trying not to trip into the gutters, which have been dug deep to capture tropical flash floods.

I lose my way and end up in the tight streets of the Arab quarter. I pass Mullah Electrics, Al-Nujim importers and Mustafa glass enterprises, then the small honey-coloured office of renowned makers of halvah, which is exported all over the Mediterranean. I pass a man wielding a wheelbarrow full of red plums, another man with a foot-peddled Singer sewing machine on the pavement, dressed in a skull-cap and a lemon-coloured *kikhoi*, the sign for kombucha — *Wild herbs cure HIV!* I catch sight of the ocean. It is striated with brown sediment that has been washed down from the mouth of the Mithi River.

I must have seen all this when I walked these streets with Storm, but I was distracted. The town appears more real to me, now that it is empty of him.

I thread my way through chickens, charcoal fires, narrow passages. Women in black veils crouch over black pots. Children sit on dirty curbs and sneer at me — *beetch, beetch!* They call. I don't know if they are saying *beach* or *bitch*.

On the beach I find the root of a doum palm and sit down. I take out my cardboard lunch box and start to eat, but wind blows sand in my food.

Two young boys sit underneath a coconut palm nearby. They frown at me through long eyelashes; their expressions are severe, for such young boys.

"Hello?" They say. Immediately they sidle closer, shuffling along on their bottoms until they are sitting next to me.

"What is your name?" they chorus.

"Rebecca. And what is yours?"

"Mohammed," says the boy in the lime polo shirt.

"I am also Mohammed," says the boy in the white shirt.

"Aha, I'm going to call you Mohammed Times Two."

"What are you doing?" They say in unison.

"Eating lunch."

I wonder if I should give them some. My chicken leg is scrawny. I don't want to insult them. Instead I look out around me. It is low tide and the water is divided into jade slices of sand bars and dark patches of seaweed. From afar it looks as if there is a pattern. In the shallows are blacktip reef sharks and cerulean damselfish.

It was early September and my last week on the coast. The wind was changing; the Kusi was waning and the skies were no longer as conflicted. We were surfing; we had to wait for the tide to come in. At low tide we passed the time snorkelling, edging over the reef that grazed our stomachs, over dark beds of seaweed, our hands sinking into its channels as we stroked, fish slipping from the shadows of their coral overhangs. Storm lifted me onto the board, his arms underneath my armpits. Our bodies never became truly familiar to each other. He felt it also, I know, that I feared him — feared what he might do to me, if he were withdrawn from my life. But it was pleasant to be handled like an object, or an animal. To be just a body in his hands.

I am still absorbing the feel of this place. Everywhere we go broadcasts a message, a current of meaning. Here, it has something to do with danger. Anything can happen and there is no protection — not from the law or its enforcers, not from the state. People sense this and live faster here, more recklessly. They drink and play because here death really could happen, today or tomorrow. It is not a distant country you are just getting round to applying for permits to enter.

I realize now that the exposure I felt here was not about this danger frequency, the realization that my life was cheap here, just like every-one else's — especially Africans' — or even what happened to me in Gariseb, or the political situation, but him. Storm had locked himself away long before I had met him. I felt an impulse to move him to feel something — anything. He had a glassiness; he was the explosion between heat and cold, like cooling lava. I understood that for his whole life Storm would deflect experience effortlessly, and emotion along with it, and felt the injustice of this. He would get off scot-free.

"What are you doing now?" the Mohammeds ask.

"Thinking."

The boy in the white shirt is marginally more bold of the two. He asks, "What are you thinking about?"

"About the last time I came here."

"When was that?"

"Two and a half years ago."

"What were you doing here?"

"I was with someone I loved."

The Mohammeds consider this with a grave expression. The tips of the boys' eyelashes are lined with grains of sand. The sun catches them and they shine like miniature jewels. We sit looking out to sea for a while. I feel reluctant in the face of the future, I real-ize. I can't judge the right moment anymore. Mohammed Times Two and I are waiting for something — to be delivered some impe-tus, for a neuron or nerve to ignite and to vault us into the next moment. We are waiting to be animated by life, but it is us who have to make the first move.

Daniel is already outside the Miombo supermarket. He sits in the shade under the awning. He must be seventy, but it is impossible to tell and impolite to ask. His nose is straight and long and wide. He has high cheekbones and large, intelligent eyes.

I greet him and tell him we have met before. He gives me an uncertain but not unfriendly look. "I'm sorry. All white people look the same to me." He laughs — a strange sound, a guilty giggle.

We agree to meet the following day at six a.m. at the gate. I make my way back to Kilindoni by matatu. As I am alighting I make a decision, or rather my legs make a decision for me. The turnoff to the Estate road is only a hundred metres from the gate of the Kilindoni Club. Soon I am walking down it, with its shattered bougainvillea bracts, the spikes of sisal plants that line it on either side.

I reach the road to the beach. This is the same road I used to run in the mornings. Everything looks unchanged: the gates of Oleander House are still flanked by two metal zebras, the mango trees along its perimeter are still there; Oleander House itself is just visible, its white bulk hidden in a grove of casuarinas. The house was protected from the looters who had free rein for a day or two in the post-election violence, perhaps, by the influence of Charles Mgura, the owner. Mgura was the Interior Minister then. We could hear their parties, two-day affairs involving loudspeakers blasting reggaeton, for which the owner's sons had a weakness. I remember his wife, who drove their two white Range Rovers very fast down the lane, the huge rings on her hands as she gripped the steering wheel as I was swallowed by a cloud of dust.

A short slip road down to the beach takes me to sandstone cliffs. The beach has been eroded since I was here last. Oleander House perches not far from the edge now. A dozen pied kingfishers emerge from their roosting holes in the cliffs and fly out to sea in fighter jet formation. I remember the camouflaged transport aircraft and fighter jets that tore along the coast. Then, the military were flying sorties to bomb Al-Nur inside its stronghold thirty kilometres from Puku. There was no mention of this on the television news, in the local newspapers or even on the BBC website. But everyone on the coast knew all the same. War is always an open secret for the people whose lives bathe in its shadow.

Daniel waits for me at the gate in the morning, his motorcycle balanced on a kickstand beside him. He tells me we are walking in a remote part of the park, that we have to drive eight kilometres down the road to another gate. We zip down the tarmac, turning heads: a seventy-year-old black man, a white woman riding pillion, clutching his ribs.

We stash the motorcycle in the trees on the side of the road and set out on foot. We enter a cool canopy of brachystegia. Immediately they are all around us, birds in every tree: weavers, drongos, sunbirds, the gorgeous bush-shrike with its panels of four-coloured feathers, the tropical bou-bou, whose bell-like call chimes through the forest. We walk over fresh elephant tracks. In the forest live three hundred small, furtive elephant.

Daniel has programmed the tour: local endemics. He leads me to the endangered pygmy tufted owl, which lives only on this postage-stamp remnant of tropical lowland forest that once stretched all the way along the coast from Somalia to Mozambique, to Graham's weaver, of which only two hundred remain, to the tiny sifaka duiker and the golden tree frog.

Nearly every creature in this forest is endangered, some of them critically. A Chinese mining company has been given a concession to flense this land of bauxite. They recently started open-pit mining in the north of the forest. Another Chinese concession claims to have discovered oil.

The forest feels unlike any other I've walked in. There is a sense of urgency emanating from it, as if the creatures know their days are numbered. The air drips with calls. We hear the bass hoot of the narina trogon, then the eastern nicator. A steel-blue whydah tears through the shadows. Gold sun-coated leaves shudder as monkeys launch themselves from the upper branches.

Suddenly, a deep-voiced, owlish call reverberates through the forest. The call crescendos, then is answered, fainter, from the opposite side of the clearance.

A flurry. We see a Napoleonic quiff. A white mask slashes his face, making him look permanently surprised.

"Fischer's turaco. They are calling to each other," Daniel says, "the male and the female."

We listen to them for a while. "Why are they so insistent?" I ask.

Daniel is regarding the bird now with a particular expression. Storm looked at birds like this, too, always, as if he were in special communication with them, as if he could read their intentions.

"They are anxious," Daniel says, finally. "They want to be together, but something is keeping them apart."

V

NUBIAN
NIGHTJAR

The sun hovered on the horizon. Within twenty minutes it would set. The patients who were well enough tied and re-tied their headscarves or washed their hands in the sterile washbasin outside the recovery ward in preparation for *Maghrib*, the sunset prayers.

They were six men from the same village near Gao, Ali among them. They spread out their prayer mats. She watched their genuflections, the way their heads touched the mats so lightly before springing away, as if the ground had delivered them an electric shock.

After prayers he found her in her office. She saw his feet first, beyond the flap of her door. They were slim and sinewy; they reminded her of leather bridles.

She asked him to sit. He folded his body with great fluidity, considering his injury, sustained a week before.

"Why do you watch us at prayers?"

"I don't know."

He nodded, satisfied, she could only suppose, with the honesty of her response.

"Why do people walk dogs in the rain?"

"What do you mean?"

"On television, once, I saw people in England, in a green space. A park." He landed upon the word as if he had only just learned it. "They had their dogs on strings."

"Leads. Dogs have to be walked. It doesn't matter what the weather is."

"Ah." His eyes flared. It occurred to her he might be hungry for conversation, nothing more. At times in Gariseb she felt this same famine blow through her, a hunger for abstract thought as much as anything. Her mind now was stuffed with facts and actions.

"How is life in Gikayo?" she asked.

"It is bad." His expression was solemn.

"Is it a big place?"

"Normally there are two thousand people. It is a large village."

"Normally?"

"Now there are three hundred refugees also. But they live apart. They have their own *quartier*."

"What are they refugees from?"

"Al-Nur."

"Why do they fear them?"

"Because Al-Nur will change their laws. Until now they have lived like *Kufir*."

"I don't think so. They have been observant Muslims, but they have had freedoms."

He considered this with a reasonable expression.

"Are they right to be afraid?"

"In Gao, yes. Al-Nur now control most of the city. Eighty percent. But you know that."

She played with the pencil on her desk. "How would I know that? We are three hundred kilometres away here."

He did not answer. Ali was the exact person the refugees of Gikayo were trying to avoid, she knew — a fighter, or a spy from the security wing, who policed social behaviour. Women found outside without their husbands were shot in those areas now controlled by Al-Nur. Or at least that is what her security briefings in the Chequers mansion had taught her. The security wing of Al-Nur were impossible to spot because they were ordinary people: shopkeepers, tailors. Spies were everywhere.

He was still looking at her.

"And your camels, are they well?" she asked.

"Very well. My father has fifty."

"Then your family is secure."

"Yes," he said. Something of him relished the word, she thought. *Secure.* Safe. His hunger for language was one of the characteristics she could relate to, as well as his precise yet unfussy speech, which gave him an instant gravitas. *You almost feel you could trust this man.* More and more her thoughts had taken on this quality: mental compositions she would later send to Anthony, requisitioned from afar. No longer her own.

"What do you think of Al-Nur?" she hazarded.

"What is wrong with my country is that it is not a country. It never has been. For two hundred years the British have been trying to turn it into something they can recognize, and so control."

She didn't argue with this explanation, even if he had evaded her question. It was broadly true.

"Have you ever thought about leaving your country, living somewhere else?" she asked.

"My country does not yet exist," he said.

"It does. But it is eating itself alive."

Ali did not shrug — the fighters she treated did not seem to have that gesture in their physical vocabulary. Instead they flared their nostrils and flashed their eyes in indifferent disdain. "I can't leave. We need to become a country. Then perhaps I will be a diplomat." He beamed at her, a sudden, innocent smile. "Before, it was possible to be a tribal kingdom or a religious state. But now the world requires countries in order to engage with you. We must be realistic. But the country needs to be under Islamic law, like Saudi Arabia."

"Why?"

He laughed out loud. Her question was that preposterous, she supposed.

"Because sharia law is a good law," he said. "The people respect it. The mosques are always completely full. There is no going back, now. The people prefer it to socialism. They remember only hunger of those years." He paused. "A country needs resources. Angola has diamonds, Botswana copper. Even Sudan has oil. We have camels and sand."

"You want to enrich your country?"

His eyes narrowed. Most people did this involuntarily. It was part of the parasympathetic nervous system, like blinking or breathing, but his reaction had a deliberateness about it. She wondered where, or how, he had learned to become so self-contained, an entity, an uncrackable egg.

There were four reasons why men like Ali became guerrilla fighters, she had learned long ago, courtesy of the army and its seminars pre-deployment and post-deployment, conversations with logistics experts, and then those long, dry weeks and months in the field. They had sent an instructor, a Sandhurst-educated strategist in sandy fatigues.

The first reason was called political but was often territorial: to dislodge an interloper, an unfair regime, a sadistic warlord. Then, to change the world, to upend a corrupt system and suspend the false consciousness that made its existence possible. "Ideology. The Che Guevara motive," the instructor had said.

The third was identical to the political motive but with a twist: religious indoctrination. Religion was a façade for ideology, which was a façade for power. Finally, the fourth: bad luck — you were caught up in events; you came to consciousness in a civil war; your parents were killed; you drank revenge like boiling petrol and it fuelled you; you had no choice. The four reasons could coexist, the army major said, but one rationale always trumped the others.

She tried to see behind the veil of Ali's eyes. She failed to find the rancid hatred of the religious ideologue, or the ordinary fury of the politically motivated. If history had not come along and bullied Ali into war, he might have been exactly what he looked like — a village

149

schoolmaster. Perhaps, with luck and the right connections, he might even have risen to be minister of education for a region or a province.

She thought of all this as he began to tell her a story. At its start she took it for a follow-up to his shark parable. The story was about his uncle — or perhaps his cousin, she missed the exact tie — "A very important man," Ali said. His name was Mohammed Ibrahim and he was a religious elder in Gikayo.

"He was about to take over the area. He was the second in command to Omaar." He said the name as if he expected her to know it. "He would have changed everything. He was educated in London; he was a real statesman."

"What happened?"

"The daughter of his cousin came to visit. He was very fond of her. He was a careful man, Ibrahim. He had everyone who came into his compound frisked, even his servants of thirty years. But Zainab didn't like being frisked by men. She told Ibrahim it was un-Islamic."

"Zainab killed him?"

"And herself." Ali nodded once, then twice, as if to seal a deed.

The diesel generators sputtered into life. It was dark now.

Ali folded himself back into an upright position with a deliberate, angular grace. She left the tent with him and watched him glide into the night. Overhead the stars were punched into an implacable, black sky. One moved suddenly, spewing a shower of light in its wake.

"It's the international space station." Suddenly, Andy was beside her.

"Really?"

"I'd show you on the NASA site if we had the bandwidth. They've passed over here before."

"There they are, twisting knobs or whatever it is they do up there in zero gravity, with us down here."

"Yeah," Andy said. "It must feel great to be above it all."

He was quiet for a moment. "I see you're getting along with Osama bin Laden."

"What makes you say that?"

"He's well educated." ·

"He is," she conceded. "But not that well resourced. Although he was in charge, definitely. Is in charge."

"How do you know?"

"Aisha recognized him." She looked at him quickly. "It's important he doesn't know."

"Sure thing."

Aisha had waited three days after he had first arrived to tell her. She came to find her on the edge of the camp, where she had gone to check on her camel.

These men, they are different. Foreigners.

· *From where?*

Arab countries. Not Africa. They use false names. Aisha's mouth sank in disdain. *They speak Arabic — pure Arabic. They have come with guns for our men. There is one man — I don't know his name. He is the leader. He looks like a schoolteacher, but he is very brave. No.* She switched words. *Brutal.*

Aisha had not actually seen him, she'd told her; she'd heard his voice on two of the nights she'd spent in the desert in hiding. It was Ali and his men she was hiding from, although neither of them knew it. As they passed nearby, Ali was speaking to his men. "Something about Gikayo," Aisha said. Aisha had passed through the town, although at the time she did not know its name, on her long pilgrimage from her home. Gikayo was where she had lost her last remaining camel, bar Montague. She had been too afraid to move from her hiding place and had to listen as he was trapped by a group of men and butchered alive.

Andy peeled away from her and walked toward the accommodation block. She never knew what to make of his visitations. She had the impression he was watching her, and not with ordinary curiosity. Or there was a more specific reason: to catch her in the act of making an avoidable mistake, maybe. Or some other motivation — something she had not even thought of.

She would talk more to Aisha tomorrow. Then she would make up her mind.

As she walked across the compound she saw Mustafa. She nearly used the greeting she'd learned in war zones. *But you are alive!* The childlike glee that powered it. There was no point in saying hello or how are you? You were there. You were not a ghost. Not yet.

"How long is it since I have seen you?" She asked in Arabic.

"Long enough, *Inshallah*."

The twenty-one-year-old had a rangy but gentle smile. He was one of the crossfire casualties from the village. He had nothing to do with Al-Nur, she was sure of it. In two days he would be well enough to go home to his goats. At this news he gave her an instant smile. All of the Bora men she had met performed these quick-change expressions, lurching from a sombreness to childish, reckless smiles.

She said goodnight to Mustafa. She didn't know what she would do that evening. She would have a tea, stare at the ceiling or just sleep. She dreaded the questions that came with these bleached hours in camp. What has she become? Has she lived a life worth living? Why did she fail to grasp the present, even when it slid over her?

She missed the city — any city. She'd been in the capital only three days before flying to Gariseb, and that was four months ago now. She wanted desperately to be in a city again. There, she could have a drink; she could watch strangers — people who she would not have to eat three meals a day beside for months on end, whose names she would never know. It was not sex she wanted. In any case sexual desire was always abstract, for her, until attached to another person. It was a moral decision, in part. But also she had never felt the kind of physical hunger that drove others to sleep with strangers.

She took intimacy seriously. But she liked to observe people who did not, who circled each other languorously in the city's bars and clubs like satiated cheetahs. She felt superior and left out at the same time. She kept her loneliness intact.

He came to find her the following afternoon. He repeated his entreaty. "I would like to listen to the radio."

"I will need to discuss with the others," she said. This was the tactic she used with impossible requests, learned from observing village elders and their dispute-settling tactics. The invitation to sit under a tree cross-legged and eat dates was like a magical potion.

He turned his liquid eyes toward her. "I had a dream last night," he said. "I was riding a black horse. There was a full moon, but around it was a green colour, like a shadow. It curled around the moon. I could not decide if this was a good omen or bad. I had a horse because there were no trucks. Perhaps it was a time before trucks. The horse was black, and we had come from the city together. What city, I don't know. There were black birds in the sky and I didn't like this either. Black birds flying toward the mountain. Where I come from, this is always a bad sign."

"Why is everything either a good or bad sign?"

"Birds are intelligent."

"They are," she agreed. "But they don't know the future."

He looked at her with an expression that might have been shock.

She was tired. The future: she felt its bully burden through these people she treated; she felt the eyes of God and his intentions. From now on she would have to stop herself from looking at a flock of migrating black starlings and seeing the dark coagulations of fate.

She ran a hand through her hair. Dust and oil coated her fingers. Water in camp was low; she hadn't showered in days.

Ali had turned to leave.

"Perhaps we can listen to the radio together," she said. "It's on my computer. I can stream a radio station once in a while. I'll have to work — I must write up my notes. But I can listen to it in the background."

She had a vision of Anthony and his team calling up the World Service for the files, listening to the broadcast over and over again in the company of two simultaneous translators from the Bora refugee community commandeered from Tottenham that morning, in a room with a smooth conference table made of pale wood and the grey snake of the Thames in the distance, trying to parse what message might be encoded in these broadcasts Ali was so keen to hear.

"Tomorrow, come at noon."

A smile spread across his face, slowly at first, then rapidly gathering force. He was a wire; he transmitted information. Even his hands and fingers were fine, like antennae.

The sun was setting. She had not had a drop to drink for three months. She had not tasted yogurt or fresh fruit, apart from pitted, hard oranges. Their bitterness was a tonic; it had within its bite an honesty, as if only in denial would she discover the true taste of sweetness.

The first casualty of the day was a camel herder who had strayed too close to a skirmish between militia and government forces. The herder was unconscious when he was brought in, but his wounds told the story. The militia had their semi-automatic weapons mounted on the back of pickups; the bullets fired downwards.

In this case, the young man his friends had brought, tearing across the plateau in a borrowed jalopy, was shot through the gut. He was stick thin; jaundice had already set in.

She and Rafael arrived in the tented triage station in the same moment. They slapped on gloves.

"You open him; I'll have a look. Then you can rummage." Rafael's words were half-eaten by the sound of fabric being cut away.

She had always been good with tissue. "Women often are," Rafael had said, when he first observed her dexterity. It was as if her fingertips had a feel for how muscles, veins, adipose tissue, epidermis, wanted to lie. She handled insides coolly, unfazed by the maze her fingers often found themselves in. She possessed the ability to keep calm even when she felt fearful and uncertain that her instincts were the right ones.

The man — a boy, really, he couldn't have been twenty — was bleeding profusely. At least one bullet had torn through the intestinal area. They poked through its spirals. The gut was bruised and shredded badly in only the descending colon. Otherwise the wounds were small punctures that could be fixed with deft stitching.

Rafael lifted his face to hers. His eyebrows went up, his *I think we can do this* signal. He was a quiet surgical companion, always, preferring to talk with his face.

He left her to close up. She joined the layers of the abdomen and sutured the epidermis. After three years doing field surgery, albeit in intervals, separate chapters in different countries, performing these procedures with limited equipment and in these conditions was beginning to feel routine. Burns was the only injury that truly frightened her, both professionally and personally, and why she sometimes cowered under her desk during rains of mortar, clutching her tiny office fire extinguisher.

"Hey, Rebecca, we're off to town." Andy yelled from outside the theatre. "Want to come?"

"Why are you going?"

"Supplies. We need UHT and the UN plane is broken. We thought we'd drop in on Lars."

"No, man," she heard the scratchy voice of Bernard, their facilities engineer, a dry South African. "Not those guys. They'll make us drink terrible vodka and I'll get a headache."

"Listen to yourself for a minute," Andy said. "These guys have got *alcohol*."

Nasir was fifty kilometres away, and hardly a town. But she felt a need for her eyes to light upon something other than camp, if only so that she could return with fresh eyes.

She forgot about her appointment with Ali. She threw her medical bag in the back of the truck and climbed into the cab for the sweat and dust of the journey.

They arrived in Nasir in time for the *Dhuhr*, the noon prayer. Women draped in cerise and orange *thoubs* melted into doorways and alleys as they drove past. Her gaze was drawn upwards, into an insolent cloudless sky. It was ringed by sandbagged rooftops of destroyed apartment buildings. The town bristled with radio masts, some cut in half by shrapnel.

Lars and Maurice were Belgian doctors. They manned the fort at a small MSF station in the town. Their role was to pick up the walking cases from the front line who had retreated this far, leaving the real war wounded for Gariseb. Individually they were mournful; together Lars and Maurice did a good impression of *The Seventh Seal*.

They were met by two gaunt forms under the arch of their clinic, which was housed in a pretty, undestroyed ex-residence framed in hardy bougainvillea.

"Lars, man, you've put on some weight." Andy encased him in a bear hug.

Lars gave them all a skeptical glance. "Not enough carnage at the front line?"

"It's been a slow day, only fifty amputations this morning."

Maurice, the warmer of the two, rushed forward to shake her hand. "What a delight to see a woman. Oh —" he very nearly put his hand to his mouth "— but you are beautiful."

"Thanks, Maurice, but that's because I'm here. Once you get home to Antwerp, or wherever, I'll seem quite plain."

Maurice smiled his wan cadaver smile. He shepherded them all through the arch. Suddenly, a crack racked the air. She knew what it was, she did not even need to turn around. Maurice was behind her, doubled over, his thin, fine hands placed in a squelching pool of blood on the floor.

"Get down," Andy pushed her down; hard, she would think later, looking at the bruise his fingers left on her neck.

They spent perhaps a minute on the floor. Maurice began to gurgle. She stood up. "Where's your theatre?" Lars had a frozen look on his face. "A bed, a table — anything!" she was shouting. She bent down and draped Maurice's arm over her neck. "Are you going to help or what?" she barked at them.

The three men leapt up. Together they dragged Maurice into a brightly lit room that must have served as their consultancy, although it would have been a pantry once. Shelves lined it at shoulder height; an old sink squatted in the corner.

"Shit, my bag."

"Where are you going?"

"It's in the truck." She was gone before they could stop her.

She leapt from the shadow of the villa's stone archway into the area of the truck's wheelbase and crouched. She heard no gunfire report, so she lunged for the door. Behind her, a ping, a puff of smoke from the stonework. They didn't have an angle on her, but they might get one, any second now.

She grabbed her bag. It nearly slipped in her sweat-covered palms, but she had it. She didn't close the door of the truck. She used it as a shield as she flung herself into the dark mouth of the archway.

An hour later it was over. "Okay, that's it. Let's leave him on the drip." She peeled off her gloves, went to put them in the pedal bin, and then remembered where she was; she had only five pairs of surgical gloves in her small travelling kit.

For the first time since the attack she ventured to look out the window. It was mid afternoon. Unfamiliar starlings swirled around the orange trunks of palms in great black eddies. She missed her binoculars. It always surprised her that these habits of the natural world continued among the mortar explosions, the rapes and clustered executions: weavers carried on weaving nests, camels drank shyly from troughs, wasps landed on her lapel, from where she evicted them with a single breath.

The birds came to rest in the tree in the courtyard. Small pendulous appendages, like an extra tongue, hung from their beaks — wattled starlings. She should have known from their waxy, excited call.

Lars sat on a wooden chair with three legs, holding his head. He looked up at her — a plaintive, unreadable look.

"He'll be fine. A nice exit wound, I showed you."

He nodded. "We've never been attacked."

"First rule of operating in a war zone," Andy said. "Anything can happen."

"This is not a war zone," Lars argued. "There is a ceasefire."

"I'm radioing Rafael," she said. "You can come with us to Gariseb or we'll get you on the medevac flight with Maurice. You're not staying here."

"You don't have the authority."

"I don't now, but I will." She took her radio out of her rucksack. The VHF would reach Gariseb. Rafael would call London on the satellite phone, London would call Brussels, and they would make the arrangements. But for that night, they would all have to stay.

They had a dinner of tinned tuna in tomato sauce, brewed up by Lars on a hotplate in the once-grand kitchen. A corner where the brickwork had been blown away was open to the sky. Through it fell the pins of stars.

Every ten minutes she went to check on Maurice, who remained stable. She thanked the walls around her that the bullet had gone clean through the muscle of his shoulder. He would have to wear a sling until his lateral movement repaired, but other than that he would be fine.

She and Lars took turns waking at hourly intervals to check Maurice's condition that night. The patient slept soundly, better than the rest of them, who for security slept together in one small bedroom, half-rusted kitchen knives under their pillows.

At dawn she braved the back entrance, which led onto an alley. She wanted to see the day come. She gambled on the snipers being asleep or at prayers.

Beyond the boundary of the ruined back garden children scurried along the alleyway. Where they were going, she didn't know — there had been no school in Nasir since the ceasefire. She had seen these same children in the streets of Kabul or in Kurdistan, playing in their dust-hemmed clothes with makeshift toys. Sometimes live fire found them. These children grew up knowing they could be killed at any time. Still they played.

The wattled starlings returned to the ex-garden. She had a better look at them, in the good light. Their plumage was grey-black. The females were quite drab. The purple-looking pendulous sacs were draped around the yellow heads of the males. The wattles looked like a growth, a deformation. She wondered what their function was.

"There is a man in my village who pays attention to birds." Ali had caught her staring at the black starlings in Gariseb, two days earlier. He stood beside her. "He consults them. If you need to know about a marriage or a battle, the birds may tell him if God approves or not."

"How? What do they do?"

He stared at the glossy black backs of the starlings. "He will not tell anyone. It is a secret."

"Great, we survived the night. Now let's blow this joint before we get killed." Andy, his eyes small from sleep, poked his head outside the shattered wall.

"There's a plane coming in at eleven. They'll be on it," she jerked her head back to where Maurice lay. "They said we need to get out of town straight away. The Nisa are only twelve kilometres to the west. They'll be here by lunchtime. The sniper we met was an advance party."

"Well, that was all very unexpected," Andy said, in response. "I think our shopping trip to town is over."

They put Maurice in the back seat of the pickup's cab. She and Lars travelled in the open flatbed of the truck. They had no helmets or flak jackets. They had to hope the snipers had moved on, to the east of the city.

They delivered the Belgians to the airstrip where the chartered plane was waiting for them. "Ah, a Ukrainian pilot," Lars said, when they had all shaken hands. "My favourite. So much less reckless than the Russians and South Africans."

She and Andy climbed back into the truck once the plane took off, with Bernard at the wheel. The trip back to camp was quiet

— no dust-smeared Toyota pickup trucks, their beds full of young men in ragtag fatigues, semi-automatic weapon rounds crisscrossing their bodies. No hastily butchered camels and goats on the side of the road. No smoothed tracks that hid a recently placed landmine. They passed groups of young men with scarred foreheads chewing *qat*. Now they stood under trees in suspiciously new green fatigues. A month before they had been cattle farmers, their hair dyed orange with cow's urine.

Andy had never looked at her before with any special interest. But on the trip back he pitched her sliding glances she found difficult to read.

After three or four of these, she said, "What is it?"

His small mouth pinched itself together. "I was just wishing I could do what you do." His eyes stayed on the road. "Save people's lives. Save Maurice's life."

"You can. You do."

He grimaced. "I'd never make it through medical school. I'm not like you. I was brought up in a two-up, two-down in Burnley."

"Lots of people from that background go to medical school these days."

"I'd have to go back and do chemistry at A-level."

"Probably," she said. "Why don't you?"

The radio jolted to life — Rafael calling for their coordinates — and their conversation was interrupted.

They pulled up in the compound at two that afternoon. "I never thought I'd be so pleased to see this shithole," Andy said.

Rafael came to meet them, his hands pressed together. He never expressed fear, but she had observed his hands making the cathedral shape they constructed now, and how he hopped from foot to foot, very lightly, when he was anxious.

She alighted from the truck, her legs cramped from sitting. "We have to be in theatre in half an hour," Rafael said. She dropped her bag in her office. Her body sagged with fatigue. She wanted a cup of coffee just to keep going through the operation, but it made her hands jittery. She had to trust her hands, or she had nothing.

The following day she had her first lie-in in a month. Rafael had ordered her to rest. She was surprised; so far he had given no sign of being the kind of man who would give an inch. She had come to almost appreciate his arid neutrality, his fastidiousness.

That afternoon Ali came to see her again, a pair of narrow feet arriving unannounced at the perimeter of her tent flap.

"I am getting stronger."

"You are," she agreed. "Soon you can go home."

He drank tea while she pounded out emails with her computer screen tilted away from his view — lists of surgical kits to be ordered, ampoules of morphine-based painkillers, anesthetic. On his previous visits she had observed a pattern. He would remain silent for long periods, drinking tea, looking contemplative, before bursting into speech. *A man without a mask is very rare.* Where had she heard this, or read it? It might have been one of the psychology books she had gorged on, five or six years ago, when she had been convinced she would specialize in psychiatry. Ali's mask was easy to guess — she had identified it already — but rather than reassure her this made her more suspicious of him.

She was still typing when he asked, "Why did you volunteer to come here?"

She stopped and turned to face him. "I felt it was my duty."

"To do what?"

"To save people who would otherwise die because they are at war."

"But you treat combatants," he said.

"We treat whoever is brought to us."

"Don't you feel more for one life than another? Do you not treat the civilians first?"

"We treat the person who is most likely to die first."

He left the tent without a word. She hadn't told the exact truth. She had become worried about Ali's attentions. Rafael, Andy, Niccolo the Italian surgeon and Eileen the Canadian nurse — the nexus of their small team — were appraised of his visits to her tent. When Ali was present one or other of them would stick their head inside the flap — *cup of tea? There's a delivery for you.* They were looking out for her, supposedly, but also they did not approve.

She heard the *wow-wow* of the Nubian nightjar. All nightjars made unearthly noises; it was on their calls that car alarms were based, an incessant mechanical fluting. She had seen nightjars singing near camp, their throats pulsating hurriedly like a tiny machine.

Night was coming. She found herself at the edge of her office, staring into the west, examining the sky for what felt like the thousandth time. She didn't know what she wanted from the land here, the way the curve of the hills sank into the sky instead of rising, the sidewinder trajectory of the moonrise, the envious sun.

She wondered about Andy. Something was not quite right. She tried to cast him as a character — the tall ginger-haired orderly who supported Manchester City, who listened to gloomy Adele songs on his iPod as he swept a bleach-sodden mop along the canvas corridors. Who now, in her memory, is still standing outside the triage tent in Gariseb, sucking on a cigarette, watching her accompany Ali as he hobbled around the bare scrub the day they spotted the lion track together, both as excited as children to see the ovoid paw and four fat digits, and Ali told her a story that may have been true or may have been allegorical, about how one day he encountered a lion stalking a man's goats, but the lion was so thin he could not bear to shoot him. "In fact," he said, "I wanted to deliver a goat to him. I thought about buying it and putting it in the truck, but then I realized I couldn't bear to see it ripped apart." Who was this man who could not watch one animal kill another, even as he held a loaded AK-47? They had watched her — all of them, Andy, Rafael — as she had laughed with Ali, with the easy complicity of people who would soon betray each other.

S he was in theatre when Ali left camp. As he'd predicted, three men showed up in a Hilux truck and took him away. There were few goodbyes in Gariseb in any case. Staff came and went on unannounced cargo flights. She went looking for Bernice, the Irish nurse who liked to play Scrabble with her, only to find she had left an hour before, never to return.

She sat in the canteen, trying to coax Aisha through a bowl of vegetable soup. She had not eaten properly in weeks, and she had to be careful to reintroduce food slowly. Her stomach would reject anything too substantial. In severe cases of near starvation the patient could convulse and die.

Lenjoh the interpreter sat with them. Aisha had holes in her memory, as she called them. She could not remember exactly when it happened, only that it was a long time ago.

"It was during the Jilal," Aisha said. "We were friends since we were girls; we fetched water together, we herded goats and, when we acquired them, cattle. There was Samira, whose family was from the very far north, near the border. She was small. She had only one possession apart from the hijab she wore — a bead necklace. She never took it off.

"There was Wanjiru. She was a mix from a highland Christian family; her mother married a Muslim. There were two other girls, Isa and Leila, they were sisters. There was not a day for seven years when we did not all see each other. There had been rain. The land was healthy." Her mouth worked from side to side, a pensive gesture, before she spoke again. This time each of her sentences came as individual eruptions. "We thought nothing bad could happen then. It was before the war."

The men were militia, she said. She never learned the name of the warlord they served.

"A man of many camels and many guns," Aisha said. "After they came, nothing was the same. We have no idea as we live our lives that tomorrow will be different."

She chewed one of the crackers, eating her way around the edges, sucking off the crystals of salt. "They tied us all down, in a circle. How you would tie livestock, or hobble camels. We tie a front to a back leg. Or goats at the neck. That was how they tied us, at the neck. They caught five of us when we were fetching firewood. Myself, Samira, Wanjiru, Leila and Iza."

Their names seemed to be a kind of incantation for her. Her eyes froze. She went into a kind of spell.

"Yes, they tied us down and raped us all together. One man for each of us, then they switched. They went from one to the other saying things like, this one's cunt is dry. This one's pussy smells."

Lenjoh hesitated. He was normally a swift interpreter. He cast her an embarrassed glance.

"We could hear our camels calling us," Aisha said. "It was night, then. I don't know how long it lasted. We never held hands or gave each other any looks of solidarity. I tried, but they all avoided my eyes. When I touched Wanjiru in the middle of it, she pulled her hand away like she had been scalded.

"About it, I was very clear. I thought: I can survive this. No matter what, I will survive. I felt very powerful. I can't describe it."

"Like it was happening to someone else?" she asked.

"No, it was happening. I had no doubt. I had no need to pull away, out of myself. The attack was terrible, but it is not the kind of thing that breaks my heart." She paused to eat some soup.

"But it destroyed us, as friends. That is what I didn't expect. We were never together again. Shame kept us apart."

"Did you try to — to reach out to them?"

"I reported it to the authorities, to the village elders. I went to each of my friends' mothers and told them how their daughter had fought to defend their honour. But my friends looked away when they saw me in the village, as if it had been me who attacked them."

"They knew you were different," she said.

"They said I was without honour, because I did not allow myself to be destroyed by it. They expected me to kill myself or die of shame. That was why I had to leave my village and look for a husband far away."

The militia, Aisha's men, came to visit her that night in her dreams. They never showed their faces. They had guns that were rusting at the edges; they didn't have enough oil to keep them in good condition. They rode up to her tent in a pickup truck and tried to get in. They were thin, weedy. She thought them incapable of doing much harm. In the dream she'd reached into a closet and found a weapon there. She had shouldered it and was ready to fire when she woke.

The email popped up in her inbox. *Doxycycline — new shipment.*

Her skin went cold — a strange sensation that would happen only twice in her life. On the inside she was burning, but her skin was frozen to the touch.

"Andy? Is anyone on the sat phone?"

"I don't think it's working."

She paced in her tent. Andy was outside, somewhere, fixing something.

She left, tearing the flap aside. She found him on his knees on the edge of their compound, wielding a wrench at the recalcitrant backup generator. "Are you the mechanic now?"

"Mark's on leave, didn't you know?"

"What, they leave us without a mechanic?"

"Just for a couple of days. He went to Nyala to get spare parts."

"Well, it's an emergency."

Andy got to his knees and dusted them off, a pointless gesture they all persisted in. "I'll see what I can do."

Half an hour later he had coaxed the phone to life. She dialed the number. She clamped her fingers around the sat phone's dense wedge.

A crisp female voice answered.

"I need to speak to Dr. Gregory."

A brief pause, then Anthony came on the line. "Your application was approved," he said. "You've been selected for the specialist training. I need you to attend a conference on early vaccination. We'll cover your travel."

"When?"

"We'll let you know."

She nearly said, *How?* But he'd hung up.

She calmed herself, or tried to. She left the air-conditioned chamber where the satellite and computer server were stored. She tried to stall the trembling before she handed the phone back to Andy. Outside she met the heat — not a wall but a compression chamber, pressing on her from behind, above. It was everywhere.

Something had happened. There could be no other explanation.

She stared into the horizon. It was well known to her now, the flattened parabola where the sun emerged each day with its burning censor eye. If there were an enemy — if Ali, or people who knew him, people who survived the attack on the town from where he and his men operated, a town now with a swathe ripped through it by a drone aircraft, came — they would emerge from that horizon, the sun watching over them.

But was there an enemy, really? She didn't quite see it that way.

She had been asked to provide information; she was a small piece in the puzzle, so small she might not exist. If she were not in her job it would have fallen to someone else. The morality of what she did could be worked out by others, by Anthony and his kind. They had been trained to do this and she was just a doctor.

She was just a doctor and she was not strong enough for the world. She wanted life to be beautiful, not the bitter shadows the thorn trees of Gariseb threw, not the unspent cartridges shoved down the throats of prisoners of war, so that they died choking on the dank taste of copper. Not the dead, bloated corpses of children, inflated like out-size watermelons that littered the desert only fifty kilometres from her cot bed.

She had tried to satisfy her hunger for beauty by going to the theatre, to art galleries, when everyone else's life had become consumed by mock exams and job applications. But her yearning was a glutton; it thrived on lacks. It would go on and on. A kind of internal savagery took hold of her then, born perhaps of self-preservation. She banished herself from any more visits to the Bush, the Finborough, the Globe theatres, the Tate Modern and the British Museum, the readings to hear pale, serious authors talk about the future and the past. She throttled her inconvenient desire until it too was a corpse scattered among the already occupied fields of the dead.

If she tried to bring her mind back to those dates on the calendar, the strangely foreign sounding name of the month — June; what was its origin again? *Juniper, Juno, Jupiter* — her mind slunk away from the word.

She knew that a certain amount of time had passed since her conversation with Aisha, since the message from Anthony, perhaps three or four days. There was no further news of the departure Anthony's message had referred to. Across the border it was quiet. No wounded fighters appeared. In fact the hospital was strangely empty; there were not even any IED injuries or wounds from cattle rustling skirmishes.

They might have changed their minds. They might have decided she was safe. She tried to find out. She rang the secure line only to be told he was not available. She realized he was probably on a plane from London at that very moment. She spoke to a woman she had never spoken to before and who would not give her name. "Sit tight," the woman said, "and don't call this number again."

She encountered Andy smoking pensively on the outskirts of camp one of those evenings. Beyond the perimeter of light thrown by the floodlights came the tinkering of goats' bells, a sound that was sibilant during the heat of day but became tinny as night approached.

"I wonder what's going on," Andy said.

"What do you mean?"

The evening was silent. They could hear only the wind.

Andy narrowed his eyes. "In Helmand I always used to distrust these lulls. I'd sleep extra light if I were you."

"I may not sleep at all."

He finished his cigarette, pummelled it under his heel. "Mark my words," he said. "Something's about to happen."

VI

AUGUR
BUZZARD

"She's crazy to come at a time like this."

"Who?"

"Delphine." Julia gave her an uncomprehending look, as if the bearer of the name were so famous it was a scandal she did not lurch at its sound. "Bill's sister," Julia elaborated. "She lives in Mozambique."

They were seated for breakfast. It was only eight o'clock, yet the morning heat gathered around them. She wanted to rip it apart, like drawing an invisible curtain, to get somewhere beyond it where she could think straight again.

"Why does she want to come now?" Storm said. "She'll have to bribe her way through twenty roadblocks. That's if they let her cross the border."

"It's your father's sixty-fifth. Anyway she's a writer. They always go where the action is, don't they?" Julia asked, to no one in particular. "When I worked with those guys" — she assumed Julia meant journalists — "I'd drive them to the airport. They'd be on their way to cover the latest atrocity. There would never be space on the plane — the army, the spies, the UN would have booked it out. You had to hand it to them, they always got a seat. Delphine's like that," Julia said. "You can depend on her to always get a seat on the plane."

"What does she write?" she asked.

"*Plains of the Serengeti*, you must have heard of it. *Lost Land of the Boroi*. Big books with lots of photographs."

"I don't read coffee table books."

"Well, nobody *reads* them, obviously." Julia scraped her chair out and rose from the table. "We don't see much of Delphine. She finds

172

it boring here. We're not ambitious enough for her."

She went to fetch one of Delphine's books from the shelf. She pulled out the one with the thickest spine. The cover shot was of a vast agglomeration of wildebeest from above — a helicopter shot no doubt. It showed a knot of burly beasts, their distribution almost geometric. Around them were tawny clumps of stone. She peered closer to see the giant shoulder muscles of the cats, perfect and rounded as loaves of bread. The knot of wildebeest was surrounded not by stones but by lions.

She turned over the book. Delphine appeared, holding a spear with a spade-shaped tip. She was tall and thin and wore her grey hair in a loose braid over her shoulder. An outline of red lipstick was her only concession to makeup. She was dressed in a battered pair of brown trousers that had perhaps once been suede. She recognized her uncle's startling blue eyes. They stared forthrightly, almost defiantly, at the camera.

"She's very beautiful," she offered.

"She is." Julia's voice was grim. She turned to Storm. "What are you doing tonight?"

"I thought Rebecca and I might do something."

She shot him a look, which he deflected.

"That's lovely, darling."

She watched him cross the living room. His muscles seemed to have their own individual life. He had the rangy architecture of a creature that spent most of its life in anaerobic blasts of effort: cheetah or impala.

They'd had a straggly herd of impala around camp in Gariseb. Once she had seen a cheetah give chase. The impala had a thin black chevron stripe down the side of its body. It leapt from side to side, bounding two metres at a time, in an attempt to shake off the cheetah, which ran so low to the ground it looked as if it were in collusion with it. Finally the cheetah dropped back. The gazelle kept going, a black blare of panic in its eye. She watched the cheetah, its flanks heaving, through her binoculars. It lay down on the ground and panted.

She felt faint; if she hadn't been sitting down already, she would have fallen to the floor.

"Rebecca, are you alright?"

She swivelled toward Julia, who regarded her with that alert yet uncomprehending gaze of hers.

"Yes, fine."

"It's just you look changed, somehow. Have you finally put on weight?"

Her eye searched for him, but he had gone. None of Storm's mystery had diminished, although a familiarity was taking root. The change in her state, renewed purpose, with the special density of intimacy, seemed to have transferred itself to Julia. Julia felt her change, was animated yet confused by it, as if she had been granted a second life, but as someone else.

At the kiosks outside the small supermarket at Kilindoni were racks of newspapers splattered with red headlines, red shirts, blood, gashed faces. In the background were faces shining in pain and fear. Red was the colour of TANU, the ruling party, which was fighting to remain in office in the upcoming elections, and it cast its shadow over the news.

The elections felt like an approaching storm. The air had the electrified, unhappy smell of a turbulence both feared and desired. *Al-Nur attack Puku*. The story asserted that the city near the border, once beloved by tourists, a mini-Zanzibar, everyone said, where Christian and Arab culture had coexisted happily for over a millennium, had been hit the previous day. The insurgents had been hoping to kill tourists but they had long fled, so they had to content themselves with killing local Christians.

174

She scanned the article while walking across the bridge that spanned the entrance to Kilindoni harbour. Five political parties dominated the landscape, the article told her. Here, in the east, the Tswalu ethnic group prevailed; they had formed an alliance with the centrist Kandinka group to form TANU, the powerful political alliance that included the most dominant ethnic group in the country, the Milau.

This was as far as she got. Without the military strategists and political analysts that her training provided, she was lost. She did not understand the blood feud intricacies of politics, whether in the UK or the countries where she deployed herself. She saw politicians as alchemists, mixing potions of power and fear. Politics was responsible for the wounds her hands prowled and sutured as much as any gun.

Her uncle, on the other hand, was a political man. He would not have arrived at his position without making strategic alliances. Now that the elections were approaching her uncle took more and more calls on his mobile phone, laying it down on the table at mealtimes where it vibrated, crawling across the table.

There is no place for the white man in the politics of this country, she heard him say at one of Julia's dinners. *You have to become black. For political purposes, I am a black man.*

She'd looked at him then, expecting to see a different skin. *You're a black man in every way, Bill*, one of his associates replied. *I think you'll even be president one day.*

She arrived back at the house and perceived her aunt's absence instantly. Without Julia the house was rudderless.

She saw a figure in the living room. As with Storm, names sounded wrong with her uncle. She didn't know what to call him.

She took her place in one of the rattan chairs opposite him.

"Am I disturbing you?"

"Rebecca, you are family. It's not possible to be disturbed by you."

"I bought the newspaper. It doesn't look good, the elections."

"Elections in this country never look good."

"Who do you think will win?"

"Rudai, of course." He named the oldest political dynasty in the country. "They are very powerful."

He stared at her, an identical note to the one she saw behind the bullish wall of Storm's eyes. It could be distrust, or tolerance. In his eyes they looked the same. She realized she had no idea how to appeal to these people's confidence, or what would trigger it. She nearly said, *I'm a doctor. I have three university degrees.*

But that doesn't matter here, her uncle would say.

"Julia told me," she ventured, "about the bank."

"Oh." Grey circles had accumulated under his eyes, smudges of ash.

"She said there's a lot of money at stake."

"Yes, fourteen million depositors in total. All of them locked out of their accounts."

"What do you think of the investigation?"

"It's equivalent of a land grab. It's the first time it's happened here, with the banking system. Our backers are in Dubai and India, where such things don't happen. Suffice to say they're not impressed."

"That's Africa, as they say," she offered.

"Who says that?" His face had a rigid cast. "The banks in the UK were bailed out by the UK taxpayer to the tune of several billion. Do you think you and your fellow taxpayers will ever see a penny of your money back? What happened to the hedge fund managers and the futures traders and the sub-prime merchants who generated that crisis? Are they behind bars? The UK is Africa."

"I think you need to rest. You look tired."

"Yes, Rebecca, thank you, I realize that."

His attention drifted away. He stared out into the garden. From the distance came the crash of the sea.

When he had turned back his face had softened. "Your mother

thought I was a crook. A man fed on colonial fat." He gave her a thin smile. "Like her, you're pointing the finger in the wrong direction. Africa is no more corrupt than Europe; there are just fewer ways to hide it, here."

She sat in silence, shocked that he had mentioned her mother. He had never referred to her before. Had they ever even met?

"*Why don't you just go back?* the Africans say to us," he went on. "But there is no *back*." The word clanged in his mouth. "There is no Europe. England is a foreign country to me. I am an African. A white black man." He pinched his forearm, puckering the skin.

"Black men are generally much poorer than you are."

His reply was quick. "Do you mean you have to be poor in order to qualify as authentically black?"

She understood her error. Her uncle had an advantage, she reminded herself. He was on home ground.

"There hasn't been a white man of significant wealth or political influence in this country for thirty years at least," her uncle said. "In case you think I'm abusing some sort of privilege. The colour of your skin has been trumped by money. That's what race and class is here, now: money. In fact you could say our white skin is a disadvantage. They see us coming and they think, we will make you pay."

She didn't ask him who the *they*, the *we*, were. She supposed it ought to be obvious, but she had noticed that her uncle rarely talked in terms of us and them, as other whites she had overheard — guests at Julia's constant soirées, people at neighbouring tables at Reef Encounters — did. She might make many judgments about him, but her uncle was not *racial* — the softened term locals used, rather than *racist*.

"Yes, we are just minor players here, now." He exhaled, a gesture that might have been a quiet sigh, or fatigue. He looked tired, she thought. He was sixty-five, he would soon begin to feel the dictates of the body, he would no longer be able to drive the seven hours to the capital without tiring or play golf for four hours in the equatorial sun. What was the advantage of arguing with this man? He had already bested her, in so many ways. When had they become rivals? Perhaps they were this from the beginning, and Bill understood this, much more clearly than she did. Any antagonism they felt was not personal, in a strange way, rather it was about the situation that engineered their meeting, his position in life — his values, choices, right back to the flash of entrepreneurial zeal that had led his ancestors to this country in the first place — versus her far less expeditionary and ruthless origins.

"You say Britain is a foreign country, yet you're happy to carry its passport and bank in its offshore islands."

"Yes, yes," he said, amenably. "That's the sum of it. I make use of my connections." His back straightened. "But I'm an African. That's all I will ever be, no matter how many times they rob my bank account, or my property is confiscated for the state, or radical Islam try to bomb us back to Europe, as they see it." He leaned toward her, his long body easily bridging the space between his sofa and her baraza, eating the distance. His eyes flared with a strange fire. She breathed in, searching for signs of alcohol, but his breath smelled vaguely of lemons.

"There is no *Europe*." He stared at her. "It's all a pretty fiction."

"But there was," she said.

"Oh, undoubtedly. But now the Chinese own Europe, and in thirty years twenty percent of the population will be Muslim. You think Al-Nur here is a problem. Just wait."

"You seem to look forward to that."

"Oh, not really. I'll be long gone by then."

She looked out to the edge of the house, where the living room dissolved into the dark garden. She would never stop expecting to see a wall there. She had been raised inside, in houses with walls and cold rooms, and this would stick.

William MacMaster had been born in Benghazi on the Libyan coast. His father, a settler farmer, was also a Royal Engineer. He had qualified before the war and spent most of it in Burma, in charge of 150 Ghurkha fighters who had bestowed upon him the ultimate honour — he had become their brother. He'd worn a turban and carried a ceremonial scabbard gifted to him by his troops.

Bill had never known this incarnation of his father. He'd grown up a prosperous farmer's son in a rambling farmhouse joined to three rondavels by cool corridors, half-open to the elements, lined with hedges of hibiscus, china sets and cutlery and gin and tonics at sundown, and a semi-insane African grey parrot for a pet who uttered "Swine" at intervals, and who otherwise spoke only in profanities. All this had imprinted itself on his consciousness: the stone farmhouse, rondavels orbiting it like satellites, thrilling grey mountains puncturing the sky and beyond these, a sere plain stretching all the way to Ethiopia.

Then, his years in the capital. There, his life is a circuit of receptions and cocktail parties. He is both in a position to choose and yet must be chosen. He raises capital, he founds an airline, then buys houses: one, two, three. He goes into business in the clothing market, making sweatshirts and jeans. Still his father's farm thrums out pyrethrum and alfalfa, managed by a foreman. His unrustled cattle grow fat on the teeth of his security operation — men are shot so that his cattle can be slaughtered. He plants experimental crops and is the first man in the country to pasteurize milk.

He is garrulous, a talker. He travels often for business. There, in Brazzaville, he meets Julia. He is ten years older than her. The puzzle of his life is complete.

Between these signposts are numberless days when little happens, when failure laps at their shores. Mitsubishi dealerships; his business importing cut-price antibiotics from France only to be overtaken by generic pharmaceuticals from India, which flood the market in the 1980s; the vitamin supplements from South Africa instantly outmoded by steroids. He makes business trips to Dubai and Johannesburg to procure machinery at a third of the import price; he pays Somali truckers to cross the border with goods undeclared. He knows every twist and turn of this country. *I know how to make things work here*, he says frequently to his family, his visitors. He does business in Saudi Arabia and in Mugabe's Zimbabwe. He looks the other way as competitors are hassled, or squashed. He imports Danish yogurt and makes a killing.

Could Storm and Lucy really have emanated from this man? Lucy, with her cool intelligence. Storm, with his austere self-containment. The truth was, Bill had nothing to do with his children. He was their father, almost certainly, he had given them his genes. They carried the outlines of his face. They might even have his ruthlessness, his restless ingenuity, his cat-like ability to get up after being knocked down. But apart from that, no trace of his character could be found in his children.

"Rebecca. I think I lost you there."

The file that was the source of this information, which she had read on Anthony's laptop in the capital only days before coming to the coast, closed itself in her mind.

She allowed her gaze to return to the living room, lit with Julia's gin bottle lanterns and filled with the small scratching sounds of the tropical night.

"You're a thinker, aren't you?"

"You say that as if it's something unsavoury."

He shrugged. "It depends on what you think. On whose behalf you are thinking."

She was too exhausted to be alarmed at this drift in the conversation, what it might mean. She was so tired, from the weight of the knowledge she had procured about her uncle, and by association about all of them. Knowledge should be empowering. But it ended crushing you. Once known, knowledge could not be unravelled, stuffed back into a box labelled oblivion. Only now, at thirty-seven, was she coming to understand the true nature of its burden.

"I think I'd better turn in," she said.

Bill's eyes, darkened with the night to the green-grey of heavy woolen blankets, were lidded, furtive.

"You're friendlier than she was. You're not as conflicted, as jealous. I'm sorry. I'm so sorry for all of this. I wish we had known her. I wish we knew you."

"We can. I'm here now," she said, but sensed her error. She was distracted by his use of the past tense. Something was over, for him. The knowing, the regret. He already inhabited the future.

"You're still here."

Margaux was waiting on the terrace of Reef Encounters. The ocean rolled ashore behind her in batter-thick breakers.

"Did you expect me to have left?"

"I just had this feeling that I'd try to call you one of these days and find you gone. Everyone else has skedaddled."

"Well, I'm not going anywhere." She adjusted her sunglasses to the noon-day glare. The beach was empty. That the tourists were leaving, or no longer coming, was an open secret. It was evident in the dark, silent bars and restaurants of Fitzgerald's and Reef Encounters.

"Have you seen the new Foreign Office directives?"

She had, she said. There was little talk of anything else. Three days before the Foreign and Commonwealth Office had changed its travel advice for the coastal zone, citing intelligence that an Al-Nur attack was imminent.

"It's amazingly effective, isn't it?" Margaux said. "Issue a random threat, Thomsons or First Choice cancel the charter flights, invalidated travel insurance et cetera, watch the tourists disappear to Thailand. Although the Italians seem more adventurous. At least they keep coming."

"Everyone seems so shocked that it's happened. You'd think they'd understand the risk of being a resort next to the biggest terrorist threat since Al-Qaeda. Anyway, I'm not in a rush to get back. I worked four months straight without two days in a row off before I came here."

Margaux flinched slightly. Perhaps she had caught her impatient tone. She was used to inhabiting zones of danger and had little interest in discussing whether or not a grenade would be thrown across Reef Encounters' deck any time soon.

"I don't know if I'd cope with people dying around me all the time," Margaux said.

"But you dig up the dead."

"That's the point. They're already dead. I've never seen anyone die. Have you ever been to talk to someone?"

"You mean a psychiatrist? When we go back to the UK we are debriefed. There's plenty of counselling."

"But it doesn't help?"

"To be honest I can diagnose myself. I've had post-traumatic stress disorder. Anxiety disorder, panic attacks, you name it."

"You must have been afraid."

She tried to keep her voice light, glancing. "Mostly when under attack from the air. That's my least favourite mode of attack. It's too sitting duck." As she said this she saw the roof above their heads at Reef Encounters shattering, splinters raining down, the raw exposure, subjected to the scattershot will of an angry air-god. "Once, the operating theatre wasn't hit but outlying buildings were. Two of our support staff and fifteen goats were blown to bits. Some of the patients started grabbing the hunks of goat flesh and stuffing them in their bags to hoard. But it wasn't all goat. They still had the skin on them and we'd taken away all their knives, so they were upset."

Margaux grimaced.

"One time we were running through a wheat field; the wheat had just been cut and it was sharp," she said. "I had paper cuts all over my hands and wrists from it. I couldn't avoid the cut stalks because we were carrying a stretcher. I was holding an IV bag with my other hand. It was strange because I knew that day would be different. The sky was yellow and the wheat was blue. *Do you see that?* I wanted to ask someone — anyone, Roddy who was with me, or Mike, my senior. *The sky is yellow and the wheat is blue.* That day everything felt etched. The way the wheat looked against the sky, it was as if they had just been drawn or sketched that morning. The gleam on their edges was fresh."

"What did you think that meant?"

"It was a sign."

"From what? From who?"

She drew a breath. She hadn't intended to go down this road at all with Margaux. She was wary of confiding in her, but her very reluctance prodded her to carry on.

"I have a theory. We all exist in a reality that is actually a vast simulation, but it's moving and changing all the time. It's a plasmic realm. As humans we see only a very narrow sector of it, as if we are in a tunnel. We just haven't got the capacity to see the entire dimension. But sometimes, in heightened situations, it's possible to leave the tunnel and be in contact with this invisible realm. If it suits it, it will communicate to us. The etched quality of everything that day was an example of it trying to communicate. It was telling us, *get out of there*."

Margaux had turned to look at the sea. Her brow had furrowed. She had never shared her theory with anyone. She knew how it sounded. She also knew she was not a good storyteller — she never started at A, then proceeded to B. There were few beginnings, middles and ends, in her experience, for all her medical understanding of cause and effect. Things that happened to her presented themselves as a pane of ready-shattered glass.

"Why were you out there in the first place?"

"We were transporting a guy out, just in front of the line. We didn't do that often, not on foot anyway. But that day there were sandstorms and there was no vis for the pilots. So they put us in by truck and we had to reach him on foot. Snipers. We knew they were there but we thought they didn't have the range. They must have had a new shipment of scopes. Likely bought from a British company in Saudi Arabia. We would have been killed by our own hardware, probably."

Behind Margaux's shoulder three kitesurfers curled into the air. Their kites billowed, levering them above the ocean. They hung there, suspended on the wind, before slapping back onto the sea.

"It can be healing, this place," Margaux said. "The nature, the swimming. You need that."

"You're saying I'm damaged."

"Life is damaging enough without putting yourself in the line of fire."

She thought this was melodramatic but did not say so. She found herself looking down at her hands, then. She saw very small brown spots littering the area just above her wrist. They were new. This had been happening lately — small changes in the depth of the lines around her eyes, a stray grey hair. These signs of ageing weren't happening gradually. One day they weren't there and the next they were.

Margaux's gaze drifted behind her shoulder. "Don't look now but we've got company."

She looked up and found the man who had sat near their table on their last visit. The sun was swallowed by his shoulders.

"Hello, ladies."

"Hi there," Margaux said amiably. "How's it going?"

"I'd like to have a word." With the subtlest of inclinations of his head, he indicated her.

"What is this about?"

"It won't take a moment."

"Unless you tell me what this is about in the presence of my friend, we're not going to talk."

Margaux darted her a surprised look. She was amazed at how her voice had changed, become upright and commanding. Even her accent had stiffened. How quickly she'd become the version of herself she had left behind in Gariseb on the weed-eaten airstrip. An instant regression.

The man put his hands on the table, his fingers forming two tents, his palms not touching its surface. She found her gaze arrested on this detail; she had seen it before. It was the way men who might take flight at any moment touched surfaces.

Margaux rose. "I'll leave you to it then." It was such an English phrasing. She looked sharply into Margaux's eyes.

To the man she deployed her clinician's voice. "Sit down."

He lowered his frame into the chair. He looked over his shoulder, then back. He wore a blue T-shirt. Across it a marlin leapt from a wave in white relief. Underneath she read, *Quepos, Costa Rica, 2005.*

"You're going to get a message from someone. Someone you knew, but not from him directly, through an intermediary. We don't know his name. They'll want you to meet up."

"Where will they want me to meet him?"

"Here," he paused. "On the coast." He moved his head. His hair shifted strangely — was he wearing a wig?

The thought blared through her: it's him. How can it be him?

"How do they know I'm here?"

"When he gets in touch, you call me." He handed her a blank card with a phone number written on it in blue ink.

She watched him go. He walked slowly, but not with that falsely lackadaisical step she'd observed in other intelligence agents who were trying hard to be nonchalant in public places. She watched him pass into the dark entrance stairs, then emerge outside, where he was immediately consumed in a blare of white sun.

She sat for a while afterwards, trying to read her reaction. It was familiar, even reassuring — that feeling of the very air drawing itself close around her.

Lucy greeted her at the door. "So what have you been up to, Rebecca?"

"Reading, running. I've been going to the ruins."

"The ruins? I haven't been there since I was a kid. That's what happens, isn't it; you start to take your surroundings for granted. Even in London."

"I've been to a couple of parties with Storm," she offered.

Lucy raised an eyebrow. "You're lucky. He never takes me anywhere. It's a miracle I ever met Evan at all."

Lucy walked into the living room. Lucy had her mother's airy voice but there was a careful, formal quality to its friendliness. Her sugary English complexion had darkened. Two inches of bracelets were now lined up on her wrist. Her nails were painted different colours; pastel green for the index and fifth fingers, purple and pink for the ones in between. She wore a new bikini every day, she had noticed, paired with a different kikhoi. She padded barefoot through the house, slightly pigeon-toed and yawning, her eyeliner smudged, like a recently deposed Cleopatra.

The friendship she had hoped for had not materialized. Lucy had so many friends on the coast. She had gone to nursery school in Moholo, had done her GCSEs in an international school in a suburb of Bahari ya Manda before being sent to England for A-levels. All this she had gleaned from Julia. "Lucy was too smart for the schools here," Julia had said. "We realized we were doing her a disservice by trying to keep her close." She was sent to a bohemian boarding school in Wiltshire that had its own indoor swimming pool.

"I was hoping you could help us out with Dad's party," Lucy said. "There are a few catering things Mum and I usually take care of."

"How many people will come?"

"About thirty. Only family and close friends."

"Your father has a lot of friends."

Lucy shrugged. "He has a lot of people he needs to keep impressed."

She watched Lucy climb the stairs now, the arches of her feet curling above steps, walking as if she was not required to touch the ground.

"Just let me know what you need me to do," she said.

"Thanks, Rebecca." Halfway up the spiral staircase Lucy turned and gave her a guileless smile. "It's so good to have you around. I wish you'd been here, with us, all these years."

She was amazed to find tears in her eyes. She didn't want Lucy to see. She turned away, just in time.

That night she and Julia were alone in the house. The wind had come up. She watched her aunt move around the living room, closing the louvers, drawing blinds and shutting doors.

When she finished, Julia came to sit next to her on the baraza. She had never been so physically close to her aunt, apart from the quick, efficient hugs Julia dispensed, or when they breezed past each other in the kitchen. Julia emitted a more muted version of the firecracker energy that surrounded Storm.

"I've broken into the wine cellar." Julia held up a bottle of Paarl sauvignon blanc she had imported from South Africa. "It seems we're on our own tonight. Storm and Lucy have so many friends."

"They seem very rooted here," she agreed.

"Yes, but they'll live their lives elsewhere, an eight-hour flight away. I'm always thinking about that, as soon as I meet them at the airport. *How long have I got?*"

"But Storm doesn't want to go."

"He'll see sense, this time." Julia paused. "I have to let go." The wine seemed to have affected her mood instantly. Something had condensed inside her.

"It's different with the first-born. I was told it would be, but I never believed it. From the beginning I felt that he wasn't just my child, my son, but also my companion. As soon as I saw him I thought, yes, I am responsible for your life. But you are also responsible for mine. We will help each other. I didn't feel burdened."

"You treat Storm as if he's the one in charge," she said. "As if you're only waiting to hand over to him."

Julia looked at her. "You sound like your mother."

"In what way?"

"I don't know. It's the way you put things. Although you're more intellectual. Or maybe more analytical. Your mother was very intelligent. She just didn't have a chance to develop herself."

She heard the heft of judgment or, worse, pity in Julia's voice. But also an implication, as if she might be responsible for her mother's arrested development.

The sea sighed against the low cliff. Julia put down her drink. "Why didn't it work?"

"What?"

"Your mother. You. You never seemed close. She was surprised by you. She wasn't ready to have a child. Not that I know much about it. She didn't confide in me."

Desperation flooded her. "It must happen sometimes, between mothers and daughters."

Julia nodded, her mouth set. "I'm glad I don't have to face that, with Lucy." She brought her gaze back and met her eyes. Her eyes had the same swooping trajectory as Storm's. They arrived on a side current, from a long way away. "You know, I had a very narrow escape. Your grandfather — " she gave a sharp shake of her head "he ruined everything."

She knew the story, at least in outline. She had known her grandparents only as separate entities. They had split up long before she was born. Her grandmother lived in a flat in Kentish Town. Her grandfather lived with his second wife in a village in Sussex topped by a brown box of a church. When Julia and her mother were teenagers he left her grandmother for another woman. Her grandmother, who had never worked, was given a paltry settlement. They had been brought up only millimetres from the poverty line.

"I don't know, Julia. It's complicated."

"It's not." Julia's eyes were indifferent. "Everyone says that, but it's really quite simple. You hold a marriage and a family together."

"No matter what?"

"Look what happened to your mother and I."

She realized she had never made the connection between her grandfather's abandonment of the family and Julia's dread of poverty, although of a genteel kind, in their case. She had missed a diagnosis.

"Your mother said, why marry into money, Julia, and be kept like a pet cheetah when women have fought for rights and independence. Why live like it's the 1950s?"

"But she was right, don't you think?"

Her aunt gave her a long, regal stare. "I don't know if you'll ever have children."

She shrank back into the sofa. "How can you say that?"

Julia lowered her gaze, in a kind of shame, perhaps. "I'm sorry. I'm very intuitive. It's just a feeling I have."

She woke the next morning with a feeling of malaise, a sensation that increased with each hour. She went for a walk on the beach to try to shake it off but managed only ten minutes before she had to lay down on the sand; her head tilted to one side in an effort to dispel a sudden light-headedness.

Ghost crabs scattered horizontally in her path, the patterns of their tracks like stitching on the sand. In the distance were two knots of children, one black, one white. At the tip of the beach, kitesurfers twirled in the air like giant water birds. Clouds advanced from the southeast in two chevrons over the wedge of Tern Island. Beyond it was a gauzy morning moon.

She put her hand to her forehead. Her temperature had shot up four or five degrees in the last half hour. She didn't know if she had the strength to walk back to the house.

"What are you doing here? I've been looking for you."

She blinked into the sky. Storm was peering at her. "I'm not feeling well."

His approach blotted out the moon's muslin. He sat down beside her, collapsing his long limbs.

"I don't want to give you this, whatever it is."

She felt a hand on her face and realized it was his. "I don't want you to be ill." His voice was hoarse with an emotion she could not read.

She felt her hand make its way to his. She gripped his fingers, held them beside her jawbone.

The screech of a child and a squawk from a roseate tern on a fly-by came to them in the same moment. They looked in the direction of the child; their hands fell away from her face. The imprint of his hand remained on her fingers.

Tears, strangely cool, drew rivulets down her hot face. "I'm sorry," she said.

"For what?"

"I . . ." There was a knot of darkness inside her. "We shouldn't . . ." She stalled.

"Let's get you back to the house." He put his hand on her elbow and gently lifted her off the beach. She resisted for a moment.

"What's the matter?"

"I have this feeling that we're being watched."

He looked toward the house. "I don't think so."

The tide tossed clumps of greasy seaweed ashore. He wrapped a kikhoi around her shoulders. They walked against the advancing tide and the wedge of steel cloud in the sky.

The world was drawing itself in electric outline. She knew what this meant: it was gathering its perimeters, taking on the etched quality that her senior Mike had taught her to be suspicious of nearly ten years ago now. It meant the future was decided. It was speaking to her from a dimension over the horizon of time.

He walked beside her, scowling into the sky. Her lungs were made of lead. She couldn't speak, or breathe, or think. She was so afraid. Was it possible to lust for something, or someone, when you possessed them? She could not withstand much passion or lust; they had the dank ring of things that could be solved only in death.

She shivered. Julia's voice rang in her head, suddenly. It sounded so like her mother's, but soldered with rage. *We gave you sanctuary. We are your family. And this is what you do to us.*

D elphine appeared in the late afternoon. She descended the spiral staircase, wearing a pair of khaki bush shorts paired with a blouse that must have been Indian, with its riot of greens and pinks. She was the embodiment of her author photograph, a willowy lean woman of indeterminate age.

"Rebecca," Delphine's voice was brisk. "Where do you come from then?"

"London."

"Well, then, let's have a drink."

Delphine had Storm's eyes, or he hers. She kept staring into them, one and then the other, looking for clues to more familiar resemblances. She had his airy indifference, too. There was a theatrical quality to both of them, which was only partially explained by their physical beauty, by the fact that faces would have been rotating toward them all their lives, as sunflowers turn to face the sun.

Delphine's eyes were on her. Her gaze was level, the sort of flensing, evaluative look she had met in military analysts. "So, what do you do?"

"She's a doctor."

Storm had appeared soundlessly, as usual. He wore a pair of sand-coloured shorts and a necklace made of bone. He came to stand beside her. Delphine's eye shuttled between them.

"Hello, Storm. Or have you outgrown your name by now?"

"I guess not." He did not move to kiss his aunt hello. "How is business?"

Delphine sipped from her drink. "Not bad. I had the King and

193

Queen of Belgium on safari last week. Although that's confidential. I had to sign an agreement not to discuss them in public. But family isn't public, is it?" Delphine pointed the question in her direction.

"Is that common, that you have to sign confidentiality agreements?"

"Only with movie stars and royalty."

"What are these people like on safari?"

Delphine crossed a pair of lean legs. "Like anyone else. Except they want cold Tattinger at four in the afternoon when you're six hundred kilometres from the nearest electricity transformer."

She didn't know what to ask next. In her professional life at least, she was used to the company of people who conversed in a series of facts and statements, who, as she suspected with Delphine, had no use for ambiguity or interpretation. But now the task exhausted her.

She caught Storm's eye. He raised his eyebrows. "Come on, I'll show you something."

They left Delphine and Julia at the kitchen table and went to stand beside the pool. The afternoon was golden. Black starlings bubbled in the trees.

"Why don't you like your aunt?"

"Let's get away from the house," he put a finger, very lightly, on her elbow. She walked with him to the cliff edge. The fruit harvest in the Estate was in progress. The rubbery smell of burned vegetation hung in the air. Its narrow roads were clogged with lorries carrying towering loads of papaya and pineapple.

A brown shape moved in a tree on the edge of the gardens. "Look," she pointed.

Storm reached for the binoculars Julia had scattered around the property; a pair was always within arm's length. They were all Swarovski, bought in England. He looked through them, then handed them to her. "He's a long way from home."

The bird came into focus. It was tawny, with white tips on its wings. Between its claws was a small creature. Purple blood spilled from ripped fur. She recognized it from Gariseb. "Augur buzzard."

She watched it pick at the torn creature trapped in its talons. It had yellow eyes and a sharp hooked beak; its neck twitched back and forth. It ate as if it was being watched, lancing the air with its eyes left and right.

The red flash of their tail was the clue to their name. They were easily spotted in the sky, long before they arrived. That was why they were called the augur buzzard — they came announced, like the future.

We are tempting fate, all of us, simply by being alive. Ali's voice said. *Life does not want us here. Few people know how much conviction you must have to remain alive.* In her mind his voice was ghostly — a dead man come back to life. But he was not dead.

"What are you thinking about?"

"A man I treated. An insurgent. He told me the reason why the augur buzzard has his name. He nearly killed me."

In his eyes she saw suspicion — or distaste. "What do you mean?"

"I'll tell you another time."

"I don't think I can compete with your secrets."

"I'm not asking you to."

"You're not here; you're somewhere else. I can't go there."

She had never seen his anguish before. She wondered if it were even within his capacity. A primitive self sensed an advantage. If she did reveal herself to Storm, he might close her as neatly as he would shut a book, leave her the way he walked away from all objects — mobile phones, rigging ropes, cars — with an impatience that was almost audible, as if these objects had dealt him a grave disappointment.

Delphine's voice reached them on the wind. It was deep, unusually so, for a woman. She had a lanky, hoarse laugh that was attractive but also harboured a threat. Storm cast a wary glance toward the house.

"She reminds me of a lioness," she said.

"Well, she could kill all of us if she chose."

"Why do you say that?"

"She was a professional hunter. She was famous all over Africa — or white Africa. The only woman who did it."

"Why did she give it up?" She imagined that Delphine might have lost the stomach for killing, after a while.

"The money's in conservation now. People want to look at animals, not kill them." Storm frowned. His face was distorted by uncertainty. "I wish she wasn't here. It's all wrong."

"What do you mean?"

"Dad's party. What's happening in the country. Everything. It feels like it could all go wrong. For the first time in my life, I think it might not be possible for us to stay here."

"Let's go out," she said.

"Where?"

"Anywhere. Some roadside bar. A place locals go. Let's get away from here."

They did not make excuses to Julia and Delphine. They got in the car and drove to Moholo. By the time they arrived the sun was setting. Storm turned off the tarmac road just before the village and took them on a gravel road she had never been on before. It headed north, hugging the coastline. The tide was out, exposing coral and mudflats. Greenshanks and herons skipped across them. The breakers had drawn back, beyond the reef. She smelled jasmine.

He turned down another road, toward the sea. This road was lined with shacks and unfinished cinder block constructions. Inside them, where living rooms or bedrooms might one day exist, goats picked at brown grass.

"Where are we?"

"Coral Bay. It's part of Moholo, but the only tourists here are Italians from the all-inclusive resorts up the road."

They drove past a row of tiny *dukas* papered with paintings that showed spindly figures in red robes poised against amber skies. She counted four shacks in a row, all selling identical paintings, interspersed with shops with tomatoes and eggs piled up outside, covered in signs for mobile phone credit.

They passed a restaurant named Les Blancs and an Italian ice cream parlour where families sat outside, the men smoking and drinking espresso as their wives and children ate ice cream. Next door the women who minded the identical souvenir painting stalls sat on plastic chairs, their legs flung out straight in front of them, gesticulating and laughing. A motorcycle with three women wedged together riding pillion streamed by her window. In the distance she could see the sparse electric lights of Kilindoni and Moholo stutter on.

They pulled up in front of a sturdy structure. A yellow and green sign hung above the entrance. *Mysteries*.

He got out of the car. She followed him through the lip of the entrance, past two burly men in black shirts and white ties who nodded to Storm, the barest of gestures.

"Storm."

"Lucio."

A tall thin man with a gold earring in his left earlobe had wrapped his arms around Storm and was beaming at her. "This is your sister! Your sister! Finally."

"No, this is my cousin."

She found herself embraced in the same frantic hug.

"Business is quiet, sorry." Lucio's mouth sank into a cartoon frown. "All the *wageni* have left."

They seated themselves at an oval bar. The waitresses wore a uniform, bosoms held tight in white shirts and micro-shorts that showed off their hamstrings. Around the bar were four or five shaven-headed men with tattoos on their forearms. Next to them young women nursed a solitary glass of white wine and stared at their mobile phones with profound boredom.

"What is this place?"

"A bar, a club. The local pickup joint." Storm shrugged. "Only Italians and locals come here."

They had a mojito at the bar then crossed the single dozy street and sat in white plastic chairs as a hard-working man brought them *kuku choma*, grilled chicken, with chapatis and *kachumbari*, a salad of tomato and red onion, from his kiosk. Storm told her about the food of the coast — *ugali*, a polenta-like grain that sat like a truck in the stomach, *sukuma wiki*, spinach, whose local name meant 'to push the week' because Africans ate it at the end of the week, when money for meat had run out.

For the first time since she had met him she felt at home in Storm's company. No, that was not quite right; she had always felt an inexplicable serenity when she was near him, which had nothing to do with what they said, or would say, to each other. She had never felt this before, with any human being, and didn't know what to call it.

After they had eaten they sat back in their plastic chairs and assumed the posture of the locals, whose cinema or theatre was the street, watching trim middle-aged men wearing loose white shirts, knee-length shorts and loafers enter Mysteries alone only to emerge within the hour with a racehorse-thin woman on their arms; a gaggle of underage girls all wearing tight red and green dresses, like Christmas presents, charmed their way in past the bouncers; the Land Cruisers piling up outside the club as the night went on. Shy girls who couldn't have been more than ten years old condensed out of the night and sat on the curb nearby, staring at them with huge, amazed eyes. Beggars came and went. Storm always gave them something. *Thank you, bwana*, black men murmured to him, calling him "Sir" even though they were more than twice his age, their hands cupped in supplication. *Thank you.*

The news reached them via the coastal newsletter, a round robin of local news sent by email. Al-Nur had attacked three villages to the north, near the border. The attacks took place on subsequent nights. A football match between Senegal and France was being televised and the Stay A While bar was heaving.

They came in pickup trucks carrying AKs. They were masked. They went from house to house, using gruff Arabic to order the women out. While the women and children were running through the night, hiding in the bush, they shot the men who could not recite verses from the Quran.

At the Car Wash bar twenty kilometres away, it took two or three seconds for the football fans seated at the tables to register that this band of men wearing balaclavas were not going to order a round of Cokes. By then they were dead; high-velocity projectiles having ripped through their livers, their spleens.

On the third night they drove even further south, ramming their way through a roadblock. They set fire to a hotel outbuilding in Bahari ya Manda and threw a grenade over the wall into the Isla Amor resort in Moholo.

"Reef Encounters is completely undefended," Julia said. "They could pull up in a pickup and kill us all. I don't know if we should go out on the dhow." This was where Bill's birthday drinks would be held — a dhow, hired especially for the occasion. They would sail not more than four hundred metres offshore. Any farther was not safe.

She heard Delphine's coppery voice say, "Come on, Julia. If you change your plans then the terrorists have won."

Now, every time Storm went out sailing, Julia was worried. There was no phone reception five miles out to sea. "I lie in bed and see the boat speeding toward them, guns sticking out. I see them climbing aboard. Storm would swim for it. He's a strong swimmer. He would make it back. These guys, they can't even swim."

"They'd shoot him if he ran for it, Julia. He's only valuable to them alive."

Her aunt stared at her, repulsion in her eyes. She regretted what she'd said, which came from her Gariseb self, who dealt with death each day as if it were washing powder. She'd imbibed enough cruelty to become cruel herself. She hadn't realized this had happened.

You're going to get a message from someone. The sentence inserted itself between her thoughts. Since the afternoon when the sport fisherman spook had approached her, she'd batted the episode away. What could he know? He and Anthony might encounter each other in the capital. But if Anthony had anything to convey to her he would have just called her. There was no reason for him to use subterfuge.

But now the air was becoming denser. She listened to herself, waiting for the moment when the giant realm she had described to Margaux might speak to her again.

She played out scenes in her mind those nights, of what was happening in those towns where they arrived to evict and murder the Bantu, the Christians, the *Kufir*, unbelievers. And if they came farther south, to the threshold of Kilindoni?

She knew how they would come: on a bus, dressed in western clothes, their assault rifles wrapped in T-shirts so as to not rattle in their holdalls. They would travel on separate buses with false documents, puffing out their drastic faces at the army roadblocks. They would leap out of the buses at the crossroads where the coastal highway intersected with the eight-kilometre-long road into Moholo and hijack two minibuses, taking the drivers with them. It would be so fast, no one would know, although perhaps one dusty boy loitering at the gas station on the corner would see, but he would not know who to phone and perhaps he had never used a phone in his life. In any case the police would have deserted their stations long ago, knowing they would be the first to be killed.

The night would be ripped open by the spin of sand on the

wheels of the approaching trucks. They would flee, stumbling down the coastal path, perhaps being stopped at the tunnel underneath the coral cliff by high tide. Charlie the dog would be shot first. They would open fire while shouting, *Allahu Akbar!* Or perhaps there would be no shouting, only the soundless rip of bullets.

She knew the pointed-nosed copper alloy bullets, their trajectories. She had plucked their lead bases out of sternums with tweezers. She didn't know how it would feel to have one tear through her thorax. It would feel like she were being punched, or perhaps she would feel just a sting. At first she would think, thank God, it grazed me. But there would be a hole in her throat and a severed carotid artery. There would be no repair. Even if she could operate on herself with a mirror, her bloodied hands would slip, she didn't have her instruments and there was no anaesthetic. For once her powers would fail her.

The sky was the colour of gunmetal. Ghost crabs scattered at her approach. The crabs scavenged the beach for turtle fledglings, for dead fish and the small blue bubbles of marooned Portuguese men-of-war that popped beneath her feet.

She passed a cart hauled by two donkeys and men dressed in kanzus and *kofia*, on their way to prayer. With the vanishing of tourists, the beach had resumed an earlier incarnation. It must have looked like this a thousand years ago; slim fishing dhows, their sails unfurled, safe within the reef for the night, greenshanks and curlews tripping along the sand with their piping cry.

A figure appeared on the horizon. As she approached she saw a salmon-coloured kikhoi and dark hair blowing in the breeze. She recognized Lucy by her stride, a sashay, childlike and winning.

They sat down on the sand and looked out to sea. A single ghost crab passed in front of them, dragging a piece of pineapple covered in sand into its lair. The recoil of the tide had exposed grey-green out-croppings of coral. The sulphureous scent of saltpetre hung in the air.

"I've been here for three weeks now and this is the first time we've met outside the house," Lucy said.

"There's nowhere to meet by chance here. There's no public space, apart from bars and hotels. And the beach, of course," she added.

"True." Lucy's long eyelashes batted shut, then open. "Not like in London, where we could have met at the South Bank or in Covent Garden. But we wouldn't have recognized each other."

She stole a look at her cousin. Lucy had been absent enough from the house that she was still taking her in. She saw dark blue eyes, a colour not unlike her own. Unusually long eyelashes framed them so that even without makeup she looked as if she had lined her eyes. Henna tattoos spiralled down her calves.

"Why do you want to be a psychologist?" she ventured.

"I wanted to be different, I suppose. It's a rebellion."

"Different from who?"

"Than the people I'd grown up among. I was fascinated by people. I don't know that most people here are. People don't count here."

"What does count?"

Lucy was silent for a while. "Race. Money." She gave her a con-spiratorial glance. "It's too brutal for me. Maybe it was an elaborate way to gain integrity."

"You didn't have that here?"

"Here, where people are running guns to Somalia disguised as maize or cement? Or shipping ivory to China disguised as furniture?"

"Is that what people do? Who?"

Lucy turned her eyes on her. She saw a dark lane within them, a path protected by an arbour of trees. "I can't tell you that. Or I could, but I couldn't prove it. So what's the point? It all becomes rumour, which is like the air here. People need it, they subsist on it."

She paused. "Most of Mum's friends don't even want to know what their husbands do, but they want the money to keep coming for the children's school fees and the shopping trips to South Africa, and that's another reason they don't ask. Their husbands prefer it that way. Everyone is happy."

"Except you."

"Me? I actually like the fact that there are rules in England, that there is an accepted code of behaviour," she gave the ocean a fierce look, "that everyone is not manoeuvring nakedly for their advantage."

"Naked manoeuvring is what made the British empire great. You could say here there's less of a moral failure in it because there was never any state to protect people. People do it to survive. Your father, for instance —" she paused, unsure of where her venture might lead, "he strikes me as the quintessential survivor."

"What makes you say that?"

"He's been flexible. He's set up farms and businesses, invested well and moved on when the moment was right." She corrected herself, "*Before* the moment was right."

Lucy studied her. "Did he tell you all that?"

"No, your mother did."

Lucy's gaze remained on her, as if something was not quite right.

"What do I know? I don't even know how many businesses Dad owns, or has owned." Lucy said, finally. "I'm just not interested enough. Don't get me wrong — he's paid for my education, he's set me up in life. I'm not going to bite the hand that feeds me. I'm very grateful. Too much so to criticize him to strangers." Lucy darted her a look. "Not that you're that." Lucy gathered up her knees under her chin. "I'm only thinking about all this now. It's taken me years to feel at home in the world, to get some perspective. Growing up here was like an extended childhood."

They listened to the wind. She had the impression Lucy was hoping she would say something to absolve her of her dilemma. Her cousin was correct, as far as she could see. That was the curse of the place, of living as a white person in Africa with all its privileges, as Margaux had said. Anywhere else the whites became ordinary citizens, and they were not prepared to accept such a demotion.

"Do you think passion for a job and passion for a person are one in the same?" Lucy asked.

"I think of passion for a vocation as something that you are driven to do, or be, out of conviction," she offered. "It's a doubtless state. Passion for a person is . . ." she looked away, toward the wedge of Tern Island. Around it white birds frothed. "Something else."

"Have you ever felt it?"

"Yes."

"For who?"

"You wouldn't know him."

"I guess I wouldn't."

"Why do you ask?"

"I don't know," Lucy said. "It's just something that's been on my mind." She smiled. "And I've got no one else to ask."

"What about Storm?"

"He's not much of a talker." Lucy smiled. "As you may have noticed. He's a good person, essentially, but he doesn't look inward. He's not very emotionally experienced."

"Has he ever had a relationship?"

"Not that I know of, but I've been away for years now. If he did I don't know that he'd tell me. He's very private. He's like Dad that way."

Her heart pounded so loudly she was afraid Lucy could hear it. She felt a ragged thrill to be discussing Storm with Lucy. He was a great mystery and she had thought — wrongly perhaps — that Lucy was his intimate, that she would be able to shed light on the perplexing emergency that had overtaken her, which had been generated by him. To get to the bottom of the mystery had become necessary, without her even realizing it, perhaps even more essential than what she felt when she watched him move, startled and rapt, as if she were watching a separate species. She did not expect what had taken place between them to happen again, or she would not be able to live if it did not. It could not; they would not allow it. They had not even spoken of it. Her hunger or terror had not diminished. She shied away from his company but felt desperate if she did not know where he was. She feared him and yet felt more serene with him than with anyone she had known. She careened between these two extremes. She couldn't imagine how she would be able to let him go.

The winds of the afternoon had abated. They watched terns fly over the ocean. The birds were bright white arrows against the blue.

"I've been wondering about you," Lucy said. "The things you've witnessed, your experiences. Mum said you were very nervous when you first came to the house."

"Field hospitals are nerve-wracking places."

"I can imagine," Lucy said.

"You think I'm suffering from something."

"Well, it would be surprising if you weren't. I mean, in psychoanalytic terms."

"I've had all the symptoms: insomnia, night-sweats, flashbacks, irrational fears, arrhythmia, palpitations."

"You're not worried by that?"

"There's nothing I can do but wait for it to pass."

"And that's what you're doing here," Lucy said, her voice grave. "Waiting for it to pass?"

"I suppose. I'm thinking, too. I haven't had time to think in years. Or to just be."

Lucy's head dipped. With her knees gathered and her bony shoulders she looked like a solemn child. "What about lust?"

"What about it?"

"We were talking about passion. Have you ever felt lust?"

"I'm not sure. Lust is primal," she said. "It's a primitive force. It has no logic or understanding. Passion can be constructive but lust is always destructive."

Lucy frowned. "So it's a mystifying element in life. You have no choice but to act on it?"

"Do you think we should always be aware, in control?"

"You're talking to a future Jungian analyst," Lucy laughed. "It's not possible to be in control. The unconscious is too powerful."

"But what is the unconscious, if it's not part of the self?"

"It is, but it's a self you're not much in contact with."

"A saboteur, or a succubus, then."

"That's a negative interpretation but it can be," Lucy agreed, "if you don't acknowledge its presence. Like anything you supress it only comes back stronger. Once you are in contact you can at least have a conversation."

She did not tell Lucy what had happened in her own life, so recently: That she had realized the self was not one coherent entity after all, but there might be several selves, and how to know which was the real one? That the discovery of the unconscious self was like the birth of a new and thrilling persona, but a persona who was far more reckless and hungrier for life than she was; she who was used to a certain security now, that of the middle-class doctor, the woman who inspired respect and admiration, the woman who had fought for and attained a place in the world.

She was alarmed at the turn Lucy's questioning had taken. Did she suspect something? Wariness crept into her. Since the moment she had met her, she understood Lucy was different from the rest of her family. It was not her profession, or not this only, that gave Lucy uncommon insight, she suspected, but rather character. She felt bested by her cousin, and also exposed. Lucy might have generated these feelings in her even if she'd had nothing to hide. Delphine was also astute, but her instincts were more primal, built of shrewdness. She didn't think she could withstand both categories of scrutiny at once.

She looked up to find Lucy's watchful eyes on her. "I try to see us through your eyes."

"And what do you see?"

"People who can't take much hardship. We've been spoiled by wealth. Life here is too seductive. We can't take the cold. We go to other countries because it's impossible to get a job here, now. We're not wanted. But when things get tough we're on a plane home where we don't wash dishes or make our own beds. And even if we move to England or America we never get this country out of our heads. It's a kind of curse, to come from such a beautiful country. Anywhere else you go is a disappointment. There's a passion in that, too, the misplaced love you can feel for a country where you're no longer of any use."

"There is," she said. People were so much more alive here than in England, characters living up to their dramatic nicknames: *Chex, Storm, Dutch.* She thought of the young women she had met at the parties Storm took her to, whose mothers and fathers had bequeathed them names from the map: the girl named after the Larsha hills, another for the Leramora wildlife park, even a girl named Africa. Romantic names, certainly, and the glossy women who bore them lived up to their epic tang. It was a country that inspired sufficient passion to make people imprint its names on their children.

Lucy smiled. "Here we are on the beach saying things to each other we'd never say at home."

"Why is that?"

"I don't know. The house is so much my mother's, I guess. It's as if it's on her side. Maybe it even is her."

They stood and walked back. The coral pools were being filled again by the incoming tide. They had been talking for an hour, perhaps. She had lost all track of time. She could never tell how much of it had passed here, or how much might remain.

Margaux stood in the entrance of Reef Encounters, inside a penumbra.

"You fit right in now," Margaux said.

She looked down at her own body to find she wore a black vest, a kikhoi folded correctly at her hips like a skirt, flip-flops on her feet. She was very tanned.

"I'm trying to go native."

"You're succeeding. Time for a drink?"

They sat at the table they always took, with the view of the beach, the scalloped sweep of the bay and the coral islets that dotted it like boats perpetually at anchor.

"So what did the spook want?" Margaux asked.

"Nothing really. He'd heard from someone I was working in the north. He wanted to know what was really going on there. From some- one on the ground — he actually used the phrase, *on the ground*." She smiled. "A real spy sentence."

"It's quite strange."

"What?"

"The way he approached you. He blew his cover. Not that he had much of it in the first place." Margaux turned her sunglasses toward her. She saw herself in them, two distant sepia selves. "It must have been important."

She shook her head. "I don't think so. There are intelligence agents everywhere, as you said."

"Just watch yourself with these guys," Margaux said. "We make fun of them, sitting here and reading their five-day-old *Daily Telegraphs*, but they mean business. The security situation here is bad now. I really think that. I'm going home myself."

"Are you?" She was surprised. This was the first time Margaux suggested she would return to the States.

"Before it gets any worse. Plus I'm teaching in the fall."

"When do you leave?"

"In two weeks." Margaux pursed her lips. "Just in time for the start of term. I'll go from sipping G&Ts on the coast to teaching Archaeology 100 to a hundred eager freshmen."

"There's something I want to talk to you about." She had said it before she knew the phrase was out of her mouth. Margaux's imminent departure had provoked a sudden panic. Before she knew it, the story, which she told haltingly, was there between them.

Margaux sat back in her chair. She removed her sunglasses. Margaux's eyes were round, like two brown eggs. "He's your cousin. That's a problem. At least where I come from."

"I didn't know him. I never knew him. He's a stranger. Or like a stranger."

Margaux gave her a delicate look. "He's still related to you. Genetically."

"It's not as if I'm trying to have a child with him."

"What are you doing, then? I think you're using him as much as he is using you."

It was as if she'd been slapped in the face. "Why does it have to be about *use*?"

"You're trying to revive yourself. You've been dead. Or you've been around death for so long it's become your life. You can't tell one from the other anymore." Margaux put her sunglasses back on. "Loving a person and loving how they make you feel is not the same thing."

She was driven to her feet. It was one of those moments when she could feel the past peeling away behind her, and another, nameless force nudging her toward the future.

"Why did you tell me, then?" Margaux asked.

"I don't know."

"I think you don't want my opinion at all. You just wanted to get it off your chest. You needed to tell someone your secret. Maybe I shouldn't have said anything. I thought you were telling me as a friend."

"I was. I am."

"Well, then," Margaux put her hands on the table in front of her and opened them, palms up.

She walked away from the table. She didn't want to — it was rude, she knew — but a force drove her away.

"See you around." There was a forlorn, perplexed tone in Margaux's voice. The waiter who had been coming to refresh their drinks stepped back and out of her path as she brushed by.

She started the engine of Julia's Land Cruiser. It was not unpleasant, this vertigo she was living in, she thought, as she drove up the drive, as the security guards in their white shirts, faces dark under Charles de Gaulle hats, raised the zebra-painted boom and waved her off. She had lost the sense of what she should be doing in her life. She had only ever wanted to not feel a fraud. Everything had been about that. And she was not. She stood firm, as if on a plinth, above all these people. After their golf lunches and their community film nights, she will return to the real business of healing the victims of war and peace.

"All my friends are going back."

"Well, it's September." Julia placed a bottle of wine on the table. "Back-to-school time." Julia kept her voice light, as if it were any other year, facing her children's return to boarding school or university.

Lucy had graduated with her Masters in June and would soon start supervised training in psychology at the Tavistock Institute. Within a week her life would be walks through Tavistock Square with its gazebo in the middle like a reposing crane, a placement in a hospital, essays and exams.

Later, Lucy would spend the night at Evan's; Delphine, her aunt and uncle would have a drink at a yacht club reception after dinner.

"What will you do?" Julia asked Storm.

"I don't know. Watch a movie maybe." He gave her the briefest of glances.

Delphine's eyes landed on her. "When will you go back, Rebecca?"

"In two weeks." The sentence settled in her stomach. She hadn't realized it was so soon.

"Will you return to London?"

"No, to my job, in Gariseb."

"Don't you find it difficult, being stuck up there with the Bora and the Nisa?" Delphine said. "Now, there are two peoples who will never make peace. They've only been warring for the last three thousand years."

"There are privations, yes."

"It can't be good, the civil war up there. Do you think it will ever end?"

Delphine's question surprised her. She knew more than anyone else in the family, who all treated the conflict in the north as a distant scrap that would never touch their lives, despite being in the same country. But then Delphine had spent a great deal of time in the bush, she supposed. She understood the enmities between peoples. She would not make the mistake of calling it a tribal or ethnic conflict. It was far more complicated than that.

"I don't know. Certainly not while the Islamists have a hold on the territory."

"Aren't you afraid there?"

A shiver travelled up her spine. "No," she said. "Why should I be afraid?"

Delphine gave her a level, dispassionate look. "You're a woman. It sounds very exposed, where you are."

"It is," she conceded, "but everyone's fears are different. The worst things have already happened to me. That's changed my relationship with fear."

"And what are those worst things?"

"Delphine," Julia intervened. "Maybe Rebecca doesn't want to talk about them."

"No, it's alright," she smiled at Julia. "I've come under attack several times, in camp. I'm most afraid of bombing raids from the air rather than a ground assault."

"And you haven't ever been singled out? Personally?"

"No," she said.

Lying always depressed her. She struggled to counter the energy they generated within her, which was as heavy as mud. She sat up straighter and injected vigour into her voice. "I've been fortunate that way."

Storm's eyes had followed their exchange back and forth. She was answering Delphine's questions, ostensibly, but really she was speaking to him.

When everyone had left they sat on the edge of her bed, their knees white in the moonlight flooding through the louvers.

When Storm was not near and she conjured up a visual picture of him, she always saw him in profile. His face carved the night in two; on one side was darkness, on the other silver moonlight caught the edges of his face. She thought, not for the first time, that her fascination might in reality be an obsession with a face; a face that in some ways resembled her aunt's, who resembled her mother, who resembled her.

"What you said to Delphine tonight, was that true? About not having been attacked personally?"

"No," she said. "I have been, but I didn't want to talk about it."

He smiled. "I knew it."

"How did you know?"

"I just sensed it wasn't the truth. You're an honest person," he said.

She turned to him. "Am I? How can you be so sure? Is what we're doing now honest?"

He never answered. They were speaking, then they were kissing. She could remember no transition, no decision. Kissing him felt the same as speaking. There was an honesty to that, too. A blue rush of power passed through her. His mouth was her mouth. She was astonished by its familiarity. It was not her own yet she knew every ridge, every hollow.

She pulled away. "What do you want?"

"What do you mean?"

"If you don't want me, then what *do* you want?"

He turned his head. She lifted her knee and sank down to the bed beside him.

"It's not what you think."

"What do I think?"

She could hear the waves, far beneath the house. The tide was coming in.

"That I'm a dilettante."

A sudden boredom crushed her. She sat up again and faced him. "I don't."

"All my life, I've been some kind of golden boy."

"People haven't taken you seriously, is that what you mean? If you want to be taken seriously you have to do something serious."

He looked away. Part of him wanted her censure, she understood: to be taught, scrutinized and found wanting. She heard the dry rustle of the wind in the palms sentinel outside her bedroom.

"It's my looks. Even you only like me for them."

"It's not the worst thing that can happen in life, that you're so good-looking you never know for certain if people are attracted to you because of the beauty of your inner self."

He would not look at her, still.

"I like you because —" she paused, trying to find something to say that would mollify him. "I feel so alive in your company. You're like the sky."

"What about the sky?"

She got up from the bed and began to pace the room, listening to the drone of the night ocean. She wished she could explain to him. how she wanted not to know, for a change. To not have the answers, to not be responsible, to not have to act. She wanted to erase herself into a nullity, to take the idea of herself back and back in time's long spiral staircase, to the double helix of DNA, to the void moment before conception, before her mother understood she might be possible. But that moment had erased itself long ago.

He hooked an arm behind her neck and pulled her toward him with a single loop, as she'd seen him grapple *filusi* onto the boat. She remembered the way the fish shimmered from blue to yellow as it changed colour, ripples of pink, brown, silver, amethyst swimming through its body, and how it paled into grey as it died.

Sixty people stood barefoot on the teak deck of the dhow. Lucy wore a backless black dress whose slip skirt stopped above her knees; a sheath of material flowed on, brushing her ankles. She wore no jewellery, other than a green beaded necklace. Her dark hair was tied behind her head in a bun. Next to her, Delphine stood in a fuchsia dress that hung off thin shoulders.

Their eyes met. Delphine had caught her watching. She felt instantly stripped bare by those cold grey eyes.

The other women who joined the party that evening were so similar in physicality and spirit she had difficulty distinguishing between them with their straight blond hair, their racehorses bodies. Their thinness extended to their narrow child's feet. Women insisted on going shoeless to restaurants and parties on the coast. It seemed a badge of honour among them. It meant they were free, she supposed. There was another possibility; in their insistence on being unshod in public they meant to show that they had tamed the country, dominated it entirely. Africans also went shoeless, but not by choice.

She didn't know if these women were as bored and underutilized as Margaux avowed they were, because they never spoke to her. They eyed her, saw that she was not from here and that most likely soon she would be gone. She had only her race in common with these women, an insufficient communion.

The captain cast off. The dhow drifted toward the reef. As the shore receded she noticed a group of men, each straddling a motorcycle. They remained under a tarpaulin shade, their motorbikes idle, handlebars turned to one side like the heads of shy cats. These motorcycle taxi drivers were so ubiquitous she'd ceased to see them. Why then did one catch her eye? He wore a helmet. That was unusual enough.

She turned back. The man had taken off his helmet. He had removed his sunglasses and his helmet was held in the crook of his arm. He was rangy, darker and taller than the rest. He had hungry eyes.

The dhow lurched on the crest of a wave. She stumbled backwards. A man in a white shirt and trousers made from kikhois had to catch her. She felt eyes on her. Everyone probably thought she was drunk.

When she turned back the man had gone. In the lane, swallowed by the dark drape of a single palm tree, she saw a retreating motorcycle melt into its shadow.

That night she always knew where Storm was, even when she could not see him. There was a new reserve in the way he moved in space, as if he were being careful not to align himself too closely. The crowd conspired in this new détente of theirs; if they moved toward each other, it generated someone who needed a drink refilled to separate them. Whenever their eyes hooked on each other people closed like a cordon around him.

On the dhow, at sea, she felt the weight of their collusion but it did not threaten to sink her. Secrets had become possible, then familiar, then necessary to her being. This had all happened over a matter of months. The withholding, conflicted slant in Storm's eye that night confirmed to her that he was new to secrets. He did not approve but was surprised to find himself enlivened by them.

She sat on a bench and leaned over the gunwale, watching the black water slip from the hull. She tried to forget about the motorcycle man she had seen and the memory he had excavated.

Storm detached himself from a knot of people and sat beside her. She had to move away from him. It was like the wind coming to sit with her.

"Dad wants me to leave next week. He's putting me on a plane. He's not giving me a choice. He says we're not safe here."

"You're not safe anywhere. It's time for all of us to go, one way or the other," she said.

He stared straight ahead. "You want me to leave."

"I want you to save yourself. It's what I would do. That way we have a chance of seeing each other again, some day."

He looked startled. It might not have occurred to him that they would see each other ever again. Even she was not sure they existed, or rather that the versions of Storm and Rebecca who knew each other here could exist in another place.

"Do you really think we could die here?"

"I'm not the best person to ask. I see death all the time."

"I know," he said quickly.

"Your mother could have been killed last week in that attack, if she'd gone to the supermarket," she went on, spurred by an instinct to shock him. "Do you really think nothing is going to happen if Al-Nur gain control of the coast?"

"That's not going to happen." Even as he said it, he looked unsure. She saw how unfamiliar he was with consequences, with remorse. He was a clean slate; he was — or had been — happy.

The dhow drifted in calm waters. The moon rose higher in the sky. In its bone light she saw faces huddled on the beach, the flames of braziers, a family's only light. They would sleep that night in one-room shacks where they would be bitten by mosquitoes and jigger worms would burrow into the feet of shoeless children. She could see their eyes, bright in the darkness. They watched as the dhow floated, hurricane lamps and garlands of bougainvillea hung across its riggings. They would see women on the deck of the dhow changing positions like chess pieces, the shrouds of their dresses billowing behind them as the dhow slid beyond the perimeter of night.

The days that followed Bill's birthday party had the feel of departure. Storm's and Lucy's plane tickets were bought, decisions about where they would live were made. Their father transferred money into their accounts and gave instructions about how to access more should they need it. The fact that Bill and Julia allowed her to overhear their talk of money she took as a sign of trust.

She began to take note of things that had slipped her attention before — the change in the clouds, for example. They had changed from the turbulent grey monoliths of the Kusi monsoon to become cathedral like, stately and serene. The beach was clean. The dawn came earlier — only by a minute or two, but on her morning runs she could do without her headtorch now. The rainstorms that had lashed the house at dawn for the nearly two months she had been in residence subsided.

She began to hoard the detail of life there. She wanted to imprint it all on her consciousness: the razors of shade the doum palms threw on the sand, the dignified Swahili lanterns Julia had placed in alcoves, the whistle of mosque swallows as they strafed the coconut palms in the evening and which sounded so much like the wind. She had at last come to a casual acceptance of time, now when it was very nearly over. All this — the detail of the land and light and sky — might one day be precious to her, she understood; it would cease to be a place and instead become a sacred code.

"Tell me how you got involved with this again?"

"At the site," Margaux said. "They do bird counts there. They'll be five people, all from the national ornithological society."

"Let me get this straight: they catch the birds to count them?"

"That's right; every year they ring them. There are guys in Ethiopia, even in Yemen, doing it too. Can you imagine? They find time in between being bombed to study the migration patterns of ringed plovers."

They sped down the coastal highway south to the estuary of the Sarara River. Margaux drove, and she looked out the window. The road was a constant theatre. Now a young man wearing a red T-shirt walked down the road with a black-and-white goat slung across his shoulders like a fur stole. Three women dozed in a makeshift shelter surrounded by baskets of pale mangoes, hoping for roadside trade. A young man approached them wearing a silver lamé suit and a gangster fedora. The sun caught his suit with the same glint as the Defenders and Prados that charged up and down the highway.

"You're thinking," Margaux said.

"Yes."

"What about?"

"About having to leave. That's why I'm watching the road. I'm storing up images because I'm already fading out of the picture."

Margaux was silent. She had not mentioned Storm since the day of their conversation on the deck at Reef Encounters, and Margaux had not brought it up, either. It occurred to her that far from feeling contaminated by her, Margaux might be entirely detached — from her dilemma, from her fate, or anyone's. Margaux had grown up everywhere and nowhere; other people's fates might not be entirely real to her because she did not stay long enough to witness them. She would become an interesting anecdote for her: the woman I met on the coast who fell in love with her cousin fourteen years her junior. The dignified woman who made an avoidable mistake.

They turned off onto a sandy road and drove through a tangle of mangroves.

The river was partly tidal, Margaux had told her. They rounded a corner and saw torn ribbons of breakers where the river and the ocean collided. The beach was a horizontal field of grey. These were the mudflats where the birds fed at night.

It was sundown when they pulled up in front of a small hut at the edge of the river. Here five men sat in the gathering evening. A man wearing a polo shirt and a New York Giants baseball cap stood up. He introduced himself as one of the professors from the national university. He bent down and produced a white-and-black bird with long red legs like stilts. "We just caught him in our test net."

Suddenly the bird was in her hands. It felt like holding a bundle of string. It was trembling so violently she worried it would shake itself free of her grip. She stroked it to reassure it.

"That's good," the man said. "We hold it like that, then we put the ring on." She saw the tiny aluminium anklet on the bird's leg, a number imprinted upon it.

"What does this tell you?"

"This is one of our rings, so this bird lives here, but it migrates to the Comoros. Someone caught it there and posted the number on the internet. That's how we know. Now it's time to let it go. Would you like to release it?"

They walked to the edge of the water. The plover trembled in her hands. Its heart beat so quickly she feared it would die.

"How should I let it go?"

"Just put it down in the water."

She walked to the edge of the liquorice-coloured mud. The light was waning and the sky was indistinguishable from the water. From afar it might have looked as if she were levitating.

She bent down and uncupped her hand. The plover took two uncertain steps in the water before bursting into flight. She watched as it was consumed by the sky.

"You need to get to the birds before the monkeys." Margaux handed her a spiral of entangling net. "They're mostly asleep by now but keep an eye out for them. Just walk along the path and let it unfurl. Keep the top loop around your thumb."

"Do the monkeys kill the birds?"

"They tear them apart alive. Then they eat them."

She shrank at the image and quickly unfurled the net in a single sheet. Once unwound the mesh was invisible against the green of the forest.

"Now what?"

"Now we wait for the birds to come. Two hours, I reckon." Margaux looked out over the estuary. "Let's go for a paddle."

"It's looking stormy."

"Don't worry. The estuary is only waist-deep."

A thin man came toward them, stepping through the shallows rigidly, his knees flexing like a stork's. Behind him a rough-hewn canoe followed obediently, towed on a rope.

They got in. There were no seats or struts; she and Margaux sat low, inside the hull. They paddled out, with Margaux in the bow. It was windy, even cold. For the first time since she had come to the coast she wished she had a jumper.

Land began to recede. Over her shoulder she saw a line of canoe-keeping men, queued up on shore, frowning.

The wind tossed wavelets of water into the canoe's hull, where they pooled, soaking her legs. Margaux paddled on into a darkening sky. Squally clouds hung above the ocean.

They cleared a headland and were immediately hit by a wall of wind. It tore off Margaux's hat. Margaux told her to paddle backward.

She understood they would tip over before it happened. She closed her eyes. The canoe struck her knee, but not hard, before righting itself. She hung on to her paddle. The water was warmer than the air. She stayed immersed. She had to convince herself to surface.

Margaux was right, it was not deep at all. She stood in the muddy river bed, waist-deep. Margaux appeared, also upright, wearing her hat.

"What do you say we head in?" Margaux said.

They hauled the canoe to shore. The line of thin men who had waved them off had been replaced by a single figure. He stood to attention rigidly, like a rake. He wore dark jeans, a dark shirt. It was his air, his alert, flexible posture, that began to convince her. She stared at him, the blare of recognition louder in her ears as they approached.

The man turned and walked toward the boatmen's hut.

"Why don't you see if you can find us some tea?"

"Sure. What's up?"

"There's someone I have to talk to."

She walked toward the hut. He stood outside, just under the makuti thatch gutter. She no longer felt that her hair was wet, that she was cold.

"So," he said.

She stopped at a distance from him. "Why have you come? I can't speak here." She turned toward the tea stall. "See that woman? She's American. She shouldn't see you. What are you doing here?"

"One of us saw you, in the town. He told me you were here. Are you working in a hospital?"

"I'm visiting — family." She wished immediately that she had not said the word and asked a question to distract him. "Why are you here? Gao is a hundred kilometres from here."

He looked into her, possibly through her. "You must leave the coast."

"Why?"

"Many people will be killed."

"How?"

"I can't tell you."

"And if I don't leave?"

"You can go to the sea. You get on a boat. There will be no one on the sea."

"What do you want?"

"I came to warn you."

She caught him looking intently at her hands. He remembered, perhaps, that she was the person who had saved his health, if not his life.

"Will you come for me?" she didn't say, again. Her chest felt very heavy. Her mouth was flooded with a taste like copper.

He opened his mouth. She was waiting for what came next. "We must pray that not many people are killed."

"Why have you followed me here?"

"We are all being followed."

· She sighed, a weak gesture, considering the gravity of the situation. She was so used to playing the role of the harmless doctor she found she could not shake it off.

"I wanted to speak to you."

"You want to speak to me because I am the only person you have ever saved."

As she said this the heaviness in her chest was transforming itself into a strange fatigue. Black curtains of dots, or grains, began to cascade over her eyes. She knew what was happening but could not stop it. The ground embraced her.

"Rebecca, Rebecca."

She opened her eyes to see Margaux's anxious face. "Well, thank the Lord, I thought you were gone there."

She sat up, slowly.

"I brought you some tea."

They were inside the hut. Someone must have placed her there.

"Do you want me to take you to the clinic? You might have banged your head."

"You didn't see me fall?"

"No."

She felt her cranium. "Put your finger in front of my eyes." She touched the tip of Margaux's finger, then her own nose. "Ask me to recite the months of the year in reverse."

"Tell me the months of the year in reverse."

"December, November, October . . ." she stopped. "I'm not concussed."

Margaux drove her back to the house. There was no one home, apart from Grace and Michael, who let her in.

It was dark when she rang the number on the piece of plain card. The phone was off. Fifteen minutes later he called her back.

"I'm sending someone." There was an urgency in the voice, a commotion in the background. "What you've told us is invaluable. You have a chance to save peoples' lives."

She said, "I save people's lives all the time."

VII

HARTLAUB'S
TURACO

The air of the capital was thin and clogged with diesel. The city sits at two thousand metres above sea level — high enough to make me light headed on arrival. The overnight flight from London landed at six thirty a.m., five minutes after sunrise. As we taxied, a red sun rose through a mesh of umbrella thorns. Smoke from charcoal fires hovered in the early morning air, casting a veil over the plateau.

I was expected at the embassy in Gariseb at ten a.m. They'd sent a driver in a black Land Cruiser with red diplomatic plates.

I was driven for nearly an hour through a morning thick with traffic fumes. We drove past new high-rise apartment complexes built in ovoid shapes; there were so many of these it looked like a city of giant eggs. These new buildings were in the suburbs, while the old downtown, the original clot of ox-cart streets, was faded now. There, Samsung air conditioners hummed in rusted cages outside buildings with tired 1950s shop fronts. On the side of the highways there were no pavements, only smooth dirt paths. Along these, neatly suited men and women picked their way to work between puddles and outposts. of rubbish. Marabou storks huddled in the grime-coated acacias that lined the main arteries to the city. *Welcome to the seat of a new African power* blared a billboard, the president's face emblazoned on it. Behind him, on the backdrop, giraffe and elephant filed across a tangerine plain.

The embassy was in the suburbs. Most of the western embassies had been moved from the city centre a decade ago, Anthony later told me. In the suburbs they could be protected by high walls topped with four tiers of electrical wire and concrete crash barriers. There, embassy staff could drive their armoured cars less than a kilometre away to the local roastery café outlet in the Baridi shopping centre with its fifteen guards wielding AK-47s.

We climbed into the Tembo Hills. The land on either side of the highway became steadily greener. Here the exclusive suburb of Hatton spread itself in the shadow of a dormant volcano. Its caldera had been dammed to provide water for the wives of millionaires who played at running smallholdings, keeping cows and chickens while gardeners laboured in their vegetable patches.

Everything I knew about the capital Anthony had told me. He was revered for the thoroughness of his briefings, both written and oral. It was rumoured his staff was composed entirely of failed novel-ists who vented their frustrated ambitions into picaresque reports on arms dealers, tax equality campaigners, Heathrow runway protestors, minor heads of state and the most prized quarry — the adherents of radical Islam.

The capital was only a hundred and fifty years old. It had begun life as a railway station where two lines built by the British using Indian coolie labour converged on an arid plateau. The water was good: clear and cold and, crucial for the European settlers, parasite free. Three streets turned into ten, then, within two years, by 1895, there were four import-export houses and three banks.

The city had been built by Germans, and some streets still bore their names, vying with African liberation heroes on others: Bismarck Avenue crossed Nyerere Street; Kaunda Avenue ran parallel to Schoenberg Allee. Then the English had come, the nascent colony was one of the bounties of the European victory in the First World War. With the English had come their obsession for domesticating the land, and the market gardens of Hatton.

It was the only country apart from South Africa where after Independence the whites had stayed in enough numbers to con-stitute an ethnic group. They were farmers, safari operators, UN consultants, high school teachers and businesspeople, running bean exporting or cheese making conglomerates, heading up the regional branch of Unilever or Deutsche Bank.

The country's whites were neither one thing nor another: no longer British or German or American, but the wrong colour to be legitimately African, as Bill would later tell me. They had made their fortunes in a country where they had little political influence, where they were increasingly seen as a freakish hybrid species whose numbers were in permanent decline. In England they would have been ordinary middle class, driving BMWs from Kent to insurance jobs in the city. Here they had become heliotropes; they would wither without the sun. They grew and grew, flaxen stalks of wheat, until they were tanned and daring.

Among the Africans there were three ethnic groups with distinct characters, Anthony's briefing informed me: the Milau, the Tswalu and the Kandinka. The Milau are wily and profit minded; they run the businesses in the highlands, and so the country. The Tsawlu are fastidious cattle herders, interested only in money and blood. The Kandinka are seemingly sweet-tempered fishermen or dairy farmers or cultivators of ostriches, but when called to war they are merciless.

Anthony's voice had begun to ring in my ears, now that I knew I would see him again. *We might not need you.* He had a voice of gravity and a honeyed accent of such patrician character that it almost sounded put on. I could not imagine him as anything other than an intelligence agent. He inhabited the role so thoroughly. Many doctors are like that, too; there is no other calling, no alternate version of themselves. Even if they gave up medicine tomorrow and set up an artists' commune in the Pyrenees, they would always be doctors.

We might not need you. But now they did.

Traffic lunged toward giant roundabouts controlled by white-gloved policemen. It was a city in love with cars. We were wedged in four lanes of solid Prados, Land Cruiser Xs, a gleaming new purple

Range Rover and even a white Porsche four-by-four slinking among the battered minibuses painted wild colours — one with green and purple ants — which conveyed armies of workers from the slums surrounding the city.

We pulled up at the embassy. It had been the home of one of the original settler families, a sprawling two-storey building with many-paned windows. The tiled roof bristled with cameras. Two armed men in army fatigues stood on either side of the building. A van with blacked-out windows and an antenna on its roof crouched nearby.

"You'll have to wait for a consular officer," a PA told me. It seemed I was just another doctor, pitching up for credentials and a logistics briefing. The PA told me I could wait in the garden.

There, huge acacias threw feathery shadows on the stone pathways. At first it was quiet. The upcountry birds — the black and Klaas's cuckoos, the African mourning dove — had finished their morning song. A cloud obscured the sun and I heard a deep hoot. A turaco — Schalow's, perhaps, or Hartlaub's, considering the elevation. It flew between the tall pines, flashing its opposing red and green on its wings, its smart anvil-shaped head.

"Dr. Laurelson."

I turned toward the PA's voice and saw him.

He stood under the building's broad verandah. He lunged forward — he had the same energetic, spring-built step many doctors have — and took my hand. "Rebecca. So good to see you."

"I can't say I'm happy to see you again."

He nodded — an understanding, practiced nod. "Come to my office. I've just come out to get a blast of light. We work in one of the most beautiful countries in the world and I never get to see the sun."

This man was tall and thin. He had a particular elliptical gait, as if his legs had been misaligned slightly with his hip joints. He tipped his head toward me solicitously as we walked. "How was your flight? Looking forward to getting stuck in your new post? We'll make sure it goes as smoothly as possible for you." He didn't wait for answers.

His office was at the back of the building. Through the window I saw the three serene crests of the Tembo Hills.

"So." Anthony fingered a blue folder on his desk. "Gariseb." He gave me a look that might have been encouraging. "A tricky place. There's no backup nearby. As you know, the nearest army base is three hundred kilometres away and we have no jurisdiction in Gariseb."

"Do you see that as a problem?"

"Not a problem. A challenge. The most important thing is to maintain your cover. These confined environments can be hard, I know. You're isolated. You have to keep your counsel, as we explained. Email once a day, satellite phone, restricted internet." He looked at me. "But you've done all this before."

I was thinking about his phrase, *keep your counsel*. An elegant stand-in for secrets.

"Not in places quite as isolated or unsupported, I have to say."

"That's right," he nodded. "You'll have to think for yourself."

"And I haven't quite been in this position before. I've always just been a doctor."

"You are still just a doctor."

He sat back in his chair. My mind slowed enough — it had been racing for so long now I hardly noticed it — for me to take him in as a person rather than a pure threat. He wore a blue shirt and lightweight trousers. I stole a look at his shoes, just visible around the corner of his handsome rosewood desk. Brogues, a sandy hue, handmade.

I never got to know any of his colleagues that well, so Anthony was my measure of the intelligence agent. In London he'd taken me to lunch, to the restaurant in the Royal Festival Hall. It was spring and tourist boats puttered down the Thames.

He was surprisingly confiding. "I have a soft spot for doctors," he'd said, before we had even ordered our starter. He had been brought up by a pair of doctors, both men, long before the days of civil partnerships. He was thirty-three, three years younger than me at the time.

"Tell me about yourself," he'd said.

"You already know everything about me."

"That's not true. The facts, maybe. Grew up in Clapham. Graduated in medicine, Cambridge, four years in the army medical corps, two years with MSF in Kurdistan. Now taking your consultant exams. Emergency medicine at St. Thomas'."

"What else would you like to know?"

He smiled. "Never married?"

"Engaged, when I was twenty-eight. To a pilot, Alexander. He died in South Sudan. But I think you know about that, too."

"I'm very sorry. And since then?"

"Since then I've been concentrating on my career."

I liked the expression in his eyes, very experienced, certain. This man knew things I would never know, was privy to information perhaps only twenty people in the world, including the president of the United States, knew. His knowledge created an authority, and this became a force field.

"I've always admired doctors," he said. "But what you do, working in remote environments, in conflict situations, it seems" — he gave me an almost beseeching look — "heroic. Really."

"Once you start thinking of yourself as a hero, you're done for. I think that applies to any profession."

"Why did you choose it? I mean, remote environments, the deprivation."

"To see how much I could take. It seemed to me a useful thing to know."

"And how much," he smiled, "would that be?"

"Everyone has a different relationship with fear. Fear is abstract, until you encounter it. Everyone has their breaking point, when they succumb to fear. Mostly you find out that what you thought you

231

feared doesn't frighten you at all, but then something comes along that you had never thought of, and you're terrified."

"I was rather hoping to learn what you might be afraid of."

"I know, and I'm not going to tell you."

A grey-hued ship, like a mini destroyer, slunk down the Thames. We watched its progress, our gaze arrested by the same spectacle.

"You know," he said, "you could be quite good at this. You have independence of mind but allegiance to your profession. You're cool, you've got good nerves. I can just tell. You can see the bigger picture."

"And what would that be?"

He sat back in his chair in a definitive, even victorious, way. "History."

"I never wanted a role to play in history. In any case I would only ever be an extra."

"That's what we all are. You don't even see us on screen. But we're here. We know we're here. That's enough."

"It's interesting how for a one-word explanation you people always reach for history, rather than politics, or economics, or power, or oil."

"You don't believe history exists?"

"After you've lived it, yes. But you have to go through it first."

"So history is posterity and the present is politics," he'd said.

"You know, I'm just a doctor. What I feel is — is that I veer between thinking politics doesn't exist and everything is political. Love is political. Sex is political. But we don't want to see it. We're resistant to history. Everybody just wants to live their lives."

"Do they? I don't."

"Why are the British so good at intelligence? Haven't you ever wondered?" I asked.

"I expect you're about to tell me."

"I have my theories. A talent for emotional quarantine, a cultural knack for treachery." I waited to see what he would make of this, but he didn't react. "Is this just a career for you?"

He shook his head. "No. It's never been."

"What do you hope to achieve?"

"Victory over the forces of evil."

I searched his voice for irony. "You really think that there is good, and there is evil?"

"Absolutely. I've seen them both, and I think they are evenly matched. More than that —" he leaned forward, "I *feel* it. I've felt it." He thumped the palm of his hand against his chest. "It's called radical Islam. I'd do anything to stop it. Anything."

"That's not quite evil. What you're talking about is threat to a way of life, to a way of thinking."

I can't remember what he said, then, if he'd argued the point with me, if we'd discussed definitions of evil: moral, religious, practical. I do remember the word, evil, rang between us. It filled up all available space, so that I wondered how everyone in the restaurant did not hear it.

The bulbuls were alarming in the tree outside his window. The kind of call they make when a raptor or a snake is nearby. *"Balaabil."*

He followed my gaze to the window. "What's that?"

"The bulbul. Its name comes from the Arabic for nightingale." The birds quietened. "I was thinking about London, the times we met. How you seemed genuinely interested in me. How I bought it, I suppose."

"I wasn't trying to sell you anything."

"I mean, I agreed."

"You're helping us out. We have three hundred people like you in North and East Africa alone. You're hardly on the payroll. Your medical impartiality will certainly not be compromised, if that's what you are worried about."

Impartiality. I heard an accusation in the word. He thought me weak and misguided for being worried about ordinary morality when civilization was at stake.

233

The future — his future — yawned open in my mind. I saw an endless civil war; a war without boundaries or end. What did it look like? I saw a seventh-century morality, a repressive religious state monitored by Iris scans and robots. Our freedoms would disappear. There would be no airplanes because they are impossible to make bombproof. Australia would become the moon. I would be stuck there in Africa, under the shoulder of the Sahara, an impassable barrier to home.

He gave me an impatient look. I was taking up too much of his time, for this stage in the game. I was getting cold feet, and he found this wearying.

"This isn't espionage like in films, Rebecca. I'm not handing you a codebook and telling you to memorize it and then burn it. I'm not passing you messages hidden in rubbish bins in parks. You know what to look for. You've seen it elsewhere. It's just that here we don't have anyone. We can't put them in. It's too risky."

"The closer I get I'm not sure I do know what to look for."

"You've been very well briefed. We won't leave you in the lurch." He rose. I followed him out of the garden and back through the corridors of the colonial mansion, into the smell of wood smoke and maize meal from the fields outside.

"The secretary will see you out." He turned and gave me an unreadable look, which came and went in an instant. It had a note of apology in it. The air became denser around me. For a moment I was arrested in its vise.

We shook hands. I was to wait for a driver to take me to my hotel. The lobby of the embassy was lined with portraits of several prime ministers and a single queen. In hushed wooden panelled offices on either side of the corridor were slim women who looked as if they'd just stepped out of a four-bedroomed house in Bromley labouring behind flat-screen PCs, their skin as yet untouched by the highland sun.

As I waited for a car, a man appeared from a darkened hallway. He wore a sand-coloured shirt and trousers. I knew right away that he was a doctor. It was the deliberate way he used his hands.

He was a little taller than me. His hair was receding. He had a long sloping nose and a fine mouth. There was something outmoded about him, I thought, a man from another era dressed in modern garb.

We stood in silence for a moment.

"You've just been through the same wringer I have, I imagine."

"Have I?"

"Are you going back to your hotel?"

I said I was, that I'd just flown in that morning.

"We were probably on the same plane." He stuck out his hand. "I'm Urs."

"Urs? As in bear?"

"That's right." His eyes were a grainy green, the same colour I would see in Julia's eyes. "Danish, or my family was. But now I'm English." He held out his hands from his thighs in an actor-like gesture. *Here I am. Take me or leave me.* "Where are you staying?"

"The Kaminski."

"Me too. I'm going to enjoy every minute of the hot showers and room service. When are you heading out?"

"In two days."

He bounced very slightly on the balls of his feet as he stood. "Listen, would you like to have a drink? It would be great to have a glass of wine before it disappears from the menu for six months."

"I'm really tired. I'm sorry. It's just — the altitude. The flight."

I saw him absorb the rejection. I saw it was unexpected. He was a good-looking enough man to be unfamiliar, perhaps, with rebuff.

"Sure," he said. "I understand."

A few months ago I would have taken his appearance at face value — what a coincidence, meeting another doctor in the same *situation*

— whatever that was — in the Embassy waiting room. We would have a drink, keep in touch, perhaps be friends or even more. We would compare notes on field directives, on the generic and brand antibiotics available; we would discover we had done the same short rotations on obstetrics and toxicology. But now I wondered.

The embassy had ordered one car for both of us. We sat in the cool leather of its air-conditioned interior. This was his second time in Africa, Urs said. He'd worked in Macedonia, and before that in Pakistan, before that Nigeria, in Port Harcourt.

We pulled up into the drive of the Kaminski, a pink and maroon spaceship in the heart of Lakeland, where the main shopping malls were located. More low-slung Porsche four-by-fours lined the driveway.

"Hard to believe we're in Africa. A far cry from one goat-and-three chickens villages, anyway." He turned his eyes on me. They were a cool but not unfriendly grey now. They changed with the light. "Are you sure you wouldn't like a drink?"

"Well, maybe just one."

We arranged to meet in the bar in half an hour. The bar was lined with burgundy banquettes and gold-hemmed champagne glasses. We were not the first drinkers of the day. Men — the customers were all men, I noticed — were dotted on the banquettes, alone or in twos or threes. I did not recognize him straight away. Urs had changed into a dark linen shirt open at the neck to reveal a tanned chest. His fingers were like the rest of his body — lean and fine.

I sat down. "It's a bit early in the day to drink, don't you think?" I looked at my watch. It was four in the afternoon.

"I've lost sense of what time it is. Or even what day. Anyway," he reached for the cocktail menu, "like I said earlier, it might be the last alcohol I see for a while, courtesy of the relentless spread of Islam. A daiquiri for under ten quid? Bonus." He raised his eyebrows. "Let's get blotto. It's on me."

236

"Okay, thanks, but I think it's better if we split it."

"Sure." He did not say, as some men might have, *suit yourself*. He fixed me with a diagnostic look. "So, what's your story?"

"Which story would you like?"

"The one where a jobbing doctor is pressured to provide information to the security services."

"Oh. That one. You first."

Urs had been contacted for the first time in Nigeria. "One of the local consular officers came to the hospital. He said there was a problem with my visa renewal, but that he was looking into it. He told me I had to come into the consulate to sort it out. Needless to say that was a ruse." There was a local separatist movement, Urs discovered. "I knew nothing about it. Nothing!"

This was the topic of interest to the security services: would this Islamist separatist movement mount attacks in a thriving, cosmopolitan part of a country that was an important ally of the UK? But why should he come into contact with information, Urs asked the officer. He was only a doctor. "He had said, 'Doctors hear many things. They have their ears to the ground.' That's the phrase he used — *ears to the ground*. I said, 'I've got my ears to people's lungs listening for TB.' How about you?"

Around us the restaurant was filling up. Men in suits sat at the bar drinking imported whisky, platinum watches glinting against their skin. Pale, tall men with blond hair — Scandinavians, unmistakeable from their sheer altitude and sail-like cheekbones — leaned against the bar. I was more alert to all this random phenomena than I would have been, now that I had been pressed into service as eyes and ears. Anthony had told me I must treat everything I saw from now on as if it were a pattern, a code. I had to crack it in order to see the shape of the true reality underneath the surface.

The address led to a slim Georgian house on one of those furtive St. James's streets that were home to think tanks and government ministries — Chatham House, the Overseas Club, DEFRA. It was November. The streets were dark chrome and slick with rain.

The invitation reached me in a barren period. I did nights mostly and slept in the day. Nine days on, five days off. By night I pumped the stomachs of fifteen-year-olds and treated graze wounds from stab attempts in some local high street — the results of what ought to have been a mild altercation: queue-jumping in the supermarket, taking another guy's parking space.

The interior of the building had been painted chocolate and rasp-berry. A grand staircase, carpeted in a deep, pulsating green, spiralled off to the left and the right. Why had I come? I asked myself as I mounted the stairs. Was I that desperate for a social life? I might not even recognize, let alone know, anyone.

If I did see someone from my college, I would be pressed to regale them with a litany of field hospital stories: grenade, mortar, evacuation, insurgency, IEDs, the duet of danger and boredom, danger and bore-dom, ticking over like a metronome. A woman among men and bombs. No one would know about the 10 mg of propranolol I hid under my breakfast plate every day, the 2.5 mg dose of valium I ingested at night, the nocturnal sweats, the hours spent shopping for clothes to wear on dates I lacked the courage to arrange, in part because I had never been on a date in my life. The few men I'd had a relationship with I'd met in the line of duty, in field hospitals or on training courses. We would sit next to each other on a hard bench one day in the camp mess to eat lunch, never having seen each other before, and that would be it.

That was how I'd met Alexander. It had been unsought. One day we were sawing through overcooked chicken breasts, the next day we sat together in white plastic chairs watching *The Day After Tomorrow* — all the films shown on base were about natural disasters or apocalyptic scenarios — on a suspended television with sixty other people. The following day we were deployed together. I'd undergone this evolution only twice in my life, beginning with being strangers, then acquaintances, then graduating to wary colleagues before slowly becoming intimates. The days in between marred by life and death. It seemed to me a good way to get to know someone.

The email had said *Dress: Casual*. When I arrived I found women in black banker dresses and heels and men in full suits. The people in the room looked as if they'd aged thirty years in fifteen. I headed straight for a mirror to measure myself against these people and their serious, straining expressions.

On that night I was so grateful that someone approached me and engaged me in conversation I was prepared to overlook the fact I didn't remember him at all.

He didn't look patrician or self-satisfied. He didn't quite have his gestures or facial expressions under control — there was a floppy, anarchic quality to the way he waved his hands, grimacing and laughing at once.

"You were in the year above me," he said. "You probably don't remember me. I'm Stuart."

"I'm sorry, I'm not sure I remember anyone here."

"I barely made it through politics," he confessed. "I'm a slow writer, as it turns out. Not good for journalism or politics. Another reason I chose the civil service."

At the end of the conversation, as we were all being called to order for speeches on behalf of the organizers who were about to harangue us to continue being perpetually successful, we exchanged cards.

A month later I received an email from Stuart. He wanted to meet, he said, to catch up. I met him in a tapas bar in Borough. For the first hour we talked about university. He listed the floor my room in first and second year was on, he reeled off the names of dinners and receptions we had both been at. It seemed plausible enough, but the fact remained I didn't remember Stuart at all.

I had meant what I had told Stuart the night we met: I remembered little of my three years at university, which in retrospect appeared as one unbroken networking session punctuated by terrifying exams. I never shook off a feeling of fraudulence at having been accepted, spending years doing cram courses and paying for private tutorials to get the necessary results from my comprehensive school education. I never lost the feeling I was there on charity, amongst the willowy issue of peers, ambassadors to somewhere or other and equine surgeons.

I twirled my margarita. It was good — fresh lime juice, imported tequila. My head spun with the combination of altitude and alcohol.

"At the end of the evening Stuart told me what he really did for a living and what he wanted from me."

"Aha," Urs said.

"Aha indeed."

Six months later I got the job that would lead to my posting to Gariseb, I told Urs. It was a routine briefing, they had said. Just come in for half a day, the coordinator said on the phone. I was at work at the time, at St. Thomas'.

"I can't get a half day between here and my departure date," I said.

"Well, it's kind of obligatory."

"You didn't tell me about this when I signed the contract."

"We didn't know."

"Alright fine, I'll have to trade a shift. Give me a day to sort it."

"It has to be Wednesday."

At this I lost patience. "Look, you call me in for a half day I'm not paid for, then give me two days' notice."

"I can't reschedule it. I'm sorry."

I went over what the organization called the recruitment process. There was nothing unusual in it — I had seen the advert on the online portal, field surgeon, I knew the organization by reputation; my friend Maria, who graduated in the same class, had worked for

them for two years in Kurdistan. I emailed her and she gave a glowing report: expert logistics, they know what they're doing, and they
keep their people safe, although there's a Christian bent, she'd said.
But you don't have to encounter that much. The Christians keep to
themselves. I'd wondered: Christian logistics in a part of the world
where proselytizing was punishable by death?

I arrived at the organization's headquarters just south of Brixton
tube. In a month's time I would be on a plane to the equatorial winter.
I thought about the privations I would endure. Washing my hair once
a week to conserve water. The desert sun which would etch deeper
the fine lines only now beginning to appear on my face. I considered
these trivial vanities, hardly worth regret. But still they got to me.

The man was seated at the table. He wore a suit which had a very
slight sheen in its fabric. A single folder crouched next to an iPad.

"Dr. Laurelson," he said, rising to his full, crisp, impressive height.
"I'm Anthony." He sat back down, motioning to the chair opposite him. "I understand you'll be at Gariseb for a year." He smiled
encouragingly.

An hour later I went straight to the pub and ordered a gin and
tonic and drank it in two gulps, his words leaping through my head.

*I believe we are entering a time of war. A war potentially without
end. The war will be dispersed. It will be everywhere. It will be between
two ways of thinking, of being. Two civilizations.*

I don't see any evidence of that.

*Within a year a new organization will emerge in the Middle East.
It will spread, first to North Africa, then to East Africa. It already exists,
in fact. It is biding its time to announce itself to the rest of the world.
When it does, all our lives will change.*

I'm just a doctor.

You will be in a position to help us, to help all of us.

*If it's that important you can put someone else in, surely. Someone
better at getting information.*

There's no one. And there's no time.

I left the office and walked back to St. Thomas', even though I was not on shift that night. I needed to be somewhere with people I knew, a stable reality. I passed by the nurses' station which flanked A&E; the senior A&E consultant was there. He was a bearded tango enthusiast with a sharp tongue. He ordered me into his office.

"Rebecca, Christ, what did you do, kill the Pope? I've just had bloody MI6 on the phone. You're to do what they want. Whatever it is, just do it. Those fuckers don't fuck around."

You have family there; they live between the capital and the coast. Anthony sat back in his chair and folded his hands behind his head, as if he had just played a trump card.

They're not family. I don't know them. I've met my aunt only once, I barely remember her. I haven't heard from her in ten years, at least.

You don't intend to visit them? Even out of coincidence? You're there, they're there. You might need somewhere to go when you're on leave.

Why does that concern you?

It doesn't, Anthony had said. *Let's call it coincidence.* And with that he closed my folder. It was a little curlicue of doubt, or threat, on his part.

"Coincidence," I say to Urs.

"What about it?"

"It doesn't exist."

"So what does, then?"

A seizure of control on the part of a deity, an engineered arrival. That there is an infrastructure to fate; in fact fate is theatre. Now I have been backstage and have seen the faded glamour of the dressing rooms, the rigs of lights and cascades of ropes, the tearful divas in the corridors. I will never watch the play in the same way again.

"You're far more valuable to them than I am," Urs said. "There's no radical Islam in the DRC. At least not yet."

"Is that supposed to make me feel better?"

"I don't know," Urs said. He deflated slightly, as if the fight had gone out of him. "I'm not very interested in secrets."

"But it seems secrets are interested in us."

"It's not about secrets, or so they say. The only secret is that we have to keep it to ourselves — what we're doing. Otherwise it's hard information. We're just part of an army of eyes on the ground — that's how they see it." He stopped. "What's your view on all this —" he cast a slightly anxious glance around the restaurant "on what we're doing."

"I feel . . . neutral. I can't imagine any information I'd come across would be that important. They know who the combatants are, where they come from, who trains them. They have satellite, communications chatter, drone surveillance. For all I know they could pick out a single camel in the middle of the Sahel if they wanted to and blow it up. They know everything." I drew a breath. My heart was racing. It might have been the alcohol. We were on our second drink. "Mostly I feel dread."

"That's *exactly* what I feel," Urs nodded vehemently. "Dread. Where will it all lead? I treat someone, I report his background, his wounds, his seeming affiliations. Where will that end?"

"Do you mean in someone getting killed?"

"It's entirely possible."

"What about you? Is your appearance today really coincidence?"

He grimaced. "Do you mean was I planted to find out if you'll be a reliable source?"

"I'm sorry. This is making me paranoid." I looked around the room. One of the Scandinavians was eyeing us. I stared back until he shifted his gaze. "I don't think I've really taken it on board, what it means, until now."

"Why did you agree to it?"

"I didn't. I never said yes, but I didn't say no, either. I was flattered, maybe. Not a very good reason, is it?"

243

"It's an honest reason."

Honesty. The word crouched between us.

"And here I am, the person who never said yes, but didn't say no, either, having a drink in a pink hotel in Africa."

Urs looked at his watch. "We have one night left in the land of the hotel mini-bar." He paused. His eyelashes fluttered, perhaps out of nervousness. "What do you say we share it?"

"Thanks, but I've retired."

"From what?"

"From . . . the whole arena of . . ."

"Of sex."

"If that's what you want to call it," I said.

"What other name does it have?"

"So many. None of them good." I tried a rueful laugh.

"I'm trying not to take this personally," he sat back in his chair. "Could you be a bit more specific? You mean, it's not about me — you find me attractive and so on. Or at least I hope you do." He gave a very English defensive laugh. "But you're recovering from a breakup, or a divorce, or some episode of bad faith."

That phrase of his is still with me now: *episode of bad faith.*

"I'm not up to it," I said. "I just don't have the conviction anymore." It hit me, a revelation. I would have liked to feel unrepentant, or say I did. But I felt a need to apologize to him. I wasn't letting him down, I was letting down my entire species. "It's too — brutal. Sometimes, when I'm kissing someone, I start to see their subcutaneous veins. I see the yellowed gums of the smoker. I see adipose tissue."

I saw a door open, or shut, in his eyes. "You know, you're quite serious."

"Being a doctor is serious, don't you think?"

"From time to time I want to be frivolous and impulsive, that's all." He looked genuinely sad. "You're like my classmates. You're one of those people who has just aced everything, as the Americans say."

"Being clever wasn't a point of personal pride for me, it was survival."

"How so?"

"To get through medical school I needed scholarships all the way. I don't have family money."

"Still, Cambridge, then the army."

"I didn't ace either of those. I wasn't really built for the army. I was just very good at putting on a front. The overachiever, the person who was not intimidated by death or aristocrats. That's Cambridge and the army, respectively, in case you're wondering."

He laughed. More people had come into the bar and dining area. Now we had to raise our voices to be heard. He swivelled his head around the room. "There's a real middle class here," he said. "It's good to see that happening in Africa."

"I don't think they're middle class."

"I was trying to be positive, I guess."

"I've only been here a day but I kind of like it, this city," I said. "It feels raw. Vital. But decadent, too. There's something heady about it."

"You mean apart from the altitude?" Urs smiled. He looked over his shoulder at the row of businessmen around the bar, the brushed chrome sheen of their suits, their pale pink shirts knotted with ties. "You can just tell there's so much new money here," he said. "I've never seen so many Rolexes and Porsches in my life. When I was driving in from the airport, it was like Knightsbridge, only with beggars at every traffic light."

"It's the fastest growing economy in Africa, that's what they told us at the briefings," I said. "Oil, defence contracts, telecommunications, finance, export agriculture, the rose and string-bean farms, even fashion, you name it."

He nodded. "A heady brew indeed. Never mind that the biggest anti-terrorism operation besides the Middle East is being run out of here. It's the sort of place that makes you feel like an idiot for taking anything at face value." We both darted suspicious glances at the businessmen then, imagining who they really were, behind the Armani suits and the Longchamp watches bought on business trips to Zurich.

Our cocktail glasses were empty. "Forgive me if this sounds like I'm making a last-ditch attempt," he began, "but we're both about to be stuck in the middle of nowhere for six months, and — "

"And it would be a shame to lose the opportunity."

I could find nothing to say against this affable, nearly handsome man. In London I might have plucked up enough courage for it. On the third date we would have gone to bed. On the sixth date he would have been posted to Myanmar.

"Well," I rose and offered him my hand. "Good luck. The DRC is tough, everyone says. You seem like a good person."

He grimaced.

"You've heard that before?"

"It's a killer, that one." He laughed lightly, a little dismissively. "But you seem resolved."

"Well. Goodnight."

"Goodnight."

He would have a whisky, he said, at the bar, beside the slim goddesses who had begun to appear next to the men in clever suits and pointed-toe brogues. I took a last glance at him as I walked toward the lifts. He was sitting on a stool, chatting amiably to the bartender. He had gotten a taste for the expat life, he'd told me. He was thirty-four, unmarried, and his life was entirely open — those were his words. He would return to London and meet a girl from Cheltenham Ladies' College in a Marylebone cocktail bar; he would be posted to South Africa and meet the cultural programmer for the Goethe-Institut at a *Mail & Guardian* literary festival event; he would marry a Congolese woman and start a local NGO specializing in scoping projects for HIV, for TB, for child-soldier rehabilitation. I would never see him again.

The next day I was driven in a similar car to the airport, to a side entrance, a departure point used only by UN, military and diplomatic personnel. In the airport were tall south Sudanese men travelling to the regional security conference in Djibouti and British Army lieutenants heading to the not-so-secret army base in the north, near the famous elephant sanctuary. I would be one of them, this nomadic tribe of international salvage experts. I would rue the fact that I had left the ordinary world. I would watch the tourists just arrived from the UK with their straw hats board planes to the coast. Julia and her family lived there, in a place I had a rough holiday brochure image of — hotels and beaches and hot, chaotic cities choked with tuk-tuks and minibuses — but I had no plan to contact them. We would remain unknown to each other. I would come and go from their country under their noses, undetected, even invisible, a ghost.

VIII

AFRICAN
SACRED IBIS

D elphine's last day in the house was one of storms. They powered in from the ocean, dark Kusi squalls. White birds keeled around Tern Island, screeching in the wind. The dark and pensive grove of palm trees on the other side of the road from the entrance to the house was lashed by rain.

The rest of the family milled about the house uncertainly, waiting to say goodbye. This energy — a stalled expectation, a sense that at any moment some sort of rupture would need to be confronted — had established itself in the house only a day or two ago, and now felt unmovable.

"I don't know why she doesn't take a boy with her," Julia said. Julia meant the part-time gardener-cum-carpenter, Marcus, who must have been fifty. "She's bound to run into trouble on the road."

"Tell her, then," she said.

"Me? Tell Delphine how to drive in Africa?" Julia laughed.

Meanwhile, Delphine stalked the plazas of the house. She got in her car and roared to the petrol station in Kilindoni, stocking up on jerry cans of petrol and water and provisions for her journey. It would take her twenty hours to drive home with all the roadblocks.

Now that Delphine was leaving, she felt safe enough to observe her. She was an ectomorph — lean and yet delicate. Her ascetic physique furnished her with drama even as it siphoned her of warmth. She was restless, always, sitting down only to stand up, clicking her fingers for the staff to help carry her things to the car. Delphine must have had lovers, she considered, perhaps many. To a man she must appear as a vault whose code was exceedingly difficult to crack.

The previous night at dinner she had found herself subjected once more to Delphine's lighthouse gaze. Julia had put her next to Storm at the table and she had spent the dinner trying to drown out the roar of his body by conversing to everyone else, by drinking too much. She was clumsy and brash; she dropped her knife twice. Each time Julia had winced. .

Delphine had been telling a story about her last photographic safari. "I was in Botswana a couple of months ago," Delphine said. "I was guiding a *National Geographic* photographer deep into the delta. We were on horseback for part of it. One of the horses was attacked by a lion." Delphine paused to accept a refill of her wine glass.

"What did you do?" she asked.

Delphine fixed her with that rigid stare of hers. "I shot it. I'd been wanting to try out my new .458 from horseback for a while. I got it in one shot. Brain." Delphine folded her napkin into two sharp panels. "I left the carcass. Wild dog, hyena, they came that night. We could hear them squabbling over her."

The anecdote silenced them all, which is perhaps what it had been designed to do. They hung their heads like penitents and finished their dinner. In the lull that followed she found her eye drawn to Bill, then to Delphine, back and forth, comparing them. How much they were sister and brother. Their heads had the same sharp slope from the crown to the back of their necks, as if they had been planed off.

She imagined Delphine's alternate English self, had her and Bill's grandparents stayed on their farm in Gloucestershire instead of adventuring in the tropics. She might be an angular home counties trophy wife, shopping at Boden and the White Company, drinking slimline tonic. There, she would have been hard and brittle, but Africa had given her a carnivorous grandeur.

"I see you two have made friends." Delphine said.

She stiffened. Storm answered. "What makes you say that?"

"When you're in the house together you are always looking to see where the other is."

"Like impala," he said. "Safety in numbers."

"More like klipspringer," Delphine said. "Which mate for life."

Julia had given them a bright, puzzled look. Then Bill's phone had rung, and the moment was dispersed.

Delphine left at eleven o'clock. They had all been up early that morning, and it felt as if it had lasted forever. As they waved her off, Delphine had called Julia over to the car. Their heads had dipped toward each other for a minute. Then Julia had drawn away. She couldn't see her aunt's face, but her posture had changed. She held herself carefully, as if she'd just been issued a warning.

It rained all afternoon. She liked the rain. Clear skies were exposure. She found protection in these wooly afternoons when the land and the sea were held inside cloud. The rain was unlike anything she had experienced. It didn't come in sheets or storms; it didn't seem to actually fall from the sky. Instead the rain seemed to be dimensionless, generated inside the air. Surely no harm could happen in its hush, in the afternoons it thickened to instant night.

The rain made geckos dive behind picture frames and spiders fall asleep in their webs. In her room she saw the ocean enveloped in a curtain of mist. The bougainvillea hung its head as if ashamed. The air smelled of metal. The house also shifted personality on these wet Kusi afternoons; it became hushed and eternal.

She fell asleep for over an hour and struggled to rouse herself. At seven o'clock she went down into the living room and walked outside. It was nearly dark. The monkeys were already asleep in the neem tree; she saw their small bulks, how they nestled close, faces buried in each other's chests.

She walked one circuit of the infinity pool, then two, three, until she had paced for nearly an hour. The moon swung over the ocean, where it carved a silver streak. The slender-tailed nightjar called, *whirr-whirr, whirr-whirr,* a purring small machine. She loved nightjars, their soft eyes like crushed blackberries.

Her eye caught a light at sea. She grabbed the binoculars. They were likely out on the boat, Storm and Evan. They went fishing at night now and then, he'd told her, when the tide was right. She had watched them carefully since the night she'd seen them together in the living room. She felt guilty about her spying, however inadvertent. What lingered in her mind was a single image of fine dark fingers in Storm's hair. Depending on the angle this picture took it was an emblem of the easy friendship of young men or something charged with almost abstract lust. If this were true, she felt less panicked than if he were with another woman. She didn't know why, only that most men were attracted to other men on some level, she judged; this was their true nature. Women were just a diversion.

She went back inside the house. Her uncle sat on the baraza. She hadn't heard a car in the drive.

"Julia." There was no question mark at the edge of the name. "Oh, Rebecca, it's you. What were you doing out there?"

She took a seat opposite him on the baraza. "Listening to the slender-tailed nightjar. Do you know how they catch their prey?"

He gave a diffident shake of his head.

"They have tetrachromatic eyesight; they see in long, medium and shortwave dimensions. They also see UV light."

"We could all use better vision," he said. A weight had settled inside him. This was what worry did to people, she thought.

The man sitting across from her was still vital, in the prime of life, really. He had expected to enjoy living off the fruits of his labour, but now he was facing the worry of his children's safety, the prospect of not seeing them for many months, having to flee the Dhow House, the coast and its life of ease for the cold city. Although fleeing one house for another was not necessarily a tragedy.

"Is Storm here?"

"No, he's out on the boat."

"With Evan." He shook his head. "Those two are inseparable."

She said it before she even thought it. "They love each other."

"We all loved each other. We had friendships like that, when I was young. Me and my best friend Dennis spent hours together walking the farm, shooting guinea fowl. We went to school together; we went on holiday with each other's families. We were never apart. Other people then were everything. We had no distractions." He paused. "Men don't have friendships like that anymore. Why is that?"

"Because it's assumed to be something else."

He laughed. His voice swung on a hinge, hesitating between pleasantry and mockery, she had observed. The hinge could swing either way. His volatility had the effect of keeping everyone in his realm hooked, uncertain, eager the wind-blown door of his mood should veer in their favour. The family had different strategies for dealing with her uncle when he was like this, she had observed — Julia mollified, Storm avoided, Lucy loved, showering her father in hugs.

"And you, have you ever had a friend like that?"

Her uncle's face was impassive, affable as always. But there was a glint of irony in his voice.

"No," she said. "Unfortunately not."

"But you have had — relationships."

"One serious one. With a helicopter pilot. He died."

Her uncle did not offer any comfort. He merely nodded.

"You must find life very lonely, then."

"I'm alright. I have my work."

They looked at each other. She might have imagined it, but something pure — some understanding — passed between them.

She got to her feet, powered by a sudden conviction. She couldn't take any more of Africa. She wanted to be back in her own country, she wanted to be somewhere things worked. She wanted to be back in her sphere of power and not beholden to circumstance.

Her uncle might have sensed the storm that had flashed through her. "You must find it tedious here, without lives to save."

His eyes burned into her. She turned. "I'll see you in the morning."

The eyes stayed with her as she ascended the spiral staircase. She shook them off only when she closed the door to her room. For a while she could hear him moving about downstairs in the living room — the creak of the fridge door opening, the rattle of ice.

She sat on the bed. Her breathing finally slowed. Bill had meant to accuse her of something, but what? He would not be plain about it. No, he wanted to see her put under pressure, see what she would do.

She had been waylaid by his charm. Storm was not like his father. He was not charming, which she associated with vanity in any case. He was not as conflicted as his father, but he had force. It was beyond charisma or sexual magnetism. She had never seen its like before, although she had felt a similar current, more brutal, emanating from some of the army officers she had met. A force that can subtract the qualities that dog her — her dismissal of fear, her fastidiousness — a force that has the ability to return her to her quiet, courageous self. Storm's danger provoked her valour. Maybe that is the truth of it: it was all wrong, but she believed that she was a better version of herself with him. No one else could have effected such a transformation.

The wind picked up. The tide flung waves at the edge of the shore. The sound of their breaking boomed in her ears.

Here she was in the house, her uncle downstairs, two solitudes at the helm of night. They were out there, an isosceles triangle, pointed at one another: Storm and Evan on the boat, Lucy at a friend's house, Julia god knew where. She felt its presence suddenly, the alternate quadrant of fate where they might never have met, let alone been family. Where they could all be strangers.

Morning sun coated the fronds of the coconut and golden palms Julia had planted in ceramic pots. The garden glimmered against the blue froth of the ocean. The yellow-rumped tinkerbird whirred in the trees.

Julia was in the kitchen, her hands busy with commands to Grace. "Time goes so quickly. You never have time to do all the things you want to."

Julia's eyes glistened with sudden tears. It was the first time she had seen her aunt cry. Julia's face held its composure. Her own mother's face had become distorted and ugly the few times she had seen her cry.

"I hate this feeling of the future closing in," Julia said. "My children are always leaving me. From the moment they were born they've been leaving."

She didn't know what to say. She had no experience with such an emotion. When she had left her mother to go to university, she had only felt relief.

She watched Julia move back and forth. Her distress made her restless. She was wearing a pair of white shorts and a green T-shirt. Her nails were painted silver. She had seen her every day for nearly two months, but even now she found new angles and details to her aunt's being — her demure feet, her thin shoulders, the swan-like curve of her neck. Her lovely porcelain face was not fragile, as such a quality would have been for many women, but expressed a broken bravado. She felt reassured by her beauty. Perhaps that was why so many strove to obtain beautiful people: their perfection soothed the world's ills. Most people could be reduced to a predominant element, she thought: air, water, fire, earth. Julia was air, Storm was water, her uncle was fire. What was she?

"It's our last chance to go out as a family," Julia said. "I want it to be perfect."

Now her aunt paced the open living room of the house. She hesitated, wondering what to do. Julia was not a person who encouraged hugs or gestures of solidarity at all. She couldn't muster the resolve to ask her the questions or suggest remedies as she would have anyone else.

She pictured her aunt in all those years she did not know her — driving the children to school, organizing charity fashion shows, her short-lived enterprise of making leather bags for export, her painting and photography classes, her attempts to maintain an innate gift. She would have been a good photojournalist. She would have lived more briefly perhaps, but each moment of her life would have been engraved on her like scripture, instead of these years she has spent waiting in paradise.

She perceived that something inside Julia was coming to its terminus, a spiritual rather than physical entity. Julia knew this intuitively but did not know its cause, which had something to do with her, Rebecca, with her infiltration of their lives. Julia must have scented her guilt, was suspicious of it, but recoiled from her own doubts. Suspicions could have little place in families, if you wanted them to survive.

Election day three weeks. Countdown to the future. Will blood be spilled? The newspapers seemed to exist only to stoke fear. But there was a countdown involved. The country was collectively holding its breath. Would a repeat of the violence that marred the election four years previously take place? Would Milau people run the risk of being killed at roadblocks while driving from the capital to the Larsha Hills, as had happened before? Would the smell of burning rubber and the sight of young men with scarves wrapped around their faces as improvised balaclavas be repeated?

Flights to London, Dubai and Istanbul were full of foreigners leaving the country. The oil executives, Food and Agriculture Program administrators, the Third Commercial Secretaries of the embassies of eastern European countries among them. But no doctors, she supposed. Doctors — at least those of her tribe — were the last to leave. They went down with the ship.

Al-Nur close in on the coast. Islamists had entrenched cells in Puku, in Lindi, in Bahari ya Manda, the papers reported. *We now control the coast all the way to Mozambique*, they claimed. In Bahari ya Manda, motorcycle assassins patrolled the streets and shot an Australian tourist at close range as he queued to board a ferry. Fifteen men, all Milau and Christian, were taken out of a long-distance bus travelling from Puku to Bahari ya Manda and shot by the roadside as vehicles streamed past.

In the north the Bora continued their advance into territory so recently annexed to give a home to their rivals the Nisa. Gariseb was fifty kilometres from the border of the annexed territory. Close enough to Gao and Port Al-Saidi — this accident of geography is what brought Ali and his men to her IV drip, after their successful rout of the Bora only a hundred kilometres from the hospital.

That conflict had been close; this one was closer. She felt the pressure she detected when she first came to the coast but which had abated, floated away from her consciousness on an unceasing circuit of beach parties at Moholo, cocktail receptions, lunches at the yacht club, dhow cruises.

The daily sorties by fighter jets returned. From the Dhow House they could see their faint outlines, high in the sky. They travelled north in the early morning to bomb Al-Nur positions over the border. At dusk different planes flew over, bombers painted in camouflage. The fact that the wheels were down meant they would land nearby, possibly

258

only five or so kilometres away, but when she inquired — to Margaux, to Bill and Julia — where these planes were going, no one knew.

The day dawned cloudy.

"He could have taken the launch." There was a complaint in Lucy's voice.

"He just wanted to swim," Julia said.

Storm was already in the boat. He had swum there as they had all watched. He was an elegant, effortless swimmer.

Bill started up the outboard motor on the tender and they climbed in. She sat next to Julia, beside a cooler full of white wine and beer. Julia had her hair cut short the previous day, a pageboy haircut that gave her a slant of androgyny. Yet she was so womanly still, with her queenly feet, the thin gold necklaces that encased her throat.

The wind was beginning to turn. Soon they would enter the Matalai, when the wind hesitated between the winter and summer monsoons. The Matalai brought doldrums and uncertain skies, Storm had told her. By November the summer monsoon would establish itself. This wind was born in China, he'd said. It travelled all the way, across India's triangle to the archipelagos of the Indian Ocean, then the blasted wedge of Saudi Arabia, to reach the coast.

They threaded through mangroves. They would motor out until they were past the reef. There they would hoist the sails. As they rounded a corner to the open ocean they disturbed a caucus of white cattle egret accompanied by a single grey heron. The birds levered themselves into the air. The heron tucked its snake-like neck into its shoulder and floated above them, before flying away.

On the boat, Storm unfurled the sail and the sailboat leapt forward. On shore the sun's light caught the tops of the casuarinas.

"Rebecca." Storm was staring at her from the prow. "I'm going to tack."

"What?" she shouted against the wind.

She felt Lucy's hand on her shoulder. "Tack. Get down."

They all ducked, touching their foreheads to the deck as the boom swung over.

She looked up to see Storm standing, the sun caught in his driftwood hair. She levered herself carefully to her feet. She couldn't walk around boats as Storm could, without once touching the gunwale or putting his hand out for balance.

She found she was walking toward him. He gave her a single frightened look. The boat heeled over. She put her hand out and found Storm's chest, for balance.

"Sorry."

"That's okay."

She saw white particles of light, dancing on her eyes.

"Here, Rebecca. Come sit down." Her uncle slid over. "You look a bit faint."

She sat and watched the land became an olive strip on the horizon. Beyond it the sun grazed the green wooded hills of the Estate. Baobabs were silhouetted, so sharp they were stencils. A white-tailed tropicbird sliced the sky.

"Look," she pointed. "You almost never see them so close to land." But no one seemed to hear.

The wind filled their ears. Storm remained at the tiller. They faced the horizon in silence. Lucy rose and padded expertly to the bow of the boat. She had been on boats since she was a small child, she supposed, and like Storm she did not reach for the riggings or the rail for balance. She folded her body next to her brother's and sat cross-legged in her bikini and her kikhoi.

Julia put her mouth to her ear, to be heard through the wind. "They need time together," she said. "They hardly ever see each other."

"But they'll both be in England soon."

Julia drew away. "You'll all be in England. But that doesn't mean you'll see each other."

She searched her aunt's face for censure. Julia wore sunglasses; her lips were pale with sun protector.

She turned her gaze to a parchment sky. The clouds of the Kusi were gone. She felt the presence of the Indian Ocean summer she would never know. Summer on the coast was a different world, Storm had told her, with nights so hot Charlie slept in front of the refrigerator. They heard trumpeter hornbills every day when they came to feed on the berries of the neem trees. Ghost crabs invaded the house and had to be chased from the curtains with a broom. Biting fleas bred in the swimming pool; Storm plucked them out with a kitchen sieve. With the summer came dolphins and Portuguese men-of-war, the jellyfish with a fierce sting and for which the only relief was human urine applied straight away. "It's a shame you won't see it," he'd said to her. She hoped he would say something else, then, of the order of what she was feeling, an abstract desolation that haunted and frightened her at once — *I wish you could stay; I wish we could stay here together; I wish we could have met somewhere else, as something else* — but he did not.

When they returned to shore she had two missed calls on her phone, a nameless number with the country's international dialing code on the screen. As if on cue, it rang again.

"Rob at Reef Encounters here." She heard the American vowels of the Costa Rica sport fishing T-shirt man who had accosted her. "I've got a friend coming to the coast to fish. Let's have a beer. Tomorrow."

She walked on the beach from Moholo to Reef Encounters. These walks were never the same. Details inserted and erased themselves — the eastern-bearded scrub robins posted in the thinnest casuarina branches, calling methodically to each other, the corpuscles of sea-weed that popped under feet. Greenshanks scanned the tideline. At the waves' edge the birds hesitated, bounded back, then scattered into flight. The two black eyes of ghost crabs appeared from holes underneath her feet, then vanished at her approach.

She climbed the stairs from the beach to the deck. At the top step she watched a figure step out from a Range Rover. His paleness shocked her. His very existence. She had forgotten he might be real.

They sat at a table. After the waiter had taken their order he remained still for half a minute, looking at the ocean in that proprietorial way she had observed before in him, as if the ocean were not real, and certainly not a marvel, as if the ocean owed him something.

"I can't go back to Gariseb, can I?"

Anthony sighed, almost a fatherly sound.

"Where do I go?"

"Home."

And where is that?

"I've already been relieved of my post, haven't I?"

"I told you that was the likely outcome." He looked at her. "Do you really want to go back?"

She could see a reflection of herself in his sunglasses, retreating, small and wan. Andy, Rafael, Aisha, Aisha's camel — she would never see them again. They would not be surprised. They would think she was traumatized. That for all her experience, she couldn't take it.

"Why are you here?"

"I have some things to attend to on the coast. You were on my way."

"You have bigger fish to fry?" There was no hurt in her voice. That would be childish. This man was not her father, she reminded herself. In fact he was three years younger than her. Yet he exerted an authority that worked like a spell.

"He found me by accident. I'm sure of it," she said.

"What did you say to him?"

"Nothing."

"We have them all under surveillance."

"What are they planning?"

"Random attacks. Soft targets — they've already done the police barracks and the traffic control cops."

Soft targets. "You mean hotels, private houses."

"Probably, but they're too intent on creating pre-election chaos to go for straight attacks. The coast is the edge of Islam. They're trying to push the edge further, as far as it can go."

She remembered this phrase, *the edge of Islam,* from the briefing he had given her after her evacuation from Gariseb, before she'd boarded the plane for Bahari ya Manda. This was a part of the world that — if you discounted slavery — had seen the peaceful cohabitation of Christians and Muslims since the arrival of the Arab traders in 800 CE. Now all that was about to change. Pop-up mosques had been established up and down the coast, everyone knew, and in the smallest villages women were suddenly pressed to wear headscarves. Tiny boys in kanzus and kofia could be seen walking alongside the road to new Madrassa, their satchels stuffed with the Quran. The edge of Islam was seeping far inland, too, to highland villages where decades before Catholic missionaries from Italy and Ireland had built tin-roofed churches.

"Can you protect us?"

"That's what I'm doing now, here, to the best of my ability. You need to leave."

"Aren't we worth protecting?"

"It doesn't work like that. You're not a head of state. We haven't got an army stationed here. We are in constant dialogue with upper echelons of government, with the military. No one wants a repeat of the election violence. No one wants an Islamist insurrection. That I can assure you of."

She recognized the detached note in his gaze, the wanton clarity of it. The cause and effect calculations he made were familiar. They almost reassured her, as if she'd made them herself. The disappointment she felt was personal — it was this that confused her. She realized she had liked Anthony. But this business had nothing to do with *liking* — a poor, cool word in any case.

"You should leave now and take the daily flight while it's still going. Your family needs to go, too. Tell them to drive. It's still possible by road, but in a week's time I'm not so sure." He paused. "You've done everything you can here."

"I haven't done anything at all. There's nothing to say. He's not involved in anything, apart from the banking collapse."

Anthony gave her a level look. "Perhaps that's the case."

"Do you know something about my family you're not telling me?" She was shocked to have used the word *family*. How easy the propriety of it sounded in her mouth.

Half an hour later Anthony rose, having delivered the information he had come to give her. They did not shake hands or say goodbye. She watched him go, in his tropical uniform of beige trousers, a beaded leather belt, light blue shirt. He could be any Englishman down on the coast for business, along with the Italian package tourists, the South African deep-sea fishermen, the German backpackers.

But they were all gone now. The coast was draining — of Embassy staff in the highlands, of the United Nations and World Bank people, who had for years come to the coast on weekend breaks in the all-inclusives, had brought their young families to play on the beach. They had been issued directives forbidding them to travel to the coast. Tourists were not forbidden, exactly, but found their travel insurance invalidated. Everyone had left, out of fear, apart from the people who belonged here.

At Reef Encounters, at Fitzgerald's or Baharini, the beachside bar, the kikhoi-wearing barmen apologize, their hands empty. A thin, desperate smile. *Hakuna wageni* they say, there are no guests. At Reef Encounters there are three waiters for each customer, who find they can't finish a bottle of beer without a man in an orange

264

and purple shirt swooping in and taking it, mouthfuls sloshing in the bottom. Up and down the coast men selling coconuts and women minding stalls selling kikhoi and khangas proffer similar pained smiles. *Hakuna wageni.*

L ucy roared through the gate at the wheel of Julia's Land Cruiser. "They've closed the road from Kilindoni," she shouted through the window before she even came to a stop.

"Where have you been?" Julia barked. "Why didn't you call?"

"I told you, I went to Tasha's. How was I supposed to know they were going to put up a bloody roadblock?" Lucy opened the door and climbed out. "It didn't seem that serious. They didn't even want money."

"That's when it's serious," Julia said.

She and Lucy stood by the edge of the pool together. On a different day, in a different country, they might have been contemplating going for a swim.

Julia peeled away to tell the servants to stay overnight in the quarters rather than run the roadblocks, even though they all knew they wouldn't — they had families to get home to, children to feed.

"Was it really that easy to get through?"

"It wasn't hard. Nobody threatened me. It's interethnic, anyway. I'm not sure how much they care about white people."

"White people are an ethnic group in this conflict."

Lucy peered at her. "How would you know?"

"Because I'm an outsider. These things are obvious to me."

Lucy dropped her eyes.

"What's the matter?"

"I just have this feeling sometimes." She raised her eyes. There was a frankness in them she hadn't seen before. "That you know things we don't. Or you know more about this place than you let on."

She swallowed. "That might be the case. But I haven't lived here all my life as you have." She returned Lucy's direct look. "Do you have any guns in the house?"

"A couple of rifles somewhere, gathering dust. Why?"

"I think we should get them."

"You can't be serious."

"We need to put Charlie inside. They'll kill him."

"You think people will come here?" The way Lucy said *people*, the word emerged a strangled version of itself.

"Yes, I do. I think they'll come soon. In the next few days."

Lucy's eyes darkened. They were like Claude glass, she thought, those small black mirrors nineteenth century aesthetes used to carry for parsing landscape. She'd seen an exhibition of them once, in the V&A. Reality had a furtive relationship with Lucy's eyes; it longed to be reflected in her, yet locked itself away.

Lucy exhaled as if she'd been holding her breath. "I knew it." She stared at her. "You should have told us."

"Lucy, I don't know anything. It's just I've worked in conflict situations. I can feel certain things coming."

She didn't reply. "I'm going to call Storm." Lucy fished in her bag for her mobile, then scowled at her screen. "He's at Evan's, I guess. It says no signal. That's weird."

"Is there a landline?"

She shook her head. "No one has landlines anymore."

They found two rifles, a .308 and a .375 — hunting rifles, the latter she knew was powerful enough to bring down an elephant — in the store room at the end of the corridor, along with two boxes of ammunition, their cardboard limp with humidity.

"I need some oil." She slid the bolt in and out of the action. It creaked with a thin layer of rust.

Lucy stood back and folded her arms over her chest. "How do you know how to fire a gun?"

"Basic training for field medics."

"Have you ever lined up another human being in those sights?"

"No, but I will if I have to."

Lucy must have heard something in her voice. Her mouth opened and closed, but no words emerged.

"I'm going to teach you how to fire the .308. I'll take the bigger rifle." She pointed the barrel to the floor, her hand clamped around the action.

Lucy flickered her eyes toward it. "I hate guns."

"It's loaded but I haven't chambered a round. You don't need to worry."

"So what exactly did they teach you?"

"Just the basics. The SAS did it. The guys who trained us could have killed any of us in about fifteen different ways."

"You're so . . . capable. We're just playboys. Play*girls*." Lucy laughed, that bright chime of hers.

"You are like me. Or you will be."

"I'm not sure I want to be like you."

She didn't get a chance to ask Lucy what she meant. The crunch of gravel signalled a car in the drive. Bill was home.

A power cut lingered into the evening. There was no diesel for the generator. She and Julia sat on the baraza, side by side, looking out to sea from a house lit by lamps.

"Did you know the name the Arabs gave this coast was The Sweet People?" Julia said. "Because the people here could be bought for the price of a piece of candy."

"No," she said. "I didn't know that."

"They carted thousands of people from here to Iraq to be slaves. They mounted a rebellion, you know, in Iraq — the Zanj uprising. So not so sweet after all."

Out to sea only two or three lights of fishing boats glinted. The ocean was black lacquer under a thickening moon. She pictured the arrival of a flotilla, a thousand dhows from Arabia come to sell them at market.

Orion hung on the lip of the land. It was coming back, from the south. By summertime — Christmas and New Year — it would hang overhead, its lopsided warrior suspended.

"The stars look strange tonight, don't you think?" Julia stared at the sky. "They're brighter."

"It's because the power's out. All down the coast, probably." The power cut would only affect the houses connected to the shaky grid, houses owned by whites. Africans would carry on with their single kerosene lamps, their makaa braziers. She pictured the coast at that moment from the air: a dark strip next to a taffeta sea, a necklace of small fires hemming its perimeter.

"You know, I never missed her." Julia gave her a barren look. "I'm sorry to say that, but it's true."

She didn't know why Julia was speaking like this now. She might have had a drink. In any case she didn't want to talk about her mother now. When she had first arrived in the Dhow House she'd been hungry for her aunt's memories, for anything at all that would link her to their family. Now she was afraid of what Julia would say about her, about them.

"She didn't approve of me marrying here, of what became of me," Julia said. "She was judgmental; she was *political*." There was an accusation in the word.

She couldn't remember her mother being political. Independent, yes, argumentative. Her mother had had a contrary streak she knew she hadn't inherited, but she did have a certain independence of mind. It struck her that for Julia, the two — independence of mind, being political — might be one and the same. That Julia's analysis would go no further than that: politics was an ornery, wayward application of the mind, one which only those who had no money, or who wanted it, indulged in.

"Your mother believed in making her own way in the world. She couldn't accept that I'd married a wealthy man. That I expected to stay married to him. The last time I saw her she said, Julia, you're a trophy wife, and when you're fifty he'll just replace you with a younger trophy wife. What will you do then? I said, you don't understand. You haven't kept a man. Family is everything for Bill. He will never leave his family, which is to say he'll never leave me." Julia gave a small, rough laugh.

"Did you love him?"

Julia gave her a blank look.

"Bill. Your husband," she added, for measure.

Julia looked out to sea. Her expression had hardened. In her anger she looked so much like her mother.

"Your mother had no luck."

"There's no such thing," she said.

"What do you call it, then, what happened to her?"

"I call it what happens."

She returned her aunt's clear gaze. She shook her head, as if to express dismay, which was real, in a sense — a bottomless sense of malady on behalf of her mother, and Julia, and the story she had told herself, the stories we all tell ourselves, insistently, until they are required reading.

After dinner they went to bed early. Storm had not come home. He would stay at Evan's, Lucy said after dinner when Grace was clearing the food away. He'd left it too late to drive home in any case. The curfew had been brought forward the day before. Now everyone apart from police, army and the long-distance lorries had to be off the roads by ten p.m.

She slept for two hours, then woke, then slept again. The house groaned in the wind. From the beach she heard the trill of curlews. She rose and looked out the window. There was no moon, no familiar lights of the fishing dhows that trawled by night for shark and filusi beyond the reef's edge.

The second time she woke, she was out of bed and on her feet in a second, running, fully clothed — she had gone to sleep in shorts, a T-shirt, her running shoes beside her bed.

It was just as she expected: the sound of wheels on the gravel, Charlie barking, the crisp retort of gunshot, Charlie silenced. Not even a whine.

She lunged into the closet, grabbed the guns. She ran to Storm's bedroom and flung it open. His empty bed answered her.

Lucy was in her room, awake. *Get up*, she hissed. *Get dressed.* Then Julia and Bill. *It's me*, she called before she opened the door. Then, as if this was not enough, *It's Rebecca.*

They appeared at the door, their faces unusually pale in the dark. "Rebecca, what's that in your hand?" Julia said.

"Stay here. Don't move. Don't resist."

Her aunt and uncle didn't question her. They didn't understand, yet, what was happening.

The house knew. The house had not let them in. The alarm system was yet to blare, the heavy wooden door stood firm. The house had been waiting for this all along, ever since it was built. It did not shudder against their onslaught. It shrank back, demure and withholding, ready to guard its honour.

But now three men stood in the living room, their faces covered with dark scarves. Their eyes glittered.

"What are you going to do with that?" his voice said. "Did they train you?"

She stared back at them.

He made a small gesture to the men he emerged from, just like that day in Gariseb, materializing out of their bodies. The others were more robust than him yet they deferred to him, subtly. She saw the right hand of one of these men twitch. He was not accustomed to staying still.

"What do you want?"

"You must leave the coast. The Kufir cannot live here."

"You will never evict them," she said. "There are too many."

To be talking to him again felt strangely calming. There was no reaction, either from him or the men who flanked him.

A noise erupted. She couldn't tell where it came from. She swivelled her head to where her uncle stood at the top of the stairs. His shirt was loose from his trousers. His face had a pallor. In the dark it was the dingy grey of the jahazi sail.

The noise was not the shot, which was nearly soundless, but its ricochet. One man lurched sideways — it was he who had fired the shot, the one she returned, on muscle memory. She will not remember shouldering, or firing. The men were running backward in the house, toward its open door, dragging the man she had hit. Ali was invisible — where was he? She looked behind to the top of the stairs. Her uncle was upright, but something was wrong.

Rebecca.

It seemed to take a long time, this glance, or look, over her shoulder. She saw her aunt trying to hang on to her uncle, his shirt ruched underneath her arm. Julia was bent over him, her fair hair and slight frame, her blond hair folded over his face. Then her uncle was on the floor at the top of the stairs.

They covered the hundred kilometres between Kilindoni and Bahari ya Manda in an hour, in a private ambulance with its purple flashing lights.

From the window of the ambulance she saw the sky pale into dawn. Outside the city were grassy, sodden rice fields. African sacred ibis nudged through them. The birds were black and white with a mask on their faces. Ibis were probers, she remembered, their straw-like beaks suction small creatures, fungi, moisture from the grass. At sunrise the ibis took flight in a stately elevation.

By dawn the outskirts of the city were awake. Men in kanzus walked accompanied by women in black buibuis, their hems brushed with dust. A wooden cart drawn by oxen was piled with green bananas. The oxen shuffled down the road as intercity buses streamed by them. There was not an angle in the town from which the sea was not visible. The grey wedge of a supertanker devoured the horizon. Bahari ya Manda had the best natural harbour on the coast. A ten-storey ship could park next to a cashew nut kiosk, where it would overlook the battements of the crumbling fort built by the Portuguese five hundred years before.

The ambulance driver veered into a wide road lined by mango trees. This was the suburb where all the expats lived, near the international school and the private hospital run by the Aga Khan.

Beside her, Bill was conscious, although sedated. He tried to rise from time to time. His eyes sought out hers, his mouth forming and reforming words. She offered her doctor's reassurances. *Be quiet, don't strain yourself. You have to rest.* Then, just as they pulled up at the emergency entrance, she heard him clearly. *I understand, Rebecca,* he whispered, over and over. *I understand.*

The hospital's cement floors were polished to a dark, translucent onyx. A warm wind that carried the tang of the sea blew down its corridors. Latticed sections of its coral frame were open to the air.

Julia and Lucy were slumped on chairs in the corridor. She was talking to the trauma doctor when Storm walked in.

"Where have you been all night?"

Julia cast a look at her. This was her question, by rights.

"At Evan's."

Storm's voice was hollow. He sounded half himself. "Why didn't you call me?"

Lucy answered for her. "We forgot about you." Her lips pulsed with a flickering distrust.

Storm walked out of the dim corridor and disappeared into the white blare of sunlight at its end. They all watched him go. He did not look back.

The drive from Bahari ya Manda was a negative copy of the one they had made in the middle of the night two days before. Now the driver overtook languidly. Julia sat in front, holding voluble conversations about the increasing price of water and petrol with him. She watched as Julia gesticulated emphatically but abstractly, unable to hear her words over the rush of air through the windows as she called people on her mobile and conducted terse, animated conversations as she made plans for the funeral.

Zebu cows grazed next to the road. Goats and their child pursuers clattered on the half-weeded paths on the shoulder of the road. She thought she saw a bat hawk slice the air, swooping from a tree to an electricity line on the other side of the road.

She missed the ordinary life of the road, which had vanished with the crisis: the mango baskets and jute bags of makaa stationed along the road, the Saturday markets, with their piles of clothing set out on the ground on burlap bags, smoke from boiled *mahindi* — charcoal roasted corn on the cob — the men who walked by the side of the road, shirts rippling in the wake of buses and trucks streaming past them. She even missed the policemen who waited in the shade next to invisible speed bumps or the motorcycle taxi drivers who flung themselves headlong onto the road without looking in an attempt to die young.

A village wedding had gone ahead despite the lockdown, she saw. They passed its tottering marquee and morose-looking guests sitting on plastic chairs with their elbows on their knees, music hurling from a hastily erected pyramid of speakers that looked as if it would collapse before the end of the day. She saw the thin minarets of mosques painted mint and apricot, the maze of roadside shambas and their cargo of bitter kale and pumpkin.

Her uncle was gone. She tried to absorb the fact. The bullet had hit his shoulder. He would have been back to normal within a month. But his heart rebelled against the intrusion. The heart attack happened as he was being prepped for theatre. Bill would have had no idea he had a heart condition. It was not at all uncommon that such conditions went undiagnosed. Left-dominant arrhythmogenic cardiomyopathy, the doctor at Bahari ya Manda had confirmed. She had studied it but never diagnosed it in a patient. They had tried adrenalin, the defibrillator, even CPR. She watched from the back of the theatre, feeling increasingly desperate. She knew — she would think this later — that he was not going to respond. Sometimes you just knew.

She felt pity for him, also a nameless emotion that panicked her if she approached it. She took refuge in ordinary shame. It was an armed robbery attempt, insurgents looking for loot, that was all. It had happened so fast and it had been as violent as she had feared, but neither had she been convinced it would really happen. She had thought she could protect them. And if she couldn't, that she would save them.

They passed the saline flats of mangroves. Giant egrets perched in their branches, looking out to sea. The mudflats shone like slate. *The coast gets under your skin*, Margaux's voice floated to her, an uncharacteristically sentimental pronouncement she made one of those nights at Reef Encounters. *You want to get away, you say it's too hot to think, nothing ever happens here, but then as soon as you leave you start planning to return.*

They turned off at the Estate road, whose entrance was flanked with two pickup trucks of armed security guards. They passed the signs for Oleander House, Zanj Mansion. Margaux was right; the coast was an anesthetic. For a while, it had been possible to forget oneself here, along with the world, and history. But Ali and Al-Nur had returned history to its shores. History had rediscovered this somnolent backwater. It would prod it into the now.

They passed through the gate of the house. On either side the servants were lined up, hands pressed together, faces drawn. As the car came to a halt she began to hear a low murmur. They were chanting a single word, so low it was almost under their breath: *Pole.*

A mound of freshly dug earth marked where Charlie the dog lay. Storm must have been there and had buried him. On his grave was a bouquet of bougainvillea. Lucy got out of the car and went to stand over the fresh earth. Julia shot out of the passenger seat and into the house.

She hesitated on the drive. Lucy's eyes were hidden behind sunglasses. Her cheeks were stained with dried tears.

"Aren't you coming in, Rebecca?"

She followed Lucy into the house. In the kitchen Julia stood with her back against the breakfast bar. She gave them a plain look. "I have so much to do."

Storm was there. He had been waiting near the infinity pool.

"The man," he said. "What did you say to him?"

"I told him not to harm the family. That no good would come of it."

"Did you know they were coming?" Storm said.

"You weren't even *here*." Lucy's face was ashen.

Storm ignored her. "Why do you speak Arabic?"

"I have to, for my work. I've worked for five years in Arabic-speaking countries."

She looked at Julia. Her thought was that her aunt might do something — take the whole thing away with a wave of her hand, with the demure diamond wedding ring that clutched her fourth finger. But Julia's eyes were glossy. Her gaze was pitched over and beyond them, out to sea.

Storm had not looked at her — really looked at her — since she had arrived. She sought him out — tried to find his eyes. He turned away. He no longer looked like himself, or he did, but like an effigy, a statue that had been abandoned in the rain.

This is what you get, the voice inside her head savage, for the first time in months, *for having anything to do with him.* He is a *boy.* Her rage was so close to the surface of her skin she worried it would spill out through her eyes.

"Don't be ridiculous," Julia said, finally. She was relieved to hear the authority in her aunt's voice. "Rebecca has nothing to do with any of this."

They stood in the living room in a triangle: her, Storm, Lucy, angled toward Julia, who now stood in front of them, who was not the same woman they had known until only two days before. It was hard to know what had changed. A hollow grandeur had taken up residence. But there was something else, indefinite, which was not engineered by grief.

Julia walked across the living room, toward the pool. She wore patchwork linen trousers and silver thong sandals with little wings on their straps, where they clutched her ankles. She walked into the garden. They watched as a trio of Amani sunbirds unruffled themselves from the neem tree and hovered for a moment in the air. They followed Julia to the edge of the garden before shooting up into the sky in a flash of a second. They watched the birds disappear into the air.

At five thirty the sun is levering itself out of the sea over the horizon, somewhere near Zanzibar. The dugongs and green turtles move beneath its mantle, wading through olive depths where the sun never penetrates. In smooth pockets of coral, leopard cowries wink and close their single eye against the day.

Today she will run on the beach. It is her thirty-eighth birthday. She has told no one in the house. Such things are irrelevant now.

They are all leaving. In two days' time Julia will fly to the capital with Bill's body. Storm and Lucy will drive, a seven-hour journey. Tomorrow she will fly to the capital and then take a flight to London. She knows now there will be no visit to the embassy in the suburbs, and no return to Gariseb.

She runs in the semi-darkness, a head torch affixed to her forehead. The sky is lightening quickly. She wants to be away, to be somewhere she can be innocent again. But she fears her departure, too. After the next twenty-four hours she may never be in the same room as Storm again. She will never be able to put out her hand and encounter the edges of his body.

The beach is empty. Not even the nocturnal spear-fishermen with their buckets full of live wounded octopus are there.

Bill's face hovers in her mind. She can see him in Storm's face now. For some reason she could not point to the resemblance while he was alive. Their likeness is in the shape of his eyes, which Storm has inherited — glass-blue eyes that look upon the world so searchingly, at times, for someone who has never been tested.

She wants to greet the day with resolve and exertion. She runs where the sand is soft, so that she has to work harder. Cloud presses in. In another minute a squall has drifted over her and she is soaked through. She will keep going because it is her birthday, and to turn away from the storm would be to gainsay the year, to live under a mantel of cowardice and lack of resolve, of failure. She keeps running, into the force of the storm as it engulfs the coral islets of the coast in its murk, into the next year of her life.

For the whole of her last day in the house they skirted each other. They were bound by an unspoken pact not to all be in the same space at once.

She barely saw Storm. All day Lucy did not emerge from her room. She saw Grace mount the stairs with a tray of tea and toast. Julia was always on the phone. As soon as she put it down she had text messages from people who had to be rung. Friends of Bill's arrived at the door and sat on the stools around the breakfast counter and stared into space.

In the evening the kitchen was still full of mourners. She went to her room and lay down. Her state of being was entirely unfamiliar to her. She felt sluggish but alarmed, tired but awake.

There was a knock on her door. She thought it might be Lucy. Of all of them, she might say goodbye to her. Her intention was to melt out of the house the following day, as if she had never been there. She had considered leaving before dawn, for them to discover her room empty, but this seemed too obvious an admission of guilt.

She rose from the bed and opened the door. She stared into his eyes and saw something raw and silent there. He stepped back from the door. She understood from his eyes that she should follow him.

In the darkened corridor they slinked through slats of light. The moon had risen early and was nearly full. From the kitchen came a murmur of voices.

She followed him to his room, closing the door behind her. He sat down on the bed and did not look at her.

A burning, a cold fire, took hold inside her. She was faint. She hadn't eaten properly in two days.

For some months afterward she will not be able to approach what happens next. The memory sealed in a ring of fire.

She sits down next to him. She knows she should not be there, that he perhaps hates or fears her, but she finds she has entered an infantile state. She has regressed. She can't move. She needs to be only a body now. There is nothing else she wants to be.

She can't breathe. For some reason her breaths can't come fast enough. She puts her head between her legs, her knees press on her ears. For a second she considers closing them and crushing her head, in a vise. When she rises he is looking at her. He wants to feel compassion, she sees, but really he just wants it to stop.

They are so disoriented, and she so exhausted from hyperventilating, that they make the mistake, for the first time, of falling asleep in his bed.

She has a dream that his father is dying. Storm gives him the kiss of life, pinching his nose, tilting his head back and blowing through his airway. Then it is her turn. She puts her lips over Bill's, stretching her mouth to avoid his lips. But Bill is dead. His hair is beginning to lose its sheen. They turn to each other and continue the kiss of life. They are kissing, his father's corpse between them.

This is how his Julia finds them in the morning.

She woke, up and up, as if surfacing from a great depth, gasping for air.

What are you doing? He is a child! He is your cousin!

Julia had been brought back to life. She was above her now, a towering blond God.

Why? Julia's eyes were black and scorched.

The three of them had levitated downstairs. She would not remember getting from the bedroom to her room, where she must have grabbed her backpack containing her passport, leaving her bag with all her possessions under the bed.

Lucy was among them, wild-haired, just woken up by shouting. *What's happening? What's going on?*

She said this over and over, but no one heard her.

Ask him who he loves? Ask him!

She would not remember the blow, but she would remember that suddenly she was on her knees. Then, like a sprinter, she was up and running.

It was eight o'clock. Already the heat was thick. The askaris sat in their security huts outside empty houses and watched her go, thinking it was an ordinary run. They had seen her before in the mornings on these dusty roads. She was the only moving thing the watchmen would see that day. There were few cars; the buses had been suspended.

She ran past Oleander House and Zanj Mansion. They were empty, their swimming pools already choked with mbambakofi leaves. In the fields of the Estate, Klaas's cuckoo called its plangent song, *Won't you come? Won't you come?* A lament, perhaps, for all those mornings on the coast when the days had dawned golden with tourists and money. She ran with her passport in one hand and her phone in the other, although it threatened to slip out of her grip with sweat. No vehicle came to follow her or return her to the house. There was the day, the heat congealing, a heron flying with its neck tucked in, wings pounding the air. Behind her, the Dhow House was affronted by her sudden departure, but also satisfied. It closed its eyes and turned to face the sea.

IX

NORTHERN CARMINE BEE-EATER

"**S**omething is keeping them apart."

Daniel squints into the early morning sun. We stare into the branches of the brachystegia forest, which dissolve against the sky. The Fischer's turacos have flown away.

I am not used to the heat anymore. I am covered in a thin film of sweat. The forest bubbles with sound around us. Green barbet, forest batis, golden pipit — the small, secretive birds of the coast. Many of them are endangered. Some species, like the Sarara River cisticola, have not been observed in forty years and are thought to be extinct.

By nine o'clock the birds have quietened. Daniel and I walk side by side down one of the sandy roads just outside the protected forest. It is fenced, to keep the elephant from trampling the crops of the villagers who live nestled against its perimeter, but also in a vain attempt to keep poachers out. As we walk Daniel stops, ducks into the holes that have been clipped in the fence's wire, shakes a tree or rattles the undergrowth and emerges with green wire in his hand.

"Snares," he says. "They are eating the sifaka duiker to extinction."

Daniel has lived and worked in this forest all his life. He knows it better than anyone alive. "Before, the elephant were never threatened. Now they are killed for their tusks, which are almost worthless anyway, they are so small." Daniel has come across the forest elephant many times when walking. "They are very shy; they vanish into the forest."

Beyond the fence the forest is a mesh of lianas, of ferns and brambles and parasitic bromeliads. Tiny amphibians suck on their moisture, curled on gold haunches. Daniel finds one for me. "Pygmy golden forest frog," he announces.

We find his motorcycle, which he had stashed in a mesh of trees so that it would not be stolen. We hop on and drive the loamy road that takes us to the coastal highway.

There we pass light blue–shirted policemen dozing under mango trees. Jute bags of makaa line the road. Motorcycle taxis driven by an army of thin young men wearing oversize sunglasses carry women in red and green khangas, yellow plastic water-carriers, baskets of fruit. The smell of the sea is never far away.

Daniel drops me at the crossroads. From here I will get a minibus back to Kilindoni. We say goodbye.

"Thank you," he takes my payment and sees my tip. "Bless you," he adds.

I wave him goodbye, this grandfather on a motorcycle. The next time I see him again — if there is a next time — he will squint at me. He will not remember. He will say, with that admonishing giggle of his, "All white people look the same."

At the Kilindoni Club not enough time has passed for the faded sign to be painted, with its yellowing cattle egrets nosing through mangroves. The seller of stale peanuts, three teeth in his mouth, is still outside the entrance though, still waving, calling after me, *mama, rafiki; mama, rafiki.*

Not enough time has passed for me to feel this place is foreign or exotic. Although there have been two and a half years in the interim — years of emergency rooms, nightshifts, serums and injections, the neat cavities of gunshot wounds, the tear of knives renting skin in A&E departments that increasingly resemble triage stations for alcoholics. On Friday and Saturday nights, men in football jerseys sit slumped between echocardiograms and water coolers, waiting for the friends they have borne to the hospital after last orders, casualties of a weekly war.

I glimpse myself in the mirror here, putting on or taking off my swimsuit. In this country the most defining feature of my existence is my colour. Ivory, albumen, sickly pale. White woman; white woman ageing rapidly; white woman thinking there is still time. Here the heat congeals time, delivers it to you like a gelatinous soup and says, drink. I catch myself anticipating the next moment: the moment when I will have a cold beer, the moment when I will bask in unreflective happiness. We live in a state of constant anticipation. Time is a surprise delivered in moment-sized parcels.

I feel more alive here. Many people do, in African countries where life is not yet governed by the delusion that we can control everything. Africa is dangerous and people of my kind — people who have been brought up in relative safety — gorge themselves on the elixir of sudden disruption. I am enlivened by its detail; goats grazing on garbage, the milky sludge of open latrines, the signs announcing free fresh water — *maji ya bure* — dispensed at mosques. Here I am jolted by a thousand injustices every day.

I go running on the same road as I did before but stop short of Oleander House and Zanj Mansion. The same askaris come leaping toward me, having finished the nightshift, raising their spears and clicking the heels of their rubber sandals in the air. They shout in Swahili: *Keep going, sister!* In the Usimama supermarket I queue behind a blond woman in a green dress. I stare at her neck, her cheek, until a slice of her cheekbone reveals it is not Julia. She divides her time between Durban and Mozambique now, Lucy told me. Bill left her more than enough money to buy a house in a suburb of the city frequented by surfers and black mambas. "You have to be careful they don't breed under the swimming pool," Lucy said. She meant the snakes, not the surfers.

Lucy didn't tell me where Storm was and I didn't ask. He could be in London, working for one of his father's business associates, or living on his legacies. The country's whites often scatter to South

Africa or Australia. They gravitate to places of warmth and beauty. Understandably.

Lately the whites are not welcome. The president of the republic has discovered the advantages of anti-colonial rhetoric. "It will never get as bad as Zimbabwe —" I overhear whites saying this when discussing the situation, their voices strident but also tinged by dread. Although the president himself has nothing against the whites — this is what Bill told me during one of those sparring matches which passed for conversations we had late at night in the Dhow House. He accepts that there can be such a creature as an African with white skin.

Even the last round of political violence failed to disperse them completely. A year and a half ago the advances of Al-Nur were repelled by the army, with assistance from the US and British military and intelligence services. This was kept quiet; it was considered an embarrassment to the government that the former colonists of the country were needed to quell the revolt. Ali and his men may have survived, melting across the border, or they may have been killed only a few hundred metres away, in Kilindoni Harbour.

But before foreign forces were brought in, Al-Nur fighters walked into the Baridi supermarket complex in Bahari ya Manda and sprayed bullets into the aisles, puncturing microwaves, jars of peanut butter, lungs and intestines. From motorbikes, they shot at random into a crowd at the market, a place where Christians and Muslims have met to do business for two millennia, killing three Christian market-stall holders and a German woman on holiday from Hamburg. The police mounted a sluggish, incoherent response, and Ali and his like sped away on the back of motorcycles, changing conveyance three times before arriving at a safe house in a suburb of the city.

I've been avoiding Reef Encounters. Now I slink in the entrance as if I expect to be recognized. But by whom? Margaux is long gone. Bill is dead. Julia is in South Africa. I wonder where Evan is? Evan might have stayed.

The place is unchanged with its serene, commanding view, the fishing boats that rise and fall on the breakers, their outriggers singing in the wind. The bar is full of people down from the highlands for Christmas. The nights are warmer now — twenty-seven degrees. A table of young women sit outside on the deck. I remember these people, their look, which I have never seen anywhere else. They look English but simultaneously not. Their hair is too glossy, their noses are small and upturned, like the noses of children, but their bodies are tanned and hard.

The last time I was here was the day I met Anthony. He had one last thing he needed to tell me. But not before he tried to allay my fears.

"What you're doing is very important to us," he had said. "You're a natural, as much as you might hate to hear it. You're one of us."

"I'm not. Wrong background, wrong accent. I don't come from a class bred for treachery."

"It's not like that anymore."

"You said you have something to show me."

He reached into the leather backpack he carried everywhere and drew out a peach-coloured folder. He swung open its front cover. Inside was a sheaf of pages. Between them, the edges of photographs peeked out.

"Your uncle knows a businessman from Bahari ya Manda; in fact he's from Dar es Salaam. He has an apartment in Shanghai."

"And?"

"Your uncle is trading in illegal wildlife parts."

"I don't think so. My uncle is a director of the biggest conservation agencies in Africa."

"But these days he can't resist making a fortune from being above suspicion."

I shook my head. "Since when do you care about wild animals?"

"Since we discovered the profits are being funnelled to Al-Nur."

"He might be into land deals, greasing the palms of politicians. But financing terrorism? That's impossible."

"He's not aware of where the money is going. The horn and ivory he's selling is being consolidated into shipments. It's the shipment we're concerned about."

"So he's not . . ." I searched for the word, "culpable?"

"Well, that depends. Implicated in illegal wildlife trafficking: yes; arms dealing and aiding and abetting terrorism: no. The problem is," he said, raising his eyes to mine, his manner ever so slightly seen-it-all-before, "when you have so many business interests, you can never quite control where their tentacles will go."

He extracted more pages from the folder. On these were email logs in small print, copies of statements from bank accounts in Guernsey, photos of Bill in Dar es Salaam with an Arab-looking man, photos of the same man meeting an Asian-looking man in Dubai. I swept my eyes over them quickly. CIA surveillance details, national security service files, letterhead bearing the logo of the US State Department.

"How did you find out?"

"Routine surveillance. Guernsey authorities have recently signed an agreement with us." He stared into the distance for a minute, his face impassive. "We were watching his contact in Dar. So it was an accident, a confluence of two circumstances, you could say. Not that this is a priority. We're too busy right now with straight terrorism."

I looked at the images again. All the details were pristine, so sharp they seemed to leap out of the photo. A breakfast buffet behind the men, papaya, pineapple, their spiny tops, the slumped postures of bona fide tourists, a woman wearing an expensive-looking watch and a crisp shirt, thin and devouring. Delphine.

"That's his sister."

"Yes, she's currently supplementing her income with wildlife trophies from Zambia and Mozambique. Bill gave her a very useful contact in the man from Dar it seems."

"What will you do?"

"I don't think we'll move on it." He scowled. "Arguably the financing of terrorist groups from illegal wildlife parts is the growing criminal activity in this part of Africa. But we don't have the capacity to tackle it, never mind the jurisdiction. We might pass it to the national authorities but it depends who they are. Everything's on hold until the election. I don't need to stress that this is confidential."

"Who am I going to tell? My uncle?"

He gave me a level look. He might think I had been converted, that I considered myself one of them now.

"Why are you telling me?" I pressed.

"Because we owe you. We thought you should know."

"I don't think you operate like that. Dues to pay, good turns to honour." I shook my head. "I've been no use to you here."

"It was never a priority, really. On the other hand, what you did in Gariseb —" his face became formal, composed "— that was very helpful."

Anthony appraised me then as they all did. I had been wrong to think they took me seriously or that I could escape my involvement with them, what I had done. I was a chess piece, a plinth of black lacquer. If he could manoeuvre me onto the right square, he could take the king. If not now, then eventually, when the moment was right.

On the walk back through the village I pass a gate I recognize. *Kaskazi*, the blue and white ceramic nameplate on the coral wall announces. In the background is a faded drawing of a dhow on the ocean. The house belongs to the man who makes the country's ice cream. We came to a party here, the four of us — Storm, Lucy, Evan, and I. On a patio by the pool people writhed and puckered like the speared octopus I saw boys on the beach carry in buckets.

In the house there is a bathroom, an ensuite off a bedroom

containing an enormous teak bed. The floor underneath our feet trembled with the bass from the speakers.

His skin was always cool and pale, even in the heat. I licked it, the hollow between his two plate-like shoulder blades, to cool my mouth. We rarely spoke. He was so much taller than me. I lost myself in his limbs. It felt not like sleeping with a man but with another species. I always wanted the light off. I was afraid he would see me in some angle or motion or moment of crisis and think *she looks old*. I feared he would see something else, too.

He lifted me easily onto the counter next to the bathroom sink. The taps were in the shape of dolphins; their noses butted into the small of my back. We stayed like that for a while, long enough for our absence to be noticed, my legs wrapped around his torso. I can see them now, my feet entwined below his buttocks, in the mirror. Not my feet but those of a much browner, thinner woman, toenails painted the blue of cuckoo's eggs.

It is strange, how we could hardly speak to each other, yet we could do this. How kissing was not an exchange of tongues and saliva at all, but a rummaging in each other's souls. He brought me closer to myself than I could. Or he took me to a nameless place, which I had just vacated, and now it was inhabited only by the wind.

We registered the shock on each other's faces. I thought she would turn and walk away. When she didn't, I said, "Lucy."

We stood, arms limp by our sides. The high-altitude sun stung me. We were prodded into action because we stood in a car park. Black cars with red diplomatic plates brushed past us as they slid into parking bays. I felt their heat as they passed.

I knew it was possible that I would cross paths with any of them. But for some reason I never thought it would actually happen. I had no plan for how I would react, what I would say.

I watched her hesitate. She mustered her resolve and walked toward me with that light-footed stride of hers.

"I thought you went back to England."

"I did. I've come back for a month to sit an exam."

"What exam?"

"I tried to do my bird guiding exam in England, but it had to be written either in South Africa or here."

The next thing I said was a kind of apology. "I never thought I'd return."

We looked at each other. We could not see each other's eyes behind our sunglasses. Her hair was lighter. She wore the same pair of dark blue skinny jeans as she did on cooler days in the Dhow House. No rings gripped her fingers. Her nails were unpainted. She wore none of the feathered necklaces and silver bangles of before.

She was talking easily; she was telling me something innocuous — how she had eucalyptus trees in her garden but was trying to have them cut down because the colobus monkeys didn't like them

— when I remembered everything. The last time I saw Lucy. Her eyes were red. The smell of rage in the room. The scene — all of us frozen in horror.

I said, "Well, I should be going."

I perceived her relief that I was not going to ask after her mother or her brother. Her mouth began to speak, then hesitated. She was swallowing some automatic pleasantry that had nearly escaped.

I felt a crushing weight on me. A bomb, another fucking bomb, and we were caught in it.

When I opened my eyes, Lucy was still there. Her face loomed in my vision. She had taken off her sunglasses. Behind her the sun blared.

"What happened?"

"You fainted."

She drove me home that day. She insisted. She negotiated the hellish roundabouts of the city, where juggernaut trucks not only never braked if you got in their way but bore down on you with relish. She was suddenly voluble. My loss of consciousness had enlivened her.

"I've been practising for a year. I came back after I qualified in England. My clients are all expats — UN types, mostly. I don't have many friends here," she said. "It's an occupational hazard of coming from such a close family."

Her hair had grown very long. She kept tugging it back when it flew out the window as she drove, veering between lanes, flinging the car at stop lights.

"I appreciate your doing this."

"You fainted in a supermarket parking lot. I'm hardly going to leave you there." She paused to let a lorry lumber through the roundabout. "I know you're a doctor, but don't you think you should be looked at?"

"I've never fainted before. Well, maybe once."

"I know it must be a shock, seeing me."

"It was. It is." I looked out the window. We were passing the hotels that lined the airport road. This was also the highway that bisected the country, lined with ragged palm trees and their cargo of Marabou storks, who sat in their branches like hunch-shouldered undertakers.

I looked at Lucy then — really looked at her. She was no different. Apart from her longer, lighter hair, nothing had changed.

We met once a week over the following weeks, usually at the Coffeestop in the Baridi shopping centre. She told me about finishing her post-doctoral training in England. She had worked at the Maudsley for six months, then taken the decision to come home. She didn't mention Evan. On these first meetings our conversation was light and friendly, as if we had only just met each other.

We sat among the bonsai palms underneath the café's awning. "Julia's coming up for the weekend," she said. "I'm not going to tell her you're here."

"I wouldn't expect you to." The mention of her name caught me off guard. *If Lucy exists, then Julia exists, then Storm exists, too.*

"When did you start calling your mother by her first name?"

"A year or so ago," Lucy said. "I decided I had to make a break. It was part of my analysis. Our boundaries weren't clear. That can happen in families. Even if she was always closer to Storm."

Our coffee sessions moved to evening drinks, although I was trying not to drink. I told her I'd developed a problem in England. On winter nights I would sit at my desk and read or write emails, and I began to need a glass of wine. Then another. Soon I was drinking three quarters of a bottle of wine a night. To end each day drunk suddenly became necessary.

"That happens. But usually only if there is something you want to blot out of your consciousness."

She gave me a look that was unmistakable. Judicious, not particularly kind. But why would I expect kindness? It was already a miracle we were speaking.

Once or twice on a Friday we went to one of the cocktail bars of the moment, located on the tenth floor of one of the new ovoid glass buildings that had sprouted in the suburbs. The bar became a club after seven in the evening, when diplomats and foreign correspondents and businessmen from Uganda or Burundi or Senegal would accumulate. The security was watertight — three private guys, armed to the teeth. "Ex–secret service," Lucy whispered as we brushed past their black-suited bulk. "I know the guy who owns the company. He's a Sikh — calls himself Killer Singh. He's rumoured to have a knife in his turban."

All the talk in the city now was about threat and defence. Everyone seemed to be carrying a weapon. In the suburbs, near the embassy, householders slept with a shotgun under their beds. People involved in minor fender-benders were frequently shot by an enraged driver; everyone had taken to fleeing the scene of accidents. People met only in areas that were well secured. The memory of Al-Nur's attack on the Usimama in Lubaga Heights a year and a half before was still fresh. Locals and expats alike now preferred to stay in their guarded compounds patrolled by Rottweilers, hosting lavish dinner parties for a decreasing circle of intimates as people abandoned the country for England, America, even Israel. "When people think Israel's safer, you know it's bad," Lucy said.

The hotel and cocktail bars were where people desperate for the random appeal of the stranger congregated. They made a heady multinational mash of people, almost none of whom were who or what they said they were: ordinary spooks, corporate spies, regional heads of the UN food and agriculture program, disgraced missionaries, doctors working in the sticks on aid contracts — we even met a couple of aid apparatchiks from Lichtenstein. Later we leaned into each other's ears and whispered — *do they really expect us to believe them? Lichtenstein?*

She understood I was not going to rake over the past, or not

295

straight away. Gradually we became more confiding of each other. "Do you have a . . ." none of the words I could choose — *partner, boyfriend* — seemed right. Directed at Lucy, who was so demure, so private, they sounded garish. I settled for *relationship*.

"I'm not that interested in relationships right now."

"But you're an intimate person," I said.

She smiled then, a smile so much like her brother's, but more wounded, and so warmer. "I need to leave the country for a while," she said. "I'm going to South Africa to do a course in working in post-conflict situations. PTSD, that sort of thing."

The crowd pressed itself around us. We watched a tall woman in a white dress and four-inch heels seat herself on a bar stool next to a Sudanese man.

"There's one thing I want to ask you."

I turned back to look at Lucy. And waited. *Why did you sleep with my brother? Did you have a hand in my father's death? How long did you know about him and Evan? What does it matter to you? Why did you try to destroy our family?*

"Why didn't you defend yourself?"

"When?"

"When Storm hit you."

"I was in shock."

Lucy looked away. "I've thought about it a lot over the last two years. After dad died we were hysterical. We took it out on you. But I didn't expect him to do that."

"He was angry with me."

"For what?"

"Everything. For falling asleep that night in his bed."

"I had the impression you were about to say something. That's why he hit you."

"I don't know," I said. "You'd have to ask him."

The music changed. The bar's DJ was nearby. He was dressed in skinny jeans and a T-shirt that said *Hoxton Brewing Company*. On his back he carried a strange contraption, like an archer's bag. Out of it protruded arrows. I stared at his archery kit, as if it offered some explanation.

"Storm has always been someone who is capable of turning people inside out," Lucy said. "He doesn't set out to do it."

I had an image then of a sweater being pulled, arms flailing, seams exposed.

"What do you mean?"

"He's a lightning rod. He turns people against their better natures. He knows he has an effect but he can't name it."

"But you can."

Lucy raised her glass in a mock salute. "That's what I'm trained to do. Although with family I'm not sure it's possible to have the necessary distance. It's like trying to analyze yourself."

The music seemed to animate the men in the bar. We were interrupted as two of them approached us. I watched their eyes flick over our faces, then settle on Lucy. She dispatched them efficiently and they moved on to easier game.

"Later I understood you didn't have anything to do with — with the attack." Her eyes slipped away. Later I would realize that not once during our meetings did she say, *my father's death*, or, *my father is dead*. She might not believe it, even now. "After you'd gone, I wanted to —" she was speaking quickly now "— to get in touch with you, somehow. Email, Facebook, whatever. But I found I couldn't. I don't know why."

"There weren't any communications on the coast for a week," I said, even though I knew this was not the reason she didn't contact me.

"Where did you go?"

"I missed my flight. Then they cancelled all flights for a week, until after the elections. I stayed at the Kilindoni Club."

I had a flash of those weeks, living on my credit card, the Zimbabwean managers taking pity on me with my one change of shorts and a T-shirt and selling me an ill-fitting linen shirt at a discount from their souvenir shop.

"That must have been difficult."

"If we'd come under attack it wouldn't have been good," I admitted.

"Julia might ask me if I've been in touch with you," Lucy said. "What do you think I should say?"

"I think you should say no. You should pretend not to have thought of me once in these two and a half years."

She frowned at my voice, which sounded odd, even to me: aggrieved and contrite at once, relieved too, perhaps. I had just realized I hadn't ruined their family after all. I was just a temporary interloper. They were stronger than any one rogue element, which they would simply absorb, as the sea swallows waves.

"I should never have armed us. I should have tried to talk them down. I've spent too long in, in . . ." I fell back on a default term, "in conflict situations."

"It was a stray bullet," Lucy said. "This is a dangerous country. Everyone's armed."

"What does Julia blame me for, then?"

"Storm."

His name sat between us. I could have asked then, where is he? Who does he love now? Who is he turning inside out?

"She saw it as a betrayal," Lucy said.

"It was."

We were silent for a minute.

"You never said what you thought," Lucy said. "About how we lived, what was happening in the country. You never said much at all."

"I'm a reserved person."

"I could see that," she said.

"But also, I didn't dare open my mouth."

"Why?"

"I was afraid of your mother."

"Afraid of Julia?" Lucy scowled — not with disbelief, if I was not mistaken, but with recognition. She might also fear her mother.

I told Lucy that while I lived in Julia's — in their — house I refrained from making judgments because Julia was the closest thing alive to my mother, or who my mother had been, that to anger or disappoint her would have been to live through my relationship with my mother again. That is why my manners became smooth and gracious and I came to feel detached. That is why I quickly stopped making private judgments about their fundraising dinners and corporate golfing outings.

"Julia liked you, you know," she said.

"Did she?"

Now that I think of it, I hardly saw Julia outside of the house. She preferred to do her shopping alone. We never went to Kilindoni village or walked through the streets of Moholo together. My life outside the house was lived alone, or with Margaux, or Storm. Perhaps Julia avoided taking me anywhere because she understood I would see a completely different reality to the one she saw.

I did not tell Lucy what I really thought: that Julia had no sense of me as an independent being; she saw me only as a riposte to her children, a rebuke, even. She papered over this unease by taking me under her wing. It was important to her that I be an innocent — an imbecile, preferably — because I had not grown up in Africa. I was unaware of its intricate power structure, its racisms, its ethnic groups and allegiances. I came from the theme park of England with its monarchs and mortgage insurance policies and self-checkout machines.

"It's my birthday next month." Lucy's mouth was set in an unhappy shape. "I keep saying to myself, you're thirty-one and alone. I ought to take charge of my life. I ought to be a person of substance."

"You are. You're a qualified psychiatrist. You're helping people."

"I'm just having to get used to the fact I won't be young anymore."

"Thirty-one is young, believe me."

I had a vision of what she would look like when she was older, her mouth puckered, her face weathered by the tropical sun. She would still be lovely, but a hardness would set her features. She had Storm's statuesque quality in her face, but in hers it was latent, waiting to emerge.

"In past generations people had three children by the time they were thirty," she said. "They were adults. I think you only truly become an adult when you have children, when you are responsible for other people's existences."

"There are many ways to be responsible for other people's existences."

As I said this, I wondered, why did we not talk to each other more in that month we shared a house — a family? We have something in common, Lucy and I: our intellect, our ambition, our interest in ideas as entities that free us from the impersonality of life. Life without ideas is just a ceaseless lurch from event to event, stimulus to stimulus.

She watched me. She might have understood the disenchantment that had passed through me.

"When I first came to stay with your mother I was recovering from an attack."

I sat back, afraid but thrilled at my admission. I'd had two beers and two daiquiris by that point. I wasn't sure of my motivation, of where I was going.

"What kind of attack?"

"When I was working at Gariseb."

She inclined her head. There was a professional slant in the gesture. "Why were you attacked?"

"Because insurgents I had treated thought I was responsible for the destruction of the town where they were based."

"Were you?"

I looked away from her gaze. It was the same look she had given me so many times in the Dhow House. A look delicately poised between the neutrality of curiosity and the scald of suspicion.

"They were angry. They wanted revenge."

Lucy had cooled. I had ignited her suspicion again. But my desire for admonition was too strong — that was what I wanted: not her forgiveness, but her condemnation.

"I knew there was something else. I mean, besides Storm. That's why I tried to talk to you on the beach. You were displaying classic symptoms of PTSD. But you knew that. I thought it would end badly, somehow, for you. Although I didn't think you would be sleeping with my brother." She huffed, a sound between a grunt and a snort. "I thought you should talk to someone."

"And if I had spoken to someone, what would they have concluded?"

"That you were angry, although subconsciously. That's why you did what you did with Storm. You wanted to get back at the family because you haven't had our lives. And also . . ." for the first time since we had met in the supermarket parking lot, Lucy's face tensed, "you wanted to fall in love, to seduce." She looked away. "That's also a way of belonging to something other than yourself, seemingly. It's a narcissistic impulse."

"Is that why you don't want a relationship? It's a narcissistic impulse?"

"I've thought myself out of relationships. I'm not unhappy about it."

"But you're not happy, either."

"I'm neutral, and in a neutral place I am less likely to do damage."

"Lucy," I said. "It was a mutual seduction."

Her eyes had hardened. Their darkness had a streak of deep blue in them, like tanzanite. Why hadn't I seen it before?

"The older person is always more responsible for it, though, don't you think?" It was a question but there was a steely, independent note in her voice. "You were going to say something. That's why he hit you. He was afraid. What was it you were about to say?"

"That he was Evan's lover. It was Evan he loved, or loves. Not me." She crossed her legs at the knees, her bare ankles pale and demure. "Did you know that?"

She didn't answer. "When Evan was adopted it was uncommon for a white family to have a black child. Now you see it all the time."

"Do you mean he wanted to be white?"

"I mean he is white on the inside but black on the outside. Storm is black on the inside but white on the outside. They're a perfect fit." There were tears in her eyes. It was the first time I'd seen her cry, since that morning.

I understood it was time to bring our meeting to a close.

"I'm going to the coast for a couple of weeks, over Christmas. I won't go near the house. I wanted you to know."

"I know you won't," she said. I watched her gather her things: a dark brown leather beaded bag made on the coast, her car keys. As she reached for them her hand hovered.

"We found your gun."

"Oh?"

"In the bag you left behind. I didn't know doctors carried guns."

"They do, sometimes. Gariseb was a dangerous place."

"Why didn't you use it the night Dad was shot?"

"I didn't have time to get it. Handguns aren't effective anyway against semi-automatic weapons."

"Neither are rifles," Lucy said. She looked at me carefully.

"I was afraid of it, to be honest. I don't like guns much, either."

"Julia has it now. She's learning to shoot in Durban. She enjoys it. Everyone has guns there. I'm sorry she took it," she said, but there was no apology in her voice.

"I wasn't going to come back for it. I'm glad Julia has it."

I watched her walk across the car park. She looked slight in the dark. The club's bouncers also watched over her. It was their job to see people arrived safely at their vehicles. After that, they were on their own.

In that last week in the house the days take on a cast of finality. I look at everything — the clouds, the mustard-coloured seaweed on the beach, the violet underwater light that illuminates the pool, the sorties of Roseate terns — with a new avidness. Soon, I may never see them again. I have only lately realized that being attentive to the detail of such a place, its ravenous beauty, creates a different state of consciousness. A different relationship with the self, even. Here you might finally allow yourself to exist.

The first light of the morning comes at five thirty, a thin glow on the horizon. In this bronze light we stared at each other, dreading his mother's step on the stairs, her hand on the door to his room. We knew that was a possibility, always. The first bird singing before sunrise was my cue to leave. It was either the common bulbul or the white-browed robin-chat. I stayed to listen to them with him. He was attentive to their existence. He did not take birds as inevitable background phenomena. Like Ali, he watched them closely, looking for clues. People who are attentive to the existence of animals have refined souls. Storm was one of those people who trusted the natural world more than the world of man. That is where his talent for wind and water and the gnarled life of the coast with its skinks and plated lizards and marine turtles and osprey eagles came from.

He knew the lives of birds were uncertain and marked by vio-lence. Raptors, monkeys, snakes, humans — they have so many ene-mies. They are lovely, small enigmas — this is what I think. Where do they go between the dawn and dusk chorus? Are they merely silent on their perch, are they dozing or do they fly elsewhere, to a fourth dimension? Such delicate little things, but their lives are a charnel house. Only two days ago I wrote an exam to attest that I can identify 250 species by sight or call. I can say their names, but what do I know about their lives?

The day dawned cold. I could see my breath in the air before I threw off the camel hair blanket and rose from my cot. I slept fully dressed those days. In that sense I was prepared.

It was late June, the beginning of winter. The days at that time of year were wood smoke and famine. I did my rounds. Diarrhea, dehydration, typhoid — the usual — but also a respiratory disease I had never encountered before and lacked the tools to diagnose. Ribcages rose and fell, squabbling for breath.

These casualties were all Bora. They came from lands controlled by Al-Nur, who had rebuffed all vaccinations as un-Islamic, a conspiracy between Christians and the West. I remembered what Aisha had said — a week, or was it two before? "Al-Nur are a plague. They are like the locusts that come and eat our crop. They want us to die. That way they have fewer mouths to feed."

I tried to reconcile this scorched earth policy with the tentative, bookish Ali. He had disappeared ten days before. Just as he'd said, his people had come to fetch him.

I remembered his intelligent eyes, his courtesy. It was not the frigid courtesy of men who hated and feared women. He seemed at ease in my company. This is what first raised my suspicion. That and his mode of transport to the camp, stuffed in the back of a flatbed. On the flatbed's gunwales were the scratches that signalled RPG mountings.

Later I learned the faction Ali's men belonged to was called SLK. Ali hinted at it once. "There is no sheik, no warlord above us," he said. Their political affiliation was a cover for straightforward guerilla activities — ambushes, IEDs, short-term mortar assaults. After his first few days in camp I had concluded he was Al-Nur. I'd been briefed on the factions and groupings of the country. *You couldn't call it politics*, Anthony had said. *What they want to do is to wage war. Politics is just window dressing.*

Are you certain the vaccine stock is complete? He'd asked me by email from his alias, which professed he was a doctor at the Geneva headquarters of the International Red Cross.

It is 100% complete, I wrote back.

When I returned to my desk from sending the email, a giant insect of a kind I had never seen before waved its antennae at me from its perch on a sheet of white paper. The insect looked like a cross between a cockroach and a beetle but it was enormous, the size of my hand. I remembered Rafael's counsel: *Anything animal here you can't identify or whose behaviour doesn't fit, back away.*

Then came the hottest interval in the Gariseb day: three-thirty. The afternoon's torpor thickened and the scorched winds dropped. Now there was only heat.

I had seen the cloud of dust on the horizon. I was at the threshold of my office, on my way to see to a man with a perforated lung I had operated on the day before. I thought it was a dust devil. They were not uncommon on the plateau in winter.

The dust cloud grew larger.

"Incoming," said Andy.

"No —"

Andy scowled, his near-handsome face crumpled by sweat. "No what?"

I looked behind me at the scrub, the thirty or so low-slung acacias that stung the horizon. If I ran, how far would I get? The guilty run.

The flatbed truck had eaten the road. It pulled up in front of the triage tent.

"What are these guys doing back?" Andy gave me a look, as if I might know.

The men were out of the truck and around me and I felt a cold glint of something at my throat. I could only see them out of the corners of my eyes. They were behind me. Now they were dressed quite differently. Their dashikis had been replaced by smart olive-coloured combat trousers.

Ali appeared from behind a phalanx of the others. Their faces were covered in black scarves but I knew some of them by the cast of their eyes — Omar, who was from Khartoum; Mohammed, a Qatari. Ali I knew by his quick, careful stride.

I held my arms rigid against the grip of the men. I could not push against them forever, but I did not want to accept their touch.

"Why did you tell them?"

"Tell them what?"

"Gikayo is destroyed. By the Americans."

"I know nothing about that. I am a doctor."

My voice is strange, I thought. I must correct it. But how? My voice seemed to have deserted me. Where was Andy? Then I saw he was on the ground, two men on top of him. How had he got there? I'd heard nothing — no altercation, no thud. It was as if the air had been sucked from around them, creating a vacuum.

A camel drifted into my line of vision. Aisha's camel.

"Tell us what you told them. What else did you tell them?" Ali's voice was serene, a little syrupy, even. The voice of someone in control.

I shut my eyes in shock. A warm viscous liquid was pouring down my face, my body. I shook my arms but could not dislodge the men. So recently I had gripped their bodies to heal them.

Someone — Omar? Mansour? — held up a jerrycan. The jerrycan had been heavier than he had expected. It had hit only my face and torso because they could not lift it high enough to pour it over my head.

Petrol filled my nostrils, mouth. I began to feel dizzy.

307

"You must tell us now," he said.

I opened my eyes. They stung. I thought: I must wash the petrol out with saline, afterwards.

The flies that had been harassing my nose and eyes vanished. I drew a breath. The air sang with its cargo of uninterested birds, who watched me from nearby thorn branches. I heard the lowing of Aisha's camel, who seemed to understand what was about to happen.

A calm entered my lungs. I'd known from the beginning that this — or something like it — could happen.

"Do what you have to do," I said, in Arabic. "I've done nothing against you. I treated you, I made you well. I am ready."

My eyes locked his. What did I see? Our conversations, or a residue of them. My error. I had failed to recognize my assassin. This seemed a crucial neglect, worthy of death even. Maybe that was it: I deserved to die.

Where was everyone? Andy was on the ground, but the petrol had cast a tobacco and purple glaze over my vision. I couldn't see.

The arms sprang away from me and I swayed in the wind like an unmoored tree. Then I fell to the ground.

They sent a plane the next day. I spent a week in the capital, in the same stylish neighbourhood where I would later encounter Lucy.

Then I flew to the coast and assumed my new role as exhausted Dr. Rebecca, bona fide cousin who Storm, Julia, Lucy and Bill had never met, never expected to know, who drifted through their house like a prearranged ghost, the forerunner who comes to signal that not all is well, that it might be time to abandon their paradise.

Ali was back across the border by nightfall of the day he decided not to incinerate his saviour. His men revered him. They did not ask questions. He would tell them, it was all a ruse. I wanted to frighten her. She could not have known anything. Or maybe, but then there would be no medical care for our people. We cannot leave them exposed.

For many weeks I would not think of Ali. He would appear only in dreams. But I knew him, better than he could have imagined. I had identified him as one of my patients, then named his town as one of the strongholds of Al-Nur. Even though he had evaded the drone attack and was still alive, I was congratulated. Twenty-eight fighters were killed at Gikayo two days before the pickup raced into the compound at Gariseb. Once back in the capital, my prize of thanks was a message from Anthony sent from an untraceable server with the report attached.

He was brought up in a village in the land of the Bora, close to the coast but inland, on the estuary of a failing river. He had five sisters. In his house there was a curtain made of beads and an ancient boxy television. Some days there was a channel from the capital, which broadcast singing competitions and quiz shows from Italy. He watched as fuzzy Catholic nuns sang from a church in the Vatican, row on row like birds on a wire. Across the road was the office for the bus company, Massimo, a leftover from the days of the Italian colonists. Within two hundred metres were three mosques. Men came door to door selling small humid bags of freshly roasted cashews. The smell of the sea was always in their nostrils, even if they had to walk for half a day to see it.

"We are pure Arabs," his mother told him, "from the Yemen." This was code for: *there is no black blood in my family; we are the original Swahili*. From a very young age he was different; he needed space for the thoughts between his thoughts. A resinous finger of sound set up home inside his head in the place he created. He couldn't say what it was — the wail of the muezzin, the chant of an inner god.

He dreamed of floods often, of moist leaves as big as chairs. He listened attentively to his dreams, recording them in a notebook he kept under his bed. He decided the dream was telling him that his destiny was to live in a moist place. Five years later he crossed the border to attend university in the coastal city of Bahari ya Manda.

He was too intelligent to be a mere religious ideologue. His goal was political change, through the imposition of an Islamic state. By nature he was an ascetic. He did not like people much. He liked to watch fires but not to light them. He never thought he would be an enemy of life. Unlike many of his friends he feared death. He felt it in the world, a physical presence. It had a resinous sheen, the solid equivalent of the muezzin's sundown call. There in the alleyway amongst the cunning cats, the stale smell of the sea, the day-old catches of fish, he had no idea that one day he would deal out this substance with his hands, like a game of cards.

No one has ever done me any damage. But if I were to meet him again here among the motorcycle taxi drivers who sleep in the shade, or glimpse him disappearing down a narrow alleyway, I am not sure what I would do. I would like to say that I can intuit whether he is alive or dead. Some people leave such an impress in the world. We are always alert to them, we can sense their existence as you would tune into a frequency on a shortwave radio. But really I don't know.

The gardeners are done for the day. Bathers are out of the water and the pool lights have come on. The lights turn the pool green at night, that watery turquoise of tropical shallows. Red fairy lights crawl up the slim palms. An unknown bird cries *piu, piu* for the last time today. The muezzin's minor thirds and fifths threads through the town, the call to evening prayers.

Last night I went to Christmas carols at the Kilindoni Club. The candlelight illuminated tanned women in red dresses, barefoot, Santa Claus hats flopping on their heads. Their husbands smoked beside the balustrades over the beach, supervising their children playing in the waves.

The beach is clean, there is no seaweed and no plastic debris. The sand has changed consistency and is looser, drier. It is so different from the Kusi, I could be in a different country, on a different ocean. The sea is calm now. It rises and recedes, advancing half an hour every day.

Other things are unchanged. Men in kanzus walk along the beach to the mosque, their feet swishing on the sand, their women seated behind them in a black clutch of shade, surrounded by children. Ghost crabs pilfer fish from our plates.

The Dhow House is empty now, through the summer monsoon, the winter monsoon. I don't need to go there to see its five young coconut palms standing guard over the cliff and wag their heads at the sea, the razors of shade they cast onto the ground. The details of the house return to me — the Japanese fishing buoys made of coloured glass Julia had scattered around the house, the chocolate and white feathers of a fish eagle she had gathered in a vase next to the bookshelf, the soap trays in the bathroom carved from wood into the shape of angelfish. I remember the house better than I remember most people.

Gunfire. Its pop-pop sound coming from the town across the inlet. In the Kilindoni Club the shroud of the mosquito net drapes over the bed. There is one power outlet for the fridge and my phone is out of battery. I try to phone Lucy but my call is blocked. Later, I will be grateful. *Please speak to him*, Rebecca would have said, then. *I am so sorry.*

But she is not sorry, other than for the outcome. That is what people mean, generally, by the phrase. She remembers in those days the difference between regret and remorse. Regret is to feel sorrow for what has happened; remorse is an urge to correct what has happened, to return to the moment before, when the future could be directed to be different, and start again.

Outside her room in the Kilindoni Club vervet monkeys fret, lying in wait in case she throws them cashews. Rebecca remembers the dreams she had, those first nights in Julia's house. In them she is burnt. Her skin desiccates and puckers like parchment. She smells the waxy scent of burnt epidermis. The skin releases itself and floats upward like flakes of ash.

In the Kilindoni Club I look at a reverse image of the scene she witnessed then: children splash in the pool, gardeners snap at the tangled creepers. Two and a half years ago there were no children and the gardeners never went home but remained in the walled grounds of the hotel complex wearing their dark green overalls, prepared to fight the insurgents with rakes and spades, their only weapons.

The power was cut. No electricity meant no water, in the whole of Kilindoni, as the mains were fed by power. The black plastic water tanks everyone has here ran dry. They huddled in the restaurant by the light of hurricane lamps sipping from small bottles of mineral water, their rations for the day. The cook made a huge pot of rice and beans because that was all that was left in the kitchen. Siege food.

By night small boys would steal across the inlet by boat and raid the shelves of the cook's relatives.

On those nights she waited for Storm to come for her. She could not believe he would not appear under the hotel's thatched roof and take her out of there.

Those last days in the house before the invasion and Bill's death they spent skirting one other. They were sluggish and resentful of his mother's presence. She could feel it. They would have dinner together and talk of what everyone was talking about — the elections, the attacks, whether the coast and tourism would ever recover. Julia would look at her, then Storm, trying to knit together the meaning of their seeming indifference to each other, his breezy tolerance, and why, too early by far, they would habitually find some urgent email they needed to send or book they wanted to read, and go to their separate bedrooms.

Now, I understand him better. We colluded against his mother and he hated me for it. I saw the flash of hatred in his eyes, from time to time. I had never been hated and loved in the same moment before and it frightened me.

It was always going to be my last night in the house — my flight was the following day — but I couldn't have anticipated my mode of exit. I hadn't packed. My passport sat on my desk underneath a sheaf of paper.

We sat on his bed. I was crying — hot, rasping tears. My breath couldn't come fast enough. He said, tell me what to do. I sat up and tried to stifle my breathing with my hands. I put my head between my legs. I remember the dream I had that night, of trying to resuscitate his father. I don't remember falling asleep. But then we never do.

You get away from my son!

As I heard the words I thought, where am I? I remembered that we had been to the hospital in Bahari ya Manda. We had left Bill behind, as if by mistake.

313

Now, I think of that first party in Moholo. That was when I decided that he was for me, that I would go for him, that I loved him, even though I knew he did not love me — I had seen him with Evan— and that he would likely never love me. The decision announced itself without bothering to ask my opinion. The heart, that muscle with its own brain, fired signals up through the carotid artery, sliding along the trachea and bursting in a spray of fireworks into the mind.

Julia was shaking. Little tremors skittering like sidewinding snakes, all over her body. Our faces were white masks of shock.

Get out. Storm's voice.

I thought I didn't hear correctly. My face must have looked like the moon. Some stupid grey orb.

I had thought he had punched me in the stomach but later I remembered Julia pulling at his arms. He must have put his hands around my neck and I'd fallen to the floor under his weight.

Get your hands off her! Julia was clawing at her son, pummelling his chest. She tried to protect me.

In the corner of the infinity pool, a pied kingfisher bathed. He shook out his piebald feathers, now stiff and wet.

This was the last thing I saw of the house — the bird in the corner of the pool, a butterscotch wall behind him and three living statues in the kitchen.

Then I was running. The Estate, the dust-fringed tired bougainvillea leaves. The morning sun gripped the leafless limbs of the baobab. A pickup truck full of men with rusted automatic weapons rumbled by. The crazy woman running in the middle of a war, look at her go. Running through an inner city, a sea of broken bodies, her future only gravity's shadow, poised on the edge of darkness.

For five days and nights we waited to be invaded, to be blown up by grenades tossed over the walls from all directions. But the terrified army recruits kept the Kilindoni Club safe, or the insurgents had bigger problems at Bahari ya Manda, where they hit five hotels in quick succession, although these had been deserted by foreigners. They managed to kill the cooks, waiters, chambermaids and reservation staff who had huddled in the generator shed for safety.

At some point in those days a transformation took place. A devouring energy sunk into Rebecca like dye. Part of her cleaved away. The rupture was soundless but she felt it happening. She was becoming me. I was born in this hotel room in the Kilindoni Club two and a half years ago: an iteration, another, more resilient, self. This happens in many people's lives, sometimes more than once — our core selves remain, perhaps, but it is not a rebirth or a resurrection. I don't know if to describe it as sloughing a skin, or a death. All I know is that the Rebecca who existed until then retreated, shocked to find herself a newly minted ghost.

I still see her, those nights when she sat with a hurricane lamp in her room, no air conditioning or fan, the door open to the night. She thought, something has been let loose inside me. A reverse self. Needy, uncontrollable. Feral. But why the state of emergency? She didn't even feel that the day Ali and his men came for her. Why the panic? The answer came back smoothly from some other self. Because someone who two months ago you hardly knew existed had suddenly become necessary to your survival. The panic comes from your realisation that you may not be able to live without him, or that you may not want to.

There were two kinds of love, Rebecca knew: conscious and unconscious. Conscious love you professed every day, reminding yourself why you loved the person, thinking fond thoughts, remembering their deeds of kindness and the security of their presence. Unconscious love was like being shot into a different dimension.

Here the world was fascinatingly altered. Here you lived in a vertigo of elation and fear and need. Once you had lived in this country it was very difficult to return to the other, safer, more reasonable, place.

I see her arriving in their house that July day, stunned and enervated by the heat and by a sudden panic that she was not about to be called upon to act at any moment, that no one — certainly not Rafael — would burst through the door of the house and shout for her to clamp an artery, to deliberate between a typhoid and malaria diagnosis, to sever a mine-ruined foot.

I see her meeting Storm for the first time, that her reaction was genuine. She really did think, oh, my younger cousin. Good to meet you. But in the same moment she perceived the transfixing hollowness at his core and this did not frighten and enervate her as it would have done in another human being, rather she understood he might be the key to a similar space within her, that he was an alternate self. His blunt stare, the sick thrill in her stomach, the defibrillator jolt of her heart: it was all a decoy for this more abstract truth.

I see her fear. She suspected that this blameless young man might lead her to purloin her dignity. Perhaps from the first moment she arrived she was accompanied by that dank chaperone, the shadow self. This creature had its own agenda. It was tired — so tired — of storing facts, of having an opinion, of knowing everything. This accompanier sank into the Dhow House as if into a leather sofa, admiring the expense of its texture. It knew Rebecca had registered its presence and that she was spooked. She had been to Afghanistan, Kurdistan, and now Gariseb, looking for ways to rid herself of her internal stalker. She had tried to extinguish it by smothering it with rational thought, with knowledge and aptitude.

I tried to talk to this buried self, to reason: you are a natural double agent, a natural spy, I told it. I know that once you have savoured the tarnish of betrayal, you develop a taste for it, a devious addiction. I won't let you ruin me.

The other Rebecca recoiled from the word, but this other self found betrayal so much easier than I did. A very long time ago, one part of her — the ambitious, belligerent, intellectually aggressive part — easily dominated the caring, sensitive person. The loss of her mother fuelled this fission. It took what she did in Gariseb to reveal how thoroughly the other Rebecca had been crushed. And then Storm. After the first betrayal, the next is easier. I wonder if that was apparent to them — to Anthony and his brethren — those professional manipulators to whom I was useful for a time. I wonder if they spotted the crack inside me, long before I did.

But it isn't betrayal itself which generates the allure, rather the discovery of the exact grain of your soul, like fine wood, pitched against itself, doubling back and back until it is more like stone, or keratin, the horn and ivory of animal lust and animal life. Betrayal is a sophisticated savagery. It brings you in contact with the self that is also wild. A predator.

Perhaps this was the self who allowed Storm to command her to crawl around the empty living room, blindfolded. Crawl, he said, and she did as she was told, if slowly, trying to fend off the legs of arm-chairs, the edges of tables. This was the self who would allow him to fall on her, drag down her underpants, take her from behind on the floor, in the darkness, where she would have to brace herself against the baraza. This version of Rebecca lay back and from behind her blindfold, on the dark screen of her eyelids, watched flint stars careen across her mind.

I know she is here, in this room in a four-star tropical hotel. Each time I perceive her she is aware of me. I see her in the mirror after I have returned from swimming in the pool with its view over the Indian Ocean. She is thinner than I am, made beautiful by her desire. Please stay, I say. She glides toward me, gives me an admonitory look, then turns and melts into the shadows.

New Year's Eve. The coast is packed for the holidays. Its beaches and resorts have returned to favour, now that the coast is calm.

In the Kilindoni Club they are taking the Christmas tree down. It is plastic, silver garlands lumped on its branches, frosted baubles. Underneath it are empty boxes wrapped in foil paper, once blue and silver, faded to grey by the sun. Families sit around the flat screen television, which beams British sport, and watch rectangles of green pitch, men running across it, hurling themselves at each other, a distant roar, people bundled in duffel coats and hats.

I go to Reef Encounters for the yearly New Year's Eve party. Four hundred people will come. I won't stay until midnight. I just want to lose myself in the crowd.

In the car park the four-by-fours are parked three rows deep. Christmas and New Year is the best time to observe this lost tribe of white people. The women with their narrow bronzed shoulders, the kikhois and khangas they wear tied halter-like around their necks. Their beaded jewellery and butterscotch faces, the faces of babies, until one point in their early thirties when suddenly they harden.

Now, at Reef Encounters, where I write staring out to sea, they are around me, talking in small groups around circular tables. It is nine o'clock; in an hour and a half the disco will begin. The waiters wear the same mint and orange uniforms.

The crowd grows. I am at the bar ordering a beer — *baridi sana*, I say, because they have a habit here of giving you a beer from the front of the fridge where the heat presses against its door, when something makes me swivel my head over my right shoulder.

Driftwood hair. Blue eyes. A tall man. The smile that is an explosion. He is standing at the far end of the bar, talking to three or four men his age. I scan the group. I can't see Evan. I can't see any women.

He is raising a bottle of Duma beer to his lips but he stops before drinking and laughs at something one of the other men has said. He throws his head back so that I can see the sinews of his neck. He wears a black shirt that makes his eyes shine like coins.

I turn back to the barman. I try to hide my body behind that of the man next to me. The crowd presses in from all directions.

Three a.m. The night I come into the living room and heard the snake, wrapped around the lamp. Two hours later a peach silk light soaks the sky. We listen to the crack of the sea at high tide, each wave an explosion. The sea fills and drains like a glass until where the coral pools have been invisible, ripples begin to appear. In minutes the tide has pulled back and the smooth ridges of coral, the actual architecture of the shoreline, appears. The snorkelling boat with its name — DESIRE — emblazoned across the side, glides into the horizon. The house broadcasts no internal sounds, no snoring or creaking floorboards, no indication that people live there at all, only the sounds of the sea, a silent oceanic cathedral.

"You two, you're always up at the crack of dawn."

Julia was lovely in the first minutes of waking, before she tidied her hair and applied mascara. She looked like the girl he could have been. All the features and quirks I found so compelling in Julia's face Storm had inherited: her broad, cruel mouth, an intelligent forehead, fine eyes which always harboured a note of hope, the strong nose, the cheekbones unfurled on either side of her face. She had made Storm, and that was an accomplishment. Julia's strange prophecy was correct: I will probably never have children. I will never know the propriety mothers can feel over the bodies of their sons.

What do you want from me? Julia screamed at me on that terrible morning in the house. *Do you want my life?*

Perhaps I did. Perhaps I wanted the barbecues and the fishing trips and the dinner parties for businessmen visiting from Mozambique, from Zimbabwe, men like her husband, who had enriched themselves in countries of great poverty. The Cordon Bleu cooking courses and watercolour and interior design and pottery courses, the sudden interest in making mosaics or applique collages which you would sell through pulling a few strings in London or Paris.

Storm didn't want any of this. He was ready to take flight from the luxurious torpor of his family. All this had failed to make him happy. I was on the outside trying to get in, and he was trying to escape. On the threshold we found each other.

How can you do this to me, to us? At the time I thought, *us*, meaning her family. But now it occurs to me Julia might have meant my mother.

I walk across the bar of Reef Encounters in full view. I know he won't see me, somehow. I lean over the railing above the ocean and drink my beer. I stare at the cheetah's uncertain face on the label. I've looked at this beer bottle a thousand times, but only now do I see the downward cast of the two black tear marks underneath the cat's eyes. The cheetah is a predator, but a furtive, delicate one. It hunts in the day to avoid confronting the leopard or lion, which often kill it. The cheetah's only defense is its speed.

Three men stand next to me. They cast me glances from time to time. The friendly, non-committal Tom emerged from just such a trio in this exact place two and a half years ago. The symmetry of the moment hits me — a reversed déjà vu.

I turn around. He is leaning against the bar, his hip curled into its rim, in the exact place I inhabited ten minutes before. That is all that separates our bodies: ten metres, the ten seconds it would take to walk across the floor.

My bird exam is behind me, my recitations of species lists, of Latin names, of passerines and non-passerines, breeding habits, reproductive strategies, distribution and habitat. I did well; I passed. I always pass.

From my perch on the terrace I see a bee-eater on a flyby. They fly acrobatically, winging up through the air, near-vertical, then yawing sideways so fast, as if they've just activated an engine. *Little, northern carmine, Somali, white-fronted, white-throated, blue-cheeked, European, Böhm's.* Family *Meropidae.* Bee-eaters are an endearing family of birds with their lollipop colours, the black stripe across their eyes that gives them the air of a masked bandit. You cannot tell the male and female apart. Bee-eaters are sally hunters; they consume their prey in flight. Their throats are lined with tough skin, resistant to stingers. What for other birds would be poison for them is sweet.

Bee-eaters have a unique trick; when bathing in water and so exposed, they lie with outspread wings and their heads twisted to the side, as if broken, one eye closed, to fool potential predators. They look dead, but are alive.

The car turns at the junction to the beachside airstrip. It is January 3rd. I arrive on time for the daily flight to the capital at three fifteen p.m. to find the plane is delayed by three hours. "Protocol!" says the airport staff, thrilled to use these words. "Very important people."

I go outside the airport terminal to wait. Women hawkers sit in the shade, baskets of mangos at their feet to sell to passengers departing for the capital.

The VIPs turn out to count among their number Charles Mgura, Julia and Bill's neighbour, and Eugene, the politico I met in the

Dhow House. As I board they are strapping themselves into business class seats. I stare directly at Eugene but his eyes do not even flicker.

The plane pirouettes and glides to the end of the runway. The sun has reached the treetops. We will arrive in a darkening capital with its nighttime thunderstorms. My connecting flight to London leaves at midnight. From my seat I watch piebald African sacred ibis peck at the ground. A heron takes flight, wings kneading the air with commanding lassitude. He flies against the red sunset.

The plane charges toward the highway. It is a short-run airstrip and the small jet needs to accelerate quickly to clear the fence at the end of the airfield.

We are aloft and climbing over the coast. I keep my face pressed to the cold of the window. Beneath me I see the scatter of lights of Moholo and Kilindoni. The long stretch of silver beach darkens in the brief twilight.

Tonight people are drinking Duma beer at the Baharini bar, at Reef Encounters, at the Sahara restaurant. Kitesurfers are reposing on the beach, stroking their thin, alert dogs. Women move through white houses, flicking lights that may or may not turn on, thinking of the hour, soon now, when they will serve their husbands a drink. Women in the backland villages light the makaa, prepare chicken for the grill; their children will study by candle and kerosene lamps.

The sea sounds louder at night. Mosque swallows pour from minarets, unfurling in curlicues above the ruins of Swahili cities now inhabited by monkeys and narrow-mouthed mambas, by madafu hawkers with bloodshot eyes.

Storm is there. What will he do tonight? He has many friends. They will gather in teal pools of darkness, drinking beer by hurricane lamp, listening to trumpeter hornbills swaying in the anaemic upper branches of casuarinas. Evening glosses the ocean. Pied kingfishers fly out of the creek, heading to their roosts for the night.

mwisho

Acknowledgements

My sincere thanks for their help in the writing and publication of this novel go to Veronique Baxter at David Higham Associates for her continued support for my work, Susan Renouf at ECW Press in Toronto for her diligent and insightful edit, Lauren Parsons at Legend for her helpful editorial input, and to Henry Sutton at the University of East Anglia, whose collegial support and reading of an earlier draft of this novel has been invaluable. I am very fortunate to work at UEA, where I am surrounded by talented writers, students and lecturers alike. Terry Stevenson and John Fanshawe's *Birds of East Africa* is the definitive field guide to the bird life of the region, and it has proven invaluable in the writing of sections of this book.

Note: *The majority of place names in this novel do not exist. The names for ethnicities and political factions are also fictitious. However the bird, animal and tree species named are generally those found in coastal or upland East Africa.*

Short Glossary of Swahili Terms

Askari: guard, watchman

Bahari/baharini: the sea, to the sea

Baraza: sofa

Baridi: cold

Buibui: a chardor, often black and decorated with colourful detailing, worn by Muslim women on the Indian Ocean coast

Bwana: sir, a term of respect

Dudu: insect

Duka: shop

Filusi: blue and yellow ocean-going fish also called dorado or mahi-mahi; the common dolphinfish

Hakuna: not any, none

Jahazi: type of dhow; can also refer to the mainsail

Kanzu: the embroidered cotton full-length robe worn by Muslim men on the Indian Ocean coast

Kikhoi: a cotton sarong-like wrap, traditionally worn by men to go to mosque in the morning

Khanga: a printed fabric worn by women

Kofia: an embroidered cap worn by Muslim men

Mabati: galvanised iron sheets used largely for roofing

Madafu: coconuts/coconut water

Mafuta ya taa: paraffin

Mahindi: roasted corn on the cob

Makaa: charcoal

Makuti: thatch made from the sun-dried leaves of the coconut palm

Mama: lady, madam

Matatu: minibus taxi

Mshumaa: a candle

Pole: sorry

Pwani: the coast

Rafiki: friend

Sana: very; well

Shamba: farm; a plot for growing vegetables

Wageni: guests

Jean McNeil has written ten books, including five novels. She has twice been the winner of the PRISM International competition, and her work has been shortlisted for the Governor General's Literary Award, the Journey Prize, the National Magazine awards, and the Pushcart Prize. She is co-director of the Masters in Prose Fiction at the University of East Anglia. Originally from Nova Scotia, she has lived and travelled extensively in southern and east Africa and lives in London, England.

The Fell Types are digitally reproduced by Igino Marini.
www.iginomarini.com

Published by ECW Press
665 Gerrard Street East, Toronto,
Ontario, Canada M4M 1Y2
416-694-3348 / info@ecwpress.com

Originally published in the United Kingdom
in 2016 by Legend Press.

Editor: Susan Renouf
Cover design: Michel Vrana
Cover images: Chris Werner/Stocksy
Type: Rachel Ironstone
Author photo: Diego Ferrari

This is a work of fiction. Names, characters,
places, and incidents either are the product of
the author's imagination or are used fictitiously,
and any resemblance to actual persons, living or
dead, business establishments, events, or locales
is entirely coincidental.

Library and Archives Canada
Cataloguing in Publication

McNeil, Jean, 1968–, author
The dhow house / Jean McNeil.

Issued in print and electronic formats.
ISBN 978-1-77041-349-8 (paperback)
ISBN 978-1-77090-997-7 (pdf)
ISBN 978-1-77090-996-0 (epub)

I. Title.

PS8575.N433D46 2017   C813'.54   C2016-906352-6
C2016-906353-4

The publication of *The Dhow House* has been generously supported by the Canada Council for the
Arts, which last year invested $153 million to bring the arts to Canadians throughout the country,
and by the Government of Canada through the Canada Book Fund. *Nous remercions le Conseil des
arts du Canada de son soutien. L'an dernier, le Conseil a investi 153 millions de dollars pour mettre
de l'art dans la vie des Canadiennes et des Canadiens de tout le pays. Ce livre est financé en partie par
le gouvernement du Canada.* We also acknowledge the support of the Ontario Arts Council (OAC),
an agency of the Government of Ontario, which last year funded 1,737 individual artists and 1,095
organizations in 223 communities across Ontario for a total of $52.1 million, and the contribution of
the Government of Ontario through the Ontario Book Publishing Tax Credit and the Ontario Media
Development Corporation.

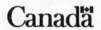

Printed and bound in Canada by Marquis   5   4   3   2   1

Get the eBook FREE!

At ECW Press, we want you to enjoy this book in whatever format you like, whenever you like. Leave your print book at home and take the eBook to go! Purchase the print edition and receive the eBook free. Just send an e-mail to ebook@ecwpress.com and include:

- the book title
- the name of the store where you purchased it
- your receipt number
- your preference of file type: PDF or ePub?

A real person will respond to your e-mail with your eBook attached. Thank you for supporting an independently owned Canadian publisher with your purchase!